Tall, Dark & Lonely

by

R.L. Mathewson

This is a work of fiction. All of the characters, organizations and events described in this novel are either products of the author's imagination or are used fictitiously.

Edited by Maura O'Beirne-Stanko

A special thanks to Jennifer Romero, Donna Ebineza and several others who took the time to make this book flow better :)

ISBN-13: 978-1479338948

e-book ISBN: 978-0-9832125-0-8

To everyone who has ever made me laugh and to my children who will always be my inspiration.

Prologue

Lancashire, England 1819

"He's the devil!" a woman cried.

"Hush, woman! Just show the magistrate your wound!" his father demanded.

Ephraim couldn't focus. His eyes were too heavy to open and his body felt limp. Everything felt so distant and fuzzy. He was so tired….he just needed sleep. A little sleep and then he would ask why they were in his bedchamber.

"This woman is obviously prone to hysterics, Your Grace. This is clearly an animal bite or she stabbed herself in hopes of creating trouble for you. I would dismiss her at once without a reference," a cold voice said.

"I ain't lying, m'lord! Look at his mouth!" the woman demanded. Was that Mary the upstairs maid? Ephraim tried to focus. She was obviously upset about something.

"First tell me who this man is," the cold voice ordered.

"Tell you who it is?" his father, sounding confused. "I told you who it is! That's my middle son Ephraim!" his father snapped.

Ephraim heard a chuckle. "That's not Ephraim."

"Yes, it is!"

"No, it's not." The man sounded annoyed.

What the bloody hell was going on?

Someone grabbed his chin none too gently and yanked it to the side. Ephraim wanted to protest, but the only sound he managed was a weak groan.

"This is Ephraim!"

"But….but….Ephraim is sixteen and he looks….well he looks….like…."

"Like a ten year old boy," he heard his older brother Henry answer in an amused tone. Good old Henry. He would have to remember to box his ears later.

"Yes!" the magistrate agreed. "This is a twenty-five year old man. Is someone playing a jest? I assure you that I do not find this funny or tolerable!"

"I would never do such a thing. This is Ephraim. I wouldn't believe it either, but I've watched over him for the last month."

"What happened to him?" the magistrate asked.

Good, that's a good question, Ephraim thought. Answer that! Ephraim had so many of his own questions. None of them seemed to be able to leave his lips at the moment so he would rely on this man to ask them on his behalf.

"He's always been the devil! We all knew it! Not natural for a man to stay a boy! Not natural and now he feeds on virginal blood!" the maid screeched.

Someone chuckled. "Come now, Mary, virginal? I think that claim is five years too late." Of course Henry would know. He had a reputation of lifting every skirt in town. Henry liked to diverse his attentions.

"Quiet!" their father yelled.

"I want to know how a boy known for his youthful appearance is sick for one month and then he turns into *this*."

His father sighed wearily. "We're at a loss. All the surgeons I've brought in are at a loss as well. They've drained him, cooled him, heated him, poured bile liquid down his throat and still he remained asleep and....changed."

The magistrate scoffed. "Changed is putting it mildly. He looks like a man. Are you positive this is Ephraim and your boys aren't playing a joke?"

"I'm sure. I sat at his bedside every day for the last month." His father sounded weary. "I watched the changes happen."

"Explain to me why he's chained to the bed."

Chained? He was chained? What the hell was going on? After several long minutes of heavy concentration he was able to force his eyes open. The images slowly changed from blurry to sharp.

He slowly looked around his room. His two older brothers stood in the corner, looking bored. Several footmen stood in the room, holding cricket bats and glaring at him. Mary was whimpering and cowering near the door. His father and Magistrate Nichols, a man in his early thirties and well known for his cruelties, stood on either side of his bed looking down at him. His father looked worried. Magistrate Nichols looked at him with annoyance.

"What's your name?" Nichols demanded.

He cleared his throat and nearly winced. It felt like he swallowed sand. "E-Ephraim."

"See!" His father thrust a hand in his direction.

Nichols leveled a glare on Ephraim that made him squirm. "Has someone put you up to this?"

Ephraim turned his head to look at his father only to have cold bony fingers grab his face and yank his head back callously. "I asked you a question."

"No," Ephraim said. "What's going on?" His voice was raspy and deep like a man's. It wasn't his voice! He had a boy's voice. Something was very wrong here.

"We're about to find out," Nichols said, nodding to himself. "Bring the girl!" he snapped.

"No! No! Please!" Mary screamed.

Ephraim watched as two footmen grabbed Mary. They dragged her kicking and screaming to his bedside as Henry and Marc started laughing.

Tall, Dark & Lonely

"Papa, this is ridiculous! This girl is just looking for a way to fatten her purse. Ephraim finally grows some hairs on his sack, albeit he did so in a coma. It's odd, but there's nothing evil about it," Marc said in a bored tone.

Henry laughed harder. "She's just adding to the gossip. You know people have always talked about Ephraim like he's some kind of freak. It's not his fault he took so long. Toss her out."

"No! I'm not lying, yer Grace! He bit me!" she screamed.

"We'll see about that," Nichols said as he grabbed her arm and thrust it in front of Ephraim's face. "Did you do this?" he demanded.

Ephraim's eyes focused on two small scabs that were less than a half inch apart. He shook his head. He'd never been more frightened in his life. They were accusing him of biting a maid, who was accusing him of being the devil? This was all so confusing. He needed to focus if he was going to make any sense out of this whole mess.

After a few minutes he felt his strength slowly seeping back into his body. He raised his arms and sighed with relief. When he dropped his arms, he was startled by the sound of chains clinking. He raised both hands again and gently turned them over, noting the changes. They were different. They were longer, tanner and muscular and he was chained! He raised his feet, too. They were covered by a sheet, but there was no mistaking the feel of cold metal chains hugging his ankles.

"Why?" he asked, lifting his arms again just to prove to himself that this wasn't a dream.

"Girl, you lied! You'll wish you never tried this!" Nichols shoved her violently to the ground.

She shook her head frantically as fresh tears trickled down her face. "No! I ain't lying! He bit me!"

His father gestured to the footmen with a weary sigh. "Get her out of here and remove Ephraim's chains."

Relief surged through him. "Thank you, father," he managed to say.

"No! I can prove it!" Mary cried.

Nichols turned around in time to see Mary shove past as she ran towards Ephraim, wielding a knife.

"Stop!" Ephraim yelled weakly.

With a determined look, she brought the knife down across her own palm as she made her way to his bed. He couldn't figure out what she hoped to accomplish by cutting herself as he struggled to push himself up in the bed and away from this deranged woman. Everything seemed to happen at once. Nichols stumbled backwards, his father tried to race around the bed, his brothers pushed off the wall and were at a full run towards him, the footmen seemed confused and were the last to react. Mary stumbled the last few feet to the bed and thrust her hand in front of his face.

"Get away from me!" Ephraim ordered, watching as blood streamed down her hand and onto his chest and stomach.

Instead of doing as he demanded, she curled her hand into a fist, forcing more blood to drip onto his chest. Ephraim eyed the blood with disgust even as his stomach rumbled at the sight. He ignored it even as his mouth began to water. His reaction to the blood frightened him more than anything.

"Get away from me!"

His father and brothers came to a skidding halt just behind her. Magistrate Nichols grabbed Mary by the hair and yanked out of the way.

Ephraim sighed, "Thank you, s-"

Nichols grabbed his jaw and yanked Ephraim's mouth open. "Dear God in heaven," he muttered. Ephraim watched in horror as Nichols' finger came towards his mouth. Seconds later, he felt pressure against one of his teeth when something sweet and delicious hit his tongue.

"Christ almighty!" Nichols pulled back a bloody finger and shook it off. "They're razor sharp!"

"What?" Ephraim asked stunned.

He watched as his father and brothers paled. He couldn't understand any of this. The only thing that he was sure of was that he wanted more of that sweet delicious liquid, badly. He ran his tongue over his lips, hoping to lap up more when his tongue came across something pointed in his mouth. He ran his tongue over the sharp tip only to find a second one in his mouth. What was going on? Did the surgeons do something to his mouth while he slept?

"I told you he was the devil!" Mary said smugly, holding her bleeding hand against her bosom. Ephraim stared at it like a man dying of thirst.

"Shut her up!" Nichols yelled before he turned to Ephraim's father. "We need to talk." Ephraim watched as his father was dragged to the corner of the room. He was sure they were whispering, but he could hear everything they said loud and clear as if they were standing by his bed.

"Is he a devil worshipper?" Nichols demanded.

"No!" his father protested.

"Tell me about his birth," Nichols commanded.

Ephraim ignored the looks his brothers were giving him and the fact that they were now swiftly moving away from his bed as if he were a leper and focused on the private conversation.

For ten years he pleaded and begged his father to tell him about his birth. The only thing he was told was that his mother died in childbirth. His stepmother refused to tell him anything. That didn't surprise him since she hated him. She referred to him as the "thing" she was forced to tolerate. He never understood that and now it seemed he was about to get some answers.

"The mother was attacked, was she not? An animal the villagers say," Nichols prompted.

He heard his father drag in a harsh breath. Odd that was. His father was over twenty feet from him. He could hear everything clearly, too clearly. It was starting to hurt his head. He heard the sounds of clothes rustling, steps, breathing, heart beats, bugs flying in the room, someone downstairs dropped a pan in the kitchen and swore. That was the oddest thing because they were on the second floor in the west wing, very far away from the kitchen, but he was positive that he could hear Mrs. Brown working in the kitchen.

Ephraim forced himself to ignore every competing sound and focus. His father looked over his shoulder to make sure no one was close enough to hear before continuing.

His father shook his head. "No, it wasn't an animal attack."

"I thought as much. I've heard rumors that a mad man from Bedlam escaped and attacked your first wife during the last month of her confinement."

"Yes, I'm afraid that's as close to the truth as we'll ever get. I was holding a coming out ball for my youngest sister, Amy. My wife was restless with her confinement. Our two boys were asleep in the nursery and she desperately wanted to see Amy dance."

"Understandable. Please continue."

"Marc, what the hell is he?" Henry asked loudly, but Ephraim ignored them.

"Shut up, Henry," Marc said coldly.

"She...she....we...." his father's voice cracked. Ephraim never once heard of his father crying. "We found the bastard bent over her body. She was so pale...and....and...."

"What?"

"He was feeding her his blood! She was drinking his blood!" his father whispered harshly.

Nichols didn't say anything. "We chased the bastard off, but not soon enough. She went into labor...but she was dead. The boy just....he came.....the surgeon couldn't understand it. He thought we were going to have to cut her."

"I'm sorry. I'm rather confused. You said she was dead? I saw her myself in the village not a week after the boy's birth. I was led to believe she died a few days later from complications."

His father looked over his shoulder again. "We had to tell everyone that....truth is she woke up the next morning like nothing happened. She tried to take the boy. She was screaming nonsense. I had to throw her out, but she came back for the boy with *him*!"

Nichols cleared his throat. "I hate to ask, but is it possible the boy isn't yours."

"You mean did my wife cuckold me?" he asked bitterly. "I...I don't know. He looks nothing like his brothers. I just don't know and at that point it would have created a scandal for the boy to disappear and I was most certainly not going to send an innocent child with....oh god, she was dead I buried her myself....I.....do you think...."

Ephraim looked at his brothers. They were not handsome men by anyone's standards. They looked so much like their father. They were as Mrs. Brown liked to say "womanly men." They had very feminine features. They were pretty boys some of the ladies said. A lot of women liked that, but Ephraim always secretly prayed that he wouldn't look like them. He always found comfort in the fact that everyone told him that he didn't look like them. The only thing they shared was their mother's black hair.

He was always told that he looked like a "little man". He was a rough little boy with a thick muscular frame unlike his brother's much thinner frames. His startling blue eyes also set him apart. Could that have changed along with everything else? It seemed ridiculous even to him at the moment, but he didn't want to look like a woman.

Nichols looked back at him and shook his head. "He doesn't look like you or your other sons except for the black hair. Does he look like the men on his mother's side or does he look like-"

"Him you mean?" His father made a sound of disgust.

"Yes."

"He has a larger frame and different eyes but...I thought...I hoped he would look like us." His father looked him over. "He looks like *him*. Do you think he's contracted whatever ailed his mother then?"

"Yes, I think it's a good chance the boy is diseased. If you truly are not the boy's father then he most likely is insane as well. Tell me what happened to his mother?"

"What do you think we did? She was dead. We burned the bitch and her lover," he said coldly. Ephraim's breath caught.

"You're not my father?" he asked before he could stop himself.

Tall, Dark & Lonely

Both men slowly turned to stare at him. Their confused expressions turned horrified at the realization that he heard their entire whispered conversation. His father's hand went to his chest as a collective gasp sounded throughout the large bed chamber.

"His eyes! They're red!" Henry shouted.

"The devil!" A footman raised his weapon and backed up.

"Father? What's going on?" Ephraim couldn't hide the fear in his voice as his vision was tinted with various shades of pinks and reds.

"Don't call me that!" his father yelled. "You're clearly not mine!"

"No, father, please!" Ephraim tried to sit up, but his restraints held him down.

"What do you want us to do with him?" Nichols asked.

His father shook his head. "I don't care what you do with him. Just get him out of my sight."

"Father?.....Father!" He watched his father and brothers hurry from the room. No one looked back at him before they walked out on him. "Father, please!"

Nichols walked over to the bed, smiling. "Tie the chains around him and make sure he can't get lose," he ordered.

When the footman hesitated coming any closer, Nichols shouted, "Now!" The men jumped and did as they were told. Ephraim could now move his arms and legs, but he was too weak to fight back.

"Please, sir, if you let me talk to my father…there's been a mistake." The men released the chains from the bed. In one smooth move they flipped him onto the floor, roughly. He felt the air rush out of him when they slammed onto the floor. They quickly wrapped the chains around his body tightly taking advantage of his weakened state.

"Stop!" he screamed, pain shooting through his chest as the chains threatened to break his ribs. The chains were too tight, making every breath a struggle.

Nichols bent down in front of him. "I'm sorry, my boy. I realize this isn't your fault, but you must realize the position you've put me in. I cannot have you running around feeding off people." He shook his head. "No, that will never do." He looked up at the men. "Take him to my estate and lock him in the dungeon."

His dungeon? Ephraim's stomach coiled in dread. Nichols was known for being one of the most religious and straightforward men in the area. He was honored and accepted by every member of the ton. He was also known for being a sadistic bastard who took his job seriously. He tortured men, slowly, and took great pleasure in it if the rumors circulating around the village were true.

"Please, sir, no! Get my father! He wouldn't want you to do this! Please!" He began sobbing.

Nichols knelt beside him at a safe distance. "I promise you that I will make this quick out of respect for your father. He wouldn't want to know that you suffered."

"Oh, god no!" Ephraim shook his head and tried to fight his restraints, but it was useless.

"Grab him!" Nichols snapped.

The footmen scooped him up, careful to stay away from his mouth. "Father! Henry! Marc! Please help me!" he screamed.

He was quickly carried down the servant's stairs, out the back door and thrown into the back of a carriage before he could put up much of a fight. When he looked up, he spotted Nichols standing at the door, looking pleased. "I promise you will not feel a thing, my boy."

He closed the door.

Tall, Dark & Lonely

"Noooo!" Ephraim screamed as the carriage took off.

* * * *

The large door to his tiny cell opened with an ominous creak that would have scared any of the other occupants of the dungeon, but the effect was lost on him. Nichols stepped inside followed by five heavily armed footmen. Ephraim pushed his long knotted hair away from his face, his bony fingers shook violently from hunger with the effort.

Nichols ran a hand over his now bald head. He sighed heavily as he looked down at Ephraim's ghastly figure. A look of disgust and revulsion spread over Nichol's features as he raised a cloth to his face, trying to avoid the stench. Ephraim dropped his shaking hands to cover his genitals. His clothes had long ago worn away to nothing. His skin was practically black now from the mixture of dirt, burns and dried blood.

"What now? Are you going to set me on fire again? Or perhaps chop my head off for the tenth time? Hmm, oh no, that wouldn't do for you. Let's see you'll want to try something new of course since it's been five years since you did anything original," Ephraim prattled on, mocking Nichols and daring the man to do his worst.

He didn't care anymore. He stopped caring about everything years ago. The pain didn't bother him, the hunger even less. They had become his friends, his companions. In an odd way, he'd come to depend on the pain to make him feel alive.

Nichols sighed behind his cloth and then coughed from the stench. "I'm tired of your mouth, boy. Before we continue today I would like to say that you have been my greatest and most frustrating challenge. It's a damn shame this has to end today."

Ephraim chuckled. "Oh, so today is the day that you finally figure out how to once and for all end me? Why, I'm impressed." He slowly dragged himself to a standing position. His body was literally skin and bone now with too much hair on his head and face. "Let's have a go at it then." He had no illusions over the matter. He would remain here for eternity.

"Bring him," Nichols barked over his shoulder as he stormed out of the room, obviously hating the reminder that he'd failed.

The footmen were careful to remain out of reach of Ephraim. He was weak and looked brittle, but they'd learned long ago to remain out of his reach or they would find themselves attached to his mouth.

Nichols waited in his favorite torture chamber with another five men and over a dozen buckets lining the cracked walls. Ephraim couldn't smell anything over his own stench. That was a good sign at least. That meant that it wasn't oil. He hated being burned alive. It was perhaps the most painful of Nichols' methods. The pain lasted for weeks.

"Over there and secure his foot to the floor." Nichols gestured to the wall.

Ephraim studied the marked wall. He could make out burn marks, bullet holes and dried blood. It was Nichols favorite spot after all. He leaned back against the wall, waiting for Nichols' brilliant plan.

A footman handed him something. Ephraim was too surprised by the action to make a grab for the man. He looked down and was startled to see that in his hand he held a long ago forgotten item, one that he dreamed of for years.

Soap.

He looked up at Nichols, confused.

"Let's get this over with. We can't very well allow His Grace to see you like this." With that, three footmen carrying buckets stepped forward and threw water on him from a safe distance.

Tall, Dark & Lonely

It was cold, but that didn't bother him. He was always cold in this damp dungeon. The water felt strange on his body as it slowly penetrated the layers of dried grime, making his skin itch. He slowly began to wash. He didn't wait for Nichols to ask him. He wanted this. It had been so long since he saw his own skin. He had to scrub hard, as hard as his shaking hands allowed him to. He was so weak he could barely move the soap against the resistance the grim presented.

"Get more water. It seems it's going to take a lake to clean him," Nichols ordered. Men scurried out of the room quickly. They always did. No one liked being in the same room as the "devil."

"You said my father's coming here?" Ephraim did his best to sound casual. He learned long ago not to show any emotion to Nichols. Nichols knew how to use his fears and his hopes against him. The man was a master to his art.

"No, I said His Grace. Perhaps this is the time to tell you that Edmund Duke of Havenville passed away in his sleep yesterday. The new Duke, your brother by your mother, has requested to see you today."

"Henry?"

Nichols flipped his hand in an annoyed manner. "Oh dear, I forgot to tell you that Henry died twelve years ago. Jealous husband. You get the picture I'm sure."

Ephraim slowly allowed the information to settle in. If he was upset he didn't show it. He knew better. This could very well be some new sick torture. He continued to clean himself as the footmen threw water on him. Slowly, so slowly he saw pale skin peek through the grime. The sight disgusted him. His skin was wrapped tightly around bone and showed every line and curve. He looked like a living skeleton. If he had anything in his stomach he would have lost it right then, but he forced himself to continue. That was after all one of Nichols' favorite tortures to starve him to death. He'd been doing it for twenty years.

He wanted to ask who else had passed away, but he didn't dare. There was no one he really cared for, not anymore. Any affection he held died years ago. All those he loved had turned their backs on him. They knew what Nichols was capable of and did nothing. They allowed it.

Shouts erupted in the dark tunnels. Nichols turned quickly. "Go see what that is." He gestured to four footmen. They took off running with their weapons drawn.

Shouts and the sound of a gunshot carried to the large torture chamber. Ephraim continued to wash. No one and nothing was going to stop him from cleaning himself. If he only had this one chance to feel and smell clean then he was going to take it, greedily. It was a sense of freedom. It was the only thing that could make him feel free in this dreadful place.

"Get in there!" a man shouted. Nichols' footmen stumbled into the room followed by a dozen armed men.

"Line up against the wall, the lot of ya!" the large man said. He pointed to Nichols. "You stay where ya are. His Grace would like to have a word with ya!"

"His Grace?" Nichols asked, looking confused.

"Aye."

"Uh oh, Nichols, sounds like you're in trouble," Ephraim said tauntingly.

He began scrubbing his face. The soap made the itch worse for a minute then slowly subsided. The grime on his skin turned to a paste, but rinsed off easily enough. "If someone wouldn't mind pushing a bucket this way I would truly appreciate it," he spoke as if there wasn't an armed siege occurring. He didn't care. It didn't mean anything for him. He knew his brother, the new Duke, was coming here to finish the job. He couldn't have Ephraim alive and threatening his position. Little did he know that the job was impossible.

Tall, Dark & Lonely

He heard a bucket scrape on the floor in front of him. The soap stung his eyes. Nichols should have done this years ago, because it stung like a bitch. "Thank you," he muttered as his hands shot out and found the bucket. That was one thing he never lost, his humanity. He hung onto it like a dying man. He refused to allow Nichols to steal it from him. He was no longer the boy he once was, but he refused to turn into the monster that Nichols demanded.

Strong thin hands ran a damp cloth across his face. Ephraim jumped at the touch. No one had touched him in too many years to count unless it was to hurt him. He opened his eyes to see a man who looked very much like his father, except for the black hair, kneeling in front of him. The man looked sad and confused. Finally he looked down on Ephraim with pity.

Ephraim cowered back. This was worse than torture. "Go away," he mumbled.

Marc sighed and dipped the cloth into the bucket again. He looked relaxed in front of Ephraim. He wasn't cowering away or keeping his eyes on Ephraim, afraid of an attack. Marc took one of Ephraim's hands into his and began scrubbing it, unconcerned for his expensive wardrobe.

The new Duke's men kept the footmen and Nichols at bay while he cleaned his brother. "I used to do this for you every night until you were twelve. Do you remember, Ephraim?"

"Yes," he answered automatically.

Marc chuckled. "Then there were the times when I had to clean you up in the kitchens after you snuck off and got dirty. Father refused to have a speck of dirt in the house. Do you remember?"

"Yes."

Marc stopped cleaning his hands and looked into Ephraim's eyes for a long moment. He looked like he had something to say, but didn't. Reluctantly, he looked over his shoulder. "I need some shears, a razor and towels in here and for Christ's sake someone get me some hot water!" With a nod, one of his footmen ran out of the room.

Minutes later the man returned with the items. Ephraim sat back and watched as his brother washed him, unafraid. The hot water made a difference. The grime washed away with the heated water. His skin turned pink before turning back to a sickly pale color.

"Are you hungry?" Marc asked.

Ephraim didn't answer. He didn't need to. Marc eyed his brother's body. He tried to hide his reaction, but there was little he could do. Ephraim's body was repulsive. "When's the last time you were fed?"

"I don't feed him! I was told to kill him! That would be counterproductive if I fed him, don't you think, Your Grace?" Nichols said callously.

Marc's delicate jaw clenched. "I'm going to have two men cut your hair so that we can wash it. Can you promise not to hurt them?"

The offer was tempting. His stomach rumbled at the reminder of that long ago memory of the sweet liquid, but he wanted to feel his face more than anything. He nodded firmly.

"Okay, I'm trusting you. Don't hurt them and I promise I will feed you," Marc said. Ephraim didn't care. He couldn't even count the number of times Nichols promised him that.

Marc gestured to two men to begin their work. Ephraim placed his hands under his backside to help ease the temptation to grab one of the men and ease his hunger.

"I appreciate that, sir," one of the men said. Ephraim nodded and watched his brother approach Nichols. This could be interesting.

Tall, Dark & Lonely

"Do you know why I'm here, Nichols?" Marc asked in a deceptively calm voice.

"To finish your brother off, Your Grace," Nichols said with his chin raised. He was making his stand. In his mind Ephraim and every living soul that entered the dungeon deserved his cruelty.

Marc laughed, taking a dagger from one of his men. He walked around Nichols as he toyed with the blade. "No, I think you've proven that is quite impossible. Of course, if I had known that my brother was still alive I would have come sooner instead of mourning him. Tell me, Nichols, who was the poor soul that you burned and buried in my brother's name?"

Nichols puffed up his chest. "I don't remember the name. Your father demanded I provide a body to go with the story and I did. It's not my fault the boy turned out to be a demon."

"Hmmm, then explain to me why fifteen years ago when I asked you about my brother you lied and told me that he was dead and then yesterday when I approached you with the same question after my father's deathbed confession you told me the truth?"

"Because fifteen years ago you weren't the D-"

"Duke," Marc finished. "Yes, I believe that is what finally allowed you to speak. You believed I was worried about my position and allowed me into this little secret. I also believe that you were hoping that I would continue to pay you what my father did to keep him here and this story a secret."

"Of course." Nichols began to fidget.

"How are we doing?" Marc asked his men without looking away from Nichols.

"Almost done, Your Grace," Marc's personal valet said. "We're done shaving him and cutting his hair. We'll wash him now."

Ephraim ran his hand over his face. The skin was thin and tight, but it was still his face. He felt like crying, but he had to place his hands back under him before he did something to stop this.

Marc watched his brother get scrubbed and then dried. He sat naked on the floor, looking like a very young skeleton. His brilliant blue eyes had lost the look of youthful innocence. Gone was the boy he once knew. This man looked hard and angry.

"Has any man been here for less than ten years?" Marc asked in a loud voice.

Only one man raised his hand. Tom, he'd been here less than two weeks and refused to be cruel to Ephraim. "How long has this man worked here," Marc asked Nichols.

"A week or two."

Marc nodded and looked at his brother. "Has he been good to you?"

Ephraim looked at Tom. The man looked frightened as he should, but Ephraim knew he wasn't afraid for himself. The man had a newborn son to raise on his own. That was the only reason he took the job. He told Ephraim that when he snuck him water to rinse his mouth late at night.

"He's been good to me. Let him be," Ephraim said dismissively. He didn't want anyone to know how much Tom's kindness meant to him in case this was a new game. He didn't want Tom dragged into it.

Marc nodded. "You have a choice, work for me or share their fate. Which will it be?"

Tom bowed. "You, Your Grace."

"Good. Give this man a weapon. Mind you if you go against me you will share their fate." Marc gestured to the other footmen.

"I swear my loyalty to you, Your Grace."

Marc nodded and gestured to the rest of the men. "Has any of them been kind to you, Ephraim?"

He didn't hesitate. "No."

The men cursed under their breath. "Good," Marc said. He gestured to the two men attending to Ephraim to move away. "Let's start, shall we?" he suggested cheerfully.

Nichols' eyes narrowed. "Start what exactly?"

Marc shrugged one shoulder and began to pace again. "The feeding, retaliation, revenge, whatever you want to call it."

He gestured with the knife to two of his men. The rest took positions and aimed their weapons at the footmen. "If anyone moves kill him."

Ephraim watched curiously as two of Marc's men grabbed a footman who'd enjoyed pissing on him, and dragged him towards Ephraim. "Please, feed yourself," Marc gestured towards the men, "These men, I believe owe you."

His stomach growled viciously at the thought. He didn't question it. He didn't care. After what these men did to him he had no qualms about killing them, but he had to make sure. For some reason he couldn't do it without hearing it from Marc. "Marc?" He put everything into that one word.

"Eat up, little man," Marc said in the same endearment he used all those years ago.

"No!" the footman screamed as he was dragged towards Ephraim. "No!"

Marc's men held him down in front of Ephraim. Ephraim's eyes narrowed on the pulse he could see clearly on the man's dirty neck. He licked his lips. His fangs dropped and instinct took over. He latched onto the man's neck, sucking the sweet hot liquid that poured out, greedily. The man screamed as he struggled. Ephraim's own shaky hands came up to hold the man.

Once the body was drained, Marc offered him another and then another. Ephraim watched in awe as his skin filled in, tanned and muscle appeared beneath the skin. By the sixth body Ephraim looked like the same man he woke up to be twenty years ago, Marc thought. With a gratified smile he looked at Nichols, who'd paled considerably. Two footmen tried to escape during the feeding. They preferred a quick death over being fed to the devil. Their lifeless bodies were hauled over to Ephraim who made use of the blood.

Four footmen remained shaking against the wall, fresh urine soaked the front of their trousers. They were sobbing loudly as they begged for their lives. "Please, Your Grace! We're sorry! We'll do what you want!"

Marc ignored them and focused on Nichols, but spoke to Ephraim. "Are you still hungry?"

"No, thank you."

Ephraim released a burp that he couldn't possibly contain in his untried stomach, earning a chuckle from Marc. Had Marc gone insane in the last twenty years? It was a possibility.

"I want my brother unchained and given clothes," Marc informed his men.

Ephraim was shocked. The chains, the same ones he woke up wearing twenty years ago were about to be removed. He was afraid of what he was going to see there. He watched nervously as the chains were removed. Then he sighed with relief. His wrists were perfect. He felt strong and healthy. He didn't hesitate in dressing as he watched Marc. He was curious about him.

"Ten years ago, Nichols, my father asked you to take care of a young lady named Elizabeth Perkins. Do you remember? I must tell you that you should not lie, because I know you remember. You brag about it in fact."

Nichols snickered. "A whore your father claimed caught your eye and played you. I did you a favor."

Tall, Dark & Lonely

Marc's fist shot out, striking him. Nichols stumbled backwards before he was able to regain his composure. His hand shot to his lip. Ephraim knew before Nichols pulled the hand away that he was bleeding. Ephraim could smell it.

"Were any of these men involved?" Marc gestured to the four men trembling against the stained wall.

Nichols nodded. "Yes, all four of them took part."

"Shoot them," Marc said evenly.

"No!" the men screamed, but it was too late. Marc's men aimed their weapons and fired. The sound was deafening. Every man except for Ephraim and Marc jumped.

Nichols looked frightened. Ephraim finished buttoning his shirt and stepped forward and halted. One of Marc's men held out a mirror. Ephraim stared at the reflection. Twenty years ago he was told he changed. Today for the first time he saw those changes. He ran his fingers over his face. The dry thin skin was gone. His face was filled in. His skin was healthy and smooth. He looked like a stranger. He was now a man, but he didn't look like the thirty-six year old man that he was. He looked like a man in his early twenties. His eyes were hardened, but still had that brilliant blue he liked so many years ago and he looked so different from his brother.

"You look good, little man," Marc said before turning his attention back to Nichols.

"That woman you raped and murdered was carrying my child!"

"Lies, Your Grace. Surely you know that."

Marc's hand shot out and he slashed Nichols across the chest. The older man stumbled backwards. "My father may have asked you to help him for fear that I was dirtying our blood lines, but you should know that *whore* as you call her was my WIFE!" he roared.

Nichols stumbled backwards. His hands were pressed against his wound. "I..I.."

"You didn't know. No one did. We married in secret so I could protect her from him. I took her virginity in our marital bed. She was not my live in mistress. Do you understand that, Nichols?" Marc said in a cold deadly voice as he followed Nichols to the wall where he was backing up. "We were married for six months. Six months! She was three months along with our child!"

"I was told...your father demanded that I take care of her."

"Like you took care of my brother?" he mocked.

Nichols froze. He didn't say anything. "You killed my wife and unborn child and you made sure she suffered. You didn't feel one ounce of guilt or shame. You bragged about it. All these years I had to sit back while you bragged about your evil deeds. You like to call my brother the devil, but we both know that it's you."

He pointed at Ephraim who was still staring in the mirror. "You starved him for twenty years. He gets a chance at three men to fill his stomach and he gave his word like a man and kept it! He is a man and you are at your end, sir!"

Ephraim tore his gaze from the mirror and walked over to his brother. He felt uncomfortable wearing clothes, but he pushed those feelings aside and focused on his brother. "Marc?"

"Ephraim, would you like to finish this? I'm sure you have more reason than I to do it." He could see what that offer cost Marc. His jaw was clenched and he looked like he was on the verge of a breakdown.

"No, he killed your wife and child. The right is yours."

"Thank you," Marc's voice broke. He lunged at Nichols and stabbed him repeatedly. Blood soon covered the wall and Marc. Still he didn't stop. He didn't stop even when the gurgling ceased.

Ephraim's hand flashed out suddenly, faster than anything he'd ever seen in his life and grabbed the knife. "That's enough."

Marc looked up at Ephraim, stunned. He took a deep breath and reluctantly nodded. "Let's go home," Marc said in a confused voice. He was clearly lost in his grief.

Ephraim nodded. It was the last place he wanted to be or belonged, but he would do it for his brother since the man was clearly hurting.

"For now."

Chapter 1

Rascal, New Hampshire

2009

"But what if she doesn't like me?" Joshua asked.

"Yeah, what if she doesn't like us?" Jill decided to ask, giving credence to Joshua's question.

Madison swore under her breath. She was going to have to take Jill aside and remind her that a fifteen year old shouldn't add to a ten year old boy's fear. Now Joshua was going to start crying, again.

After four days on the road with her siblings and mother, Madison was ready to flee from the car, screaming. This trip couldn't end fast enough and apparently it wouldn't. She had a feeling that the U-haul trailer attached to the back of her car was the reason.

She shot another annoyed look at her mother who was curled up in the passenger seat of the small beat up car with the latest gossip rag that Madison paid for of course. Her mother was broke and never worked more than a day at any job she ever held.

Candy, that's what her mother liked to be called. Her real name was Emma and she hated it. She hated everything about herself unless a man liked it. That's how she ran her life and the lives of her three children. If a man liked it then it was okay. If the man didn't then Candy took it upon herself to make the change happen and if it didn't, god help them all, because her mother was not above throwing a tantrum, yelling, hitting or manipulating her three children.

Tall, Dark & Lonely

Madison took a deep breath and counted to ten in her head. She was pissed and for good reason. After twenty-three years of hell, Madison thought that she was finally going to make a real break for it. Candy promised to sign over custody of the kids and this time she was going to do it. Madison couldn't wait. She had money in the bank, her college degree and plans. She was moving out of their trailer, their dumpy broken down crowded trailer, and taking her brother and sister with her. Her mother had agreed.

Hell, Candy practically threw a fit and demanded that Madison take them years ago. It was her turn for a real life she said. Madison owed it to her. After all it was all Madison's fault this happened in the first place. Her mother would have been a model by now if she hadn't got pregnant at sixteen. Candy believed Madison owed her gratitude for not getting an abortion and she reminded Madison of that at every opportunity.

The only clue to Madison's father's identity was that she was clearly half Native American. Her hair was jet black and her skin was naturally tanned and she had brown eyes that reminded people of caramel. That gave her mother the only clue to her paternity. Thankfully, her mother was a racist and only "slummed" with a colored boy, what she called everyone that wasn't pure white, once. So, her father was Andrew Soloman, a boy from the local tribe. Unfortunately, he died after Madison was born. He wanted to raise Madison and Candy had been overjoyed to get rid of her burden.

When Madison's father died in a house fire, Candy threw a fit and stormed out of her mother's house. She took her infant daughter and headed out on the road towards California, but only made it as far as the next state over. There she began a life of worthless jobs, welfare, affairs with married men and drugs. They traveled all over the country until Jill came along and then they settled in New Mexico where Madison took over the care of her siblings and ran the house, well, trailer.

Madison had counted the days down until she turned eighteen and could escape her mother. She never planned on leaving her siblings, but she desperately needed to get away from her mother and her manipulative ways.

Candy dreaded her daughter's eighteenth birthday. It meant her freedom to run around would come to an abrupt end. She would have to find a job or someone else to take care of the kids. So, when the morning of Madison's eighteenth birthday came, Candy did what every self-respecting woman would do when faced with real responsibility for the first time in fifteen years would do.

She hightailed it out of there.

She left a note for Madison of course. She wished her a happy birthday and thanked her for taking care of the kids. She found her true love and was heading to Vegas to be with him. Madison didn't know whether to laugh or cry. She finally rid herself of her mother, but was now faced with supporting her two siblings sooner than expected.

So, for the past five years Madison raised her little brother and sister. No one missed their mother. In truth, Madison had played mother to them both since birth. Candy took on the role of the older sister who didn't like her siblings very much and was never there. Everyone had a role to play after all.

Madison took on menial jobs to put herself through college as well as put food on the table and clothes on their backs. She avoided her real life. Her only friends were from the Reservation where she spent her free time when she had any. There was no time for boyfriends. Well, no steady boyfriends. She was afraid of turning into her mother so she refused to allow herself to get serious about anyone.

Candy fell in love with every man she met. She became obsessive and pathetic and Madison was not her mother. Any man she started to care for was pushed away. It was safer that way.

Tall, Dark & Lonely

Less than two weeks ago Madison started her new job as a history teacher at a public high school. Everything had been going perfect for the first time in her life and then suddenly Candy swooped back into their lives without notice.

Joshua woke her up at three in the morning, crying. A drunk woman was puking in their living room/kitchen/dining room/Joshua's bedroom. Madison went to the aforementioned room with a baseball bat and cursed.

Candy was back.

Candy was back with a vengeance it seemed. Stewart, the man she ran off with five years ago, never married her. They lived in hotels all over the country. Candy loved it. She had pictures and of course magnets from every state except for those in New England, Hawaii, and Alaska of course. She hated New England, refused to return to it.

Everything was going fine until Stewart discovered Candy was not a natural blond. She bleached her hair. Madison knew of course and thought it was obvious. Apparently Stewart hadn't realized her mother's golden locks came from a box. He didn't realize a lot of things like Candy was not her real name and she was not twenty-eight but thirty-nine, which again Madison thought was obvious, so he started screwing around. Candy came home one night from a club to find Stewart "Breaking her heart by fucking that whore Jennifer from the strip club on their bed of love." Candy actually used those words to her and the two younger children, repeatedly.

Madison refused to allow her mother's presence to alter her plans. She demanded that her mother sign the custody papers. Candy refused, saying she missed the kids. She loved them. Then she applied for welfare and was refused. Seems the state of New Mexico was no longer willing to give her a free ride. So, Candy inquired about New Hampshire. They were very willing to give her funds only because Candy's mother was a resident and Candy had been claiming residence there for the past five years. That surprised Madison.

Candy wouldn't listen to reason. She wanted the kids to come with her. She needed them. She cried, threw tantrums and threatened Madison with keeping the kids away from her. They were her only chance since Candy didn't want to work.

She pointed out to Madison that she was too delicate for such labor. Madison broke down in the end when her Grandmother accepted. She was anxious to see her three grandchildren. Candy never brought any of the children to see her and wouldn't allow any contact. She frequently tried to blackmail her mother with the kids. It never worked. It seemed now Grandma had the upper hand and knew it.

Thank god for that. Two weeks ago the sweet, well behaved sister she knew and loved started to disappear. Jill now saw their mother as her best friend, her idol. She liked how Candy didn't work and flirted with men. Madison discovered her sister making out with a man in his twenties just before they left. Candy gave the man permission. She also turned a blind eye when Jill got drunk with her new buddies. Madison flipped out and chased the man out of the house and threw the drugs out. He punched her for her efforts, blackening her cheek.

This nightmare needed to end soon and her grandmother was about to do it. Grandma put her foot down. She had Candy where she wanted her. Candy bragged that her mother was a desperate, lonely, old woman and would do anything and everything to see them. They were going to live like royalty, Candy told Jill. Joshua hated Candy and let her know it. He was Madison's little boy as far as everyone else was concerned. Candy didn't care, Joshua was just a welfare check.

Grandma threatened to inform the authorities of Candy's lies. Candy was to bring the two little ones to New Hampshire immediately and sign over custody. Madison could come, too. In return, they would be given rooms in their Grandmother's large ancestral home that had been turned into a boarding house when their mother was a girl. It was large, clean and ruled with an iron fist.

Tall, Dark & Lonely

Her mother was going to have a difficult time living like a queen, Madison suspected. A week ago, Grandma sent a certified letter laying out her expectations. They were to earn their keep with cleaning and cooking. Grandma laid off her employees with the expectation that they were going to work for her in return for a roof over their heads and food on their plates. Madison had a feeling it wasn't because she was cheap and expected slave labor like Candy claimed. She suspected it was her Grandmother's last effort to straighten Candy out and fix the grandkids before it was too late.

Even with her grandmother there, Jill was in danger of turning into their mother. Much to Madison's dismay, Jill announced proudly that she was not planning on remaining a virgin for much longer. She was planning on losing it as soon as possible. Candy was encouraging it. It would just get in the way of a fun time, Candy said.

The woman was crazy.

For the last week Madison watched her sister like a hawk. The only times Jill was out of Madison's sight was when she was asleep in the hotel room Jill shared with Candy. It was fine with her since she didn't want to sleep with either of them anyway. She spent most of the night making sure Jill didn't leave the room. Once she was sure her fifteen year old sister's virtue was safe she went to sleep.

So here she was driving into their new town instead of filing for custody. She didn't feel like competing with their grandmother on that. It would be better if they worked together, because something told her she was going to need all the help that she could get.

* * * *

"It looks like a mansion!" Joshua announced as he stumbled out of the car.

Candy stepped in front of him with her arms out. Joshua ran past her and into Madison's arms. He wasn't stupid. He knew she was trying to use him to look like the perfect mother for Grandma. Of course, he probably picked up on the not so subtle clues she dropped about that. If Grandma thought she was a good mother then Grandma would leave her alone to take care of the kids. She did not want to clean or cook. That was okay for Madison, but not for her. Candy was meant to make men happy.

Madison looked around. The sun was shining. Birds were chirping. The leaves were a beautiful multicolor and she was freezing her ass off. She was shivering. How could it be this cold if the sun was out? It was freezing!

"This is where we live?" Jill said in the same bitchy tone Candy used. It grated on Madison. She hoped her grandmother worked miracles otherwise she was afraid that she would be beating some sense into her sister soon.

She took one last look at her young sister's new wardrobe. Everything was too tight and too small. Jill was short for her age and underdeveloped. The clothes made her look like a child prostitute. This miracle better happen fast.

Madison kissed Joshua's cheek. "Go knock and remember to be polite."

Joshua nodded. He ran to the door and knocked loudly. A minute later the door opened wide. He walked inside with his head held high. With a slight hesitation, the three of them walked in after him.

A tall woman in her late fifties stood in the foyer. She didn't look anything like Madison imagined she would. She expected a short, plump, gray-haired grandmother like the one on that cookie box back home. This woman was strong and capable and had a no nonsense air about her.

Candy pushed past Madison and headed for the woman. She dragged the older woman into a hug and gushed. "Oh, Mama, I'm so happy to see you!"

Tall, Dark & Lonely

Grandma pushed her back and dismissed her. "I bet it is." She focused on the three grandchildren. She took in Joshua and smiled, then Madison and beamed, then Jill and frowned. The breath Madison hadn't realized she was holding left her body. Her grandmother didn't like the looks of Jill. She was going to help thank god.

"Well, let's go into the living room and have a talk."

Madison sat on the loveseat. Joshua took the seat next to her. He reached for her hand and held onto it tightly. He was afraid. She knew why. Candy told them over the years how horrible and violent this woman was. Her only prayer was that Candy lied, again.

Grandma clasped her hands together. "I just want to say that I am very pleased to have you children here. This is going to be your home for the rest of your childhood." She leveled a look on Candy, reminding her that Jill and Joshua were now legally hers. Candy pouted. It was an act. She found another sucker to raise her kids and give her a free ride.

"Now, Joshua and Jill, you each have your own rooms."

"Really?" Joshua asked excitedly. He'd never had a bedroom before never mind his own room.

"Yes, your rooms are near mine so I have a few rules. No loud music. Joshua, you have a bed time of…" She looked at Candy expectantly, but she only continued to pout.

Madison gritted her teeth. She was tired of this game. "He goes to bed by eight," she said.

Grandma nodded. "Sounds reasonable. If you're a good boy and do your homework and get good grades then we can add a half hour later on. How does that sound?"

Joshua eagerly nodded. Grandma turned her attention to Jill and looked over her outfit with a sigh. "You are expected to be in bed by nine. No curfew yet. If you want one you earn it. Understood?" she said firmly.

Jill snorted and looked at Candy. "Candy, do something!" Candy only pouted and looked wounded.

Grandma cleared her throat. "You will refer to her as 'mom' or 'mother.' She is not your friend. She is your mother and her name is Emma," she said this last part looking at Candy. Candy had enough sense to keep her mouth shut at least.

"Madison." Madison looked back to see her grandmother studying her. She looked so different than her brother and sister. Joshua had light brown hair and green eyes and Jill had wild red hair and blue eyes, two different fathers of course. Grandma smiled warmly at her. "You turned out beautifully, Madison. You look so much like your father," she said proudly. Madison wanted to ask her about her father, but not in front of Candy.

"Thank you, Grandma," she said. It was weird saying Grandma, but this woman fit somehow. If anyone should be her grandmother it was this woman.

"You're welcome. You are welcome to stay here as long as you want, sweetheart. All I ask for is the occasional hand and to keep your bedroom and the bathroom you share with one other boarder clean. Does that sound okay?"

"I like to earn my keep, Grandma. How much per week for me and the kids?"

Grandma waved it off. "The kids are in my custody, therefore my responsibility. As for you, you are my granddaughter and I've missed you. I'm glad to have you. Just do as I ask and we're settled. But since we're on the subject of pay I found you a job. You start tomorrow."

Tall, Dark & Lonely

Madison forced a smile. Another menial job. After nine years of working the worst possible jobs by the worst possible people she thought she escaped, apparently not.

"I talked to Professor O'Shea who had some connections with the local high school. They contacted your last employer and I gave them the resume you sent me last week. They liked what they saw and decided to take a chance on you. You have a position as a teacher in the history department at Rascal High School."

That was not what Madison expected. She was out of her chair and hugging Grandma before she knew it. "Oh thank you, thank you!" she said.

Grandma laughed and hugged her back. She whispered fiercely in Madison's ear. "I'm proud of you, kiddo. I'm sorry you had to do it on your own for all these years."

Madison nodded and wiped a tear away as she sat back down. "Now, as for you, Emma, you're welcome to stay as long as you follow the rules. You start at seven in the morning and stop at four in the afternoon. Room and board are included. I'll pay you five dollars an hour." Candy opened her mouth to interrupt, but Grandma kept going. "I've already filed the papers and it's legal so you don't have to worry about the kids." It was a threat and a promise and Candy knew it. She wasn't going to be able to hide behind the kids any longer.

"There are no drugs, no drinking, and no men in your room. Also, we have three male guests. You are not to become involved with any of them. Am I understood?"

The pout was gone. It was replaced by the bitch look. Candy's eyes narrowed, her arms were folded over her chest and her jaw was set. "And if I don't agree?"

Grandma smiled. "Then don't let the door hit you in the ass on your way out."

Candy ground her jaw once again. There was nowhere for her to go and no money. She was trapped. She nodded, slowly.

"Good." She turned to look at Madison. "I almost forgot, if you give your mother any money I will throw you out. You're not doing her any favors by letting her take advantage of you and you're not helping yourself. You've done enough and you don't owe her anything. Am I understood?"

Madison could only stare and nod.

"Good. Well, let's get you to your rooms."

Chapter 2

She absently ran her fingers over the quilt that covered her queen size bed as she looked around her new room. It was very large, beautiful, spacious and all hers. It overlooked a large backyard. Their old trailer overlooked a tire factory and smelled horribly. This room overlooked an apple orchard and swimming pool. This was like the Ritz for her. Even sharing an adjoining bathroom with a strange man didn't dampen her good mood.

Grandma swore the man was nice, clean and hardly ever home. He was only home to shower, which Grandma admitted he did two or three times a day. The man was a shower addict as she liked to put it. He was also a detective for the state police and was assigned locally.

For the past two years the detective rented his room and her room, but had lived here for three. He couldn't tolerate sharing the bathroom with anyone and hated having anyone close by. He needed peace and quiet. The three people that rented the room before he took it over were anything but quiet. As soon as the last one moved out he informed Grandma that he was paying for the room so that it would remain empty.

A week ago Grandma asked the man for a favor. She needed the room for her granddaughter. The man knew about the situation and was sympathetic. After Grandma promised that Madison was a quiet and respectful, he agreed. He seemed to think that any woman who raised her siblings and put herself through college deserved a chance. His only stipulation, everyone leave him alone. Apparently, he was a loner.

Grandma said he was nice and helped her out, but didn't talk to anyone and didn't join the rest of the house for meals. Grandma liked the detective. He helped take care of troublesome renters in the past and as a thank you, Grandma made sure that everyone left the detective alone.

It was more than fine with Madison. Their rooms were on the back addition of the house above the large storage room her Grandmother used to store everything from her old motorcycles to extra tables. They were well away from the rest of the rooms which meant peace and quiet. They also had their own entrance off the short hallway that connected their rooms to the main house. Her grandmother was really going out of her way for her.

There was a room near her mother that was open, but Grandma was trying to give her some freedom and a much needed break. The kids were forbidden to come to this section of the house out of respect for the detective. That's what Grandma said. In truth, it was probably for her as well. She understood that Madison came here not out of desperation, but out of love for her brother and sister, who Madison hoped she could save.

She walked back to her laptop computer and scrolled down. "Finally," she mumbled.

Last week she discovered that her mother memorized her account number and password. She transferred two hundred of Madison's hard earned dollars to her own account. She had a feeling Jill helped her, seeing how both of them came home later that night in matching outfits. If her grandmother hadn't stepped in she would have pressed charges.

This was probably why her grandmother made the statement about her money in the living room. Madison asked her grandmother without giving too many details to open an account for her at the local bank. She did and thankfully set up online access for the account. Grandma thought of everything. Now she just had to make sure that Jill and Candy didn't get their hands on her new debit card or account information.

It was still midmorning by the time she was done bringing her things up. She liked having her own entrance. She didn't have to haul her meager possessions through the house and up the stairs and down the hall like everyone else.

Tall, Dark & Lonely

She took another look around her room. Not surprising that it was dusty since no one had used this room in two years. Their small hallway could use a bit of a cleanup as well, she decided. Both areas smelled dusty. Her neighbor as she liked to think of him, asked Grandma not to allow anyone in this part of the house. Her Grandmother readily agreed. She felt a man should have his privacy. Well, a police detective should at least. Madison had a feeling that Grandma didn't feel the same way about her other renters. There were five in total counting her neighbor, two women and three men.

"Damn it." She forgot to find out her neighbor's name. She had no plans of bothering him. He wanted to be left alone and she wanted to feel alone. She sighed on the next breath. "Oh well." She got over things easily. It was the only way to tolerate Candy and raise two children without losing her mind.

"Now let's see, she said the vacuum cleaner was in the closet." She opened her closet and nodded. Sure enough it was there. "And the cleaning supplies are in the bathroom." It still felt weird that she was sharing a bathroom with a strange man, but beggars couldn't be choosy. It was a new experience, she told herself.

She opened the bathroom door and gagged. It was a new experience all right. The bathroom looked as though it hadn't been cleaned in years, two probably. She pulled the top of her shirt over her mouth so that she could breathe while she made her way to the window above the toilet. She yanked it open, desperate for fresh air.

With that done she slowly turned around and took in the horror. This was a massacre on hygiene. The room smelled of mold, mildew, body odor, dirty clothes, public toilet and dozens of stale cardboard air car fresheners. The combined odor was vomit inducing. She looked around the room. Hanging off every available surface was an air freshener. Some looked pale and old while others looked bright green. That explained the car smell.

In the corner, a large pile of damp, mold covered towels took up residence. The pile came up to her hips. This would not do at all. She kicked the pile and gagged when the top of the pile dumped over onto the ground, leaving a rotten pile of black, slimy fabric. This was the perfect setting for a horror movie.

She moved her attention to the toilet and quickly away. The rings in the toilet were a dark red tint, strange. The toilet was covered with grime and smelled bad. The sink was covered in hard soap scum, dirt, and upon closer inspection she discovered beard trimmings were trapped against the counter in some weird street grunge mosaic. Old rusty razors covered the counter with other discarded trash. Madison looked down at the trash can and laughed. The small trash can looked brand new. Well, it had a small layer of dust, but other than that it was the cleanest thing in the bathroom.

She dreaded turning around and seeing the tub. She already knew the floor needed scrubbing, desperately. The tub as she dreaded was an equal match for the sink. There was no trash here. Instead there were several high piles of discarded soap bits. It was scary. She would have nightmares for years after this experience.

Her grandmother said the cleaning supplies were beneath the sink. She swore up and down that she stocked the small cabinet right after the last renter moved out. Madison had a sneaking suspicion about what she was going to find. Sure enough the cabinet was filled from top to bottom with brand new cleaning supplies. She had to laugh. This really would be a new experience. Not one she was willing to repeat.

Donning the one size fits all rubber gloves, she got started. She threw the dirty towels into trash bags. It took four large trash bags to get rid of them all. She had a feeling that her mysterious neighbor used his towels until they were beyond use and then threw them onto the pile. That theory was confirmed by the towel hanging by the shower. It was wearing away in some places and smelled bad. She threw that one away as well, might as well do a thorough job, she decided.

Tall, Dark & Lonely

She spent the next four hours scrubbing, scraping, gagging, pleading, and polishing. By the time she was done, it was passable even by her strict standards. Every surface shined and the room smelled of fresh lemon. She unloaded her things and left the room. She had too much to do to stand around and admire her work. She could only hope that her neighbor wouldn't take the cleaning job as a challenge. She didn't want to do this every week.

* * * *

"You look silly, Madison!" Joshua giggled as he ran past her, bouncing the basketball she bought him for his last birthday.

Madison feigned a horrified look. She looked down at her oversized sweatshirt, which covered four other layers. It was freezing. Dear god, the outside thermometer read seventy, seventy! Where she lived cold was eighty. This was hell backwards.

She wiped her grease covered hands on her baggy jeans that covered leggings and adjusted her baseball cap and pony tail. "What?"

He giggled some more. She did a little model walk, swinging her hips in exaggeration and pursing her lips. "I think I look fabulous darling," she purred. Joshua cracked up even louder.

"You have oil on your face!" He laughed.

She waved it off. "The oil simply adds texture and illusion, darling," she said in a snooty voice. Joshua giggled some more as he returned to his bouncing.

Madison returned to the task at hand, making her engine run for another day. Tomorrow she would trade it in and buy a new car since she no longer had to worry about supporting the kids. She wasn't going nuts. She would spend less than half her nest egg in case something happened, but she really needed a reliable vehicle for work.

"Madison!" Jill screeched.

"Looks like her royal highness didn't get her way again," Joshua muttered. For a ten year old he was rather perceptive.

"Why do you say that?" she asked as she fought to loosen a bolt. The damn thing was rusted on tightly. It wouldn't budge even with WD-40. It had to come off.

"That's the way she acts now that Candy is around. She's a total pain." He bounced the ball. "I don't understand why she wants to be like her. She's gross!"

Madison agreed, but didn't say anything. Her mother dressed and acted like a hooker. She was half worried that she looked that way for a reason. Now Jill was taking after Candy. Speaking of Jill…

"I want to go home right now!" Jill demanded near Madison.

"Lower your voice I can hear you fine." She continued focusing on that damn bolt.

"That woman told me I can't wear make-up. *I have to earn it*, she said," Jill said mockingly.

"That woman as you like to refer to her is our grandmother so you will call her 'Grandma' or 'ma'am' and if I hear you disrespect her again, you're grounded," Madison warned. She was usually easy to get along with, but Jill's spoiled attitude was doing a real number on her nerves.

"Fine! *Grandma* said that I can't wear makeup or tight clothes!" she said in a whiny voice.

"Good."

"Good?"

"Good. That was ending today anyway. You're starting school tomorrow and you aren't going like that." To make her point Madison looked her sister over. Dear god the girl was wearing a plastic mini skirt with a fluffy tight top that showed off her small breasts and she was shivering. She used to be so reasonable.

"You just don't want me to embarrass you," Jill snapped.

Madison laughed. "First off, we look nothing alike. Secondly, we have different last names and *you* will call me Miss Soloman like everyone else. Thirdly you're not going around looking like a slut for the rest of your life. Have some self-respect."

"Madison, what's a slut?" Joshua's young voice chimed in. She forgot he was there. She winced as Jill gave her a superior look.

"Yes, Madison, what's a slut?" Jill asked. She was going to kill her. That was it. No one would blame her.

"Ah....that is....er..." She was vaguely aware of a car engine shutting down close by. All her focus was on Joshua's question and how to answer it in such a way that he didn't use it to tease Jill in front of people like he was known to do.

"Come on, Madison, you're a teacher, so tell me what a slut is." Joshua demanded in a louder voice. That was the normal progression of events when he would ask an embarrassing or difficult question. The longer she took the higher his voice became.

"I believe, young man, that name is given to a woman who gives her affections too freely to men," a deep voice said.

"Oh my," Jill gasped in a sultry voice, a little too sensually for Madison's sanity. That could not be a good sign.

"Who are you and why do you have a gun?" Joshua demanded.

"What?" Madison startled by the question jumped back and caught her wrist on something sharp. "Ow!" Damn it, she cut herself. Thankfully the area was clean, well was before. Now it was covered in blood.

* * * *

The scene that met him when he walked up the long driveway was amusing. A little boy ran around a piece of shit car, bouncing his ball and asking someone named Madison about sluts. He had to stop himself from chuckling. This Madison person was in a tight spot.

The next thing that caught his eye was a little girl dressed like a whore. She reminded him of the light skirts that used to work the docks when he was a child. She wore too much make-up, too little clothing and had an air of experience around her. She wasn't aware of him yet.

The last thing and the most important thing that hit him was the smell of a pure blood, virgin blood. He knew it wasn't from the little boy. Men, even little boys, never gave off that scent. That particular scent was saved for women. It was enticing and mouthwatering.

It had to be this little girl. She couldn't be more than fifteen, maybe fourteen years old. He eyed the girl. Nope, this little girl was not a virgin. He wasn't surprised. Things changed dramatically over the past century. According to the media, it wasn't popular or normal for teens to remain chaste until marriage or even adulthood.

Even if this young girl had been a virgin she would have been off limits. He didn't eat where he lived and these children were clearly the grandchildren of his landlady. He remembered they were to arrive today, which is why he stopped off on the way home and picked up some more air fresheners for the bathroom. He also never fed off a child before. Never had and never would. Children were innocents in his eyes no matter their sexual experience.

Tall, Dark & Lonely

That left this Madison, probably another child. She would be safe as well under his rules. He couldn't remember the last time he fed off a virgin. Was it sixty years? Probably. He had one rule when it came to virgin woman, and that rule had not been needed in the last sixty years. He only took blood, not her innocence. There were plenty of willing women for what his body needed. Christ how long had it been since he had a woman? December back in 1880 or the 1890's he thought. Sex became boring and useless. He never escaped his nightmares and never felt close to the woman. It always felt like he was fucking air.

"Come on, Madison, you're a teacher so tell me what a slut is," the little boy said impatiently.

He couldn't help himself. He had to answer. "I believe, young man, that name is given to a woman who gives her affections too freely to men."

"Oh my," The little girl turned to look at him. She licked her lips invitingly, letting him know that he was going to have to lock the connecting door at night to the main house. This was all he needed, he thought dryly.

"What?....Ow!" a woman's voice said, suddenly, drawing his attention to the little girl running her eyes over him.

The smell of that virgin blood hit him hard. He stopped himself from stumbling back. That wasn't the worse part. Hunger ripped through him, viciously. That was odd since he just finished two bags of blood on the way home. He wasn't hungry, but the smell of her blood was intoxicating.

At the moment he wanted her blood more than anything on this earth. Her blood screamed for him. His hands clenched tightly as he fought against the urge to attack her in front of these two children. *Get it under control!* It didn't matter what this girl looked like, he wanted her blood. He'd never felt this intense need before, not even those twenty years he spent in Nichols' dungeon.

His fangs descended. He learned long ago how to control his eyes, but it was a losing battle. He needed to get away from this woman whoever the hell she was.

He stepped back the same time a young woman, he guessed since he certainly couldn't tell by the way she was dressed, stepped out from behind the front of the car and looked first at the little girl then at him while she was holding her wrist tightly. The sight of the "Ow," Ephraim guessed.

She rolled her eyes in the direction of the little girl. "Jill, go on inside please and help Grandma with dinner."

"But-"

"Go," the woman said firmly. Ephraim studied the woman. He couldn't discern her age, but he was sure that she was not a child. She wore an old baseball cap backwards and her face was smudged and dirty. He couldn't really make out any features. The only thing he could make out on her face was her eyes. They were brown, but not normal brown. They were rather bright.

His eyes roamed down her body. She was figureless. She was probably also flat-chested by the looks of it and fat. He confirmed his opinion by her baggy pants. In his experience women wore large clothes to cover extra weight. The only thing attractive about this woman was her blood. If he didn't get out of here soon he would find out if her blood tasted as good as it smelled.

"Are you a policeman?" the boy asked.

"Joshua, you're being rude," she chastised the boy. She turned to look at him and smiled. "I'm sorry. This is Joshua and I'm Madison."

He nodded. His fangs were throbbing painfully in his mouth for a taste of her. "We just arrived today," she said when he didn't make any attempt to introduce himself.

Again he nodded.

Tall, Dark & Lonely

"Well, who are you?" Joshua asked.

He only turned and walked away. If he didn't go into the house right now he would regret it.

"What's your name?" Joshua yelled.

"Ephraim," he answered without looking back.

He made his way to the back of the house and up the backstairs. It wasn't until he dropped the small bag on his desk that he remembered that he was supposed to have a new neighbor.

"Shit."

It was Madison. She would be close by to tempt him day and night.

He ran his hands through his short black hair. He could do this. He could live here with this woman. They only shared a bathroom. She would keep both doors locked at all times. Any woman with sense would lock the door when she lived in a boarding house even if it was run by her grandmother.

Not that a locked door would stop him. He could push the door down with a pinky finger, but it would serve as a useful reminder to him that she was off limits. He didn't want to leave. He was happy here. No one bothered him. He liked his job. He liked living in the boarding house. He didn't want to have his own place. He liked the idea of being alone, but not alone.

No, he would suck it up and wait. She had a new job according to Mrs. Buckman. She would save up and move out. Most young woman wanted to be on their own. Yes, that was it. He just had to wait her out.

He shook his head, trying to clear his head, grabbed the air fresheners and headed for the bathroom. He opened the door and froze. What the hell happened to the bathroom? Did Mrs. Buckman have it remodeled for her granddaughter? He knew she was anxious to have the young woman here, but he didn't know that she would go to this extent.

He closed his eyes and inhaled deeply. No, he smelled cleaning supplies and synthetic lemons. She cleaned. Everything including the floor beamed. Gone were his air fresheners, dirty towels, garbage and that disgusting odor. Now it was clean and organized. The shelves were filled with large fluffy towels. The shower was sparkling and held his shampoo and soap as well as her bathing products. He turned his attention to the medicine cabinet.

She took it upon herself to designate sides, made sense. His side held his razor, shaving gel and cologne. That little collection took up half of a shelf, leaving the other two shelves empty. Curious, he opened her side of the medicine cabinet. It was well stocked with cleaners, soaps, lotions, over the counter medicines, tweezers, ear swabs, nail polish remover and a pink razor. Pink. What difference did it make if it was pink? The other stuff was just as confusing. Why did she need the rest of it? Was she building something out of all that shit?

He closed the cabinet and opened the first drawer beneath the sink. Extra toilet paper. Okay, she would need that. He didn't, but she would. That was reasonable. He closed that drawer and opened the bottom one and froze.

"Oh.....fuck me...." His hands shook as he reached down and picked up the pink box, menstrual pads. "Fuck."

He should have anticipated this when Mrs. Buckman told him that a young woman was moving in. He forgot about women's courses. He stood up and studied the box. It was a mixed box whatever that meant. He looked it over only to discover that it was a super and regular box. He had no clue what that meant, but it couldn't be good where he was concerned.

His eyes closed and he prayed for control. The woman, no, the human whose blood attracted him like no other would be bleeding once a month next to his room and discarding blood soaked cotton in the trash can. This was hell. Pure hell. It would take every bit of control not to suck on those discarded pads. Even to him that sounded disgusting.

"Fuck." There was nothing else to say. He dropped the box back in the drawer and kicked it shut. He braced his hands on the counter and looked in the mirror. His eyes were a fiery red. His teeth were lowered and he was drooling. Great. His only hope was to stay the hell away from this Madison person and pray that she moved out before her courses came.

Chapter 3

Madison was ripped from her pleasant dream of warmth by rap music. "What the hell?" She forced her eyes to focus on the alarm clock by her bed. It was three in the morning. Who the hell was playing rap music at three in the morning?

She pulled her knit hat down on her head and jumped out of bed and immediately began shivering. Her baggy sweatshirt and tee shirt weren't doing the job. The sweatpants might as well be made of paper for all the warmth it provided. The only thing that seemed to keep her warm was the thick socks. She wrapped her arms around her stomach and looked around. That horrible music was coming from her room, but where? It was loud and annoying.

Why was it coming from her room? She stumbled over her unpacked boxes as she tried to find the source.

"Ouch!"

The bathroom door flew open, banging loudly against the wall. Madison was so surprised that she stumbled back and fell over a box. She quickly scrambled to her feet just as the light was turned on.

There in the doorway of the bathroom stood a very pissed off Ephraim. His eyes narrowed on hers before moving down to take in her outfit. He seemed pleased by something as he walked into her room, wearing nothing but a pair of boxer briefs. No hello or what is that? He walked in like he owned the place. The music stopped suddenly.

"Good," she sighed with relief.

He shot her an irritated look.

Tall, Dark & Lonely

"I'm sorry if that woke you. I have no idea what that was." The words rushed out of her mouth. This man intimidated her. He was big, very muscular from what she could see now he was handsome, too handsome. She never dealt well with handsome men. She preferred to deal with average looking men. It made her feel safe. This man made her feel anything but safe.

She didn't care if he was a cop. He was dangerous. She felt it. Everything in her body screamed for her to be careful. Of course her mother was going to set her sights on him. She loved dangerous men. Her sister was already making plans. Madison walked in on her sister and mother talking about birth control. It seems her sister didn't like the feel of condoms.

That was a nice way to twist her heart and shatter it. Her sister somehow in the last week managed to lose her virginity and her mother knew about it. Candy smiled sweetly up at Madison and winked. This was just a game to her. Madison had been too upset to talk to Jill at that moment. She walked out of the room and made her way back to hers where she cried for a good hour. Then she forced herself to focus on the task at hand, she was starting a new job tomorrow.

Using the text book and notes the school sent over, she spent the next five hours creating a lesson plan. Finally, she finished plans for the next two months and had the following week's lectures created. Then she took a shower, a long hot shower. She heard Ephraim pace his room the entire time muttering about something that made her rethink taking the room next to Candy's.

* * * *

Just then the rap music started again. Ephraim threw her another irritated look. She looked even more unattractive with that ridiculous knit hat pulled all the way to her eyebrows and down around her ears, ending around her cheeks. Her skin was tan and clean, but that's all he saw. Her scent hit him hard, making it hard to focus on anything but her. He needed to shut off that annoying music and get the hell out of her room.

Now.

He focused on the sound and ignored her overwhelming scent. It didn't take long to figure out that the damn music was coming from a box buried in the back. He moved quickly towards it, throwing boxes and bags roughly out of his way.

"Hey!"

He ignored her. He found a box with a large pink heart drawn on it. He ripped it open and found the offending object on top, a cell phone. "A 'Carl' is calling for you," he said evenly.

For the moment she forgot that she was mad at him for throwing her things around and took the phone. "This isn't my phone."

"Don't care. Tell Carl to fuck off or I will," he snapped.

She seemed not to hear him or care what he said. "He's a friend of Candy's." Friend was putting it mildly. He was one of the guys her mother managed to screw in the short two weeks since she was home. He was in New Mexico and it was one in the morning there. More importantly it was Jill's phone and Carl was thirty-five years old.

When Madison opened the phone her finger accidentally hit the speaker button. "About time you answered, baby."

"Carl?" Madison answered, confused. "Why are you calling this phone?"

"Stop fucking around, baby. I'm horny. Come on over, I could go for one of your special blowjobs."

Every muscle in Ephraim's body froze. This woman was a virgin, he was sure of it. Some other unknown emotion ripped through him as well. It was weird. He wanted to reach through the phone and rip this guy's head off and that unnerved him.

Madison's jaw clenched. Was she embarrassed? "Carl, why are you calling *this* phone?"

Tall, Dark & Lonely

"Jill baby, don't fuck around. I'm coming to pick you up. Sneak out your window and meet me by the tree, same as last week."

She took a deep breath and spoke evenly. "Carl, listen to me very carefully and don't hang up before I'm done or I will have the police at your door in fifteen minutes."

"Oh shit.....Madison?"

"Yes, my sister is fifteen years old. *Fifteen*, do you understand what that makes you?"

"I..I..."

"You are a child molester."

"Hey, whoa! She came on to me. It wasn't my idea anyway. Your mother asked me to do her a favor. Your mother and Jill told me that she was eighteen. I swear to god I wouldn't have touched her if I knew. I swear to god, Madison. I am so sorry...I...oh my god, she's a kid..." They heard gagging sounds. "I'm going to be sick," he needlessly announced as the sounds of vomiting soon accompanied the sounds of his gagging.

Having had enough, Ephraim snatched the phone from her hands. "Carl, surely you knew she was a kid. One look and you can't miss."

"I...they said she just looked young. I asked. They showed me an ID. I swear. Please! It was in a pink wallet. They showed me!" he pleaded desperately.

Madison shoved Ephraim aside none too gently and made her way to the box. He took a deep breath and closed his eyes, fighting for control. This woman, a tomboy from the looks of things, was going to be the end of him. If he didn't leave this room soon he was going to drain her. He hadn't drained anyone in nearly fifty years. He took only what he needed. There was no way he would be able to that with her. The smell of her blood was too powerful. His hands began to tremble.

"Got it!" Madison held up a pink woman's wallet. She stumbled over a box while opening it. She found a school ID and a driver's license hidden behind it. "That bitch," she muttered.

"Let me see that," Ephraim said through tight lips. His fangs were dropping. He forced them back with his tongue, but he didn't want to take a chance that she would see them.

"Here." She handed it to him without looking at him, completely oblivious that her life was on the line at the moment.

"Well?" Carl asked nervously.

"It's fake, Carl."

"Shit." He started sobbing. "But see, I didn't know that. I really thought she was an adult. Madison, I'm so sorry!"

"Carl, don't call again," Madison said.

"I won't I swear. Tell her to stay away from me."

"It won't be too hard, Carl," she said, ending the phone call.

He tossed the ID onto the bed. "Looks like you need to have a little talk about the birds and the bees with your little sister," he said a little harsher than he intended, but it couldn't be helped. He needed to get the hell out of here.

Now.

Cold glimmering brown eyes narrowed on him. She nodded firmly and spoke evenly. "I'm sorry this woke you up. It won't happen again. Now if you'll excuse me I have something to do."

Tall, Dark & Lonely

As far as dismissals went this one was good. It had the opposite effect on him of course. He hated authority and hated being told what to do even more. Unfortunately for him, his teeth were throbbing in his mouth and if he didn't leave soon he would give himself away. So with a tight nod, he turned and left, closing the door firmly behind him. Let the tomboy handle it. He didn't want the drama and most certainly didn't want to deal with a fifteen year old who couldn't keep her legs closed.

Madison traced the pink heart with her finger. This was Jill's box. She must have grabbed it by accident, she realized, dreading what she was going to find. She took a steadying breath before she dumped the contents of the box onto the bed.

Her hand shot to her mouth as she gasped. Who knew it only took two weeks to change a person this much? She froze on that thought. Did she change or maybe Madison missed something. She pushed the condoms, cigarettes and nips of alcohol to the side and sat down. She went over in her mind everything she could remember about how Jill behaved over the past couple of months. There wasn't that much to remember since Madison had been busy with her new job and looking for a new place for them and Jill had been busy with school and helping with Joshua.

There had to be something she missed. If Jill was really the responsible, level headed kid she thought she was then two weeks and Candy wouldn't have been enough to change her. No, Madison failed. She missed something some time ago and Jill slipped. It took Candy for Jill to feel comfortable with acting out in front of Madison. Until then the behavior was hidden.

"Shit," she mumbled, hating herself for not being able to be there more for Jill, but between school, work, and doing her damndest to keep them all together her time had been limited to the basics like making sure that the kids were taken care of.

She picked up the packs of condoms and grimaced. Part of her wanted to throw them away, reasoning that if Jill didn't have them then she wouldn't have sex. That was stupid since she already knew that Jill apparently hated using them. Of course if she didn't have them available when she was able to sneak away she would go ahead and have sex without them. Then there would be more problems than just a fifteen year old having sex. She could catch something or get pregnant. Jill was just like Candy now. She shouldn't have a baby. No, there was no choice, she threw the condoms, clothes and phone back in the box and closed it.

The alcohol and cigarettes were a different story. She gathered those up and went into the bathroom. She emptied the bottles and cigarettes into the toilet and flushed. That took care of that supply. In a week she was going to search Jill's room once she was settled in. Until then, she was going to have to keep a close eye on her. One thing was certain, Candy had to go.

* * * *

"I'm sorry, miss. This car is shot." Earl, the mechanic of Earl's Garage, wiped his sweaty, dirty face with an equally dirty and greasy cloth.

"Oh no!" Madison pushed her long black hair that everyone said looked like silk back over her shoulder. Up until this point she hadn't been sure if she was having a good day or a bad day. Ten minutes ago she would have said it was fifty-fifty. Now it was easily seventy-five to twenty-five in odds of a bad day.

Her day started off good. She wore her most professional skirt, which ended just above the knee, and her favorite lavender blouse that somehow survived the trip without wrinkles. There was even hot water left after her neighbor finished his half hour shower. She'd spent the entire time cursing him to hurry up so that she wouldn't be late for her first day of work.

Jill dressed appropriately, but only after Grandma handled her. Joshua was happy and Madison was able to eat breakfast despite her nerves. Her car even started on the first try. Then things became a little iffy.

Tall, Dark & Lonely

Her new job was in a very nice school. The building was new. She had an excellent parking spot. The head of her department was an old woman who never stopped smiling and her classroom was well ventilated. Her desk was made of oak and completely blocked the view beneath so that no one saw her fidgeting. Everything in her room was brand new. The students however were a different story all together.

The males kept staring at her all day. She could practically feel their eyes running over her backside and down her legs. Every time she talked to one of her male students she had to work to keep their eyes on her face and not on her breasts. She couldn't understand it. The skirt wasn't too short and her blouse didn't show that much cleavage.

Actually, compared to the way many of the female students dressed, her clothes should have been considered conservative. Some of the girls in her class reminded her of the half naked groupies that starred in music videos. Their boobs practically hung out, many of them including Jill to her horror, stuffed. They wore thongs and low cut jeans so that their thongs could be seen. It was a scary sight indeed.

The girls in her class, the ones who dressed to impress the male population, hated her on sight. They snickered and whispered when one of the more popular males made eyes at her. It was annoying to say the least. She ended up assigning a paper just to get control of the room. Now she was feared, that was good.

To her horror the students were not the only males with wandering eyes. The teacher's lounge ended up being worse than the classroom. The men spoke to her and asked questions, but their eyes remained fixated on her breasts. Halfway through her break she excused herself and returned to her room to eat in silence.

What was wrong with men? She didn't have this problem in New Mexico. All the men knew her there. She spent most of her free time on the Reservation with her friends. It had been her safe haven since she was ten. They all knew her and treated her like family. It's not that she didn't have the occasional admirer there. She'd dated several men from the tribe. It's just that they were more respectful. They were her friends as well as her family. They taught her everything about life and her culture.

The males from this new school were a little bit more obvious about their attentions towards her. Back home if she caught a man staring he usually had the good sense to look guilty and mutter an apology. Not here, oh no, here she seemed to be eye candy. The men started with her face and she could see the appreciation in their eyes as their eyes ran down her body, hungrily.

Finally, she resigned herself to this situation. After a few weeks this would end. They would be used to her and treat her with more respect. She just had to hang in there. There was one man who didn't look at her like that, Nick. He was in her department and seemed nice. It didn't hurt that he was gay. At least she could count on one man behaving himself while she was at work, she thought with a small, frustrated groan.

The rest of the day seemed to go downhill after lunch. Jill, her little sister, decided she was going to make a splash on her first day. She changed her clothes sometime between breakfast and first bell. Her bra was overstuffed, her thong was high, her clothes too tight and she wore too much make-up. She flirted with every boy in class, in *Madison's* class. It was like watching a horror flick. Madison of course gave her detention for a week. She hid her smile. That felt good. Jill scowled at her for the remainder of the class, but didn't say another word, smart girl.

She decided to run home and change before looking at cars. Halfway there her car started to sputter. It seemed like she was getting a break when her car died in front of Earl's Garage. That had been a tease, she was sure of it now. Someone was laughing at her no doubt about it.

Tall, Dark & Lonely

"So, there's no hope?"

Earl twirled a toothpick in his mouth. "Not a one. I'm surprised it lasted this long."

She sighed, "Me too."

Earl walked around the car muttering to himself. "Earl?"

"Yes?"

"Do you want the car? You can take it apart and sell it for parts or whatever."

He nodded slowly. "How much?"

She shook her head. "Just take it. It's yours."

"You sure?"

"Yes."

"Okay," he readily agreed, giving her a tobacco stained grin.

Madison grabbed a few items from the car and stuffed them into her backpack. After signing over the title and saying goodbye to the car she decided a walk for the last three miles was in order. She needed to clear her head.

She took her heels off and walked along the road. It didn't matter that it was cold out. The only things that mattered were the sound of the birds, the feel of grass beneath her feet and fresh air in her lungs. She loved to walk. She spent hours at home walking. It cleared her head and helped her relax, something she desperately needed on a day like this.

* * * *

"That's enough of that."

Ephraim turned the radio off making the purr of his car sound louder, but not loud enough to destroy the peace and quiet of driving along on an old country road. Silence was golden. He missed the days of true silence when birds chirping, children's laughter and the sounds of horses filled the air.

That's why three years ago he moved to New Hampshire. He was sick of the loud noises in the city. He wanted to spend his days quietly so he took this job. He was on duty five days a week with two days off. It was perfect.

With the radio shut off he could think. This weekend would be perfect for some fishing. He could rent his usual cabin and relax. There would be no tomboy to tempt him. What was it about her blood? he wondered. Was it because she was a virgin? He didn't think so. The virgins he used to drink from didn't make him insane with hunger. There was something off about this Madison woman and finding out what that was, was not an option.

She was too tempting. She was plain as far as he could tell, but that was just the outside package. What lay inside was driving him insane. All night he tossed and turned, trying to fight the urge to go back to her room and have a taste. When he couldn't take it anymore he kicked off the covers and ended up taking a long cold shower to clear his head.

Now he just had to go home and avoid the woman. It shouldn't be too hard. He never ate meals with the rest of the house and didn't go into the main house unless Mrs. Buckman needed him. Tonight he would relax in his room and file his reports for the day on the computer. When that was done he would catch up on some sleep.

His eyes narrowed on something two miles down the road, a woman. There was no doubt in his mind about it. His eyesight was perfect. He smiled. That was a good thing in this case. This woman was perfection. "Holy shit," he mumbled softly as he slowed down so that he could take his time appreciating this beauty.

Tall, Dark & Lonely

Her hair shimmered in the sun. It was beautiful and black. Generous hips swayed gently beneath a short skirt. Her backside was perfectly curved as well and her legs were made to wrap around a man and hold on tight. Her skin was a beautiful golden tan. Damn, this woman was hot. He was willing to bet the front would be just as inviting.

He shifted in his seat and laughed. It looked like his body was interested. Perhaps this beauty would like to help end over a hundred years of celibacy. It seemed he no longer thought that sex was boring. He quickly checked his breath and hair before he sped up, wondering if he should bring her back to his room or just go rent a hotel room.

Ephraim didn't look at her as he drove past. He pulled his car onto the shoulder twenty yards ahead and watched her approach. His groin hardened painfully. She was even more beautiful than he imagined. Her face was raised to the sun while her eyes were closed. She looked like she was enjoying the sun, well that was fine because it allowed him to enjoy the view.

Her face was stunning. She was so damn beautiful that it hurt. Her black hair and tan complexion meshed together perfectly. She was shorter than him, but he liked his women shorter. Her breasts were good size, but not too big. They looked like they would fill his hands perfectly with no waste. Her waist was narrow while her hips were wide. He was imagining her legs wrapped around him as she walked past his car.

It had been a very long time since he wooed a woman. He was sure it hadn't changed that much, flirt, keep eye contact, and make a suggestion. No wait, they went on a date first nowadays. Okay, so he had to get her to agree to a date, dinner and a movie. That was the new mating ritual. He bought her some entertainment and then she would provide him with some. That's how they did it in the movies at least.

First, he had to talk to her. He stepped out of the car as he adjusted his gun and tie. "Excuse me, miss?" he said, using his most charming smile and tone.

The woman stopped and slowly turned around, prolonging the torture. Beautiful brown eyes met his. They reminded him of someone, but he couldn't think past how beautiful she was to figure it out. She was so beautiful that she left him speechless.

"Ephraim?" She looked worried. "Are you okay?"

She knew him? Impossible. He would never forget meeting someone like her. He didn't want to let her know that he didn't remember her. He seemed to remember that women hated it when men forgot their names.

"What are you doing out here walking?" He gestured to the long stretch of road.

She bit her lip. "My car finally died. I left it with Earl. He promised me a proper burial." She smiled and he couldn't help smiling back.

He gestured to his car. "Do you want a ride?"

She looked up at the sun and then back at him. "No, thank you. It's too beautiful a day to waste." His thoughts exactly. "It's only another mile. I'll be fine. Don't worry." She sounded like she was saying goodbye. He didn't want her to say goodbye that meant he wouldn't be able to look at her for much longer.

A mile? She gave him a clue. His brain raced to figure it out. He needed something else to talk about before she walked away. The only thing a mile down the road was Mrs. Buckman's boarding house, a few other houses, and a convenient store. He knew she didn't live near him. Was she visiting?

Ephraim gave her a lopsided smile that he hoped would charm her into giving him a little more information. "I don't feel right leaving you to walk by yourself, but if you insist I would feel better if you allowed me to check on you later to make sure that you arrived safely."

She gave him a weird smile. "Sure....that's fine," she said slowly as if she was a little confused.

Tall, Dark & Lonely

He cocked his head to the side and studied her. There was something very familiar about her. Even fifteen feet away he felt like he was missing something. He decided to push for more answers. Maybe something would remind him of her identity.

"I'm afraid I've forgotten your address, perhaps you could take pity on me and remind me so I can do the gentlemanly thing later."

She laughed.

At him!

He wasn't being foolish, he was sure of that. Sure he was out of practice, but he felt that he was being charming. Her eyes were shimmering with humor as she shook her head. "I'll see you later, Ephraim." She turned, still laughing and began walking away from him.

He was about to ask her what was so funny when a gust of wind swept her beautiful black hair up. The wind carried her fragrance to his nose and it hit him hard. He stumbled backwards and landed his ass on the hood of his car. It couldn't be.

She looked over her shoulder at him and smiled. Those damn brown eyes. It was her. Madison laughed again as she turned her head around. He could only sit on the hood of his car, watching her go.

He dropped his head in his hands. "This is not happening." This woman was supposed to be a tomboy. She was supposed to be unattractive to help keep them both safe. It was bad enough that he craved her blood, but now he desired her body. This was not good. This was a test. This was a test to see if he could resist temptation. It had to be.

No woman should be this tempting. It was too much. And what the hell was she doing still being a virgin? When he thought that she was a tomboy he understood her predicament, but now.....hell. A virgin? It made it worse. The package was too damn tempting. A surprising beauty with blood that sang to him and was untouched by another man? She might as well place a target on her neck.

He pushed himself away from the car. No, no this was fine. As long as they both remained at the boardinghouse she was safe. He had rules after all and he never broke them, ever. He did not feed where he lived. He just had to get the rest of his body inline and he would be fine because feeding from the virginal Madison was not an option. She was the only woman he would not be content with just a feeding, he would take her body and life as well. That would wreck everything.

Things were different these days. Back in his day he could feed off as many whores and criminals as he wanted. If he took their lives it was no big deal. No one would miss them. Occasionally he overfed in one area and had to flee. Over the years he learned to control his feeding by using more than one victim so that he could feed without taking a life. Today, if he fucked up and killed someone the authorities would be able to track him down.

Her body wouldn't be seen as a feeding. It would be seen as a depraved lunatic's attack and they would hunt him down using his fingerprints, hair and anything else they could find. He didn't want to be forced into hiding, but that was exactly what would happen if he touched her. No, Madison was safe from him.

Chapter 4

Madison shook her head, laughing softly as she walked inside the house ten minutes later. That was really weird. She couldn't deny that she found the little episode endearing. He'd been so cute when he was trying to flirt and there was no doubt in her mind that he was trying to flirt. She bit her lip trying to stop herself from laughing.

His attempts at flirting were obvious, awkward and unpracticed and unbelievably adorable. There was really no other way to describe it. The big brooding man was utterly adorable. She recalled the expression on his face the last time she turned around and sighed. He'd looked completely stunned.

She ran the conversation through her head, worried that she might have said something to upset him. She couldn't recall anything. Perhaps he was overly sensitive and wasn't happy that she hadn't played along? Whatever it was she didn't have time to play around.

Madison spotted the reason as she walked past the living room. Jill was sitting on the couch, painting her nails while she talked on her cell phone. Madison took a deep breath and stalked forward unable to hide the menacing grin. Jill looked up. When she spotted Madison closing in on her, her eyebrows drew together in confusion.

As soon as she reached her sister, she snatched the phone away from Jill's hands. "Whoever this is, you'll have to call back in a month." Jill's mouth dropped in shock. "Jill will be enjoying a month long grounding and I'm afraid her phone will be going bye-bye for a very long time."

Jill shot to her feet, holding her hand out in a silent demand for the phone.

"Oh, I don't think so." Madison dropped the phone in the backpack she still carried. "When you earn this I will *think* about giving it back to you." With that, Madison turned and walked towards the door. "Oh, by the way, you're grounded for a month in case you didn't catch that little tidbit of information."

"I didn't do anything!" Jill shrieked.

Madison didn't bother looking over her shoulder. "Found your alcohol and cigarettes. Incidentally, be prepared in an hour we're going drug testing." This time she did look over her shoulder and grinned mockingly. "Should be loads of fun."

Jill's face paled. "You c-can't do that," she muttered.

"No, but I can," Grandma's stern voice came from the doorway. "You be prepared *now*, young lady. The two of us are taking you for a drug test. God help you if it comes back positive."

Jill's mouth opened, but no words came out. Madison jogged up the stairs, eager to get this over with. "Let me go change. I'll be right back."

Five minutes later Madison was downstairs in a pair of hip hugging jeans and a tight tee shirt. In this weather she would have preferred wearing several layers and possibly a blanket or two, but she needed to be able to move freely for the fight that she knew was coming.

She found Jill huddled in a corner, refusing Grandma and begging Candy, who looked nervous, to help her. This wasn't the time for games. Out of fear that Jill would somehow get out of this, and she definitely was not getting out of this, she moved in and grabbed Jill's arm and tugged her forward.

Just as she expected, Jill tried to fight back. She yanked her arm back trying to get free. Madison tightened her grip and quickened her pace. They were out the door and heading towards Grandma's Volvo when Jill moved to her second assault, girl punches. They were wild and weaker than a slap, but annoying as hell.

"Let me go!" Jill demanded, yet again.

"No," Madison snapped back, not even bothering to look at Jill as she answered her.

Tall, Dark & Lonely

Grandma hurried past them to open the back door of her car. Madison didn't see Jill's arm arch back and she certainly didn't expect the powerful half slap-half punch that slammed into the side of her mouth. She felt the bite of metal in her lip. Damn Jill and her gaudy costume jewelry.

Jill stumbled away and made a mad dash towards the front door. Oh no you don't, Madison thought as she ran after Jill and tackled her to the ground.

"Oh my god, are you insane? Get off me now, you bitch!" Jill screamed.

Madison climbed off her sister as she pulled Jill's arm behind her back. "Ow, ow! Stop!" She twisted it more. "Fine, I'll go!" Jill snapped. Madison did not ease up on her hold. For some odd reason she just didn't trust her little sister at the moment.

"Ow! Madison! Stop!" Jill pleaded.

Candy ran out of the house and jumped in front of them. "Madison, let her go!"

"Get. Out. Of. My. Way," Madison bit out each word, more than eager to slap her mother if that's what it took to fix this horrible mess.

"But…" Candy looked nervously from Madison to Jill. Whatever she saw on Jill's face made her act in self-preservation. She inhaled deeply and looked down her nose at Jill. "I told you not to bring drugs into the house again." Jill and Madison's mouth dropped open at the same moment.

"I'm sorry, Jill, perhaps I didn't do you any favors by letting it slide last time, but," she nodded to herself, "this is for the best I think." With that she stalked back to the house, leaving everyone stunned. Not for one second did anyone believe that Candy hadn't given Jill drugs.

A sob broke from Jill that had nothing to do with the Madison's hold. "I-I did pot last week and I-I tried ecstasy a week ago as well….." she choked out. "I'm sorry….I…..I didn't think….I just wanted Candy to li-like m-me."

Madison released her hold on her sister's arm and pulled Jill into a fierce hug. "Shh, it's okay." She was going to slap Candy one of these days. Madison swore inwardly, she knew that was the major reason Jill had been acting like this over the past weeks. Jill wanted Candy, her mother, to like her.

"I won't do it again. You don't have to worry," Jill said bitterly. Madison sighed. It finally happened. Jill realized in that moment that their mother didn't love them or care about them. It took Jill fifteen years to do it and Madison felt like someone stabbed her in the heart. She never wanted her sister to feel this pain. It hurt more than anything. She knew that better than anyone. Her eyes shot over to Joshua who was watching them with bored interest. He already knew.

She forced herself from that knowledge and pushed Jill towards the car. "What? I told you what I did and won't do it again?"

"I know," Madison said softly. "But I wouldn't be doing my job if I took your word. I don't want you to end up making mistakes that you can't take back."

Jill's eyes watered. "Too late," she mumbled. Silent tears streamed down her young face as she walked to the car on her own and climbed in. Grandma closed the door and threw a sympathetic look in Madison's direction before she climbed into the car and drove off.

Madison forced herself to smile as she turned to look at her brother. "You feel like going car shopping with me?" she asked brightly, hoping that it would be enough to distract Joshua from worrying about Jill.

Joshua's little face lit up. "Heck yeah!" His little face scrunched up, looking thoughtful a few seconds later. "You should wash your face first."

"Why?"

"You're bleeding," he said casually with a shrug.

Her fingers went to her lips and found hot moisture. She pulled her hand away and frowned. Damn that girl can hit. "Give me ten minutes and then we're off."

Tall, Dark & Lonely

* * * *

Ephraim walked into his room and froze. He inhaled deeply and then again. Blood. *Her blood.* He closed his eyes and followed the scent into the bathroom. His eyes darted to her door, making sure it was closed. He locked it before looking for the source. After a moment he found it, tissues.

His hands shook as he reached into the wastebasket to pick up one of the many bloody tissues. He snatched up all of them, afraid they would disappear. In less than a second his eyes were closed and he was inhaling the mouthwatering scent. The scent of her blood was overwhelming. His fangs dropped in his mouth, aching for a taste.

He licked his lips, imagining what it would be like to taste her blood. In a moment he would know. It was fresh. All he had to do was squeeze a drop from the discarded tissues and he would have his taste. His head dropped back and he held the tissues over his waiting mouth. He opened his eyes, making sure that he didn't miss a drop. His hand began squeezing the tissues together with inhuman strength, forcing the red liquid to separate from the cotton. His tongue darted out, prepared to catch the drops he saw forming. So close…so close…

Out of the corner of his eye, he caught his reflection in the mirror and froze. His eyes were glowing red while his fangs glistened. His features were harsh and he'd never looked more like a monster in his entire life than he did at that moment.

Slowly, he lowered his gaze. After a moment he could no longer look at himself. He threw the tissues into the toilet out of disgust and flushed. He looked at his hand and coiled at the thought that hit him, lick it. His hand was smeared with blood. He'd never been more disgusted with himself.

For years he hated himself, hated what he was and hated what he wasn't. None of those moments could compare to this one. He was a monster. A blood thirsty monster who was preying on an innocent woman. How he hated himself. The need to lick his hand only increased.

"No!" he growled. He would not give in to it. He dropped to his knees and opened the cabinet. A moment later he held his hand over the sink while he poured bleach over it.

Pain shot through his arm while the skin on his hand began to dissolve. He ground his teeth as he continued to pour the entire gallon over his hand. This would remind him that he was nothing more than a monster. He was nothing, just an unwanted accident and everyone would be better off if he remembered that.

* * * *

Ephraim took a deep breath and bent over. "Hurry up, hurry up, hurry up," he mumbled to himself. He really needed to take a piss and she was still in the shower. If she didn't get the hell out of there soon he was going to be forced to piss out the window.

He stopped himself from knocking and asking how long she was going to be. For the past month and a half he hadn't said a word to her. He hadn't let his presence be known. It was safer that way. He was afraid of what he would do if she spoke to him or even looked his way.

He was drinking two extra pints a day, hoping it would be enough to take away the temptation. It wasn't. He found that out the hard way. Even a stomach uncomfortably full of blood didn't stop the reaction she created. He discovered that every time he caught her scent. This was hell. This was worse than anything Nichols put him through.

He groaned. He was too old to piss his pants, but that's exactly what he was going to do if he didn't get to a bathroom soon. That was it. He was going to break down the door. He raised his fist and froze when he heard knocking from her side.

The water shut off. "Yes?"

Jill's voice answered, "You told me to tell you when it was five."

Tall, Dark & Lonely

Ephraim's eyes shot to his watch. Well, her sister was a prompt little thing. It was five on the dot. "Oh, damn it. I'm coming!"

He closed his eyes and listened to her every movement. She wrapped a towel around her, unlocked his door, scooped up her dirty clothes and went into her room, closing her bathroom door behind her.

"Shit!" He was really about to piss himself. He hurried into the bathroom, careful to lock her door on the way to the toilet since there was no need for either woman to see him piss blood. It would probably send them screaming or fainting. He flushed the toilet all the while listening to what was going on in the next room. Ephraim moved around purposely making noise, no need for them to think he was creepy or anything.

Madison could hear Ephraim walking around in the bathroom. She sighed, thinking that he was probably getting ready for one of his extra long showers. She hadn't seen him in over a month since the day she walked home. It was almost as if he was avoiding her which was strange. He'd seemed very friendly that day. Of course, she was being ridiculous. He was a police detective, a very busy man. It only seemed like he was avoiding her.

She put the blow-dryer down and spritzed hair gel through her hair as she watched Jill lounge on her bed with a magazine. "I really like your outfit, Jill."

Jill's face lit up. "Really?"

Jill wore a very cute understated blouse and skirt. Her boyfriend of two weeks was coming over tonight. Seth was a straight "A" student and a down to earth guy and Jill was madly in love with him. When she dressed like a slut he avoided her so she tried another angle, being herself.

Madison made a bet with her. She challenged Jill to dress like she did before Candy showed up and forget everything Candy taught her about men. Reluctantly, Jill tried it and three days later Seth showed up for dinner. He was a nice kid and Madison thought he was a god for getting her sister back in line. A feat she thought would take a year and a convent to accomplish.

Candy did not take the change well. She pouted around the house for days. She let Jill know that she was so upset with her and went as far as refusing to eat with "the boy who wrecked her daughter." Yet she was willing to get drunk with a thirty-five year old man moments after he took her fifteen year old daughter's virginity. Go figure.

It took a few days, but soon Candy happily ignored Jill's presence the same way that she ignored Joshua. She also quit working for Grandma and found work in the next town over. She still lived here, but only until she had enough to move out which should be soon. Candy wouldn't admit it to Grandma, but everyone knew that she was working as a bartender at a strip club. She took a fit the night she was hired. They told her that she was too old to strip or wait tables. Money helped her get over that disappointment real fast. The patrons always tipped her well to keep them in drinks.

"I can't believe we finally get to meet prince charming," Jill said teasingly.

She laughed. "Stop calling him that! His name is David!"

Jill giggled. "Okay, I'll call him David to his face then."

"Thank you."

Jill went back to her magazine while Madison dressed. She decided on a dress, something casual. She looked up to find Jill watching her with interest.

"What?"

"So, are you going to tell me what he looks like or do you want it to be a surprise?"

Madison rolled her eyes. "I'm surprised you don't know. The three times we went out you were waiting by the window."

Jill sighed. "We tried, but we couldn't see anything. The way this house is setup is so inconvenient. The only thing I know is that he drives a black car."

Tall, Dark & Lonely

"Then you know enough."

Jill jumped off the bed. "That's not fair! Come on, please!" She placed her hands together in a praying gesture and jumped up and down.

"Oh all right, sit down before you pass out from excitement."

"Sure thing!" Jill crawled back on the bed. "Well?"

"Don't rush me. What do you want to know?"

"Is he a good kisser?"

They heard something crash in the bathroom followed by a curse, but they ignored it. "He's okay I guess."

"Is he handsome?" Jill nibbled on her lip.

"Yes."

Jill looked up at the ceiling deep in thought. She wasn't happy with the answer and needed a comparison. "Is he better looking than Ephraim?"

She wanted to lie, but Jill would see for herself in less than twenty minutes. "No, he's not as handsome as Ephraim." She continued quickly. "He's really nice. He's an expert on British history and he's a perfect gentleman."

"He sounds dull," Jill said.

"He is not!"

"Do you think…that you know he'll be the one that you let…you know?"

She did know. Being a twenty-three year old virgin was starting to grate on her. She wasn't saving herself for marriage or anything. "I don't know. I can think of worse men to take a chance on. If I did, I think he would be gentle and respectful."

"So, you think you might with him?"

"Yes, I think so. If things continue the way they are."

"Do you love him?"

"I think I like him," she hedged. She just met the guy, but couldn't say that because Jill would think she was putting down her relationship with Seth.

Jill nodded. "Just don't rush into it. I know I messed up and I regret it. I wish I hadn't. I wished it had been with a nice guy. Just….just be sure, okay?" Jill finished, looking close tears.

Madison hated seeing her sad. She knew Jill cried at night over what happened. She really wanted to slap Candy upside the head for this. Instead, she threw a balled up pair of socks at Jill. "Hey, come on, no crying. You don't want that boyfriend of yours to think that you cry over him."

That got her attention in a big way. She jumped up and ran to the mirror, pushing Madison over to check her lip gloss. She looked very pretty and very fifteen.

Jill smoothed down her dress. "We should go downstairs. They'll be here any minute."

"I can't wait!" Jill giggled.

They walked downstairs as they talked and laughed, clicking the way that they used to before Candy showed up. Grandma met them in the foyer and smiled. "One of my favorite guys is in the living room waiting for you, Jill." Grandma loved Seth as well. He made her job easier and who wouldn't love that?

Grandma lowered her voice. "We have a surprise guest tonight."

"Who?"

"Oh, you have no idea how happy I am that he's eating with us. Listen, I know your special friend is coming over tonight, but I need to sit him between you and Joshua. The two of you seem to irritate him less than everyone else. I'll sit your friend across from you, which is more proper for a dinner anyway."

Tall, Dark & Lonely

"Who?"

A buzzer went off from the direction of the kitchen. "Oh, that's my roast!" Grandma hurried down the hallway, leaving Madison to wonder. It had to be Reverend Michaels. Grandma was constantly trying to get the man to stay for a meal. He was nice and she did enjoy talking with him and Joshua loved playing chess with him. Hmm, having the Reverend here wouldn't be bad. Candy was too much of a coward to make a scene in front of him.

Joshua walked out of the living room, fidgeting with the tie Grandma most likely made him wear. "You really should go in there. It's rude to make your friend wait for you."

She froze. "He's here? Why didn't Grandma tell me?"

He shrugged. "Probably 'cause I'm the one who let him in and she didn't know."

"Joshua, you are enough to drive me to drink." She playfully pushed him on her way to the living room.

David sat on the couch, making conversation with Mrs. Adle, the resident widow. She was a sweet old woman who liked nothing better than to talk about her grandchildren.

"Oh, look who's here." Mrs. Adle smiled in Madison's direction.

David's blue eyes lit up. He pushed his shoulder length blond hair back as he walked over to kiss her on the cheek. Madison ignored Joshua's gagging noise. "I'm sorry. I didn't know that you were here yet."

"It's fine. I've had the pleasure of talking with Mrs. Adle so I can't complain." Mrs. Adle beamed. Madison ran her eyes around the living room. The good Reverend wasn't here yet and thankfully neither was Candy.

David didn't know much about her. She really should have warned him, but she couldn't force herself. This was a nice guy and Candy would send him running for the hills. He was so old fashioned. He already told her he hated guys that went to strip clubs. What would he think if he found out that her mother worked at one?

Grandma poked her head in. "Dinner is on the table."

David gestured for her to lead the way. She led him into the large dining room. It was the second largest room in the house, the kitchen was the first. It was custom designed for Grandma years ago when she decided to turn the house into a boarding house. The table was long enough to sit sixteen.

"David, why don't you sit here? Oh, and Madison you sit here." Grandma gestured to the third seat away from the end where she sat.

Madison stepped around the chair and was about to sit down when the chair was pushed in behind her, helping her scoot forward. David was such a gentleman. She looked over her shoulder, smiling "Thank you,-" the last word caught in her throat as she looked at the one man she hadn't expected.

Ephraim.

Chapter 5

"You're welcome," Ephraim said. He took the seat between Madison and Joshua. Joshua grinned hugely at Ephraim.

"I mashed the potatoes!" Joshua announced.

"Then I believe I shall have a double helping," Ephraim said, making Joshua's day.

Madison couldn't help but notice David and Ephraim eyeing each other.

"Help yourselves, please," Grandma said as she started passing the bowls of food around. That reminded Madison that she needed to make introductions.

"Grandma, this is my friend David. David, this is my grandmother, Mrs. Buckman."

"It's a pleasure to meet you," David said smoothly.

"David, this is Ephraim." David's smile faltered a touch before he managed to pull it back.

Ephraim stood and extended his hand. "I reside here as well," Ephraim explained. David noticeably relaxed at the announcement.

"I'm sorry you probably won't have the chance to meet my daughter Emma, Madison's mother, she called and said she would be delayed."

Madison exhaled slowly and relaxed. "Are you okay?" Ephraim whispered.

"Yes," she whispered back. David was talking with John, another renter, while he eyed Ephraim.

"You'll have to introduce them sometime. It would be better if you just got it over with," he whispered back in a mocking tone that irritated her.

Annoyance shot through her. "Mind your business," she hissed.

He chuckled softly as he loaded his plate with mashed potatoes and then handed them off. Ephraim looked at his plate and sighed. The food looked good and smelled great. He hated what he would have to do later. If he didn't force the food from his system, it would just rot in his stomach. He hated when that happened.

It couldn't be avoided tonight. After what he heard her announcement tonight he couldn't sit back. Curiosity was a bitch. It had him running down the stairs before them to tell an excited Mrs. Buckman that he would like to join them for dinner tonight. She was thrilled. He was impatient. He wanted to see the man that Madison had settled on.

So far he was not impressed. This guy seemed too conceited. He was hiding something, Ephraim was sure of it. Everything in him was telling him this guy was full of shit. He just had to find out what it was. He was doing Madison a favor by finding out. She obviously held off losing her virginity for a reason. If she lost it to this prick she wouldn't be happy, he was sure of that. Only thing to do was help her see it.

"So, David, what do you do exactly? Madison tells me you're an expert of British history." Mrs. Buckman started the conversation rolling.

He could kiss her.

"I'm an author. I'm currently writing a book covering nineteenth century England." Meaning someone loved Ephraim. It was fate that this guy chose the century that he was born in. Now he just had to use it to his advantage and help Madison see that this guy was a douche bag.

"How do you make a living if you're writing a book?" Joshua asked. The boy was getting a bike for Christmas that's all there was to it.

David squirmed in his seat. "It doesn't pay anything yet."

"So, then what do you do to pay the bills?" Joshua asked. Forget the bike he was getting a go-cart.

Tall, Dark & Lonely

"Joshua! That's rude!" Mrs. Buckman, Madison and Jill said in unison. Ephraim had to fight a smile. This was fun. He should do this more often.

David put his fork down and held up a hand. "It's fine." He smiled warmly at everyone. "I actually work in a book store in the next town over. I enjoy the work."

"Oh," Joshua mumbled, sounding disappointed and making David squirm even more. He really liked this kid. "So, do you have to live with your parents then?"

Several of the other boarders coughed, trying to hide their chuckles. Mrs. Buckman looked embarrassed. "Joshua, you're being very rude tonight," Madison said.

Joshua bit his lip and looked like he was about to cry. Ephraim took pity on the boy since Joshua was doing his dirty work for him. He put an arm around Joshua and gave him a small squeeze. "The boy's just making conversation. I would take it as a compliment, Madison. He's the man of the family." Joshua sat up straighter with those words and puffed out his chest. "He's just trying to get to know David." Ephraim shot David a smile that was anything but friendly. "You don't mind, do you? He doesn't mean any harm after all." Not like Ephraim.

David gave them a tight smile. "No, of course not." From the look the man was sending him, Ephraim knew that David did not like him. Good. "To answer your question, I rent an apartment." He looked straight at Ephraim when he spoke. "Most men over twenty live on their own in apartments or own their own home." He didn't realize that he immediately lost any respect he might have earned from the rest of the renters and from the looks of it Mrs. Buckman was not too happy with the comment. She viewed her renters as friends.

It was up to Ephraim to save face for everyone, but then again he didn't have to when Joshua was around. "That's not true. John is an excellent carpenter and he only lives here because his house burned down years ago and he likes it here and Brad," he pointed to the middle aged man sitting between John and Jill's boyfriend. "He lives here because he sends half his money to his sister whose husband died. He could live on his own, but he doesn't so that she can put food on the table for her three kids," he said proudly. Brad winked at him.

Joshua jerked a thumb at Ephraim. "He's a police detective. He likes living here. He doesn't have to."

"It's okay, little man. He didn't mean to offend anyone," Ephraim said, but he knew that wasn't true.

"No, I didn't. I apologize if it sounded otherwise." David looked apologetic so everyone laughed it off and told him it was not a big deal.

Within minutes everyone was back to chatting quietly while they ate. Madison ignored him and focused on David who kept throwing Ephraim triumphant glances.

Jackass.

"What did they call police in England during the early nineteenth century?" Joshua asked David, loud enough to draw everyone's attention. A peculiar question, Ephraim thought. What was he up to? From the look Joshua threw him, he was definitely up to something.

"They were called coppers, because they copped criminals," David said arrogantly.

That did it. He couldn't stop himself from laughing. Madison elbowed him in the ribs, but that only made him laugh harder.

"What's so funny?" David asked him.

He stopped laughing, but kept smiling. "I'm sorry I thought you were joking."

David looked pissed. "I was not."

"Ephraim, do you know?" Joshua asked as he poured a gallon of gravy over his food.

He sighed. He did know.

"What was it like back then? Did they have the same setup we have with police and judges?"

David sat back, folding his arms across his chest, arrogantly. "I'm interested in your opinion as well. Perhaps you learned something in the police academy about the history of law enforcement that I would find useful."

Ah, a challenge.

"Well, they didn't have police officers like they do today in the early nineteenth century." David scoffed and everyone ignored him. They were all eager to hear what Ephraim had to say. He was known as a man of few words and he never spoke freely. This was a treat for them.

"What did they have?" Mrs. Buckman asked, eager for him to talk as well.

"They had the tradition of Constables from early history, but it wasn't until the early 1800's when people realized that a police force was needed. They weren't as organized or law focused as we are today. The men who would have done my job were called Bow Street Runners and the police force were called Peelers or Bobbies in the 1820's."

"Cool!"

Ephraim chuckled at the boy's excitement. "It was considered a lower class job. Something looked down upon. They mostly worked for private pay, but they could expect a shilling or two from the government for public work. The men they answered to either bought a commission, meaning they paid for a position in the government, or they earned it through reputation. Those positions were government based."

"They helped people then?" Joshua asked.

He sighed, "No, not really. The whole lot was rather corrupt."

"And today's police force isn't?" David demanded in a snide tone.

Ephraim ignored him. He was focused on the woman by his left who was watching and waiting. "You have to understand something, Joshua. Back then things were different. Nobility and money ran everything. They were above the law. The Bow Street Runners, the group that made up the policing unit and the other government positions were only created to control the masses and keep the nobility safe and happy. If a noble man broke the law it was only viewed as good gossip."

"A nobleman, let's say a Duke for instance could kill his wife and no one could do anything about it. It would just be talked about. If that man had any children it might wreck their chances of making a good match, because a good family wouldn't want to be linked to such scandal."

"That's messed up," Joshua said. "So, they protected the nobility?"

Ephraim nodded. "And those who could pay them. They were for hire. They mostly went after the poor or did the duties of a private detective. A rich household hired footmen to protect the property. They used the footmen to get their own justice."

"Who protected the poor people?"

"No one. They were at the mercy of the magistrate and the government. If they were in some way hurt by the nobility there was no real way to win. They could appeal to the magistrate, but the magistrate would always take the side of the nobleman. They wouldn't want to get on bad terms with someone of peer."

"The peer?"

"Noblemen."

"Oh. Did they have jails?"

Madison watched Ephraim's hands clenched tightly on the table. "Something like that. The cells were small, overcrowded and inhumane. Some of the smaller districts used dungeon from earlier times to keep criminals."

"Cool! What did they do to people in the dungeon?"

Madison saw Ephraim's hands shake before he dropped them onto his lap where they continued to shake. What was wrong with him? She looked around, surprised to find that he had everyone's undivided attention.

"The magistrate was a power onto himself. The further away from London the more powerful that man became. He had the power to grab a man, woman or child from the street on a whim and throw them into a cell. He mostly followed orders from the noblemen, but sometimes he was the highest ranking nobleman in the area."

"Innocent people were thrown in the cells?"

"Yes."

"Well, what if they proved they were innocent?"

Ephraim chuckled without humor. She watched his hands shake harder. Something was clearly upsetting him. Without thinking, she reached over and covered his hand with hers. His hand almost immediately stopped shaking, but he didn't look at her. He continued speaking instead.

"They didn't care. You were in that cell until someone paid on your behalf or someone higher up with more powerful blood spoke on your behalf. You were starved, deprived of liquid. If you were lucky you were placed in a cell with a small opening for a window so you could count the days. That was one of the worse things about being in a cell without light. Days and nights went by and you couldn't keep track. It was torture not to know how long you were in the cell." He spoke as if he knew. She could actually feel the dread of his words.

She didn't notice his thumb caressing her hand as he spoke. "If you were smart you could follow the hours by the sounds of the guards changing shifts or figure out when night came based on the rats."

"Rats?" Mrs. Adle asked, sounding horrified.

"Rats rarely came out during the day. They mostly came during the night when the guards were asleep and no one was walking the corridors with a candle or oil lamp. Rats hate light."

"How did the prisoners get rid of the rats?" Joshua asked.

Ephraim turned his hand over so he could lace his fingers with Madison's. He continued to run his thumb over her skin. He was surprised he could be this close to her and control his hunger even with her blood screaming for him. He wanted nothing more than to taste her, but he controlled it. Every now and then his fangs would begin to lower and he would run his tongue over them, sending them back. She had so much control over him and she didn't even know it.

"If you were in there long enough you would pray for a visit from a rat," he said casually.

"Why?" Brad asked.

"Food. The guards didn't give much food, not enough to live on and not often. Most families couldn't afford to feed a relative in the cells. A rat provided liquid from the blood and nourishment from meat."

"Gross!" Jill's boyfriend said.

Tall, Dark & Lonely

"So, they just sat in their cells?" Joshua asked.

"No, they were often taken out of the cells for the amusement of the guards or punishment from the magistrate."

"What did they do?"

"The prisoners were whipped, caned, tortured in any and every way possible or they were killed. Most didn't survive a beating. The cuts became infected and that's usually how they died if starvation didn't get them first."

"How sad," some of the women said.

"That sucks." Joshua said plainly.

David laughed. "He's kidding. It wasn't that bad and it wasn't like that with the nobility at all. The nobility cared deeply for the lower class. They were the backbone of the society after all. They would want to keep the workers happy so they would produce."

Madison saw Ephraim's jaw clench. "You really believe that, don't you?"

"Yes, I've studied it for years."

Ephraim released her hand and sat back. "You're the expert." With that he picked up his fork and continued to eat. After a minute everyone else returned their attention to their plates. She could tell from their expressions that they trusted and believed Ephraim.

She looked down at her hand. It felt very warm. She could still feel the hot path where his thumb caressed her skin. Her entire hand tingled from his touch. What was it about this man?

David could hold her hand and all she felt was discomfort. She didn't like his touch, but he was polite and attentive. If she was honest she'd admit that he was a little arrogant. She knew from some of her own research that Ephraim was correct. The justice system back then was inhumane.

Everyone ate, but kept looking back at Ephraim, hoping he would talk again. Joshua leaned in. "Are you okay?"

Ephraim forced a smile. "I'm okay."

"I believe you, you know," Joshua said in a loud whisper.

"Thanks. Eat your vegetables. I heard your Grandma made a chocolate cake."

Joshua dug in. The boy loved cake. Ephraim ate slowly and kept his eyes down. Madison noticed Grandma watching him. She looked worried.

"Joshua, I was planning on taking your sister to Boston next weekend. The museum is holding an exhibition on nineteenth century art if you want to come. It depicts what life was *really* like back then if you want to know."

"No, no thank you. I was hoping to go fishing again with Ephraim.," Joshua said without looking up from his plate.

Ephraim nodded, keeping his eyes on his plate as he pushed his food around. "You're always welcome to join me as long as your Grandmother and Madison say it's okay."

"Why wouldn't he ask his mother?" David asked, looking confused.

Madison opened her mouth to answer, she really needed to tell him the truth, when the door to the dining room opened.

"I'm so sorry I'm late. One of the other bartenders called in sick and....David? What are you doing here? Crystal is looking everywhere for you!"

"Who's Crystal?" Joshua asked.

David opened his mouth and then shut it. All eyes moved between David and Candy.

"Crystal is David's girlfriend of course. She works with me at the, er..club."

Tall, Dark & Lonely

All eyes fixed on David as Candy walked around the table, oblivious to the change in the room.

"Oh, before I forget, she told me that if I ran into you tonight to ask you to pick up more diapers for the baby."

Chapter 6

Ephraim dropped his fork on his plate. He leaned back in his seat, keeping his eyes on David. David fidgeted in his seat. He was sweating profusely and looking around the room nervously.

"Everyone, leave now," Ephraim said in a cold level tone.

David stood up.

"Not you. Sit down."

"What's going on?" Candy asked, sounding confused.

"Why don't you stay, Candy?" Ephraim's voice was gentle, but everyone knew it wasn't a request. It was an order.

"Okay." Candy sat down in the seat Brad vacated. The men threw David a glare as they left the room.

"I want to stay, too!" Joshua said.

Without taking his eyes away from David, Ephraim pulled his wallet out and opened it. He pulled out two fifties. "Since it's my fault that no one was able to finish this lovely dinner that your grandmother cooked I'll treat. Go order enough pizza for everyone."

Joshua looked at the money in his hand and back at David. He wanted to stay, but pizza was pizza after all. "Can I get a meatball and mushroom pizza?"

"You can get whatever you want," Ephraim said. "And if you keep everyone out of here then you can even keep the change."

"Cool!" He ran out of the room, leaving David, Ephraim, Mrs. Buckman, Madison and Candy alone.

David started to stand up. "This is just a misunderstanding that's all....I swear....I...I'll just be going," he stammered.

Tall, Dark & Lonely

"Sit down, now!" Ephraim roared, causing everyone to jump. David practically fell back into his chair.

Madison's face was bright red. She'd never been so embarrassed or felt so used in her life. Part of her wanted to run, but she needed to find out who this man was. The man she considered giving herself to. Oh god, she wanted to curl up into a ball and die. This was so humiliating.

"Mrs. Buckman, if I promise to answer all of your questions later will you leave the room now? I promise to handle this properly." Still he looked at David.

Her grandmother sighed and nodded. She trusted him to handle this situation the same as any of her other problems. "Thank you, Ephraim."

"Come on, this is just a mistake!" David pleaded.

"Candy, I have a few questions for you and then you can leave as well, okay?" Ephraim asked, eyes still locked on David.

Candy looked confused, but nodded. "Do you know this man?"

"Yes."

"From?"

"He comes into the club most nights. He lives with Crystal and they have a baby. Why? What is going on here?"

"Where does he work?"

"A bookstore."

"Did he go to college?"

Candy laughed. "Are you kidding? He just got his GED last month."

David's face turned bright red.

"What is going on here?" Candy demanded.

"Nothing. Candy, why don't you go make sure that Joshua is ordering enough pizza, please." She stood up and left, throwing one last curious look at them. "Lock the door from the inside," Ephraim softly ordered.

He waited until he heard the door click shut before he stood up. David jumped to his feet. He grabbed the carving knife from the roast beef platter and held it up in front of him while he backed away and moved towards the locked door.

Ephraim gently took Madison by the arm and pushed her against the wall. Without any hesitation he stepped in front of David. "You owe the lady an apology and an explanation."

David licked his lips nervously. "I'm leaving."

"No, you're not. You're apologizing. Why did you lie and date her if you had a girlfriend and a baby at home?"

David looked at her and gave her a weak smile. "I'm sorry it was just a bet."

"A bet?" she asked, stepping forward. She was going to slap him!

Ephraim took another step, placing himself directly in front of David. David held the knife up with a shaky hand. "Get that damn thing out of my face, *boy*," Ephraim snapped.

David shook his head. "No, you're going to hit me!"

"Of course I am and you're only pissing me off more with that damn knife!" Ephraim reached out and grabbed the knife by the blade, ripping it out of David's hands and tossing it behind him and away from Madison.

Madison scrambled to pick up the knife before either man could pick it up again. She grabbed it and quickly stepped away from the men, looking at the blade, shocked by all the blood dripping down the blade.

"Now, you were telling us about a bet?" Ephraim prompted. If his hand hurt it didn't show. He stalked forward as David retreated.

"It was stupid. She came into the bookstore a month ago and the guys and I took a bet who could nail her." He held up his hands. "I didn't know it would take this long! I didn't mean to keep up this act this long. I swear it was just a bet!"

Ephraim shot a quick look back at Madison. She was crying. Ephraim fought for control as his teeth descended. "Your eyes…what's wrong with your eyes?" David asked nervously. Ephraim turned his head before Madison could see.

"Madison, please leave," he said in a soothing voice.

"No." Her voice broke.

"Madison, now!" he roared. He couldn't control it any longer. He ran his tongue over his fangs, trying to send them back, but they refused to go. His hands shook with rage and the need to tear this bastard apart.

Madison took a deep breath. She couldn't leave, she just couldn't. "No, I'm staying."

"Damn it, Madison, leave now!"

"No!"

Ephraim opened his eyes and turned back to look at David. "Oh my God! What the hell is this?" He grabbed a chair and flung it at Ephraim and ran for the door.

"Where do you think you're going?" Ephraim demanded as he moved in front of David, cutting him off. David stumbled back against the table. His entire body began to shake.

"Please, I'm so sorry…so sorry…I'll never do anything like this again I swear!" He sobbed uncontrollably.

Ephraim grabbed David's shirt with one hand, raising him off the ground until David was looking down at him. His arms and legs flailed wildly.

"If you ever talk to her or about her ever again I will get you. I don't care where you are I will come for you. There is no window I can't crawl through, no door I can't open, no place is safe from me. I know your scent now. I can hunt you down anywhere that you go. Do you believe me, David?" Ephraim asked in cold calculating voice.

"Y-yes!" he cried uncontrollably.

"Good. I'm going to let you leave now. You are not to speak of this to anyone. If I find out you spoke of me I will kill you. Do you understand?"

"Yes!" The scent of urine hit the room. Ephraim looked down at the floor and stepped back away from the pool of urine forming on the floor, taking David with him. This man was not going to talk.

"Is this real?" David asked in a high pitched voice.

Keeping his eyes locked on David, Ephraim grabbed one of David's hands and brought it close to his face. "Stick out your finger."

"No!"

"Do it!"

His hands shook violently as he stuck out his index finger. Ephraim brought the finger to his mouth and ran it over one of his fangs.

"Ouch!" David whimpered. The man was weak. It was no more painful than a needle prick. Several drops of blood hit Ephraim's lip. As David pulled his hand away Ephraim licked the blood and cringed. He turned his head away from Madison and spit the blood back out.

He turned his head back. Things were different now. He had to handle this differently. "David, I don't know how to tell you this," he said in a much calmer tone than the emotions raging inside of him demanded.

Tall, Dark & Lonely

"What?"

Ephraim placed the man down. "You need go see a doctor, immediately."

"What?" He clearly hadn't expected that.

"Tomorrow go see your doctor," Ephraim said. His rage was doubling. If this son of a bitch touched Madison he would have given her a death sentence.

"What's wrong with my blood?" David pleaded. He held his finger against his chest as if it were a life threatening wound.

"Just go see a doctor. Take your girlfriend with you to get tested and anyone else you've been with."

David's chin trembled. "You're not going to tell me?"

"No, just go." His body was still trembling. He prayed to god Madison didn't do anything with this man. She was still a virgin, but that didn't mean they didn't do other things.

"You're letting me go?"

Ephraim turned his back on the man and faced Madison. She was hugging herself tightly and staring at him. She'd seen everything.

* * * *

His eyes were bright red. They were so bright. She couldn't imagine why he would carry around red eye contacts. It didn't make sense.

Then he turned around. This couldn't be real. Her body screamed for her to run, but she couldn't. She watched as Ephraim ran faster than any human she'd ever seen. She watched in horror as he picked David up with ease with only one hand. This wasn't happening.

This was so not happening.

He looked like a vampire. They weren't real. This was a game. Someone was playing a joke on her. This couldn't be real. She'd watched enough movies to know the rules for vampires.

She went over the list of what she knew in her head and compared it to Ephraim. He just ate for one thing and vampires couldn't eat food. Granted, this was the first time that she ever saw him eat food. He also went out in the sun. Vampires were supposed to fry in the sun. She didn't remember the logic behind that, but she was sure it had something to do with them being dead and all.

Then there was the whole dead part. He wasn't! He breathed air for Christ's sake and he was warm. She could still feel his touch on her skin. He wasn't dead and vampires were supposed to be dead.

Then he went and proved it. She was a foot away, watching. She watched in amazement as his tooth sliced through David's finger. If it was fake it would have fallen out of his mouth and it certainly wouldn't have cut David's finger. He tasted the blood! That was disgusting. She couldn't believe this. She had to get it together.

She was about to turn and run for it when Ephraim started to tell David to go see a doctor. As she contemplated that, David ran out of the room leaving her to face Ephraim.

"What the hell…." she murmured against her better judgment.

He gave her a lopsided grin. "I don't suppose there's any chance that you didn't see that?"

She shook her head. His smile disappeared as he sighed, "I didn't think so."

He turned to face her. "I need to taste your blood."

She backed away from him. "I'm not letting you sink your teeth into me, you bloodsucker!"

Tall, Dark & Lonely

As her back hit the table she reached back for a weapon. She found the roll basket and picked it up quickly, hugging it to her chest. She began throwing rolls at him while she retreated away from him. "Get back!"

He ducked out of the way easily. "Or what? You'll throw butter at me?" he teased.

"I'm not kidding....I'll....I'll..." She looked around the room, but there was nothing that she could use, no crosses, no holy water. Damn it, why hadn't her Grandmother found religion? That would be really helpful at the moment.

Ephraim held his hands up. She was out of rolls. "Listen, I know you're frightened and I understand that. I'm not trying to scare you, but I need to taste your blood."

She threw the basket at him. "Are you crazy? I'm not letting you bite me!"

"I don't want to bite you. Your blood is the last thing I want." He looked pained.

That stopped her short. "My blood's not good enough for you?"

"That's not it at all." He didn't try to walk after her. Ephraim remained where he was, but they both knew that he could get to her before she made it to the door so she didn't try to run, yet.

"Wait, you do drink blood, don't you?" This was getting really confusing.

He ran a frustrated hand through his hair. "Yes!"

"You don't have to snap. It was just a question."

He held up a hand in a placating manner. "My apologies."

She nodded her acceptance. "Why isn't my blood good enough? I bathe, I eat healthy, I don't use drugs, drink or smoke. I'm not a vampire or anything, but I would think that would make my blood attractive."

His jaw dropped. "Are you trying to get me to bite you?"

"No!"

"Then why-"

"Because you insulted my blood!"

He pinched the bridge of his nose and laughed.

"You think this is funny?" Madison demanded.

"No, I think this is the most trying conversation of my life."

Madison grabbed the bun from her grandmother's abandoned plate and chucked it at him, hitting him in the chest. She pulled a chair in front of her to keep it between them in the false hope that it would be enough to stop him. She knew that it wouldn't. It just made her feel better to do something.

"Hey! What was that for?"

"You keep insulting me when really you should be explaining to me why I shouldn't scream at the top of my lungs for help."

He sighed as he pulled out a chair and flopped down on it. "You want an explanation?"

"Yes, I think," she waved frantically around the room and then at him, "that I deserve one, don't you think?"

Ephraim shook his head slowly. "No, I think you owe me a thank you."

"A thank you?" she asked in stunned disbelief.

"Yes, a thank you. I just got rid of that douche bag for you."

He was an arrogant son of a bitch. She half stepped out from behind the chair to tell him so when she remembered what he was. Something was different. "Hey, why are your eyes blue again and where did your teeth go?"

"Would you believe me if I told you that none of that happened and that you were hallucinating?" he asked, sounding hopeful.

Tall, Dark & Lonely

"No!"

He sighed heavily. "I didn't think so."

"And *you* didn't get rid of him. Candy did when she spilled the beans."

Ephraim cocked his head to the side to study her. "You really think so?"

"Yes."

"Are you sure?"

"Yes! How many ways are you going to ask me? Now tell me about your eyes and teeth?"

He shrugged. "I believe you said they're blue and my teeth are white. What's to tell?"

She groaned and stomped her foot. "You are so infuriating! You know what I want to know?"

"No I don't," he said innocently enough, frustrating the hell out of her.

"Yes, you do!"

He shrugged. She glowered. He glowered back. Finally she threw her hands up in the air. "Fine! You're obviously playing a game so just tell me what you want and then answer my questions."

"You're awfully demanding," he noted.

"And you're annoying!"

"Fine, I have a few questions for you before I tell you anything."

She held her hands. "Wait, why do you get to ask your questions first? I'm the one with the information. I know what you are and could tell everyone."

He raised one arrogant eyebrow. "Go ahead."

"What?" She hadn't expected that.

"I said go ahead. Open the door and go tell them that I am a bloodsucker. I'm sure you'll give everyone a good laugh."

"But...." He was right she would look insane. "Fine I'll get David to back up my story."

Ephraim laughed. "David will never be able to look at you again without pissing himself and running the other way." His expression became serious. "Besides, you should really leave him alone. He's going to have enough to deal with."

That reminded her. "Ephraim, I need to know what's wrong with his blood."

"No, first I need to know some things."

"Like what?"

"I know you didn't sleep with him. I need to know if you did anything short of sleeping with him." It pained him to ask her.

Her mouth dropped open. "You what? How would you know that I haven't slept with him? Wait, where do you get off? It's none of your business what I've done with anyone!"

He seemed unconcerned with her questions. "I know you're a virgin. I can smell it." He tapped his nose. "Heightened senses and all that."

She didn't think it was possible, but she was more embarrassed now than she was twenty minutes ago at the dinner table when Candy made her announcement. It made her angry that he knew. It was none of his damn business.

"I'm not telling you a damn thing. If your sense of smell is heightened then you tell me what I did or didn't do," she said in clear challenge.

Mistake. It was a mistake.

She saw a flash of color and then felt a cool breeze caress her arm the same time she realized that Ephraim stood directly in back of her. She shrieked and tried to run when two large, warm hands gripped her shoulders. "Hold still. This was your idea, remember?"

"I..I...didn't mean…"

"Shush and hold still. I'm working here," he mumbled, his tone filled with amusement.

He shouldn't be doing this. He really shouldn't. She was his weakness in so many ways, but she challenged him and refused to answer his questions. He didn't have the patience for this game. He had to know if she was sick, too.

Holding her still by her shoulders, he used his face to push her smooth hair away from her neck. The feel of her hair against his face was erotic. He had to close his eyes and fight for control.

"No biting!"

"Shh, I'm trying to focus." He ran his tongue over his fangs, sending them back. It was too tempting to be this close to her neck so he needed to work fast. He skimmed his nose down her neck, ignoring the impulse to run his tongue over her skin. His nose skimmed down her back and then over her backside.

Thank god she couldn't see his huge grin as he did *that*. He considered staying there for a minute, but felt her tense beneath his hands. She would probably slap him or throw those damn lumpy potatoes at him. He released her shoulders and ran his nose down her leg.

"Finally-*hey*!" She yelped as he took her hand into his and smelled it. He released it and walked away from her.

"Well?" she asked expectantly.

He didn't turn around as he made his way to the door. "You're fine. That's all I wanted to know. Thanks," he said dismissively. He opened the door, keeping his eyes lowered as he disappeared to the left.

"What? Hey, that's not fair! Get back here! You didn't answer my questions!" She ran after him, but he was already gone. That's fine. She knew where he would eventually end up. She turned to the right with every intention of going there to wait for him when she literally ran into Grandma.

"Whoa!" Grandma grabbed her to steady her before she fell backwards. "What's going on? Where's Ephraim?"

Madison looked past her. The foyer was empty. "Where is everyone?"

Grandma waved a hand in the air in a dismissive gesture. "They're in the living room watching movies and eating pizza They settled down once they saw David leave." Grandma studied her for a long moment. "Are you okay?"

"Yes, I'm fine. Why wouldn't I be?" Her eyes ran to her destination, the stairs.

"Because of what that awful man did."

Oh, that. She shrugged. "I'm over it." And onto new things like finding out the answers to all her questions. He was going to answer her and that was that.

"Hmm, you don't look too upset."

She shrugged. "I'm not. What I am though is tired. Can you tell everyone that I'm sorry about tonight and tell them that I'll see them tomorrow?"

Grandma looked reluctant to let her go, but in the end she nodded. "Okay, goodnight, Madison. Make sure you get enough sleep."

"I will." And all of her answers.

Chapter 7

"Good," he mumbled as he stepped away from her door. Her light snores were even. For the last four hours he drove around waiting for her to get tired and go to sleep. He knew she would try and wait up for him. Sure enough for the first two hours when he drove by the house he spotted their small hallway light on. She was waiting.

She wanted answers. Answers she thought he owed her. He didn't owe anyone anything. As far as he was concerned, he did her a favor tonight and that was the end of it. She could ask as many questions as she wanted. He wasn't going to budge. This was none of her business.

He only hoped that she didn't get obsessed with him and start sprouting tales about him drinking the blood of babies or anything. He would hate to see her locked up in some mental hospital.

It had been a long night and he was tired. He stripped out of his clothes and headed for the bathroom. Even after all these years he couldn't go to bed without washing first. The feel of that grime still haunted him. The few times he tried to go to bed or go to work in the morning without taking a shower first were mistakes. He spent all night itching from the imaginary grime and all day bitching and snapping at people.

The only good thing about taking a shower at two in the morning was the hot water. There was plenty of it. He stood beneath the showerhead, savoring the feeling of scalding hot water running down his scalp and back.

A small click was the only clue he got that his night was not over with yet. Great. He sighed and shut the water off. "You're never going to give up, are you?"

"No," she said in an offhanded tone.

"Are you going to hand me a towel?"

"No."

"Fine." He didn't care. He wasn't shy or modest. He flung back the shower curtain and stepped out onto the small bath rug.

Madison's eyes widened in surprise. "What are you doing?" Her eyes dropped to his hips and widened even further.

"Getting a towel since you denied me one." He grabbed a towel from the rack and unhurriedly dried off.

"But..but.." she sputtered.

He sighed. "Let me guess, you thought you would keep me trapped in the shower by not handing me a towel or any clothing until I answered your questions, right?"

She looked guilty, but admitted nothing. "You owe me some answers."

He wiped his face off. "Really? How did you come to this conclusion?"

"Because you stole answers from me! Now you owe me."

He shrugged. "You're welcome to sniff me."

She gasped. "That's not what I meant."

"Well, that's what I did so if we're being fair that's what you should do." His eyes dropped to his still naked form and then to her very clothed form. "Of course, if we were being completely fair you would let me see you naked." He wagged his eyebrows.

"I will not! You know what? I bet you didn't get any answers from me. You just did that because you're either a pervert or you're trying to trick me into telling you things."

He chuckled. "Yeah, that's what I did. I tried to trick you into talking. Of course my leaving then kind of put a stop to that plan just like now." With that he dropped the towel and stalked back to his room. She followed.

"You don't know anything! You only guessed that I'm a virgin…." she gasped, "wait, you were in the bathroom tonight while Jill and I were talking. You didn't guess. You heard!"

"I don't have to go into the bathroom to hear what you say. I have perfect hearing as well." He looked guilty though. She knew that look. It was the same look Jill and Joshua had when they got caught doing something bad.

She leaned against the wall, satisfied that she had him for once. "That might be true, but you wanted a closer spot. You were eavesdropping on me. Admit it, that's how you found out. You didn't find anything out about me just by sniffing me."

He threw her an exasperated look. "Fine, you want to play this game?"

"Yes," she said firmly, straightening up from the wall.

Ephraim pulled a pair of underwear on. He really should walk around naked to make her feel uncomfortable enough to leave, but she was starting to make him feel uncomfortable enough to hide his response to her.

"Are you sure?"

"Yes!" she stressed.

He sat down on the bed and leaned back on his elbows. She did her best to concentrate on his face and not his well shaped chest or abs. It would really help if he put a shirt on. "Aren't you cold?"

"No, I'm fi-" He stopped talking and grinned hugely. "Is this bothering you?" He gestured to his stomach.

"What? No, don't be ridiculous." She sounded annoyed, but she was really embarrassed. How did he know?

"Then I see no reason to cover up since it doesn't bother you," he teased.

"You were going to tell me what you found out from smelling me." She hoped it distracted him from her discomfort.

He sighed. "Okay, but remember you asked me to tell you. Very well then. From just smelling you I know that you showered an hour before you came down for dinner."

She scoffed "You knew that already."

"May I continue or are you planning on interrupting me continuously?"

She waved a hand in the air. "Continue."

"You're too kind," he said dryly. "I know that you are wearing Calvin Klein perfume, but there's still a hint of cucumber and melon body spray on your skin from this morning. You use Tide to wash your clothes and you were near someone today who smoked cannabis a week ago." Her mouth dropped open.

"Also, in I would say in fifteen days your period is going to come. From the smell of your skin I suspect it will come in the early morning." She felt her face flush. "I also know you are not on any type of birth control which means that you weren't really considering sleeping with David any time soon which is a very good thing."

"How do you know I wasn't-"

"You're responsible. I know how you feel about Candy's sexual escapades and how upset you were about Jill's mistake. You're the type of woman who would start birth control the minute you even thought you might take a man to your bed."

She bit her lip and very much wanted to leave the room, but she stayed. She wanted answers and this way he might feel that he owed it to her. "May I continue?"

"Yes," she said quietly.

"Okay, I also know that David never laid a hand on you. I know he touched your breast from the outside of your shirt, I would say two days ago, but that touch didn't last long just like his kisses didn't last long."

Her embarrassment forgotten momentarily she asked. "Wait, how do you know that? You smelled me from behind?"

Ephraim lazily scratched his stomach. "Messages travel over your skin. Think of it as a network. Anything that happens in front will be transmitted to the back. I only need to run the length of you to get my answers."

"Oh..."

"As I was saying. You don't like his kisses. From what I can tell you break off the kiss whenever he tries to invade your mouth. He grabbed your breast when he thought you were distracted. Very amateur."

"Oh, and I bet you're an expert?" she snapped.

He gave her a lopsided smile. "I'll admit it's been a while, but a man never forgets."

"How long?"

He shook a finger at her. "No, we're talking about you now, Madison. Let's see, your skin.....ah, I also know that no man has ever touched you intimately." He tilted his head to the side and studied her. "You're a very strict date I take it."

She nodded so he continued. "Good for you, especially now since it probably saved your life."

Madison shifted uncomfortably. "What do you mean? What was wrong with him?"

He sighed. "Madison, he has HIV. You're lucky that he didn't win that bet."

"Oh my god." She felt breathless.

"You're fine, Madison. I didn't need to taste your blood to get my answer."

"Are you sure? Cause if you need to," she held out her hand, "you can take some just to make sure."

He flinched back as if she struck him. "I'm not going to bite you!"

"Why not?"

"For fuck sake, Madison, you're a virgin! You've only kissed men. You're safe."

She waved that aside as if it weren't important. "I get that, but you seem rather adamant that you aren't going to drink my blood."

"I'm not! Stop trying to push it."

"No, there's obviously something wrong with my blood and you won't tell me. If you're worried that I'll be grossed out don't be." She walked towards the bed, holding her hand out. "Just take a taste. It's okay."

Ephraim climbed over the bed to get away from her. "I'm not going to drink from you so stop it!"

She stopped. "Why?" Suspicion rose up, causing her eyes to narrow on the man looking close to jumping out the window to get away from her. "You're not a vampire at all are you? That was some kind of trick. Either you're insane or you and David were in this together."

He threw his hands up in the air in irritation. "No, I'm not a vampire and I would never do anything with a dickhead like David. What you saw was real. Be that as it may, I have no intention of drinking from you."

Understanding dawned on her. "Ah, I see. Okay, I'm sorry I understand now."

He didn't like that tone. "Understand what exactly?" he asked slowly, suspiciously.

She wasn't looking at him. She was looking past him as if in deep thought. "That makes sense...." she mumbled quietly.

"What does?"

She ignored him and paced back and forth in front of the bathroom door while she talked to herself in a low voice. "You've been here three years and all that time you've never brought any friends home. You've never been seen out at night with anyone except other cops at a bar. You go fishing, sometimes bring a friend from work, you're secretive, you only came downstairs tonight because you heard I was having someone over."

"What are you babbling about?" he asked harshly to cover his nerves.

She didn't seem to hear him. "No one's ever seen..." she didn't finish that thought. "You tasted his blood, let him stick his finger in your mouth. The idea of tasted my blood repulses you....focused on him......hmmm."

He stood nervously, waiting for her answer. She didn't say anything for several minutes. Then she turned and faced him. "I know why you won't drink my blood."

"Oh, do please enlighten me," he said mockingly.

She smiled cheerfully as she announced, "You're gay."

* * * *

She took a step towards him. He hadn't moved a single muscle in the last two minutes. "It's okay. It's not a big deal if you're gay." It was okay, but she was oddly disappointed.

He looked so serious. "H-how did you know?" he whispered.

"It's kind of obvious." She felt so bad. But he didn't need to hide who he was, the bloodsucking part, yes, but not this.

"What do you mean it's obvious?" he asked in a guarded tone. All he could think about was his brothers and their feminine features and gestures. There was nothing feminine about him and they weren't gay.

"Well, you're secretive."

"That's because I'm a Pyte," he said before he could stop himself.

"What's a Pyte?"

"Don't change the subject. You're telling me how you knew," he said hastily.

"Well, you only spend company with other men. You don't bring anyone here. You don't want to share space with a woman. You readily tasted David's blood, but the thought of mine disgusts you. It just seems rather obvious," she said with a shrug.

He covered his face with his hands. "Oh my god...I can't believe you found out." His voice was thick with emotion.

She walked over to him and wrapped her arms around him. She was safe. He didn't like women and wouldn't feed off her. It was the only reason she felt comfortable enough to touch him now.

It was too bad that he was gay. He felt so good right now. She forced herself to focus. "It's okay. You don't have to go through this alone. It won't be so bad. There are plenty of gay cops these days. As long as you don't bite anyone you should be fine."

He chuckled softly.

"I suppose you're right." His hands dropped from his face and wrapped gently around her waist. "You really don't mind?" he asked as he nuzzled her neck.

Tall, Dark & Lonely

His breath felt warm and teasing. There was no fear. She was safe. He was a gay whatever the hell he was and she was off the menu in many ways.

"No, I don't mind. It's okay, Ephraim." She ran a hand down his back, trying to soothe him. She stretched up on her toes and pressed a kiss to his cheek. "It's okay."
He returned the gesture by pressing a soft kiss against her neck. It sent shivers down her spine. It was really a shame, she thought. She froze as he continued to press soft kisses to her neck.

"Tell me something," he said between kisses.

"What?" her voice cracked. She tried to pull away, but his grip tightened, holding her against him.

"You discovered I'm gay." Relief shot through her. For a minute there she thought that she was wrong. "This was mostly based on the fact that I refused to feed from you, correct?"

"Yes," she said slowly.

He nodded against her neck and pressed another tender kiss. "What if I told you that the reason I refused to feed from you isn't because I'm gay, but because your blood and your blood alone is my biggest weakness? What if I told you that in the last hundred and ninety years I have never come across someone whose blood drives me to distraction, that just the mere scent of your blood in the air is enough to send me into bloodlust. That I have to stay away from you, because I want your blood more than anything else on this earth and that it takes everything I have not to go into your room at night and take my fill? What would you say then?"

"You're not gay?" There were several other questions floating in her head at the moment, but she focused on that because if he wasn't gay then…then he was telling her something.

He chuckled as he peeled one of her arms away from around him and brought her hand between them. He pressed her hand against the front of his boxers and moved it over his very large and very hard erection. His deep moan sent heat through her body. She gulped as she yanked her hand away and he allowed it as he wrapped his arm back around her and pulled her back against him. His tongue ran from her neck to her earlobe. He took her earlobe between his lips and gently sucked on it. "No, baby, I'm not gay."

Madison somehow managed to pull her head back. Ephraim raised his head and looked at her hungrily. For which hunger she wasn't sure, but both scared her. His eyes were red again and she knew that she was in trouble.

"Let me go, Ephraim," her voice shook.

He shook his head. "No."

"Ephraim, I'm only going to tell you once to let go of me," she warned.

He ignored her and leaned down to kiss her neck again. These weren't innocent little pecks anymore. He was pressing hot open mouthed kisses to her neck. She could feel the tips of his fangs brushing against her skin with each kiss. His hands were rubbing her backside slowly, creating an ache that she would never allow him to relieve. A small moan escaped Madison, causing Ephraim's hips to jerk forward.

Just a bite. A little taste. That's all he wanted. She felt so warm and soft in his arms. The taste of her skin was for lack of a better word, magical. It was just a tease, just a sampling. His mouth found her pulse. He suckled the area before the tips of his fangs pressed gently against her skin. Just a taste then he would stop, he told himself.

"Don't say that I didn't warn you." She'd been swept up in his kiss and touch until she felt the two sharp points at her throat. Human or not, he was a male. She held onto his hips to steady herself and with a grunt she brought her knee up hard between his legs.

Tall, Dark & Lonely

He roared in agony as he released her. She pushed him away and ran for the door, too afraid to look back. She threw her door shut and locked it before diving under her bed, praying as she went that the boogie man wasn't real.

Chapter 8

"Shit," Ephraim muttered after the last of the nausea left him. He spit the last of the vomit from his mouth and sat back, still cupping his throbbing balls. "Damn," he groaned, "that was a more effective method than sticking a finger down my throat." Not that he planned on doing it again.

Keeping one hand on his balls, he pulled himself up. He didn't know what was worse, the taste of human food going down or coming up. He grabbed Madison's bottle of mouthwash and chugged it. He had to get the taste out of his mouth. There was a reason why he avoided eating human food. It had to come up. After the last drop, he burped and winced. The sensation sent a piercing pain to the tip of his penis.

He cringed with the knowledge that the next time that he took a piss he would be urinating pure mouthwash. Still holding himself, he stumbled into his room and retrieved his personal firearm. He checked the chamber and stumbled back into the bathroom with it.

Using the butt of the gun, he knocked on Madison's door. No answer. Not a surprise after what he just did to her. He still couldn't believe how close he came to taking her. Thank god she kneed him when she did and took him off guard. He hadn't reacted to pain since the dungeon.

"M…Ma…Ma…" He had to swallow as a fresh wave of nausea tore at him. "Mad…Ma-*oh shit*!" He stumbled back to the toilet in time to see the mouthwash splash all over the toilet seat and floor. "Fuck," he whimpered.

At least it was a minty mess. He chuckled until it hurt. Ignoring the mess he went back to the door. "Madison," he said through clenched teeth. It hurt so much to speak, but he had to do it. He could hear her whimpering, probably under her bed. He couldn't stand it.

Taking in a deep breath he forced himself to speak. "Madison, I know you're upset. I'm," another deep breath, "so sorry. I apologize….I don't want to hurt you…..I *won't* hurt you. I promise! I swear it!"

Tall, Dark & Lonely

"Liar! *Ooops!*" she muttered.

He had to smile. "I promise you're safe here. I promise, but if it makes you feel better I am leaving something for you on the bathroom floor. Put it somewhere safe, somewhere the kids won't look. If you have to use it don't hesitate. I won't be mad." He remained at the door for a minute longer. "I'm sorry." He stumbled out of the bathroom to his room where he collapsed on the floor.

* * * *

"Come on, come on….come on!" She blew a dust bunny away from her face as she waited. The faint sound of a car starting had her moving. She crawled out from beneath the bed and made a mad dash towards the bathroom. She had to pee, badly.

She jumped over something black on the floor and found her way to the toilet just in time. Going to sleep with a full bladder wasn't easy, but somehow she managed it. Where was that lemony scent coming from? She looked around the bathroom. It was close by. Ephraim cleaned? She was stunned.

There wasn't enough time to contemplate what would motivate him to clean. She stripped her clothes off and jumped in the shower, trying to get the smell of dust and sweat off her. Two minutes later she jumped out of the shower, hoping to brush her teeth and hair in the same amount of time. Her hand froze mid-grab for her toothbrush.

A note was taped to the mirror.

Madison,

I cannot apologize enough. I will never bother you again. I also don't want you to feel afraid. Please use my gift. It's yours. Please hide it as soon as you find it. I cringe at the thought of the one of the children finding it. I wasn't kidding when I told you to use it. If I give you any reason to fear for your life, use it. Do not hesitate . You will not kill me but stop me long enough to save yourself. I don't foresee any reason for you to use it.

Your Servant,

Ephraim William Howard Adlard

"Adlard? I thought his last name was Williams." She pondered that while she brushed her teeth. What did he mean about a gift? She didn't see a gift. She heard him say something last night. It was hard to tell what he was saying. It sounded like he was speaking through clenched teeth. She looked around the counter. There was nothing out of the ordinary except that she was out of mouthwash. Damn it, she just bought some yesterday.

"What the..." The black thing she jumped over caught her eye. She choked on air. *That* was the gift? She picked the gun up cautiously, afraid it would go off in her hands. She looked around as if help would come. What was she supposed to do with a gun? A wooden stake would have made her feel better, maybe even a bottle of holy water.

She ran with the gun into her room and whirled around looking for someplace to hide it. Her closet. The closet was perfect. She yanked the door open and placed it on the top shelf beneath the extra blankets. Was he crazy giving her a gun?

* * * *

"Detention blows."

"No shit, asshole," came another voice.

Tall, Dark & Lonely

Madison looked up from her computer. "Hey, none of that now. You're here to learn from your mistakes...whatever they are. You only have another hour to go so I suggest that you do some homework." She looked over her small group of detentionees.

The group consisted of some of her favorite students. They were termed stoners, losers, and assholes by the students and even by the faculty. She didn't care. She liked them, even the kid in front giving her the most exaggerated pout she'd ever seen.

Chris, her constant detention companion, was laid back and didn't give her any problems. He was pretty funny and didn't bother trying to suck up. She was honest with him and didn't play any games. They respected each other.

"Come on, Chris, don't give me that look." She chuckled at his pout.

He was a funny kid. He was what some of the kids called trailer trash, but he was nice. Well, as long as you were on his good side. There was no doubt that he could be a mean son of a bitch and no one in their right mind would provoke him, but from what she knew about him he never threw the first punch and he never got in someone's face without a very good reason. Otherwise, he was one of the most laid back kids she'd ever met.

"Miss Soloman, come on now. You know this is bullshit. That little preppy bastard beats the shit out of his girlfriend over the weekend and we're paying for it." Chris gestured to his friends and the two unfortunate bystanders who got pulled into the fight. They were decent kids too, very quiet so she was very surprised when she found out that they voluntarily got into the fight.

Madison leaned back in her chair. "Tell me what happened."

Chris nodded. "See, it's like this. That little shit Mike gets away with too much. He steals, he cheats on every test, his parents hire tutors who do his homework, all the teachers know, but they look the other way because of his old man and he's on the football team." She'd heard rumors before, but no one was ever willing to confirm them.

"He also likes to slap girls around. I warned him in the past to watch it, but clearly he thought I was fucking kidding. I found out this morning the little shit beat the hell out of Carol. When I asked him about it, he told me to fuck off and no one would believe me. Carol tries to hold him back and right in front of me while the teachers' backs were turned, he shoved her to the ground."

"He's not lying, Miss. Solomon," Ed, a very shy boy, said. He hardly ever looked up from his book. That in itself let her know Chris wasn't lying. Plus, Chris never bothered lying to her in the past. He took his punishment like a man when he got caught. Not once since she'd taken this position had he complained over the circumstances of his punishments.

"I don't understand why Mike isn't here along with you," she said.

They all scoffed in disbelief. "Look at us," Chris gestured to their worn out clothes. "They're not going to listen to us over that preppy prick. He and his friends come from money. They don't care what we say and they lied about Carol. They said Mike was protecting her from me if you can believe that shit." She didn't. Chris would never hit a woman. Everyone knew that.

She nibbled on her lower lip and looked at her classroom door to make sure that it was closed. "Okay, guys, everyone move to the back. Talk quietly and you can play those video games I know you have hidden in your bags. If that door opens, pretend you're doing something constructive."

Chris winked at her. "Heart of gold, Miss Soloman." They quickly went to the back of the room, leaving her to her search.

She scrolled down the webpage she found on the Adlard family. Surprisingly there was a lot of information on the family. The family was old and noble. It could be traced to the Roman invasion, but thankfully she didn't need to go that far.

After two months of avoiding each other she got tired of waiting for answers. So this morning she dug the note he'd left in the bathroom out of her purse and decided to see what she could find.

Tall, Dark & Lonely

It was his fault. Every time she waited to talk to him or left notes, he ignored her. He walked right past her with only a polite hello. If that was the way he wanted to act so be it. She could find her own answers. She didn't need him.

She limited her search to the nineteenth century. Ephraim probably used a fake name on that note. He probably forgot what surname he was currently using. She would find out.

"Aha!" she said, smiling triumphantly when she found his name.

"Is someone coming?" Ed jumped.

"No, it's fine," she said without looking up. He probably stole the name. That was it. She read about his supposed father first, a Duke. Yeah right. According to this webpage his first wife was attacked by a mad man when she was pregnant with one Ephraim William Howard Adlard.

She read on. The Duke remarried a woman who was rumored to beat Ephraim and call him "the thing". Odd. His second wife gave him five more children, three girls and two boys. According to family history she pushed the Duke to disown Ephraim to line her own son in third place for the title. The Duke initially refused.

Hmmm, interesting. Ephraim suffered from a weird medical condition that left him looking like a little boy until the age of sixteen. At sixteen he went into a coma. The website at this point touched on some rumors.

One story stated that he woke up from his coma changed into a man. He didn't resemble his brothers or father. He attacked a maid and was dragged off by Magistrate Nichols. She wrote down that name. His second brother inherited the title and brought his brother home twenty years later. He still looked young, but unfortunately died a few years later.

The second story was simple. They had him dying in the coma. Nothing helpful there. The third story continued from the first, but had him die at the hands of Nichols. The author believed the first story because of compelling evidence below.

"Oh, a picture." She clicked the thumbnail. A large portrait popped on the screen. It was of a man and woman and eight children. That wasn't helpful. She was about to close the page when she saw the "next" button. She clicked it and gasped loudly.

She didn't need to read the description to know who the young man was standing next to a much older man, woman and five kids. It was Ephraim. His hair style and clothes were different, but that was him. According to the caption he was posing with his brother, sister-in-law and their children. Ephraim was reported to have died two months after the portrait was finished.

Shaking her head in disbelief she typed in Magistrate Nichols. What she read there turned her stomach. The man was sick. He was compared to Jack the Ripper several times. He lived to torture and kill and loved the fact that the government encouraged him. He went missing in 1835. Years later a secret entrance was discovered leading to his famous dungeon where skeletons were found in small cells. In a room that could only be described as a torture chamber they found a dozen skeletons. One of those bodies they believed was Nichols' body based on a pendant found among the bones.

It dawned on her. Ephraim lived in the dudgeon. He lived in one of the tiny cells she looked at now. He survived years of torture and somehow came out whole. She couldn't believe it. It broke her heart to think of the things that he lived through.

"Are you okay?" a voice whispered.

She jumped, startled and looked up into kind green eyes. Chris was leaning over her desk, watching her. She cleared her throat. "Yes, I'm fine, Chris. Why?"

Tall, Dark & Lonely

He picked up the box of tissues off the desk and handed them to her. "You're crying."

"Oh!" She wiped her face quickly. "Just a sad story on the web."

Chris nodded slowly. He didn't believe her, but he wasn't going to push. "Stick with puppies and rainbows then, Miss Soloman. I don't like seeing you unhappy." With that he walked back to his friends, pausing only long enough to throw her a worried look over his shoulder.

A loud knock at the door sent the kids scrambling for their text books, except for Chris that is. He leaned back in his chair with his hands folded behind his head.

"Yes?"

Principal Mason stepped inside. "I'm sorry to do this, but it seems that we have a bit of a problem."

She stood up cautiously. "Problem?"

"Yes, seems Carol's parents came home today from their vacation. They saw her face and demanded to know what happened. So they called me and the police. We need to settle this now," he addressed everyone in the room.

Madison watched Chris's jaw clench. She knew what he was thinking. He was about to get the finger pointed at him. "It's okay, everyone," she spoke to the class, but looked at him. He nodded firmly.

"The six of you I want on this side of the room and behave yourself," Mason said, warning lacing his tone.

Carol walked in the room, huddled by her parents. They brought her to the other side of the classroom. Mike, his parents, a man Madison had no doubt was a lawyer judging by his expensive three piece suit, and several of the boys Chris liked to call "preppy" walked in.

"Please have a seat," Mason said.

The lawyer gestured for his clients to go to the end of the room. "I'm sorry this should be cleared up soon." Mason glanced at Chris.

This could not get any worse. Correction, it could. Ephraim strolled into the room, looking very much like a man not to cross, seconds later.

* * * *

Ephraim walked into the room. He walked past Madison, taking a deep breath as he passed her. He missed her. It surprised him, but he did. He never missed anyone. He'd outlived his family and every friend he ever made and never once thought of them once they were gone, except for Marc. He missed his brother when he allowed himself any emotion.

It was the way things were supposed to be. He understood it and accepted it. Everyone's time would come, except his. Hers would come, too. He would have to deal with that one day. His chest tightened every time he thought about that. This woman was killing him.

He sat behind her desk and leaned back looking relaxed. His eyes slowly ran over everyone in the room. He knew a few of the boys to his left. They were good kids, troublemakers, but good. The last two on that side he would guess were bookworms. His eyes met Chris's for a mere second before moving on.

The football player in the back had his attention, but he wouldn't show it. With less than a half hour after his call he lawyered up. He did a quick search before he left his office and found several domestic violence calls from the boy's house that went nowhere. There was talk about the boy. His eyes passed over the computer screen on her desk quickly before fixing on the young lady who looked like she went nine rounds with Tyson.

His jaw clenched as he looked back at Madison's computer. It seemed he wasn't the only one that did his research today. Without taking his eyes off the group he clicked the back button to see what else she'd discovered.

Tall, Dark & Lonely

What he found didn't make him happy. It only added to his temper. She knew. He knew it had been a mistake to write his full name on that note. He clicked again and sat up straight.

"Hey, can we get this over with? I have practice," Mike, one of his suspects, said.

"Shut it," Ephraim said. He forced himself to relax as he got up. He strolled over to Madison, giving his back to the room.

"You've been busy," he said softly.

She swallowed loudly. "Yes, you wouldn't answer my questions."

"Print the pictures for me, would you?" he asked softly.

"Are you going to answer my questions?"

He groaned.

"Hey, I have practice!" his main suspect complained.

Ephraim looked over his shoulder in time to see Mike being pulled back down by his father. The little shit thought he was going to walk out on him, did he? Interesting. "Get out of that seat again and I'm hauling you in for questioning."

"Don't move," his father whispered harshly. "And shut your mouth."

Ephraim looked back at Madison. "Well?"

"What do you mean, well?"

"Will you do it?"

"What's in it for me?"

His eyes dropped to her lips. "Whatever you want."

"Tonight, we talk for two hours and you answer my questions."

His eyebrows arched. "Two hours?" He could do a great deal in two hours preferably with her beneath him. Shit. He had to stop thinking about her.

She nodded. "Two hours, and I'll have those pictures blown up for you."

"Okay," he said slowly.

"Hey, should we have a lawyer too?" a boy asked.

Ephraim turned around. It was Chris. A funny laid back kid who found his way under arrest every now and then for petty shit, mostly for beating up his mother's boyfriends after they laid a hand on him or for defending himself on the street. Three years ago, the kid caught his attention and he'd made it a special point to keep an eye on him.

"No, right now no one is under arrest. I have a few questions to ask. Since your parents aren't here I've asked Mr. Mason and Miss. Soloman to stand in to make sure that your rights are not trampled. Is that choice fine with you?"

Chris shot a look at Madison. The boy trusted her. Good. He was smart. "If I feel that I need to question you further after this then we will make sure your parents are involved. Is that understood?"

"Yes," Chris said. He was the clear leader of his group. The other boys looked at him expectantly.

"This is bullshit," Mike said. "I'll miss practice."

"Yes, you've said as much," Ephraim said dryly. He looked over at the young girl. She refused to go to the hospital until after this was settled, but she wouldn't name anyone. That was interesting too.

"I'm going to ask you again before I talk to these boys. Who hit you?" He'd rather ask her in private again, but her parents demanded they do it this way. They expected their daughter to be strong and do the right thing. They obviously didn't understand real fear.

She shook her head.

Tall, Dark & Lonely

"That's what I thought."

Mike shot to his feet. "See, this is a waste of time. I'm going to practice." He ripped his arm away from his father's grip and stalked down the aisle towards Ephraim.

The boy was six feet tall, large and obviously an asshole. Ephraim was used to dealing with assholes. With his jaw set tightly, he walked forward. Mike paused, unsure of what he should do. He probably wasn't used to people staying in his war path.

Ephraim stalked forward, pointing towards the boy's parents. "I am not going to tell you to sit your ass down, again." Mike crossed his arms over his chest in an act of defiance. "*Now!*" Ephraim snapped. Mike jumped and scrambled back to his seat. "Don't move again."

Principal Mason stood next to the football players. He was clearly showing who he was supporting. Not smart. Ephraim found Madison leaning against the wall next to Chris and his friends. She was whispering something to him. Chris looked tensed for a fight, but nodded. He heard what she was saying and she knew that he did.

He stopped himself from grinning. She told Chris he was a nice guy and to trust him. He already knew that Chris was innocent. He knew that the moment he stepped into the school and saw Mike. The scent of the girl's blood was permeated into the boy's skin. The little shit liked to hit girls.

"Detective Williams, if I could be of service?" Mason said.

This should be good. "Please do," Ephraim said as he leaned against Madison's desk.

"These are fine boys." He gestured to the football players. "Not one of them has a black mark on their files and they've never been in trouble otherwise."

"What the hell are you saying, Mason?" Chris demanded. Madison put a hand on his shoulder. If that boy hurt her, Ephraim would kill him. The boy looked up at Madison and nodded before he sat back down.

Mason held up his hands. "I'm not trying to point fingers here. I am just pointing out that these boys," the football players, "are not involved in this. It's just a misunderstanding."

Ephraim leveled his eyes on Mason. The man obviously wanted to get in good with Mike's parents. They were wealthy and connected. If memory served him correctly they were also on the school board. Mason was being led around by his wallet.

Chris jumped to his feet. "Look at her face! You call that a misunderstanding? He beat the shit out of her!"

"Sit down this instant!" Mason snapped, giving Chris a look of disgust.

"No! You're talking about her like she's nothing. Look what he did to her!" Chris yelled.

Ephraim ignored the little drama and focused on Mike's reaction. He was chuckling and grinning like an idiot. His buddies were dumb enough to clap him on the back in front of Ephraim. That gave him an idea.

"Carol, I know you're upset and you don't feel comfortable telling me who did this. I have a favor to ask that won't force you on the issue. Is that okay?"

She cast a look at her parents and reluctantly nodded. "Good." He looked at Chris. "Come here and sit in the front." Chris looked to Madison, silently asking her what to do. She encouraged him to go. Smart.

He looked back at Carol and pointed at Chris' friends. "Now, from what I understand these five gentlemen became involved this morning. Do you mind if I allow them to leave? If one of them is involved just say no and you don't have to say who it is. I'll keep them here until I figure it out."

"No," the word came out on a rasp. She cleared her throat. "They can go."

The boys noticeably relaxed and filed out of the room, wishing Chris luck. The football players stood up expectantly. "So, we can go too?"

"No," Ephraim said flatly.

"What? That's not fair."

"Life isn't fair. Get over it." He looked back at Chris. "Chris, if memory serves me correctly you're sixteen years old, correct?"

"Yeah."

Ephraim nodded. He looked over the football players. They were all seniors. "Are any of you boys under the age of eighteen?" They shook their heads. "Good. Come up here and sit down, you too, Mike. You're eighteen, right?"

He nodded. "Carol, unless you are going to tell me what I want to know now you and your parents will wait in the hall."

"But we want to stay," her mother protested.

"I'm sorry, but you need to leave." When the mother opened her mouth to protest he held up his hand. "I'm sorry, but I want her out of here for a reason. I also have paperwork in the hall that I need you to fill out. Please," he gestured towards the door. With a nudge from her husband they left.

Ephraim watched the boys intensely as he continued. "Mr. Mason, unless you are planning on staying on behalf of Chris who is the minor in the room I have to ask you to leave."

"I'll stay." Mr. Mason moved to stand next to Madison.

"Miss Soloman, I'm assuming you're staying for Chris as well?"

"She doesn't need to, I'll handle this," Mason said. Of course he would want her out of the room. She was the only one there to protect Chris.

"She stays," Chris said firmly.

"I agree." Ephraim nodded.

"Mike, your parents can leave. You are of age and I do not need them to question you. However, if you feel you need your lawyer then he can stay."

"He stays," Mike said firmly.

"Fine."

Mike's parents left without a protest. They trusted Mason and the lawyer to keep him out of trouble.

Ephraim casually made his way back to Madison's chair. He sat down and watched the boys for several long moments. Chris looked pissed and kept staring at Mike like he wanted to attack the boy. Mike looked cocky and carefree. His friends looked a little anxious, but seemed to think that this was a joke.

"Miss Soloman, would you please see if the officer in the hallway has some papers for me?" Ephraim asked, his eyes never left the boys.

"Sure." She stepped out into the hall and returned a minute later holding a file. She brought the file to him.

"Thank you," he murmured as he took the file. His fingers ran over hers, sending heat up her arm before he pulled the file away. She went back to the wall, but not before he opened the file on the desk. It held several blank pieces of paper, but no one would see that unless they were standing in front of the desk.

He made a show of looking down and nodding at the papers. "Good. They signed," he said quietly.

"Who signed what?" Chris asked.

Tall, Dark & Lonely

"Mr. and Mrs. Goodwin signed the release form for a rape exam," Ephraim said, focusing his eyes on Mike. Mike fidgeted, twice. The girl was underage so he really didn't need her parent's permission, but if it helped this to move along he would play it up.

"What?" one of the football players asked, stunned.

Ephraim nodded. "Let's cut the shit, gentlemen. I already know what we're going to find. She confided in her mother that this was not just an assault, but a rape. In one hour I will have her on a table and examined and an hour after that I will have a warrant with all of your names on it."

"You will be brought to the emergency room under custody where your mouths will be swabbed for DNA." He paused to run his eyes over the boys. "In twenty-four hours I will have a match. I will also have several accessories if my hunch is correct."

"What do you mean?" another football player asked. He looked like he was about to cry.

"Exactly what I said. If it turns out that it was Chris, he will be headed off to Juvenile hall where he'll probably stay for a year. Not too bad. If it's Mike, well since you are all over eighteen you are looking at prison."

"That's enough of that," the lawyer snapped.

Ephraim's calm façade didn't change. "Your client is of age. I am explaining the possibility of going to prison to him and his friends. The boys were involved in her attack this morning. I won't have a hard time joining the rape charge to the assault if it turns out that Mike was the culprit."

"She hasn't talked and won't talk so you have nothing," Mike said.

Ephraim chuckled. "Is that what you think?"

"Yes."

"She doesn't have to talk. She's fifteen years old. She isn't old enough to consent to sex. If any semen is found, the owner of that deposit will face rape charges."

The boys looked back at Mike. He shook his head. Oh, the boy was a liar. Ephraim knew the boy raped her.

"How about it, gentlemen? Care to tell me anything or would you like to do a little time in prison." He looked over the boys' neat haircuts and fresh handsome faces and smiled. "You boys will brighten up the place. I bet you have five guys each the first day offering you protection...for a price of course." He winked.

"You said she had sex with you! You didn't say anything about rape," one of the boys said, jumping to his feet. The threat of a gang rape was usually enough to scare young men into doing the right thing.

"Shut up, asshole," Mike hissed.

"No." The boy stood up. "No, I'm not going to jail because you're a prick." He looked at Ephraim. "He hit her this morning. I can give you that much at least."

"Go into the hall and give the officer a statement and thank you." The boy nodded and rushed out. The rest of the boys got to their feet and followed, leaving Mike and Chris.

"Madison, I want you to take Chris and go into the hall." He stood up and walked around the desk as he pulled out a pair of handcuffs. His eyes never left Mike.

"No, I'm staying. I want to see. That bastard has this coming." Chris pulled away when Madison reached for him.

Enough was enough. He wanted Madison out of here. He looked at Chris, hoping a stern look would be enough. "Chris, I want you to-"

Tall, Dark & Lonely

"Chris!" Madison screamed.

Ephraim turned his head in time to see Mike rush Chris with a large buck knife. "You little shit! This is your fault!"

Madison jumped in front of a very stunned Chris and pushed him back. A second later, Chris snapped out of his momentary shock. He grabbed Madison and shoved her out of the way.

Ephraim reached out and grabbed Mike by the collar and yanked him back. Mike twirled around, surprised by the sudden jolt. He collided into Ephraim. "Get her out of here now!" Ephraim demanded. Chris grabbed Madison and pulled her towards the door with a very frantic Mason on their heels.

He had Mike on his stomach and cuffed in less than a minute, leaving his lawyer utterly stunned. "I...I...I..." the lawyer rambled on.

"Good, very helpful thanks a lot," Ephraim said sarcastically.

Mike tilted his head up and looked at Ephraim. "Oh shit....oh shit...I'm in so much trouble!"

Ephraim looked down at the black handle sticking out of his stomach. "Fuck," he muttered. Just what he needed, a ride to the hospital for stitches he didn't need just to make sure that this prick didn't get away with it.

It also meant he had to put on a show. He couldn't walk around like it was nothing. It wasn't. It hurt like a bitch. The little shit. If the lawyer wasn't in the room he would kill him.

Ephraim grabbed Mike by the arm. "Get up, asshole. You're under arrest." He dragged Mike to the door and pushed him off onto another officer. Everyone's eyes lowered to his stomach. He heard several gasps and a few "oh shits."

He placed a hand over his stomach. "It's fine. Just a little flesh wound," he said though clenched teeth. At least he didn't have to pretend how much it hurt.

Madison's eyes widened and then rolled back. "Somebody catch her," he said. She fell against Chris who did his best to lower her to the ground without hurting her. He would have caught her himself, but he was twenty feet away from her and people probably would have noticed him flashing to her. Sometimes it sucked to play human.

Chapter 9

"Stop squirming!" Mrs. Buckman snapped.

"You would squirm too if you had a mad woman trying to shove a bedpan under your ass! I told you that I can walk to the bathroom. I'm fine!"

Mrs. Buckman narrowed her eyes on him. "Fine." She placed the offending bedpan under her arm, he didn't want to know where she got it, and headed for the door. "Just so you know, I know the doctor ordered you to stay in that bed for a week so that's exactly what you'll be doing," she threatened.

"Come on!" He threw his hands in the air.

"You heard me."

"I can't stay in bed for a week!" Ephraim said. The battle was lost and he knew it. Still he had to try.

She pointed at him. "You heard me."

"Fine then, get the hell out of here and let me rest!"

She just pointed at him again before she left, closing the door behind her. Her helpers were cowering in the hallway as they should be. He'd been screaming at everyone for the past week. They were scared of him and for good reason.

One whole week without blood. No, correction, one whole week stuck in the hospital with a healthy supply of blood and no way to get to it. It was pure hell, especially in his condition.

The little prick nicked both his heart and his lung with that knife. It would have been simple enough to handle. Three bags of blood would have been enough. Unfortunately, the rape charges against Mike were tricky enough without any testimony and they couldn't press the battery charges since Carol still wasn't talking. So, it fell on his shoulders to put the little prick away.

Attempted murder on a New Hampshire State Detective was no laughing matter. Mike was facing federal charges now. More importantly, it would be a long time before he used his fist on another woman. That was the only reason Ephraim played along.

He had to pretend to be knocked out by the medication the doctors injected into his body when in reality that medicine was poison to him. Every single drop of medication had to be destroyed internally. The more they pumped in, the weaker his blood ran until his veins were filled with nothing but poison. He reached that state four days ago.

That operating room was just a clean version of Nichols' torture chamber. He had to force himself to remain limp while the poison burned his blood and the surgeons sliced him open. He felt every nick, every pull and prod. The pain was unreal. He didn't know what was worse though, the medication or the surgery.

His only hope was a transfusion. New blood would have diluted the poison in his system. When that cocky surgeon announced that he wouldn't require any transfusions because they'd stopped the bleeding he wanted to reach out and bitch slap him. He couldn't. He had to pretend to be out. He'd been in so much pain that he'd begun sweating halfway through the surgery.

The doctors took that as a sign of an impending fever and pumped more poison into his system. It successfully paralyzed him. Every movement set off fire in his body.

Blood, all he wanted was blood and no one would give it to him. He told them he was hungry and they brought him Jell-O and broth. What the hell kind of meal was that? After the second tray they tried forcing on him he began throwing the trays at the offending deliverer until they stopped bringing them.

Tall, Dark & Lonely

So, for six days he was stuck in a hospital bed with no chance of escape. Tubes and monitors were stuck in him. On all four of his escape attempts the damn things went off and people came running. He almost cried. He needed to eat and a variable buffet came running in and he couldn't have any of it. It was agony.

As was the first two days of visitors. Endless visitors came. People he didn't even know came. They all wanted to see how "their" hero was doing. After the first minute of each visit he "nodded off". It was either that or let them see how hungry he was. Finally, he put his foot down and demanded to be left alone. Mrs. Buckman was not happy with that and told the nurses to ignore his wishes.

For the last four days he had to put up with Mrs. Buckman and a few of the other renters. The children tried to come, but ran off within the first thirty seconds when he started screaming. Screaming was good, screaming made him feel better.

Screaming was also the only thing that saved them. He was so hungry. He just needed a few pints to force the poison out and heal his wounds. God, how they itched. His entire body itched. Six days of sponge baths. That was bullshit. How could they call that a bath? He smelled like a hospital, itched and felt gross. He could feel the grime on his skin again.

Blood.

He needed blood. If he was going to be stuck here for a week then he was out of luck. He hadn't been here to accept his blood deliveries in a week. Every two days at three in the morning blood was delivered by an unmarked van.

After two no shows they wouldn't make another attempt to deliver until he contacted them with a new safe drop spot. He needed to call them to setup new delivery. So, now he had no hopes of blood being delivered. He had to suffer for another week. But that wasn't his greatest fear. If he didn't keep everyone out of his room he was going to attack someone. The urge to feed was overpowering everything else. His control was almost nonexistent.

It would only take Madison for the last thread of control to snap. Of course, it wasn't likely that he was going to see her. She hadn't even tried to see him in the last week. She sent her apologies and flowers, but didn't come. He tried to tell himself that it was for the best. If she came he would have begged her for some blood, either hers or some stolen blood. At this point in his suffering he wouldn't beg. If she came into his room he was going to take.

His eyes drifted to the adjoining bathroom door. She could at least check and see how he was. That wasn't too much to ask. After all, he did take a wound for her. She probably didn't think much of it. She knew that he couldn't die, but did she realize that he would still feel every ounce of pain and nothing in the world could take the edge off his pain but blood? He was suffering and she couldn't even bother to see him. He was pissed on top of already being pissed.

"Fuck her. I don't want to see her anyway." But he did. He really did. Never mind that it was her blood which he craved night and day. He wanted to see her. He wanted to see her brown eyes light up when he annoyed her.

She was so cute when she'd attacked him with those biscuits. He liked everything about her. She was funny, smart and kind. But, she was a human, a human whose blood screamed for him and him alone. He could never have her. She would never be his, he reminded himself.

He wanted to kill someone. He needed to hurt someone. This was too much. There was a reason that he didn't allow attachments and Madison proved him right. Once he was healed he was going to leave and start over. He couldn't handle the pain and disappointment.

"Wow, you stink."

Ephraim forced his eyes open. "What?"

"I said you smell," Madison said matter-of-factly.

Tall, Dark & Lonely

Even before his brain registered who was in his room his body did. His fangs dropped as his hands shot out and grabbed her. He dragged her down. He couldn't fight it any longer. He was starving and his obsession was here. He didn't even stop to consider if they were alone or if he could stop in time. He needed her too damn much.

Some part of his brain registered the fact that she wasn't screaming. Actually, it felt like she was coming on her own. That was odd.

"Here you go, open up," she said as she stuck something in his mouth. He froze, shocked at the sensation.

His eyes left her neck and moved down to the object in her hands. He chuckled weakly. She stuck a straw in a bag of blood and stuck the tip of the straw in his mouth. He suckled, slowly savoring the taste of type O blood hitting his lips, his tongue, the roof of his mouth and finally down his throat. He closed his eyes and moaned in relief.

"That good, huh?" she chuckled. He nodded, but didn't stop sucking. The straw was too slow. He took the bag away from her with trembling hands. He pulled the straw out of the bag with his mouth and spit it across the room before slamming the bag to his teeth. He chugged the red liquid down until he had every drop. "More."

She laughed softly. "Here you go." She sat patiently by his side while he finished ten bags of blood. He couldn't help but notice how adorable she looked in those cute little cotton shorts of hers. Finally he burped and sighed. He was done.

"Feeling better?" She ran her fingers through his greasy hair.

"Almost." He jumped out of the bed with ease. All his strength was back and then some.

Madison gasped.

"What?" He looked down expecting to discover his dick was sticking out or something. Instead, her eyes were glued to his chest. The wound was now completely gone, dissolving the stitches as well.

He ran a hand over the area. "It itches like hell. I need a shower."

"That's putting it lightly," she returned automatically. She looked dazed as she watched the last evidence of his wound disappear.

"Er, thank you for the blood."

She shook her head. "You're welcome. Just glad that I was able to intercept your deliveries."

He paused. "You intercepted my blood?"

"Of course. I figured that you had to have blood delivered otherwise there would be an epidemic of neck bites. It was just a matter of waiting." She gestured towards her room. "I bought a mini fridge to keep it cool for you."

Her concern for him made him uncomfortable. "Thank you. I'll pay you of course. I appreciate it," he said more harshly than he intended.

She rolled her eyes and walked past him towards her room. "Forget about it. I'll see you around."

"Wait!" he said suddenly. He didn't know what to do or say, but he wanted, no, needed for her to stay. An entire week without seeing her practically killed him. There he admitted it to himself. He missed her.

It was easier when he was here and avoiding her mostly because he watched her from afar. Hell, he made it a point to watch her. Something other than her blood mesmerized him and he couldn't understand this need to see her. If he didn't think fast she was going to leave him now.

"Well?" she asked.

Tall, Dark & Lonely

He half stumbled towards the bathroom. Okay, he faked it, but desperate times called for desperate measures. "Sorry," he mumbled as he made an exaggerated effort to walk into the bathroom.

Ephraim risked a quick glance at her and had to look away to hide his grin. She bit her lip. Madison looked so adorable with an expression full of worry. He had to use this against her of course. He stumbled again.

"W-what do you need?"

He looked back at her, giving her a weak smile. "Could you wait until I'm done with my shower to make sure that I don't black out before I get back in bed?" There was no way he was going to pass out, but she really didn't need to know that. It would only be counterproductive to tell her.

For a moment she looked as if she was going to refuse. In the end she sighed and waved him forward. "Go ahead. I'll wait." She sat on the edge of his bed, prepared to wait.

"Thank you," he said softly before continuing into the bathroom at an exaggerated rate. Once the door was shut he took the quickest shower of his life.

Ten minutes later Madison's eyebrows shot up as Ephraim walked slowly back into the room. What the hell was he up to? She wasn't an idiot after all. This little trick had been attempted by Jill and Joshua over the years. The whole "I'm too sick to go to school" bit was wasted on her.

If he was going to play then so was she. "You poor thing," she gushed. His lips twitched, but he didn't smile as she helped him into bed. She made a big show of fussing over him.

"What can I do for you?" she asked softly.

Christ that was unexpected. "Umm.....my back is sore?" He had to buy himself some time to think up something to keep her here.

She cooed, "Of course it is." She gently gripped his shoulders and pulled him forward so that she could reach around him and run her hands down his back. He'd only suggested it to buy some time until he figured out a way to make her stay longer, but once her hands started running down his back he couldn't get enough of her touch.

It had been so long since someone had touched him with any amount of affection. Other than the occasional hugs from his brother, sister-in-law and nieces and nephews there had been no one to show him any sort of compassion. The women he slept with showed him nothing but desperation and need. They only touched him if it would somehow lead to their own pleasure. He'd never felt any sort of affection in their attentions.

Madison on the other hand, her touches were unmanning him. There was no way that he could miss what a kind, selfless and loving woman she was from the way that she was touching him. It felt so good and he prayed that she would never stop.

She had to stop herself from licking her lips as she ran her hands over his back. Since they moved here she imagined what it would be like to run her hands over his body and now she was doing it.

This was meant to mess with him, but it wasn't turning out that way. She loved the feeling of his warm, smooth skin beneath her hands. It was amazing how firm his back was. She leaned over him so she that could rub further down his back. It took a soft groan to snap her out of her daze, he was playing with her and he was enjoying it.

Madison pulled back. "I'd say you were fine," she said coldly.

He looked up and gently grabbed her arm as she moved to pull away from him. It took everything she had not to gasp. His clear deep blue eyes were filled with unshed tears.

"D-did I hurt you?" She somehow managed to ask.

"No," his voice was hoarse. He looked away for a moment before looking back at her. Her heart broke at the sight of such a strong man looking so vulnerable. He looked so sad and lost. "Please, don't stop," he pleaded softly. "I-I know I don't deserve it. I lied about being unwell…I just…" he licked his lips. "I'm sorry."

He shook his head before releasing her arm. "I'm so sorry about everything. The way I treated you that night when I…" He winced at the memory of shoving her hand over his erection. "I was an asshole. You didn't deserve to be treated like that and I am truly sorry."

"Would you please continue?" he asked softly. There was no doubt in her mind that it had cost him to show her any weakness and it humbled her.

She sighed as she leaned over him once again. "It's fine," she said, ignoring his apology. She knew what he was talking about and didn't think it deemed an apology. Sure, he'd been crude, but she….well….she pushed it out of her mind and focused. "I'm sure you're sore from a week in the hospital," she mumbled.

"Thank you." She ignored him and focused on the warm smooth skin. After a moment she couldn't deny that it felt good, really good to touch him so freely. She bit her lip to stop herself from leaning over and rubbing her face against his shoulder or inhaling his scent. She was in big trouble here.

Her hands drew back until they reached his shoulders. Then as if they had a mind of their own they ran down his arms and then up again. She enjoyed the feel of his biceps twitching beneath her hands so she did it again and again.

Ephraim slowly laid back until he was sitting against the pile of pillows she placed behind him. They locked eyes as she ran her hands once again up his arms then she allowed them to run down his chest until she found herself massaging his chest and stomach. Hard muscle rippled beneath her touch.

She was dimly aware of him pulling her leg over his lap until she was straddling him. Her eyes focused on his. He ran his hands slowly over her thighs, giving her a chance to stop him. She didn't, she didn't want him to stop. In fact, he was going too slowly for her taste. She unconsciously adjusted herself on his lap, making him gasp softly.

It wasn't until then that she realized where she was sitting. Her hands stilled over his stomach as she realized that she was sitting directly over his arousal. She licked her lips, trying to stop the soft moan that threatened to escape her as his hands moved up her sides until they cupped her breasts through her thin shirt.

His eyes never left hers as he ran the pads of his thumbs over her hard nipples. Her eyes threatened to close in pleasure, but she fought against the urge. His expression was unreadable as he gently massaged her breasts. She watched as his eyes slowly turned from a beautiful calm blue to liquid red.

Madison willed her hands to move as he teased her breasts. It felt so good. Several men groped her in the past, but it never felt this good. He gently squeezed her breasts, directing her to lean into him. Her hands slid up his chest into his hair.

"God you're beautiful," he groaned as he leaned in, taking her mouth in a gentle kiss. He didn't push to deepen the kiss even though his body was screaming for it. This was too important to rush. He knew if he did that she would run away. Instead, he focused on pleasuring her through touch.

Purely on instinct, she began to rub against him. His hands released her breasts and shoved her shirt up until her breasts were free. He moved his mouth away from hers and latched onto one hard nipple, sucking hard while she moved against him.

Her movements were frantic as she searched for a release that she desperately needed. Hot liquid was pooling in her painfully swollen sex. She had to get it, needed it as she increased her movements. Ephraim reached down between them and ripped his towel open so that she could get closer.

Tall, Dark & Lonely

She felt the difference immediately. Mere seconds ago he felt good but now that the towel was out of the way he felt heavenly. Without the towel, his hard shaft was pressed firmly between the lips of her sex. The only thing separating them was the thin material of her cotton shorts. She couldn't get enough as she panted and moved desperately on him.

Ephraim's eyes rolled in the back of his head as she rode him. Never in a million years had he expected this. The virginal Madison was wild on his lap. He could smell how excited she was and it made him harder than he'd ever been in his very long life. He gripped her hips and moved her harder against him.

Suddenly his mouth released her nipple as he dropped his head back and groaned loudly. "Ah fuck, Madison, fuck you're so wet, baby."

She'd be embarrassed, later. Right now it felt too damn good to care. If possible, she began grinding against him harder. His grip tightened on her hips as he exhaled loudly, "Fuck it, my turn."

Before she could say anything he had her on her back. His hand held one of her breasts firmly, pushing it up so he could lick and suck on it while he began grinding into her.

"Ephraim!" she cried out as he positioned the tip of his erection against the wet cloth that covered her until it was pushing between the folds. He thrust gently against her, teasing her center with the cloth covered tip of his erection.

He grunted and groaned as he worked to pleasure her. Madison spread her legs even further for him while she ran her hands down to his bare backside and cupped him. He growled against her breasts.

"Oh, please don't stop," she whimpered.

He growled louder and moved harder against her almost savagely. She wasn't overly concerned when she heard the sound of fabric ripping. His erection was quickly creating a hole in her small shorts. It felt too good to complain.

In seconds the large tip of his cock was inside her. A loud growl filled the room as the first sensation of being inside of her shot through him. She was unbelievably tight and so fucking wet and hot. He forced himself not to push further, knowing that she would hate him. Madison's head dropped back as she moaned loudly. He raised himself up, making sure not to push further into her and reached down to rub his thumb over her clit.

She grabbed the bed spread and started thrashing beneath him. Her hips rolled up, trying to push him further in, but he pulled back just enough to stop that from happening.

"Ephraim...Ephraim!" He licked his lips as she climaxed. It was the most erotic thing he'd ever seen. She was still climaxing as his fangs dropped. He pushed them back. This was for her, not him.

When she was finally done she closed her eyes and steadied her breathing. She became aware of several things at once. She just had the most powerful orgasm of her life. The tip of Ephraim's penis was in her. Worst of all, he watched as she came. Her cheeks heated as she gently pushed her hands against his chest.

He felt the change in her at once and knew all he had to do was kiss and touch her again and he could have her. Instead to his own surprise, he backed off and watched as she righted her clothes and walked out of the room without looking back at him. At the door she paused and mumbled, "Please forget this ever happened."

"Okay." He reluctantly agreed to give her some comfort, but he would never forget. Couldn't. Even now he wanted to bring her back into his bed. For the first time in his life he didn't just want sex with a woman. He wanted all of *her*.

Chapter 10

"Is he still there?" Madison whispered. She didn't know why she even bothered whispering since *he* would hear her.

Jill laughed. "Yes, I don't think hiding helps."

Madison straightened up from behind the clothes rack. "It couldn't hurt," she mumbled, kicking herself inwardly for her choice of escape tonight. She came here to walk around just to get out of the house. It wasn't as if she had any money to buy something. Damn it, she should have just hidden in her room, again.

"Well, apparently it couldn't help, because he's coming over now." Jill grinned wickedly. "I think I'll go see who's hanging out at the food court now."

"Jill! Don't you dare….Jill? Get back here! Traitor!" Madison hissed at Jill's back. She would get her back one way or another.

Ephraim stopped two feet in front of her. His jaw was set, his eyes were cold. "You've been avoiding me," he blurted out.

She looked away, pretending to look at a dress. "No, I haven't."

"Yes, you have."

"You're imagining things," she said in a condescending tone.

"Am I?" He stepped closer, she retreated. "That's what I thought."

"What? I'm shopping," she said in an innocent tone as she turned her back on him. He looked so good. He was wearing a blue shirt, black tie and his trousers that made him look hot. His gun made him look dangerous.

"No, you're avoiding me."

She scoffed. "Someone thinks highly of himself."

"It's not that. For the past month you ran every time you saw me or ducked behind something." He gestured to the clothes rack. "You hide in your room, you ignore my knocks, and you leave an hour early in the morning or wait until I leave just to avoid me. You started eating in your room when I started coming down during dinner time, and you haven't used our bathroom in three weeks."

Madison casually walked to another section. This close proximity was messing with her head. She needed some distance just to think clearly. He had this affect on her. He was the only one. It would be so much easier for her if she feared him.

"You're doing it again!" he pointed out, walking after her.

She chuckled weakly. "I am not. I'm looking at...at...." she stammered. What the hell was she looking at? Ha! She was still in the woman's section, although the clothes seemed to be a bit bigger here.

"So, when's the bundle of joy arriving? I assume we're talking Immaculate Conception."

Her face turned red. He was an awful, awful man. "I'm looking for a friend," she lied.

"How kind of you," he said dryly. "I thought women bought for the baby."

She shrugged and decided to go with the lie. "There's no law that says I can't buy something nice for my friend."

"Of course not. So what's this friend's name?"

"Uh...Betty?"

"*Betty* is very fortunate to have a friend like you," he said casually.

"At least she's not stalking me."

"Who's stalking you?" he asked as he thumbed through shirts.

She turned on him, fists on hips and hissed. "You are!"

He threw his head back and laughed.

"Stop that!"

Still chuckling, he said. "I'm sorry but-"

"As you should be."

"I came here to find some new shirts. I didn't know that you were here and I'm not following you. You're just paranoid," he lied, partially. He did need new shirts. When Joshua told him where she was that need became urgent.

Her eyes narrowed. "So, you're saying that you're not stalking me?"

He did his best to look innocent. "Of course not."

She pointedly looked at his empty hands. "Then where are your shirts?"

Damn. "I saw you before I found any."

"Which entrance did you come in?"

"What is this, the Spanish Inquisition?"

"Just answer the question."

"Fine, the front entrance."

"Ha!" A woman with a small child walking by jumped and hurried away.

He chuckled. "Easy now, you're scaring the natives."

She gestured calmly towards the front of the store. "If you truly came in through the front exit you would have come across your shirts and you wouldn't have seen me."

Damn it. "I didn't have to see you, Madison." He leaned in, placing his mouth next to her ear. "Your scent calls me. It screams for me."

She swallowed. "It…it could be anyone."

He exhaled, bathing her skin in his hot breath. It sent goose bumps down her spine. "No darling, no one and nothing calls me the way you do. You're my siren calling me to shore. My beacon. You're the only thing I desire."

"I don't understand. It's just blood," she whispered.

He sighed heavily, sending another rush of warm air against her skin. "No, I see that you don't." He ran his lips over her nape. She smelled so good.

"I'm not afraid of you," she said firmly.

The scent of female arousal hit him hard. He groaned against her skin. "No, you're definitely not afraid of me." He pressed a kiss against her neck. "I don't want you to be afraid of me." He pressed another one.

"Because you want my blood," she gasped, biting back a moan of pleasure.

His kisses made her squirm. He felt so good. She liked everything about him. It was driving her crazy. She didn't want to feel this way about any man. She didn't want to be her mother who fell for every guy that looked her way and made her life all about a man. She couldn't lose herself like that and with Ephraim she was very afraid that she would. "Ephraim, if you want some of my blood I could donate it. That should solve your problem."

He shook his head slightly against the crook of her neck, running his lips over her skin in a more delicious manner. "It would never be enough."

"I could do it once a week," she added, sounding hopeful.

His hands took hers into his, entwining their fingers. "It would never be enough for me." He kissed her neck greedily.

She closed her eyes and her head dropped back of its own accord. "When," she licked her lips, "when will it be enough?"

"When you're *mine*," he growled against her skin.

She gasped as cool air suddenly hit her neck. She looked around in a daze. He was gone.

"As far as exits go that was a good one," she muttered.

* * * *

His words rang through her head. What did he mean by when she was his? Did he expect her to become his cow? Available for a feeding whenever he felt so inclined? Maybe he meant to drain her all at once. If all of her blood was in his stomach then that would certainly make her his, she would imagine.

She punched her pillow, trying to make the damn thing behave and tossed over onto her side, again. If he said it to keep her up all night, well then he certainly succeeded. She sat up suddenly, kicking the covers off.

"That's it!" If she was going to be up all night then he was going to answer her questions. He still owed her two hours. She had those pictures developed and blown up as promised. She even had them framed and hung up in his room. He owed her and she meant to collect, now.

He wasn't getting out of this tonight. She stormed over to the bathroom door and threw it open and gasped.

Ephraim stood in the doorway. Every muscle in his body was clenched tightly. His eyes were a fiery red and he looked so very dangerous. She took a step back.

"I told myself that if you opened that door." He looked at the door and then back at her, running his eyes over her baby pink top and matching panties. "That I could have what I wanted. I waited three hours….I couldn't leave, Madison. I had to wait…I had to…" He took a step into the room.

For the first time since the incident in the dining room she feared him. He said her blood was his weakness and she ignored it. She thought that she was safe as long as she kept her doors locked and avoided him, but she was wrong. She was so very wrong.

She stepped back, slowly. She had to get out of here. He was too fast, she knew that. The gun. She needed the gun. *Slowly, move slowly.* She took another step back towards the closet.

"Go away, Ephraim," she said, hoping to distract him with conversation long enough so that she could grab the gun. Also, she said it on the off chance that he would actually listen.

He took another step towards her. "I can't, Madison, don't you see that? I need you."

"No, what you need is a pint of plasma. Go back to your room, Ephraim, and drink it from a bag."

He shook his head. "No."

"Ephraim, think about what you're doing. You don't want to do this." She took another step and then another. Thank god Jill rummaged through her closet earlier. She left the door wide open.

"I do. Can't you tell, Madison? I want you so badly I can't breathe. I can't think. Every thought is about you. Day and night I think of nothing but you. It's distracting, annoying and hell. Don't you see? I can't hold back any longer. I want you so badly, Madison," he said in a sultry voice.

She moved closer to the closet. She just needed to reach up and grab the gun. Then shoot. He would be knocked out, hurt, but he would live and so would she.

"I want you to leave, Ephraim. Now." She was in the doorway of the closet now.

"No, I know you want this, too. I can smell it on you every time you're near. You want me just as much as I want you. I'm done playing this game, Madison. I've come to take what's rightfully *mine*."

"I'm not yours, Ephraim!" she snapped as she reached for the gun. He grabbed her, pushing her back the last few feet until her back was pressed against the wall. She gripped the gun tightly in her hand.

She could make out the outline of his body and his red eyes. "You are mine, Madison. You've always been mine. You just didn't know it and neither did I, but you're mine, sweetheart, all mine and I'm never going to let you go." He shook his head slowly as he leaned in. Oh god, he was going to bite her!

The sound of the gun cocking was his only warning that she had the gun. He should have known, but he hadn't been thinking clearly. She pressed the muzzle of the gun into his side.

"Step back from me. The kitchen's closed so you'll have to find your meal somewhere else," she said coldly.

He slowly pulled his head back. "Madison?"

"I said move back, you're not going to drain me tonight!"

"That's what you think this is about?" he snapped. He was angry. He wanted her so much and she thought he wanted to feed off her. Didn't she know that he wanted her? Didn't she want him as badly as he wanted her?

"Step back."

"No, I don't want your blood!"

She scoffed, "Liar."

He grabbed her free hand and brought it to the front of his drawers and guided it slowly over his erection. He moaned softly. "That's why I'm here, Madison." He ran her hand down his long length several times and she let him. She was so shocked by the turn of events. She was also very curious.

She would never admit that she enjoyed the last time they did this. He was so…so big. His erection was straining against the material of his boxers and she wondered if it would burst through. His forehead dropped gently against hers. He was panting and she realized that she was, too. She never wanted anything more than she wanted him at this moment. The pain in her body from denying herself for so long was becoming too much. She needed him. Ephraim would take the pain away.

He dropped his hand away, but she didn't stop moving her hand.

"That feels so good," he groaned. He lowered his mouth to hers and kissed her gently, taking his time getting her used to the feel of his lips. Without breaking the kiss, he took the gun from her putting the safety on and returned it to the shelf.

His lips felt so good. It was too good to be true. Any second now he would force his tongue inside her mouth and then it wouldn't be so nice. That's the way it always happened. She prayed it wouldn't happen, but she knew it would. It made her feel almost sad.

Ephraim's thumbs hooked into the waistband of her panties and pulled, quickly snapping them without hurting her. She gasped, opening her mouth wide enough for him to slide his tongue inside and he did. He gently licked her lips and slowly darted his tongue inside.

His tongue was warm silk. He moved it confidently in her mouth. It wasn't rough and awkward like the other men. He teased and caressed her until she was moving her tongue against his, making him groan with satisfaction.

The cool air on her breasts was her only clue that he ripped her shirt off as well. His hands gently caressed her back and bottom before moving to the front where he slid his hands up her stomach and over her breasts, brushing her hard nipples with his palms.

She moaned and squeezed his erection. He groaned into her mouth. Curious at his reaction she stopped touching him and pulled down his underwear, freeing him. It sprang free, slapping against her stomach.

He brushed her hand away as she reached for it again. She wanted to feel it.

"My turn."

"What?" She sounded dazed.

"My turn," he simply said as he pressed hot open mouthed kisses down her neck to her breast. He kissed and licked under her entire breast except the nipple. He ignored that, driving Madison crazy. The nipple became painfully hard. She squirmed and moaned, desperate for his touch. His hands joined his mouth and cupped her breasts, gently squeezing and caressing her, but they too ignored the nipples.

Just when she thought he was going to finally relieve the tension in her nipple he moved his mouth to the next breast and did the same thing. She closed her eyes and nearly whimpered. "Please, Ephraim!"

He chuckled against her skin. Seconds later, his wet tongue flicked her very hard nipple. She gasped and moaned loudly.

"Is this what you want?"

"Yes!" she practically yelled. His mouth closed over the nipple, pulling it into his mouth where he suckled it hard while flicking his tongue against it. He pinched and twisted her other nipple between his fingers. Her lower stomach felt like it was swelling. It was so painful that she needed relief.

Ephraim's mouth left her breasts to his very capable hands. He licked and nipped his way down to her legs. She tried to close her legs out of embarrassment, but he wasn't having it. He pressed kisses around the area that was bare to him above her mound. When he began lapping at the area with his tongue she moaned his name and slowly opened her legs for him.

He traced the slit with the tip of his tongue. She was so wet and swollen. He couldn't get enough of her flavor. He had to have more. He pushed his tongue inside her. She moaned as her hips reflexively pushed against his mouth. He ran his tongue around her opening.

Every muscle in her body was tense. She was stopping herself from moving against him. At that moment he wanted nothing more than for her to ride his mouth. The very idea caused his cock to jump with anticipation.

He pulled his mouth away, making her whimper. "It's okay, baby. Put your leg over my shoulder." When she didn't move, he moved her leg for her, hitching it over his shoulder. She looked confused and a little bit nervous. "It's okay."

His hands left her breasts to cup her bottom. He slid his tongue into the very core of her, making her moan loudly. His hands gripped her bottom tightly, moving her against his mouth. It took only a few seconds for Madison to follow his lead. She used her leg on his back as leverage to tentatively move herself against his mouth. Soon she was moving on her own.

She couldn't believe she was doing this. Later when she thought about this she would die of humiliation, but right now she would die if she stopped. It felt heavenly. His tongue was strong and firm inside of her. He moaned, sending delicious vibrations through her core. She moved harder against him, she couldn't help it and he didn't seem to mind. Actually, he seemed to love it judging by his moans.

"Ephraim," she moaned with her eyes closed as she ground herself against his mouth in a circular motion. He flicked his tongue inside of her hard, making her grab onto his head for both support and to keep him there. She looked down to see two beautiful, glowing red eyes watching her. It sent her over the edge.

Tall, Dark & Lonely

She held on for dear life as a powerful climax ripped through her. She screamed his name over and over again until she was too weak to move. Still he didn't stop. He licked her more softly. He focused on teasing her. It was too much. Her body couldn't handle that again so soon.

"Ephraim..no...please....I can't do that again....it's too much," she panted.

He pressed a soft kiss against her slit. He wiped his mouth with the back of his hand and stood up. "Shh, it's okay." He scooped her up in his arms and carried her to the bed. He crawled in next to her, pulling her into his arms.

She pressed lazy kisses to his chin. "Mmmm, that was so good, Ephraim. Thank you," she said sleepily.

He chuckled. "You're very welcome."

"You're eyes are still red," she mumbled followed by a long yawn.

"Are you tired, sweetheart?" He pressed a kiss to her forehead.

"Mmmhmm." Her eyes closed.

She wasn't going to sleep. Not yet.

"Can I have a goodnight kiss then?" he asked softly.

She turned to face him with a sweet sleepy smile. "Yes."

He placed his hand on her hip, holding her steady as he leaned in and brushed his lips over hers in a teasing kiss. He moved his lips over hers until hers moved against his. He slowly deepened the kiss and waited while she slowly woke up and the kiss turned hungry.

Madison felt her body stir once again. It didn't have a choice with Ephraim slowly grinding his hips against hers. He held her securely against him as he slid his erection against her slit.

She was wet again. He could feel the evidence as it coated his hard shaft with each passing. She moaned into his mouth, letting him know she loved the friction just as much as he did.

"Lift your leg," he said quietly.

His hand was already pulling her leg up as he spoke. He pulled his hips back and moved forward, changing the angle until he was pressed against her slit. He lowered her leg. It felt funny having his erection trapped between her legs and poking out the back of them.

It stopped being funny when he began moving. "Oh god!" she gasped. It was an entirely new sensation. He was rubbing against her clit with every movement and teasing her core.

He cupped her breast as he kissed her and thrust gently between her legs. New moisture pooled between her legs. Didn't he understand what he was doing? It was too much. It was more than last time. She needed more. "Please! Ephraim, please!"

"Please what?" he asked against her mouth.

"Please!"

He thrust harder yet slower between her legs. "Do you want me inside of you?"

"Yes!"

"I want that, too," he said quietly. Using his body, he rolled her onto her back. Her legs came up around him, holding him tightly against her. She was afraid he would stop. There was no chance of that happening.

"This is going to hurt," he warned.

Chapter 11

"I don't care, Ephraim! Just do it please!" she begged.

He chuckled softly as he positioned himself. He could see her. He could see everything. Darkness meant nothing to him. He saw everything as clearly as if it were day only in blue tints and he was never happier about that than right now.

She could see his eyes in the dark. They were bright and intense, but she couldn't see his jaw set tightly or the look of possession on his face. She was his. She just didn't know it yet. He slowly pushed in, watching the expression on her face. He slipped past her entrance and continued to push.

It was the tightest hold he'd ever experienced. He always dealt with women with experience. He was too afraid to be any woman's first and he wouldn't do it anyway. He was brought up to believe that if you bedded a virgin that you stole from her future husband. No, back then you married the woman you deflowered and that rule stuck with him even to this day.

He had to stop when he came across the evidence of her virginity. Once he broke through it, she was his. That wasn't what stopped him though. Once he broke through her maidenhood there would be pain and blood.

Madison's blood.

He didn't know how he would react once her blood hit the air. Why hadn't he thought about this before? All he thought about since the day on the side of the road was burying himself to the hilt in her body. Of course, he would start to think clearly once he was inside of her, he thought dryly.

"Ephraim is something wrong?" her voice was pained.

"I can't do this," he said, pulling back from her.

"Ephraim?" Her voice shook. "Did I do something wrong? Is it me?"

Oh god, she was breaking his heart. "No, baby, you didn't do anything." He pulled out of her body. It was the most difficult thing he'd ever done in his life. He turned his back on her and sat on the edge of the bed. His hands clenched into fists as he fought for control. He dropped his head and tried to calm down as his body shook with need for her.

"Ephraim?" She moved across the bed until she was hugging him and in the process, pressing her breasts against his back.

He shook his head in agony. "Baby, please stop you're killing me."

"Stop what?"

"Touching me."

She pulled back. "You don't want me to touch you?" her voice broke.

"I want you to touch me so much, baby. It's all I think about, but we forgot something."

"Condoms?"

He chuckled harshly. "No, I don't need them. Disease can't live in my body."

"Then what?"

"Blood, baby, you're going to bleed when I take away your virginity and I'm afraid of my reaction once that happens. I don't trust myself not to give into bloodlust."

"Have you ever slept with a woman when she was bleeding?" she asked curiously.

He cringed. "I don't want to talk about other women, Madison. I haven't been with a woman in a very long time. They didn't mean anything to me then and they mean less now." He heard her breath catch.

Tall, Dark & Lonely

"You're the only one I've ever cared about. Believe me if I didn't I would have taken your virginity just now without a second thought. I can't hurt you." He dropped his face into his hands.

"Answer the question. Have you slept with a woman while she had her period?"

He sighed, "Yes." It used to be one of his favorite times to be with a woman. He loved tasting blood mixed with a woman's juices.

"Did you ever have a problem with bloodlust then?"

"No, I was always in control."

"So, you never bit any of them?"

He ran his hands through his hair in frustration. "I never said that."

Madison moved away from him. She sat in the middle of the bed and brought her legs up, hugging them. "If you bit them then why would it be a problem if I bled a little bit?"

His hands dropped back into his lap. "I bit them for pleasure and hunger. It was a way to get what I wanted and give them something in return."

"Something in return?" She was confused.

"A bite during sex makes the orgasm more intense. It also makes a woman's blood rush faster so I can feed faster without the woman realizing that she'd just been my midnight snack."

"But you never killed any of them," she guessed.

"No."

"So, then we should be safe."

He laughed without humor. "No, we would not be safe. Do you remember the day we met?"

"Yes, at the car."

"Do you remember what happened at the car?" He looked over his shoulder to watch her.

"Yes, Jill hit on you. Joshua took ten years off my life with that question about sluts and you were very rude."

He nodded. "Yes, I was, but you're forgetting the most important thing."

"What?"

"You cut yourself."

"So?"

"So, it was only because the two children were there to make me pause and think, step back and allowed me to focus. The only thing I could think about was getting the hell away from you so I went inside. The further I walked away from you the clearer I was able to think. I had to fight the urge to go back. I remembered what I had at stake and what would happen if I took you. Madison, you have no idea how bad it was."

"No idea about what? What did you have to stop yourself from doing?"

He only looked at her. "What, Ephraim? Tell me what the big deal was?"

"I would have jumped over that car and ripped your throat out with my teeth and there wouldn't have been anything in this world that would have been able to tear me off you until I had the very last drop of your blood on my tongue."

"Oh, I guess that explains it," Madison said wryly, trying to lighten the mood after that confession.

"I tried to explain it to you, Madison."

"Yes, you did."

"I'm sorry."

Tall, Dark & Lonely

"Don't say that."

"I don't know what else to say. I can't take any chances with you. I don't want to hurt you."

"And if I bled you would lose control?" she asked.

He nodded. "If you cut yourself right now you would have to run to get your gun and pray to god that I could hold myself back long enough for you to put a bullet between my eyes."

She winced. "If you bled while I was inside you, while I'm already out control I would probably fuck you until you were drained properly."

"Thanks so much for the gentle words," she mumbled.

"I'm not going to sugarcoat it for you, Madison. You need to understand the dangers of being with me. You of all people need to know."

"I still don't understand that. Why me? What's so different about me?"

He looked away from her. "I don't know. I've never heard of this happening to anyone else before."

"So everyone's blood tastes the same?"

"No, everyone's is different."

"How so?"

"Baby, can we do this at another time?"

"Are you okay?"

"No." He shook his head. "I can't think of anything but you right now. I need to leave the room before I do something stupid."

"Oh, can you just answer that question?" She noticed for the first time that his body was trembling.

She heard his quick intake of breath before he answered her. "Some people taste bad, really bad. It could be because of disease, age, there are a number of things that could go wrong in the human body and they all show up in the blood."

"Makes sense," she agreed, quietly.

"Let's say a person indulges in sweets then their blood will be sweet. The same could be said about alcohol or drugs. I would taste that. Others...well, think of all the things that you do during the day, what you eat, what you drink, the air you breathe, the people who surround you. All of that influences your blood. It makes each person's blood unique."

"Okay, so all we have to do is figure out what's making my blood unique then I'll stay away from it." She felt relieved. This should be simple enough. She would change her diet and cleanse her system. It might take a little while but she could do it.

Ephraim stood up. "Madison, it's not that simple. There is nothing that you're eating or doing that is causing this."

"How do you know? I might somehow be doing the correct assortment of things that makes me irresistible."

Ephraim kept his back to her. She didn't need to see how aroused he still was. It was beyond painful. "Madison, it's nothing you're doing. I can guarantee that by the fact that you are still alive. If it was solely based on your blood you would have been killed long ago. Just going out at night would put you in danger if that was the case."

"Maybe I've never come across a vampire before."

"Madison, do you remember two months ago when I was at the bar and some of your friends dragged you in there?"

"Yes." She wasn't likely to forget that night. Every woman there seemed to have eyes for him. And every drunk seemed to have loose hands for her.

"There were five vampires in there that night. If your blood had held one tenth the power it holds for me, I would never have been able to keep them away from you. They would have ripped through me and everyone that got in their way apart."

"Wait, you protected me?"

"Yes, of course."

"If my blood doesn't hold the same value to them as it does to you then why were they after me?"

He sighed. "You're a virgin, Madison. Your blood is pure. It's a treat. Plus, you are a very beautiful woman. They'd be fools not to want you."

"So, I'm still a-"

"Yes, I didn't take you." He moved towards the door. "I'm sorry about this, baby. Goodnight."

* * * *

He was near tears. Twenty minutes after leaving her room and he still couldn't find relief. No matter how much he thought about her, the way she felt, the way she tasted and moved on his mouth, relief wouldn't come. For the last ten minutes he'd been stuck on the verge of release.

"So this is hell." He dropped his hand away and took a deep breath. He needed to think about something else, something to distract him. Fishing. There was nothing sexual about fishing. Hooks, worms, dirt, rocking boat…..rocking…motion…Madison. God damn it!

Madison's bathroom door opened. He waited to hear the click of his door. He listened as she turned on the shower. He looked at the clock to see that it was two in the morning. She never took showers this late.

A sinking feeling tore at his gut. He hurt her. Somehow he hurt her and she needed hot water to soothe any aches and pains that he caused. Shit. Thinking back he may have been a little forceful with his hands and mouth. He knew he hadn't cut her with his fangs. He definitely would have noticed *that*.

He heard movement against his door. "What the…" Why was she stuffing a towel beneath his door? He sat up on the bed and threw his legs over the side, watching the door intently. She was up to something.

She was breathing hard and muttering something even he couldn't hear. He walked over to the door and listened closely. Water was splashing off her skin, okay she was in the shower, nothing nefarious about that. Thankfully she started mumbling louder.

"Just do it…don't be such a wimp….okay, no I can do this I can….okay….." He waited with anticipation. What was she doing that required a pep talk? He found himself holding his breath. After a long moment she sighed and muttered, "I'm such a chicken." He wanted to smile, but he was becoming a little concerned.

"Madison?"

She squeaked. Yeah, she was definitely up to something and she didn't want him to know about it.

"Be out in a minute." Her voice was strained.

"Are you okay?"

"Oh, I'm fine. Er, could I bother you for something?" She sounded more cheerful.

"Of course."

"Could you run downstairs to the kitchen? I'm really hungry."

She wanted him to leave. "Sure, what do you want?"

Tall, Dark & Lonely

"Um, could you make some toast with butter? And a Coke?" She wanted him gone for a while. She knew he didn't know how to use the damn toaster.

"Sure. I'll go right now."

* * * *

Madison listened as he opened his dresser drawer, probably to get some clothes. She held her breath as his door opened and closed and she heard the sound of his footsteps fading away.

"Oh thank god," she mumbled.

It was hard enough doing this. She didn't need Mr. Supersonic hearing outside the door. She looked at the vibrator in her hands. It was Candy's idea of an appropriate Christmas gift for her virginal daughter. Not that Candy knew she was a virgin. If she did Madison would never hear the end of it.

Candy would push men in her direction. She would have to dive into the street to avoid them. She laughed at the image. No, she had to focus. She held the thin long white vibrator in her hand. It was hard and looked like it was going to hurt.

Maybe she should select a different one. She only picked this one because it was the thinnest and didn't really resemble a penis. She wanted this to be thought of as a purely medical procedure. Her hymen needed to be broken. With that gone she could lose her virginity to Ephraim.

Breaking her hymen with a plastic vibrator that reminded her of a long finger was not losing her virginity, she told herself. She was just making it possible for them to make love without him worrying. She looked at the hard tip, again.

"Oh, this is going to hurt so much," she nearly whimpered. The other ones didn't look like they would do the job. Her mother bought her an assortment of sex toys for Christmas because of the David situation. Candy didn't want Madison to rush off to some "loser" because she was horny, her words, her exact words. It was a little flattering that Candy thought she was too good for men like that.

"Just do it," she said to herself.

She'd never used any of the toys Candy bought her. She just threw them into a shoe box and hid it, too embarrassed to risk throwing them out. What if her Grandmother saw them, or Joshua found them and took them and thought they were toys? She would die of humiliation if she found him playing swords with them.

She kept them and now she was using one of them to break her hymen so that she could sleep with her boyfriend. Well, he wasn't exactly her boyfriend, but she wanted to sleep with him, desperately. He talked about his desperate attraction to her blood, but he didn't understand her obsession with *him*.

He was like a drug for her. She craved him night and day. So of course she avoided him as long as she could, but now that she finally had a taste of him she couldn't hold back. She needed him. If this was the way to do it then she would just suck it up and get it over with.

She took another deep breath, wondering if she was going to suck all the air out of the room while preparing to do this. She squatted down and placed the tip of the vibrator between her legs. "Just a small pinch," that's what she read on the internet. She jumped on her computer as soon as he left her room, trying to find ways to avoid bleeding. The only decent advice that she found was breaking the hymen on her own or going to see a doctor to do it. She would only bleed when it broke and that only happened the first time so here she was crouching down naked in the tub with a scary looking vibrator. Ah, a Hallmark moment.

Tall, Dark & Lonely

After making sure that her feet weren't going to slide, sending her flying on her butt, she pushed the vibrator in further and gasped. This wasn't how it felt when Ephraim did it. When he did it, it felt good, smooth and wet. This was…this was….none of those things.

She felt dry and it hurt. It felt like she was getting rubbed raw. "Ow..ow…owie..ow…" She pushed a little further and found resistance. Finally. She looked up, not that she couldn't hear and feel the water splashing her, but she wanted to make sure that it was running.

As soon as she broke through, she was pulling this horrible finger out of her and washing herself. She needed to delude the blood quickly so the smell wouldn't carry over to Ephraim's room. She just hoped the towel that she stuffed under his door helped where she failed.

"This is it," she said, trying to sound brave. She ran her tongue over her bottom lip and took several quick breaths. "Just do it."

"What the hell do you think you're doing?" Ephraim's voice abruptly thundered in the small room.

She twisted too quickly to the side to look up at him and slipped, landing on the flat bottom of the vibrator, thus forcing it in completely. Sharp agonizing pain ripped through her. She released a blood curdling scream.

"Oh shit!" Blood streamed from beneath Madison. It took everything Ephraim had to ignore it and his fangs, which were throbbing at the sight and the smell. Madison was crying and somehow that was enough to keep him focused, somewhat.

He dropped to his knees and gently pushed her back. Something white, well white covered in blood, was sticking out of her. With two fingers, he gently pulled it out of her. It looked like…well, he wasn't exactly sure what it looked like. It was a cross between a nailless finger and a pen cap. This wasn't a pen, was it? He turned it over in his hands, noting that the blood was already gone thanks to the water.

"What is this?" he asked.

"What do you think it is?" she snapped. It brought his attention back to her. She was covering her face with both hands and crying. Thankfully the blood stopped running from between her legs.

It was clear that she broke her hymen. From the looks and smell of it, very painfully. She wasn't aroused. It must have been so painful for her. This was his fault. He should have known she would do something like this. He plugged the tub and released the shower switch, hoping that a hot bath would help her.

Madison curled up on her side, facing away from him and sobbed into her hands. This was his fault. It should have been special for her and she shouldn't be crying. He would have made this good for her. He already made sure she came first and that she was wet. He just couldn't finish. She had to do it for him. He felt like less of a man for that.

"It hurts," she whimpered.

He leaned over and kissed the top of her head. "I know it does, baby. I'm so sorry."

"Should it hurt this much?"

Should he lie? No. "No, baby, it shouldn't hurt this much. It should have hurt at first and then if you were with the right man the pain would have gone away, leaving you with pleasure. You'd be sore afterwards for a day or two."

"Oh, you've done this before?"

"What? Taken someone's virginity?"

"Yes?"

"No. My brother was married twice. We talked about it, and of course other guys talk about it. No, I purposely avoided virgins."

"Then why does it hurt for me?" she asked through a sob.

He kissed her again. "For one thing, you weren't aroused. For another, you shoved this weird plastic thing inside you and if you're dry that would really hurt. Then of course you practically slammed it into yourself."

"That's because you scared me!"

"I'm sorry, baby." He kissed her head again.

"D-do I smell different now?"

"Huh?"

"Do I smell like a virgin still?"

He ran his nose over her neck. "Yes, but you smell slightly different. You still smell pure, but in a different way."

"Oh, so I suppose this didn't change the way my blood smells for you?"

"No, it didn't, sweetheart. I still want you." He saw her shiver. "Come on, sweetheart, let's get you to bed before you catch your death." He drained the water and picked her up, wrapping her in a towel. She couldn't uncurl her body, because it hurt too much to move.

He laid her on his bed. "Ephraim?"

"Yes?" He crawled in beside her, wearing jeans.

"Can you make this feel better?"

She wanted him to make love to her and make it go away. "No, baby, I'm not touching you tonight. I don't know what damage you just did to yourself. So until we do I'm off limits for you."

"Damn it." She sounded so disappointed and cute that he had to bury his face in her hair while his body shook with silent laughter.

She swatted him on the arm. "I know you're laughing! You're so mean! This is the most embarrassing thing that's ever happened to me and you're laughing!"

Chapter 12

"Oh, god this is the most embarrassing thing that's ever happened to me," Madison grumbled behind the curtain of hair that hid her face as she leaned forward.

She hoped to come in and sneak out quickly. She waited two days for this appointment, too embarrassed to go the emergency room. Two days of pain and discomfort. Two days of staying home and lying to everybody about what hurt. Worse, two days of not being allowed to touch Ephraim.

For the past two days he'd been so attentive. He stopped by the house as often as he could to keep her company or bring her something. He was so sweet and kind that it was killing her. To start their relationship like this was killing her. Not being allowed to touch him was torture. True to his word, he didn't try anything. He wanted to, she knew that.

For the past two nights she fell asleep in his arms with the evidence of his arousal pressing into her back or thigh. He never pushed her or offered anything. The only thing he allowed her was heavy make out sessions. Then he would stop abruptly before things got out of hand and head to the bathroom for a cold shower. So now she was sore and frustrated beyond belief, but that still wasn't the worse part. Not even close. Ephraim's laughing and joking about it was the worst.

Once he discovered what that nailless finger was and where it came from, he couldn't stop laughing. He wanted to see the box and wouldn't stop pestering her until she showed him. Then for the next half hour he made her laugh with his jokes and observations. He heard of vibrators and sex toys of course, but never saw them first hand.

Every time someone asked how she hurt herself or when Grandma offered to kiss the booboo better, the booboo being an upset stomach, her cover story, Ephraim would start laughing uncontrollably until she was laughing with him. He felt bad of course, but he found the whole thing funny until she cried that is. Then he became deadly serious and held her or placed her in a hot tub, begging her to let him take her to the emergency room. When she refused he doubled his efforts to make sure she was comfortable.

"So, you've actually been in the delivery room?" He held her hand loosely in his while he ran his thumb over her hand, but his attention was clearly elsewhere.

The older man across the room beamed. "The first time she had to have me dragged into the room," the man said, chuckling. His very pregnant wife gave him a playful slap on the arm. "The last two times they couldn't keep me out of there. It's so amazing. You're going to love it."

Ephraim seemed relaxed, but his hand told her a different story. It stopped moving. "Are the two of you expecting?" the man's wife asked.

"No, not yet," Ephraim said smoothly. She was the only one that heard the longing in his tone. "So, do they really let you cut the umbilical cord?"

"Yes, but you have to ask ahead of time or they'll do it for you."

"Not to put you on the spot or anything, but do they let you watch the baby be born or do they use curtains?"

They laughed. "It's fine. They can do either. It's up to us to tell them how we want the birth to go."

"Really?" Ephraim seemed enthralled with the subject.

"Murphy," the nurse called.

"Oh, that's us," the man said, grinning. He helped his wife stand up as he threw a smile at Madison. "Good luck, Detective."

Tall, Dark & Lonely

Madison stopped a groan. The man thought they were trying to make a baby. Well, it was probably better than the truth that she hurt herself with a sex toy.

"Simply fascinating," Ephraim murmured.

"It's just childbirth, Ephraim. You can probably watch it online."

"Really?" he asked, asked sounding excited.

"You didn't know that?"

"No, I got bored with the internet when it came out years ago. I just use it now to send in my work. You'll have to show me later."

She sighed, "I promise."

"Excellent," he said cheerfully.

From beneath her veil of hair she said, "I don't understand why you're so excited about it."

He looked around the room happily. "Marc would have loved this."

"Your brother?" He never spoke about his family and she didn't feel comfortable bringing it up, knowing it was probably a painful subject for him.

"Yes, when his wife Hannah was in her first confinement he was really excited. We both were. We thought he could go in during the birth."

She pushed her hair away from her face to watch him only to find him watching her. He brought her hand to his mouth and kissed it.

"So, what happened?" She didn't want him to stop talking. Granted, she didn't want him to stop kissing her either.

"Well, we made plans. He had his favorite chair brought into the room so that he could sit back and watch." He chuckled. "Hannah found out and made sure that we were both kept out. She hired five footmen to guard the door to keep him out."

"I bet he didn't like that."

He laughed louder. She liked hearing him laugh. It sent pleasant shivers down her spine. "No, he yelled and threw a fit. He reminded them that he was the Duke and he would not be kept out."

"Did it work?"

Still chuckling, he answered her, "No, his sister-in-law came out. Bertha, a big woman, threatened to box his ears and told him to sit down or she'd make sure that he'd never get another chance to put a babe in his wife's womb again."

"What did he do?"

"Oh, he sat down of course. Bertha was a formidable woman" He leaned in closely and whispered, "She scared me." She smiled, forgetting her pain and discomfort for the moment.

"So, he gave up?"

He shook his head. "Oh no, not Marc. He bid his time wisely. For the second and third babe he feigned disinterest in the births. We went to his study to drink and play cards and told the servants not to bother us until the babe was out and ready for holding."

"What happened with the fourth?"

"The fourth, that one was the key. The servants were now used to us hiding out in the study. That baby was part of his big plan and trust me when I tell you that he worked damn hard to make sure she got pregnant again. He was anxious to see a birth."

"When Hannah's water burst, I helped him hide behind the changing screen. I made sure that all of the candles were brought forward so that no shadows were cast. I wished him well and headed for the study where we were supposed to be playing cards."

"So, he saw the birth? He must have been so happy."

Ephraim chuckled. "Oh no, sweetheart, he was very angry."

"Why?"

"He passed out as soon as the head appeared. Flat on his back and no one even knew that he was there. I found him two hours later while the house was in an uproar searching for him."

She laughed softly. "I'm guessing that's why they had another child."

"Yes, he wanted another chance. This time when he went into the room to hide, Bertha was ready for him with a broom stick. She chased him out of the house and through Rotten Row." His whole body shook with laughter. "I've never seen him run so fast in my life."

"Did she get him?"

He leaned over, laughing harder. She saw his head nod. She couldn't help laughing along with him until it hurt. "Ouch!" That stopped his humor. He sat up, putting his arm around her.

"Are you okay?"

She nodded. "It's just a little pain."

"Madison Soloman," the nurse announced.

"That's me," she said before turning to Ephraim. "You don't have to come in."

"Are you sure?"

She nodded. "I'm sure."

"Okay, I'll be waiting for you here."

She stood up and bent over quickly, clasping her stomach as pain shot through her lower body. "Ow!" Before she could sit back down, Ephraim had her scooped up in his arms.

"Which way?" he asked the nurse.

"T-This way," she answered nervously.

Madison buried her face against his chest. "I know, sweetheart, this is more embarrassing. I'm sorry."

"It's okay," she mumbled against his chest.

* * * *

"You can help her get dressed now," the doctor said. She turned her back to give them privacy. Ephraim didn't understand the need for that. The woman just had her head between Madison's legs, but he wasn't going to say anything since Madison seemed relieved.

Once she was dressed, Ephraim leaned against the exam table while she sat with her legs hanging over the side. "Is she okay?"

The doctor turned around. "Tell me how this happened again."

Ephraim cursed under his breath. He knew she wasn't going to believe that he'd been too rough taking her virginity. He hated it more because it made him look like an asshole.

"Huh?" Madison's cheeks turned a fiery red.

The doctor folded her hands in her lap and leaned back in her chair. "I can only help you if I know what happened. I know what didn't happen. I know this did not occur during natural intercourse."

"Huh?" was the only response Madison could manage. She was so embarrassed.

"This doesn't leave the office, am I correct?" Ephraim asked.

"Of course."

"I don't want it written down either," he said.

"We'll see if it's pertinent, but I need to know."

"Huh?"

Ephraim cursed again and wrapped an arm around her shoulders. "It was an accident. She was...she...er..." He looked back at the closed door to make sure that it was still closed. "She used a device to break her hymen. She slipped and landed on it, pushing it all the way in rather quickly."

The doctor winced. "And why did she do that?"

Okay, this was time for the big lie. Something more believable than Ephraim was afraid bloodlust would take over if he did it. His mind froze. Why did women do that?

Madison came back to life. "He didn't want to hurt me. I-I freaked out in the beginning because he felt too big." He had to stop himself from grinning, he really did. "And I was crying and he said he didn't want to hurt me. So, I thought it would be better if I did it myself, only I slipped in the tub and landed on it. I just wanted to break through so that it wouldn't hurt my first time."

"I see." Ephraim saw the humor in the woman's eyes, but she didn't laugh. He had to give her credit. "That makes more sense."

"Really? So, what's wrong?" Madison looked more relaxed since the truth came out.

She looked at Ephraim. "You may want to hold her hand for this."

Ephraim took her hand. "What is it?"

"You bruised yourself. I'm guessing you went down at an angle, because you're only bruised on the right side."

"So, it's not my cervix."

"No, I'm afraid it didn't get that far."

"What do you mean it didn't go that far? It went all the way in."

"Madison, you have an unusually thick hymen."

"Meaning?"

"It only stretched a little bit to the right. The penetration was incomplete. This is very rare."

She dropped her face in her hands. "Even after that it's not complete?"

"No, I'm sorry. If you want, we could perform the procedure right now. I can complete the tear with an incision."

"I guess I don't have much of a choice," Madison whispered, sounding unhappy.

"If you'll get undressed I can give you a little shot and in ten minutes I can take care of it."

"And the pain will go away?" She sounded hopeful.

"Well, I believe a good amount of it will. The area is swollen and pulling at the hymen, what's left of it. I think this will help yes, but you will still be sore."

"So, it just needs to be broken?" Ephraim asked.

"Yes."

"Will it hurt her if it's done in another method?" He didn't want to see her hurt and he most certainly didn't want this to be a medical event.

"I would say it would have to be done very carefully at this point. With great care." She gave Ephraim a meaningful look. "I'm afraid it's going to hurt her a lot more this time around."

"Ephraim, just let her do it please. It really hurts."

He pushed a loose strand of her hair over her ear. "I'm really sorry about this, baby."

"I know."

"I can't stay in here for this." He pressed a kiss to her forehead.

"I know that, too. Call my Grandmother and ask her to come get me please. There's probably going to be some bleeding and I want to get home as soon as this is done to relax. I know you have to go back to work," she said a bit slowly as she tried to get her message across.

His jaw clenched, but he didn't argue. "I understand. I'll see you later tonight."

"Hold up. Doctor Hahn, will I still be considered a virgin?"

"Of course, this is just a matter of stretching tissue. In your case it needs more help because of the unusual thickness, but you are still very much a virgin."

Oddly enough that made him feel better. He would still be her first, he would see to that.

* * * *

"She's all set."

"Is she okay?" he asked.

Dr. Hahn nodded. "It's better this way, trust me. With her problem she would have ended up here no matter what."

"Thank god." He felt so relieved. He didn't like the idea of her being in there alone. He wanted to know what was happening to her and to hold her hand, but he couldn't. He would hurt her if he smelled her blood.

"Where is she?" Mrs. Buckman asked as she hurried over to them. Candy was close behind, looking equally concerned. That was a shock.

"Dr. Hahn, this is Mrs. Buckman and Emma Buckman, Madison's mother and grandmother."

"Madison is fine. She has prescriptions, one for pain and one for anti-inflammatory. Since she doesn't have insurance her best bet is to pick them up at the pharmacy on Reynolds Street. Also," she pulled out a pamphlet and handed it to Candy, "she asked about a payment plan application. Have her fill this out and she'll need a co-signer."

He pushed off the wall he'd been leaning against for the last half hour and approached the doctor. "What do you mean she doesn't have insurance?"

"I'm sorry, Detective. I can't discuss that any further. You'll have to ask her. I can only say that some of the school unions have harsh contracts."

"Thank you," he murmured. He wasn't going anywhere until he saw her. He would have to hold his breath the entire time and rely on the women to ask the questions.

"Yes, thank you, doctor," Mrs. Buckman said.

Candy looked over the pamphlet. "I can't co-sign this. I have bad credit." She handed the pamphlet to her mother rather hastily. Ephraim doubted Candy would have helped her out even if she did have the money.

Mrs. Buckman sighed. "Don't worry I'll figure something out to help her. I don't want to see her stuck in a payment plan, but if it's over five hundred dollars then I'm afraid she'll have to use it. I need to have the foundation fixed and a new roof put on by next month."

Tall, Dark & Lonely

"She should be out soon," Ephraim said, hoping to change the topic.

Mrs. Buckman looked suspicious while Candy looked resentful. "Ephraim, what is going on here?" Mrs. Buckman demanded.

"You better not have made me a grandmother, Ephraim. I'm way too young to be a grandmother." That was why she was upset. It wasn't over Madison. "I'm trying to find a good man and if I'm a grandmother that won't happen."

"Hush now, Emma, this is about Madison not you. Now you tell me right now if my granddaughter is in some sort of trouble and you tell me now."

"Mrs. Buckman, she's fine. She hurt herself. That's why her stomach hurt so I gave her a ride here today."

"How did she hurt herself?"

He shook his head. "I don't know. You'll have to ask her. I think she was too embarrassed to tell me." He hoped she came up with a good explanation.

Mrs. Buckman pointed her finger at him. "I'm trusting you with my granddaughter, Ephraim. The only reason that I haven't asked her to move her room is because I don't want to treat her like a child. If I feel for one minute that you are mistreating her or making her unhappy in any way, I will-"

"I'll move out in that case. I wouldn't hurt her in any way," he finished. That wasn't what she was about to say, but it was better and the truth.

The door leading to the patient exam rooms opened. The scent of her blood hit him. Ephraim gasped and stumbled back against the wall. The blood was too strong, too concentrated. He closed his eyes and fought for control.

"Ephraim, are you okay?" Mrs. Buckman asked, but he could only nod.

"Are you sure?"

He nodded as he exhaled, slowly releasing the tainted air. His body slowly relaxed, but he didn't dare take in any air.

"Ephraim, what are you doing here? I thought you went back to work." He opened his eyes. He couldn't not look at her. It was as simple as that.

He reached up and cupped her cheek. "I'm fine. It didn't hurt. Now I feel better." He nodded and pressed a soft kiss against her lips.

It was starting to become a little uncomfortable not breathing, but he was fine. He didn't need to breathe. It was just a habit. The longer he held it though the more uncomfortable he would become.

Madison looked at her grandmother and mother. "Oh, I'm sorry everyone rushed down here. I didn't mean to make anyone worry."

"Just tell me you're not pregnant and I'll be very happy," Candy whispered urgently.

"I'm not pregnant, Candy. I slipped in the bathroom the other day and let's just say that I didn't land well. There's internal swelling."

Both women cringed. "Enough said," Mrs. Buckman murmured. "What's this about you not having health insurance?"

Madison's cheeks flushed scarlet. "I have to be there for a full year before I'm eligible for that benefit."

"Oh, what about sick days and vacation?"

She looked away from Ephraim. She missed the last three days and thanks to the doctors note in her pocket she would miss another two, but her job was protected. That was one small favor.

"No, no sick days or vacation days for a year."

Tall, Dark & Lonely

"Honey, you can't afford to miss work. You're still paying off your student loans, not to mention car insurance and your other bills. Do you still have your savings? Please tell me you have your savings. I know you didn't spend it all on that Jeep of yours."

"Grandma, can we talk about this later?" Her eyes darted to Ephraim. He looked oddly composed. Was he breathing?

"No, do you have savings to cover this?" She gestured to the bill in Madison's hands.

"No, I put it towards my student loan, but it's okay, Grandma. They have a payment plan here and it's really not that much. Don't worry about it."

Mrs. Buckman's eyes narrowed on her. Her mouth twitched as she considered her granddaughter. She wasn't satisfied with what she saw there so she snatched the bill from Madison's hands.

"Nineteen hundred dollars for a doctor's visit?"

Madison grabbed it back. "I had to have a sonogram to see the extent of the damage, blood tests, an x-ray, an exam and then a procedure. It adds up quickly I guess. Don't worry about this I'll be fine."

"How? You're not going to be able to pay your bills this month. I saw the note on that bill, young lady, it said no work for two more days," Mrs. Buckman said.

"I'll be fine."

"No, you won't. Even without that bill you're going to be tight. Oh, sweetie, I wish you had come to me sooner. I would have tried to get you on my insurance."

Madison quickly wiped the tears from the corners of her eyes. "I'll be fine. Please stop making a scene."

Well, the women certainly did his work for him. At least Mrs. Buckman had. He knew enough now. Besides, his lungs were starting to cramp from not breathing for the last ten minutes. He snatched the bill from her hands.

"What are you doing?" Madison asked.

Without looking back, he walked over to the cashier and handed the bill and his bank card over.

"All on this card?" she asked. He nodded and stood there waiting while she ran his card. "Sign here....all set. Thank you, Mr. Williams. Have a nice day."

Once again, he nodded.

"Oh wait, here are her prescriptions." He nodded, taking the papers and walked back to the woman.

He handed Mrs. Buckman the copy of the paid bill and the prescriptions. He wasn't stupid. If he gave it to Madison, she would go back in there and demand they credit the money back to him. Then she would go and buy the prescriptions and put herself further in debt or worse, she wouldn't get the medicine because she couldn't afford it.

"What are you doing? I can take care of myself." Madison's voice rose.

He arched a brow in her direction and shook his head as he pulled out his wallet. He pulled out two hundred dollars and pressed the money into Mrs. Buckman's hands.

"We'll pick up her prescriptions on the way home. Thank you, Ephraim," Mrs. Buckman said with obvious relief.

He nodded and gave them a small wave on his way out. He held his breath for another twenty minutes, making sure the scent of her blood hadn't lingered on his clothes. He had a bitch of a cramp when he took in his first breath.

* * * *

"Well, I think it's very sweet," Grandma said.

"Sweet? He just paid for my doctor's bill. Sweet would be flowers or candy, not a nineteen hundred bill and my prescriptions."

"He likes you. He's trying to help you," Mrs. Buckman said.

She groaned. "I know…I know. I like him, too. It's just that…well, it's a lot of money and it just doesn't feel right. I'm going to pay him back. That's all there is to it."

"Hey, isn't that Ephraim?" Candy said from the backseat of Grandma's station wagon.

"Where?"

"Over there. He just came out of the insurance office."

"What on earth is he doing there? The police force pays for his insurance."

A sneaking suspicion was forming in her brain. She groaned again. This was definitely getting out of hand.

Chapter 13

Chris looked over his shoulder and groaned. "Miss. Soloman, can't you do something? She's really bringing me down."

Madison looked past Chris. Jill was still sobbing loudly into the crook of her arm. Frowning, she turned her attention back to Chris. "You're in detention. It's not supposed to be fun."

"It's usually more fun than this," he muttered.

Jill continued to cry as if they weren't talking about her. Madison had to admit that it normally was more fun and today of all days she didn't need this.

The big two-four and everyone forgot. There was no birthday breakfast, no birthday kisses, not one word, nothing. All she got this morning was frustration from not laying in Ephraim's arms. This afternoon she was gifted with a sobbing fifteen year old sister and her repeat offender.

"Maybe this will finally be punishment enough for you to stop acting up," Madison said, knowing that it wouldn't be.

"What it's making me think about is punching that puke face Seth in his face. It's all his fault." He ran a hand over his short brown hair to smooth it down.

"Don't say his name!" Jill wailed from the comfort of her arm.

"Touchy," Chris mumbled. He made a big show of looking around the otherwise empty room. "Come on, Miss. Soloman, let us go home. It's obvious that Jill needs to go home and cry and you need to go apologize to Detective Williams."

Her eyes shot up from the paper she was grading. "What are you talking about?"

He laughed. "Oh puhlease, I saw you guys yesterday at the pancake social."

"You were at a church social?" she asked in disbelief.

He waved it off. "Free unlimited pancakes, Miss. Soloman, focus. You wouldn't give the man the time of day. I saw the way he watched you and the way you treated him every time he tried to talk to you. I also saw the way you reacted every time one of those pretty little things came up batting their eyes in his direction. You were seeing red each and every time."

"You have way too much time on your hands, Chris," she said dryly.

With a huge grin he nodded. "Tell me I'm wrong." When she only glowered at him, he continued. "That's what I thought."

"Don't you have homework to do?" she asked.

"Nope," he made the word pop out of his mouth.

"So, what did he do to piss you off? It has something to do with last week, doesn't it? You were gone a whole week." His face puckered up thoughtfully. "You know I still haven't forgiven you for that. Mr. Darling ran detention in your place."

"He's nice."

"He's a tool."

"Chris!"

"What? He is," he said unashamed. "He actually made us get into a circle and express our feelings."

She cringed. She could just imagine Chris and his friends, the usual occupants of detention, getting into that. "And what feelings did you express?"

He shrugged. "I told him that he was a tool." She laughed. She knew she shouldn't, but she couldn't help it.

"I'm glad you're both having such a wonderful time when my life is over!" Jill said in high drama that would have made Candy green with envy.

Chris snorted. "You're fifteen. It's high school. Get over it. It's wasn't love, it was infatuation. He got over it sooner than you and you didn't take it well. Get over it. Learn from it and move on and stop wrecking detention for me."

Madison could only shake her head in wonder. Chris was a smart kid with a great deal of common sense. If only he could apply himself, she had no doubt that he would do well.

"I love him!" Jill cried.

Chris waved it off and turned his attention back to Madison. "So?"

"So?"

"So, tell me what happened."

She sat back in her chair. "Chris, at what point did we lose the teacher and student relationship and wind up here?" She gestured between the two of them.

He shrugged. "You don't cut me any slack and don't take my shit. I respect you too much to treat you otherwise."

"I'm taking that as a compliment."

"As you should." Chris gave her a lopsided smile.

A loud knock at the door made them both roll their eyes. "Come in," Chris said loudly.

Ephraim walked in carrying a tray with two beverages and a white bakery box. "Detective Williams, have you come to make an arrest?" Chris asked pleasantly.

"Ah, Chris, I knew you would be here."

"Bullshit."

Tall, Dark & Lonely

"Didn't I?" Ephraim pulled one of the beverages out of the tray and placed it in front of Chris. "What's written on the cup then?" he asked as he shifted the cup so that Chris could see his name written on the side of the cup.

"I'll be damned." He shot a glance at Ephraim. "You spit in this?"

"Yup."

Chris shrugged. "As long as you're honest." He took a sip. "Damn that's some good hot cocoa."

"I hear it's the best."

He placed the other one in front of Madison. "Are you still mad at me?"

"Yup," Chris answered for her.

"I thought so." He turned back to Chris and placed the box in front of him. "Eat up."

"I wonder what you've brought us," he mused. He flipped the cover open and gasped, "You are the best Detective, *ever.*"

Ephraim reached into the box and picked up a large gourmet chocolate chunk cookie and brought it to Madison. "I'm really sorry."

She took the cookie from him with a sigh. "Now's not the time. I'm at work. I have to watch these kids." And he did forget her birthday! Granted, she didn't remind anyone, she never did. She liked it when her brother and sister remembered on their own and made a big deal.

Chris spoke up around a mouth full of chocolate brownie. "I don't mind."

She waved an annoyed hand at him. "Go offer one to Jill."

"No way. She just got dumped. She'll eat the whole box."

"Oh, and what are you planning on doing?"

He looked affronted. "That's different. I'm not eating out of depression, I'm eating out of starvation. I was in the principal's office during lunch if you'll recall."

"And whose fault was that?"

His expression turned serious. "It's the man's fault. He's keeping me down."

She looked heavenward. "Oh, heaven help us."

Ephraim walked over and butted fists with Chris. "Fight the man," Ephraim said.

"Damn straight."

"Hey, don't encourage him!" Madison snapped.

"I don't need encouraging. I do well enough on my own," he mumbled, devouring another brownie.

Madison looked down at her cookie and then back at Chris. "Why did he get a brownie and I only got a cookie?"

"Because I love him unconditionally and you're making him sweat." Chris stuffed the rest of the brownie in his mouth.

Ephraim reached over and smacked Chris upside the head. "What?" he mumbled around another brownie.

"Give the lady a brownie. A good one."

Chris mumbled something else, but did as he was told. Madison took the peanut butter brownie Chris was eying. He huffed at her and returned to his seat. After taking a long sip of his cocoa he spoke.

"Before we were so rudely interrupted, you were telling me why you were mad at Detective Williams," Chris said in a conversational tone.

Tall, Dark & Lonely

Jill sobbed louder.

"What's wrong with her?" Ephraim looked back. Jill was still sobbing into her arm. Her red hair was spread out across her small desk.

"Girl and boy date, think they're in love then one day teenage boy falls for new girl in school with a big rack and her own car. Boy dumps girl, girl dumps contents of tray on said boy's head." He made a dismissive gesture with his hands. "Typical high school drama, now let's move on to the good stuff. What did you do?"

"What makes you think I did something?"

Chris snorted. "You're the guy. Of course it's your fault. Even when it's not your fault, it's your fault so dish."

"Stop asking. He's not going to tell you." Madison fidgeted in her chair. He's also not going to remember.

Chris looked expectantly at Ephraim. Ephraim reached up and loosened his tie and unbuttoned the first button of his shirt. Madison watched with anticipation. She had to remind herself that she was mad at him.

They'd been fighting for six days. Well, she had. He just smiled and listened to her ranting. Then when she was done he had the audacity to nod and apologize, each and every time. He only got upset when she refused to allow him to sleep in her bed. Cuddle her ass. He wanted more than that judging by the way his eyes devoured her.

So, she started to ignore him. He didn't like that at first. Then he just shrugged and ignored her back. Now, he had the nerve to show up while she was at work, looking handsome and bringing her delicious cocoa and snacks. Damn that man.

"Well?" Chris prompted.

"It's nothing. He stepped up and helped her. He paid all her outstanding debt and she got mad at him, because she doesn't like owing anyone anything, especially a man. He told her it's a gift and not to worry about it and that she didn't owe him anything. She's hell bent on having a fight about it and he's too thick to see that. It's not complicated and it doesn't compare to my problem. Now give me a damn cookie I think I earned it," Jill snapped.

Chris grinned like it was Christmas morning. "Yes, you did." He brought her a cookie. "Very good, my young one. You've made Chris very happy with this little tidbit of information."

"You have a very big mouth, Jill, did you know?" Ephraim asked.

"Yes," she said unashamed.

Chris rubbed his hands together in anticipation. "Now, let's see. You had a fight over money. I take it she doesn't have much being a single woman who put herself through college and raised two kids. That's understandable and even commendable. And then we have the dashing young police detective-"

"Please you're making me blush," Ephraim said dryly.

"Who lives in a boarding house, drives a state car, and has no real financial responsibilities, so I'm guessing he has a decent amount of money and he wanted to help you."

"Chris," Madison said tightly.

He ignored the warning. "Obviously something happened last week that put a great financial strain on you and he stepped up. He probably didn't want to see you struggle anymore. It was a very nice gesture, one that can be seen in many different ways, but I doubt very much that he expected anything from you or did it to hold it over your head." He ended with a shrug and another bite of cookie.

"Oh? And pray tell, o' wise one, how you have come to this conclusion."

He swallowed loudly. "Just common sense. He's a good looking guy, not as good looking as me of course."

"Of course," Ephraim agreed.

Chris winked at him as he continued. "He moved here three years ago and obviously has had money since then or before then. There are plenty of women in town, beautiful women I might add, who have expressed an interest in warming his bed."

"Chris!"

He held up a hand. "All I'm saying is he's not lacking in looks or offers. If he was the type of guy who was just interested in sex he could have gotten that from anyone. He's not trying to control you and seems laid back. I'm just saying that I don't think he did it to hurt you. He should have talked to you about it I'm sure, but I have to say he meant no harm."

"Thanks for the help, Chris, but I think you just got me in a boat load of shit," Ephraim groaned.

"Why? I'm just saying how it is. If you ask Jill, I bet you she would come to the same conclusion."

"And why is that?" Madison couldn't keep the irritation out her tone.

Chris shrugged. "Because she's female and she doesn't think it's a big deal. Usually females that are prone to drama can sniff out a problem if there is one and blow it up. She clearly doesn't see one."

Jill nodded.

"You both suck," Madison said bitterly.

"Hey, can you say that to us?"

"She just did," Ephraim pointed out.

"Okay then." Chris said happily, grabbing another cookie.

The door flew open and Principal Mason stepped inside. He came to an abrupt halt when he saw Ephraim.

"Detective Williams, to what do we owe the pleasure?" His greeting was cordial, but his tone was cold.

Without missing a beat, Chris spoke up, sensing his favorite teacher might get in trouble for a social call. "Detective Williams is here for me."

"Oh?" He eyed the white bakery box and cup.

"He's trying to butter me up so I'll talk, but I'm not telling him shit." He finished off the last cookie.

"Watch your mouth, boy," Mason warned. He turned his attention to Ephraim. "In the future please remember to let my office know that you're here."

"I signed in as a guest, Mason, but I'll remind you that as a State Detective I can come and go on state grounds as I wish."

"Fine." He knew Ephraim was right. He was still angry about losing the support of Mike's parents after the conviction.

"Well, it's clear he's not going to talk and there's still an hour of detention left. So, if you're done…"

"I'm afraid you're right." Ephraim stood up. Chris dropped his head back and groaned.

"Another hour, if she starts crying again I'm jumping out the window. I'm sure Principal Mason will join me, seeing how he hates the sound of a woman crying," he said a little loudly.

Jill picked up on the non-too-subtle hint and began crying again in earnest. Mason looked flummoxed. "I'll just go now. It seems as if you have this under control, Miss. Soloman." He leveled a look on Ephraim. "Detective."

A long shrieking sound came from Jill that sent Mason running for the door. Jill immediately stopped once the door closed behind him.

"Well, well, well, I do believe that I've found someone that Mason hates even more than me," Chris said thoughtfully. "Good to know."

"Jealous?" Ephraim chuckled.

"Puhlease."

Ephraim straightened his tie and bent over Madison's desk for a kiss. She backed up. He sighed, "So, I see Dr. Phil here was correct. You are mad at me."

"No, I'm not. I'm at work Ephraim." She avoided his eyes.

"Don't you see that I care about you too much to stand by and watch you suffer?" He was reaching the end of his rope. Six days. Six days of nonsense over money of all things. He couldn't believe it.

"Ephraim, please just go. I'll see you tonight at dinner, okay?"

He backed off. "Don't count on it." He left the room at a quick pace.

She dropped her face in her hands and took a deep breath. This was not turning out to be the best birthday ever. This couldn't get any worse.

"Unfucking believable." Chris shook his head in utter amazement. "I'm stuck with two drama queens."

Chapter 14

"Detective Williams, is everything okay?"

Ephraim turned his attention from the shop window to the elderly man behind the counter. "Everything's fine, Mr. Watson. Is my order ready?"

Mr. Watson smiled. "Both of them are in fact." He opened the large shop safe and pulled out a small velvet box and a long thin wooden box and laid them on the counter. "I wish you luck, my boy.

Ephraim placed the boxes in his jacket and nodded. "Thanks again."

"No problem, my boy. You have a good night."

"No chance of that happening," he mumbled to himself.

He walked past the line of shops to the parking lot. Today was not going as he planned. He hoped she was over this so he could give her a good birthday, but she clearly wasn't. Chris was right. She was looking for a fight. He wanted to avoid one at all costs. She didn't understand and now he was pissed off.

How he was going to smile through the next three hours of her surprise party he didn't know. One thing was for certain, she wasn't going to be happy with the gift her bought her. She'd just see it as an attempt to buy her.

His hand froze on the door handle of his cruiser. "Shit," he muttered. He dropped his hand and turned around. A hand shot out to strike him, but Ephraim caught the very feminine hand before it made contact.

"What the hell do you want?" he growled.

The small petite blond just smiled as she pulled her hand back. She looked him over slowly. "I see the years have been very good to you, Ephraim."

"What are you doing here in Rascal?" he demanded.

She gestured casually. "This and that."

"Uh huh, why don't I believe that?"

Eve placed a hand to her bosom. "Me lie?" She gave him a wicked smile. "Never."

His eyes narrowed. "It's just a happy coincidence that you're here."

She stepped up to him and wrapped her arms around his neck. "Why? Didn't you miss me?" She pulled him down and pressed her lips firmly against his.

* * * *

This day was just getting better and better. She paced the front of the school again, making sure to avoid Jill's eyes. Jill seemed to take any eye contact as a signal to start crying. "I think your mom forgot to pick you up again, buddy."

Chris threw the pebble he'd been toying with across the school's front lawn. "She didn't forget, Miss Soloman. No need to soften the blow for me. I told you a half an hour ago not to worry about it. You could have gone home then. You didn't have to wait." Chris' usual calm facade was gone.

She considered him for a minute. He did tell her not to worry about it. Normally he practically browbeat her to sit with him and wait for his mother. His mother was usually either late or sent someone else to pick him up, whatever loser she was sleeping with at the time. This was the first time that he told her not to worry about it.

He'd been in a good mood until she mentioned his mother. Then he slowly sank into himself. "You knew she wasn't coming, didn't you?"

"Yeah, so what?"

"Where's your mother, Chris?"

"Doesn't matter," he mumbled.

"Chris."

"Just leave it alone, Miss Soloman. I'll be fine." He stood up, brushing his hands off and tried to walk past her. She grabbed his arm.

"Chris."

"Let me go."

"Not until you tell me what's going on."

"Nothing."

"Don't give me nothing. Where is your mother?"

He turned his head and rubbed the back of his sleeve across his face. "Nothing," his voice broke.

She gently cupped his chin and turned his face towards her. He was crying. She never thought she'd see the day when Chris cried. He was a tough kid. He had to be with his upbringing. He had a mother who abandoned him on a whim and no place to go but foster homes where rumor had it, he wasn't treated very well.

"What happened?" she asked softly.

"Nothing." He wiped his face again and tried to walk away. "Nothing important anyway." He forced a smile. "Did I forget to tell you that I'm a man now? Yeah, good old Mom declared two weeks ago that I was a man now and didn't need her. She was just waiting for the right moment. It didn't hurt that the right moment came when Eric Bell left his wife and decided to shack up with her. Fortunately for me on that very day I suddenly became a man. Good thing too, because Eric didn't want me around. Isn't that great timing?" he asked bitterly.

"Oh Chris." She released his arm and pulled him into a hug. "Where have you been staying?"

He took in a deep breath. "The trailer. It was paid up until last weekend."

She pulled away. "Where have you been staying since?"

"Here and there."

"Chris, you need a home. You need food." She looked him over. "You didn't eat today because you didn't have any money not because you were in the office. Mason might be a jerk, but he wouldn't starve you."

He shrugged out of her hold. "It's fine. I have a line on a job. I can manage until I have enough money for my own place."

She shook her head. "No, you're sixteen, Chris. If you start working now you'll quit school. No, you need a home. Does anyone else know about this?"

His tone turned harsh. "I'm not going into foster care."

"No, I wouldn't send you there. Is your mother still in town?"

"Yes, she's staying with the bastard in the same trailer park. Can you believe that?"

"No, I can't," She sighed and looked at Jill. "Well, it's time to go home."

Chris mumbled, "I'll see you tomorrow."

Madison grabbed his arm. "Let's go."

"Where are we going?" Chris asked cautiously.

"Home. Congratulations, Chris, you're now a boarder."

He smiled weakly. "Really? I've always wanted to be a boarder. Do we have any special powers?" he asked jokingly, but she could hear the tremor in his voice.

* * * *

"Why does he get to sit in front?" Jill whined.

"Because my mommy doesn't love me and you won't stop bitching. Now sit back and let me enjoy shotgun." Chris gently pushed Jill back with a finger to her forehead.

"Jerk."

"You know it."

"Will you two please stop it?" Madison was getting a headache. For the past hour she had to deal with this bickering. That wasn't as bad as dealing with the manager of the trailer park who confiscated all of Chris's things when he kicked Chris out a week ago.

She had to kick herself. If she'd been at work last week she would have noticed that he was wearing the same clothes every day. When she asked him why he didn't smell, he nearly fell over with laughter. Seems Chris was sneaking into the school every morning to take a shower.

After threatening the landlord with child services, the manager bitched and whined, but cowed. A large thrash bag full of Chris' clothes now kept Jill company in the back seat.

His mother was another issue. Madison didn't know what possessed her or if it was even legal, but Madison refused to leave until the woman wrote a letter handing over custody to her. God, she was an idiot. Eric Bell and the manager were only too happy to sign it as witnesses. She groaned. What was she supposed to do with a sixteen year old boy?

"So, I was thinking since you're my new guardian and all that I should call you Madison. Just seems more natural, don't you think?"

She waved a dismissive hand. "Whatever, just not at school." She wanted to go home and curl up in bed and forget this day.

"Of course, Madison. I would never call you Madison at school, Madison."

"You're enjoying calling her Madison, aren't you?" Jill asked.

"Yes, I believe I rather am," he said with a sniff.

Tall, Dark & Lonely

"Oh my god, Madison, pull over!" Jill shrieked, making Chris and Madison jump.

Madison hit the brake, bringing the Jeep to an abrupt stop in the middle of the street. She looked around the street. Oh no, did she hit someone? "What's wrong, Jill?" she asked as her eyes ran frantically around the front of the Jeep.

"Megan's over there." She pointed past Madison. "I need to go talk to her."

"You just scared the shit out of us for that?" Chris threw her a disbelieving glare.

Jill opened the back door. "I have to talk to her so get over it. See you at home, Madison." With that she closed the door and beelined for her friend.

"I didn't want to say anything before, but your sister is a bit of a spoiled brat."

"Shut up," she groaned.

Chris laughed. A few minutes later they were driving through the center of town. "Whoa! Hold up! Go into that parking lot!"

"Chris!" she warned, she was not in the mood for games tonight.

"Go in the parking lot!" Chris sounded more urgent.

She stopped the car. "Fine." She started to turn in the parking lot. "What the-"

"-hell is he doing kissing another girl that's what I'd like to know." Chris bolted out the door and started running towards Ephraim.

* * * *

Ephraim pushed Eve away. "Get the fuck off me."

She kept herself pressed tightly against him. The window behind him shattered. He tried to jump away, but Eve tightened her grip and kept him pushed against the car. Two large hands shot out and wrapped tightly around his arms and waist. Another set appeared from beneath the car and hugged his legs. Yet another was suddenly around his neck. He heard the movements, but too late it seemed.

Eve backed up, laughing. Her fangs dropped as she eyed him. Ephraim was normally stronger than any vampire, but three vampires holding him with vice grips was too much even for him. They were crushing him. The one on top had him in a good choke hold.

He couldn't move. "What the hell do you want, Eve?" He tried to struggle against their holds, but they wouldn't give an inch.

She laughed lightly. "What the Master's always wanted of course, Ephraim. Your blood."

"I told you, Eve, my blood will not change any of you. You're not the first vampire to steal my blood. It won't work!" It would kill her, but he wasn't about to tell her that.

"I don't believe you." She moved back in and pressed a kiss to his neck. He tried to struggle. "Don't be selfish now. I think you can share. Just think how nice it will be to share the sunlight with your closest friends. I just want a little taste before we bring you to the Master." She sank her teeth into his neck.

He squeezed his eyes closed and half screamed, half groaned. She was sucking on his neck, viciously, greedily. She was afraid she would be stopped before she took enough. What she didn't know was that a spoonful of his blood would kill her, slowly. The amount she was stealing would probably kill her within a few minutes.

She pulled back. "Well, boys, don't be shy. If you wait until I'm done there won't be any left." She struck his neck again.

Tall, Dark & Lonely

On the other side of his neck a new set of fangs sunk it. The man hiding in the car sunk his teeth into Ephraim's side and ripped the skin violently. The one holding his legs did the same. They were too greedy to do this right. The blood was going to come out too fast for them to catch it all in their mouths.

"Hey, asshole!" Chris suddenly yelled.

Ephraim forced his eyes opened and looked over Eve's head to see Chris running towards him. Madison drove up right behind him. The headlights hit him full blast. He knew the instant Chris saw the entire scene, because he froze on the spot.

Madison jumped out of the car and started running. Chris grabbed her around the waist and pulled her back.

"Get out of here!" Ephraim yelled. "Go now!"

"They're eating him!" Chris yelled.

"Let me go!" Madison fought against his hold.

She watched helplessly as four vampires fed from him. It didn't look like they were being gentle. Blood was streaming from their bites and onto the ground quickly. All the color in his face was gone. His head dropped back and she got a good look at a black man on the right side of his neck and a blonde woman in front of him, latched onto his neck. She was holding Ephraim by the back of his head so that he wouldn't disturb her bite again.

Loud growls filled the air. She watched as the black man shook his head violently while keeping his teeth in Ephraim's neck. Blood began pouring from that wound at an astonishing rate.

His eyes closed as he roared, "Go now!" It was soon followed by a scream of agony. The man on his torso pulled back, dissatisfied with the flow of blood and ripped into Ephraim's arm.

"No! Ephraim!"

His head dropped to the side. He was out. The vampires tightened their hold on him so that he wouldn't drop to the ground. They weren't about to lose any blood when they were this close to their goal.

"We have to get help, Madison!" Chris tried to drag her back.

The blonde woman pulled back, smiling. The bottom of her face was covered in red blood and shined grotesquely under the headlights. "Oh, don't rush off on our accounts we'd….we'd.." Her hand went to her stomach as her smile slowly disappeared. She moaned softly and then groaned. "Why does it hurt?" She dropped to the ground and started screaming.

One by one the men released Ephraim to grab their stomachs. They were thrashing and screaming as Ephraim fell to the ground with a loud thud.

"Grab him!" Madison finally managed to get away from Chris. He was too stunned to hold her at the moment.

Madison reached Ephraim. "Oh, god no." His throat was practically ripped out. He was covered in so much blood. "Chris!"

"Madison, you have to leave him! He's going to turn into one of them." Chris's eyes were focused on the blonde's open mouth as she screamed. Her fangs glimmered in the light.

"Chris, I need your help!" Madison cried.

That made him jump and reluctantly focus on her. "Okay, okay, okay, let's just get out of here. We'll bring him to the emergency room."

"No, I have something else in mind."

* * * *

"A tub? Are you crazy? I can see his fucking windpipe and you put him in a tub?" Chris' body shook. "He's going to die, Madison! We have to get him some help!"

Tall, Dark & Lonely

"No, he needs to be here." She left him to go into Ephraim's room and grabbed the key hidden beneath his DVD player and unlocked the mini fridge.

"I'm calling 911, Madison. He needs help." Chris grabbed Ephraim's phone and began dialing.

Madison lunged for the phone. "No, trust me."

"Trust you? He's dying and you want to do what? What the hell are you going to do?"

She turned her back on him and packed her arms with bags of blood. "I'm going to feed him."

"A-are those what I think they are?" his voice sounded weak as he stared nervously at the blood in her arms.

"Yes, don't worry, Chris, he's a good guy."

"He'd better be," he mumbled.

Madison went into the bathroom. She heard wood snap behind her. "What are you doing?"

Chris walked into the room, holding a homemade stake. "Sorry about the chair, but you understand." He stood protectively over Madison with the stake raised and ready to drive it into Ephraim should he make a wrong move.

"Let me feed him and everything will be fine."

"No one's stopping you."

"Punk," she mumbled.

"How are you going to feed him? He's unconscious," Chris pointed out.

"Good question. I could pour it down his throat, but he wouldn't swallow. I need his fangs to come out."

"*He has fangs?*" Chris squeaked.

"Yes, now if I could get them to drop we'd be in business." She gently pried his mouth open and pressed the bag to his teeth.

"What are you doing?"

She sighed. "I was hoping his teeth would come out if he felt the bag against his mouth."

"He needs to smell blood I bet." Chris pulled out a pocket knife. "Here, cut the bag."

She opened the knife, but paused. "He needs something stronger than bagged blood to get him going."

"What are you talking about?"

Madison pressed the knife to her wrist. "Just trust me."

"What are you doing? No! Madison, don't!" He reached out for the knife too late. She nicked her wrist. Blood began welling up in the area.

"Now what?" Chris asked.

"I-"

Two strong hands clasped around her wrist, pulling her into the tub. She fell on top of Ephraim. Seconds later, her wrist was in his mouth. She felt two sharp points pierce her skin and tried to yank her arm away. One hand released her arm, but the other tightened to the point of pain.

She looked up to see Ephraim stare at her with fiery red eyes. He looked pained.

He watched in agony as Madison tried to pull away from him. He couldn't stop. He couldn't. Bloodlust more powerful than he'd ever known was taking him over. His brain was screaming to release her, but he couldn't.

Tall, Dark & Lonely

The scent of her blood called him out of the darkness. He didn't know what he was doing until her blood rushed down his throat. It was the sweetest, most enticing flavor he'd ever experienced. It was a thousand times better than he imagined it would be.

"Let her go!" Chris yelled. He brought down a stake aimed at Ephraim's chest and Madison's arm. Ephraim's hand shot out and pushed Chris away, hard. He would have hit Madison's arm and even in bloodlust, Ephraim would never let anyone hurt her.

"Please, baby, let go!" Madison was whimpering.

Ephraim pulled harder on her arm. He was going to kill her. He brushed his free hand down her cheeks before dropping his hand away.

It hurt so much. If felt like her arm was stuck in a powerful vacuum with teeth and she couldn't pull away. She was starting to feel light headed. She closed her eyes, waiting for the darkness to come. She heard a click and forced her eyes open, half afraid that Chris was going to try something foolish.

Ephraim held his gun against his chest. He squeezed his eyes shut before he pulled the trigger. The bullet pierced his skin and bone like a hot knife through butter, making a path through his heart until it slammed into his spine. His body slammed violently against the tub. Her arm fell away and she instinctively moved to cover her ears as Chris dragged her limp body out of the tub seconds before a river of blood would have soaked her pants.

Chapter 15

"Wakey, wakey," Chris's taunting voice said.

Ephraim opened his eyes and swore. Chris stood at the end of his bed, holding his gun.

"Put that down before you hurt yourself."

"Sure thing. As soon as I know that you won't attack Madison again I'll just go ahead and do that."

His head shot off the pillow. He tried to sit up, but was pulled short by his arms. "What the hell?" he asked in a daze as he looked at his hands. Both wrists were handcuffed to the iron frame of the bed. Four pairs of cuffs attached to each hand. "A little over kill, don't you think?" He looked pointedly at the cuffs.

"Oh, I would say that anyone that could shoot themselves in the heart and fully recover two hours later should be tied to the bed with as many handcuffs as we could find."

"Where's Madison? Is she okay?"

"You mean after she passed out from the shock of you shooting yourself and of course let's not forget the blood loss? Yeah, she's peachy."

"Chris, I'm not in the mood for this shit. Tell me where she is."

"You're no fun." He gestured towards the front of the house. "After the gun went off, grandma came running. Thankfully Madison convinced her that the gun you gave her for safety accidentally went off." He cocked his head to the side. "By the way you're in deep shit with Mrs. Buckman for giving Madison a gun."

"That's the least of my worries right now, wouldn't you say?"

"True. Anyway, Mrs. Buckman, or Grandma as I'm allowed to call her," he grinned, "dragged Madison downstairs for a surprise birthday dinner. But don't worry, I stayed and mended you to health when Grandma wouldn't take no for an answer from Madison. We told her I was upset from my mom abandoning me and all that jazz."

"So, she's okay?"

"Yup."

"Your mom left you?"

"Yup."

"What a bitch." Ephraim managed to pull himself up a little on the pillows.

"That she is, but not to worry, Madison is taking over."

"God help us," Ephraim muttered.

Chris placed the gun in the top drawer of the bureau. "She thinks you forgot her birthday you know."

"Fuck, I didn't forget her birthday."

"I know."

His eyes shot to Chris. "Wait, how do you know?"

Chris rolled his eyes as if it should be very obvious. "I found the boxes when I was taking your clothes off."

Ephraim looked down at his body and for the first time noticed that he was clean and naked. "You cleaned me?"

"Hell no!" Chris said, disgusted. "Madison snuck back up to do that. Then she helped me put you in bed."

"She didn't see the boxes, did she?"

"No, I put them under your pillow before she turned around."

"Good, thank you," he said, relieved. "You think you could uncuff me now?"

"Sorry, man, I have orders not to do that. Madison said she would bring me a huge slice of cake if I left you cuffed."

"You're leaving me like this for cake?" he asked dumbfounded that cake held that kind of power over the boy. He wondered if it was like bloodlust.

"Well, that and you are a bloodsucker."

"Shit. Did Madison explain it to you?"

He nodded. "Pretty much. I got the basics down. I'm to keep my mouth shut. Vampires really exist. You're a Pyte, which I don't completely understand what the hell that is except that you can go out into the sun and all that shit."

"Anyone ever tell you that you swear too much?"

He pondered that question. "I believe it may have been mentioned a time or two."

"What is it you want to know?"

"You're going to answer my questions?" he sounded surprised.

"In exchange that you keep what I tell you between the three of us."

"I will. I promise!"

"Okay then, ask away." He laid back and tried to get comfortable.

"Okay, um how old are you?"

"Two-hundred and six years old."

Chris's eyes shot up. "Little old to be dating a twenty-four year old wouldn't you say?"

"Chris." That one word held a world of warning.

Chris put his hands in surrender. "Relax, big guy, I'm just saying."

"Say something else quickly if you want answers."

"Hmm, where were you born?"

"London."

"You don't have an accent."

"I lost it seventy-five years ago. Next."

"How did this happen to you?"

"You mean how did I become a Pyte?"

"Yes."

"My father was a vampire and my mother was a human. Somehow she became pregnant with me. I think he feared for her giving birth to me so the last month of the pregnancy he did a blood exchange with her. It worked. She lived and I lived."

"Did you come out with fangs?"

"No!" he said, chuckling. "I was a normal boy, well a little weak and I didn't age properly. Until I was your age I looked like a small boy."

"Really? What changed?"

"I went into a coma."

"For how long?"

"A month. Then I woke up looking exactly as I do today." He looked at the handcuffs and smiled wryly. "Actually, I woke up very much in the same situation. I was chained to the bed after biting a maid."

"So, I'm guessing you can't die."

"No."

'That explains it."

"Explains what?"

"Why you shot yourself. You knew you weren't going to die so you did it. Didn't hurt you much, did it?" He guessed.

"Chris, it hurt very much I can tell you that. I felt every single movement of that bullet as it broke through my skin, my breast bone, my heart and then when it stopped in my spine. If I had been a human there would have been an instant death. That pain wouldn't have been felt. Trust me when I tell you that I do not want to repeat that particular event again."

"But you passed out!"

"No, Chris, I didn't. My eyes may have closed and my body might have gone limp, but I was not entirely out of it. I couldn't focus on anything going on around me. I was in the beginning stages of bloodlust when I realized I was hurting her. If I hadn't reacted when I did, when I had some semblance of control, I would have been lost and Madison would have died."

"The blood lust keeps me from thinking straight. If I'm deep in bloodlust the only thing that will stop me is blood or violence. When the bullet shot through me my body appeared to be shut down but my mind was kept in a haze. I was aware of all the pain and the scent and taste of Madison's blood. Time and blood were the only things that kept me from waking up still in bloodlust. If I had, I would be right now tearing through the house in search of her."

Chris sat down on the edge of the bed, taking in what Ephraim was telling him.

"Did you know it was going to hurt like that?"

"Yes."

"But you still did it."

"Yes."

"Why?"

"What do you mean why?"

"I mean why did you purposely put yourself through that much pain if you knew how badly it was going to hurt?"

"Because I was hurting Madison."

"Why didn't you just let go? I know she said her blood was your weakness and all, but if you knew you were hurting her you could have let go."

"Not with bloodlust I couldn't. I wasn't in control."

"But you were able to shoot yourself."

"I had to while I still had that little amount of control of my arm."

Chris looked at the bedroom door. "What happened to those others things? They were vampires, right?"

"Yes, they were after my blood. I'm what you would call a day walker. Living forever is a plus too I suppose. They wanted my blood and it killed them."

"So, that's why you let them do it."

"They trapped me."

"You mean when you kissed that skank?"

Ephraim sighed, "I didn't kiss anyone."

"Are you sure? It sure looked like that to me."

"Does Madison think that I kissed her?"

Chris stood up and paced the room. "Don't know. She wouldn't tell me what she thinks happened."

"That would explain the handcuffs I suppose."

"You think she plans on keeping you there until you talk?"

He sighed, "Yes. I still owe her two hours of answers."

"She has two full hours of questions?"

"Well, probably not anymore." He looked thoughtful.

"Why do you say that?"

"Because she's been standing outside the door for the past ten minutes."

"Is that why you answered my questions, because you knew she was listening?"

He nodded. "That and you had a right to know if you're going to keep my secret."

Madison stepped into the room. "What gave me away?"

Ephraim raised an eyebrow. "I heard and smelled you."

"Hey, where's my cake?"

"It's in your room. Go eat up and take a shower. You have school in the morning."

"I have to go?"

"Yes."

"Damn it."

"Goodnight, Chris," Ephraim said.

"That cake better be worth it." He closed and locked the door on his way out.

Tall, Dark & Lonely

Ephraim gave her a lopsided grin and tried to look innocent. "Happy Birthday, baby."

"Don't try sweetening me up. Why didn't you tell me that vampires were after you?"

"Well, in all fairness you never asked your questions. I can't very well be in trouble for something that you didn't ask."

She pressed her hands to her forehead. "You know what, it's been a very long day, a very scary, long day. If you're going to joke around let me know now so that I can go to bed. I just want this day to end."

"I'm really sorry, baby. I did try. I was trying to surprise you with a nice dinner and cake with your friends. I had to stop off to get your gift. I didn't know she was there until it was too late."

"What was she to you?" she asked softly. She was afraid that she wasn't going to like the answer.

"Nothing. No one. She was the servant of a Master."

"So, you never slept with her?" She met his eyes. They were a bright blue.

"Is that what this is about? Why you have me chained? I did not kiss her. She kissed me quickly before I could push her away. She did it to pin me to the car so the others could grab me." He frowned. "I take it they're all dead."

"I don't know. We didn't stick around long enough to check. You know you just avoided answering that question."

"What question is that?" he snapped. "This is getting a little old, Madison. Just ask the fucking question and get it over with."

She pulled back a sob. "No need. I think I just got my answer." She turned her back on him. "Goodbye, Ephraim."

"Goodbye?"

"Yes, goodbye."

"Look at me!" he snapped.

Madison slowly turned around and gasped. His eyes were red, his fangs were down, but that wasn't the problem. He was free. Somehow he escaped the handcuffs without making a sound.

He climbed off the bed and stalked forward. "Do you think this is a game for me? Do you think I enjoy playing these fucking games of yours?"

She set her jaw stubbornly. "I'm not playing any games."

"Aren't you?"

"No, I'm not." She refused to take a step back. She held her ground firmly. He stopped a foot away from her. Every muscle in his body was flexing with anger.

"You've been playing me since the first time that you realized that I wanted you."

"How?" she demanded.

"You keep yourself distant from me and you look for every little reason to fight."

"I do not!"

"Oh no?" His eyebrows arched. "You're mad at me because I paid off your debt so that you wouldn't have to struggle for the rest of your life to fix your credit or scrape to get by."

"I was doing just fine without your help."

"Bullshit, I know the amount of debt you were facing."

Through clenched teeth she spoke evenly. "I was doing fine. I didn't need your help!"

"Oh no? I know you lied to your grandmother about using your savings against your student loan. If that was true they wouldn't have been threatening to take you to court for nonpayment. Four months, Madison, four months you missed payments. You have the same problem with the insurance company. They stopped your auto insurance four months ago. They just forgot to tell the police that or I guarantee that someone in my department would have come for your plates."

She looked away. "This is none of your business, Ephraim."

"The Jeep is the only thing you own outright. What happened to all that money, Madison? You had over twenty grand saved up. The Jeep cost fifteen so what happened to all that money four months ago? Whatever it is you haven't gotten out of trouble yet, because you fell behind on all of your bills. You don't spend any money on yourself. You don't put money in the bank. Hell, you never seem to have enough money to put gas in your car. Tell me where the money is going?"

He leaned forward when she didn't answer right away. "Tell me."

"No."

"You're sending twelve hundred dollars a month to an online account."

She gasped.

"Yeah, I know about that. Who does it belong to?"

"That's none of your business!"

He pulled back, smiling. His eyes were hard as stone. "Really? Not my business? Then you can explain how you plan on taking care of a sixteen year old boy on the meager two hundred dollars that you have left over after you send away the twelve hundred dollars?"

"Shut up!"

"Is Chris going to have to continue getting his food in the same manner after all?"

"What are you talking about?"

He crossed his arms over his bare chest. "Oh, you don't know? Here I thought you knew everything. Chris's mother doesn't give a fuck about him. She won't send a cent to help him out."

"She gets food stamps and has a job at a bar," she said, even though she wasn't counting on any help from her.

"Yes, she does. One would think she would use those stamps to buy the boy some food."

"She doesn't?"

"She trades them for money. For a lot less than they're worth. Whatever she doesn't spend on herself she spends on those losers she drags into her bed."

"He looks healthy. I know he's eating."

He shrugged. "He waits until dear old mommy is on her back keeping the men busy while he lifts their wallets. She takes a cut of course and I've been dropping food off on their front steps when only he's home for the past three years. He thinks the church has been leaving it."

"I-I didn't know." She backed up now. He stalked forward.

"Tell me something, Madison, since you're intent on pushing me out of the picture, are you planning on fucking for your cut as well? Might come in handy."

She slapped him, hard. "I hate you."

His tongue darted out to lick up the blood on his lip. "You didn't answer me. How are you going to take care of a sixteen year old boy when you can't even take care of yourself?"

"Not that it's any of your business, but I talked to Grandma tonight and she's going to give me some hours here."

"Scrubbing toilets? Yes, that's perfect for someone with a college degree and a full time job."

"Candy offered to help me, too."

"How?"

"She's going to see if she can get me a position waiting tables."

Ephraim didn't dare move a muscle for fear that he would put his fist through something. In a deceivingly calm voice he asked, "Oh, and what percentage of your tips does she want if you get the job?"

"Twenty-five percent," she muttered.

"Wow, you have a great mother, Madison. First she overlooks you to fuck everything with a dick and then she leaves you to raise her two kids. Now she's willing to have you strip so she can make a profit. I can see now why you keep your legs closed. She'd probably sell the grandkids on the black market the first chance she gets."

When he expected another slap she scoffed, "I don't think we have to worry about that when it comes to you."

He suddenly turned his back on her. "Go away, little girl. I'm sick of these games and I'm done with you."

She didn't move as Ephraim viciously yanked on a black tee shirt and jeans. He sat on a chair, pulling on socks and shoes. "What are you still doing here? I told you to leave."

"Where are you going?"

"You don't get to ask that question anymore." He grabbed his wallet, keys and left her standing there feeling like her world just ended.

Chapter 16

"I told you already that I'll pay you tomorrow. It's just been hectic at work. They screwed up on the checks, but I'll have it by tomorrow," Jason, the man who moved in over a month ago, promised yet again from the hallway.

Everyone in the dining room pretended they couldn't hear Mrs. Buckman in the hallway practically begging for the rent.

"She's going to have to raise the rent," Mrs. Adle said. "I heard her talking on the phone to someone from the bank last week. She's thinking of getting a mortgage."

Madison dropped her fork. Great, just one more thing to worry about. Her grandmother was under too much financial pressure as it was and they were adding more. She should be paying her way and for the kids. Her eyes shot to Candy. *She* definitely should be paying for Jill and Joshua and her own way. Guilt twitched in her gut as she looked at Chris. One more mouth she added to the already straining mix.

His cheeks flushed as if he knew what she was thinking. "Madison, do you think you can get the school to give me a work permit? I'd like to pay for my own room and food."

They heard the door close. "I won't hear any of that nonsense, Christopher. You belong in school fixing your grades, not pushing fries in some fast food joint."

"Grandma, I don't feel right about this," Chris said as he looked guiltily at his food.

She slapped him upside the head. "Ow! What the hell was that for?"

"I said to drop it. You are part of this family so stop it and put some more food on your plate. I won't have you losing weight and looking like a skeleton when I've been working so hard these last two weeks to put meat on your bones."

When he didn't move fast enough to eat, she raised her hand to hit him upside his head again. "Okay!" He took more corn and potatoes. "Slave driver," he muttered.

Grandma sat down at the head of the table. "Everyone, eat please."

"Grandma, I was thinking that with us here that's five rooms you're not collecting on and five mouths to feed. I think I'm going to get another job to help out."

"Madison, you already work a full time job and you clean here ten hours a week, that's help enough." She shot a look of warning at her daughter. "And don't even think of suggesting my granddaughter go work at that obscene place again, Emma."

Candy pouted. She hated being called Emma and she hated not getting her way even more. She threw a fit when Madison declined the job offer. She'd really been looking forward to her cut.

Grandma pointed a finger in Candy's direction. "I looked the other way when you started working there, but when you tried to bring my granddaughter there," she shook her head in disgust. "You're lucky I didn't throw you out on your backside then and there."

"But, mama, I was just trying to help." Candy's pout deepened.

Grandma narrowed her eyes on her only child.

"I wish Ephraim was here," Joshua mumbled.

"Has he called?" Jill asked, jumping on the change of topic.

"No, can we talk about something else, please." She pushed her meatloaf around her plate.

"Did you try his cell phone?" Chris asked, drawing her attention.

Chris looked so uncomfortable. His clothes were already too small and worn. They looked even smaller after two weeks of eating properly for the first time and a growth spurt. He needed new clothes and she didn't have the money. He didn't complain though. He probably knew. She would have to get another job to keep clothes on his back. Jill and Joshua's clothes were in the same condition as Chris's. They all needed new clothes. Great, now she felt even more depressed.

Grandma's eyes roamed over all three children's state of clothing as well. Her frown deepened. This was bad, but Grandma was in denial and she did what she always did when something unpleasant occurred. She tried to hide her feelings from everyone and move on, dragging everyone with her.

"Everyone, please leave her alone and finish dinner. Chris and Jill, you both have dish duty tonight."

"I thought you loved me, Grandma?" Chris pushed his lip out in an expert pout.

Grandma reached over and pinched his cheek. "Oh, it's so nice having a con artist join the family." He winked at her and reloaded his plate like a good boy. That and he was probably afraid that she was going to whack him again. Madison considered it for a moment and agreed that Grandma probably would.

"He's been gone for over two weeks you know," Jill decided to comment.

Madison pushed away from the table. "If you'll excuse me, I have some papers to grade."

"You have a big mouth!" Chris snapped.

"It's fine, really. Goodnight, guys." She took her time walking upstairs. She was in no hurry to hide in her room and cry herself to sleep again tonight.

He broke her heart. There was no other way to describe it. The area around her heart ached day and night for him. It felt like a part of her was destroyed.

She paused in front of her door and looked back at his when she heard something. She could see the lights were off in his room, but weird noises were coming from inside. She couldn't fight the hope that soared to the surface. She turned around and raised her fist to knock on the door only to freeze.

"You like that, baby, don't you?" a woman asked.

A man grunted. "Mmm, I'm going ride you all night, big boy." Realization dawned on her. The weird sound was the bed springs squeaking.

She put her hand over her mouth. "Oh god." Tears spilled down her face.

"Mmm, these handcuffs were a good idea," the woman said. "I can keep you on your back and up all night." A loud masculine moan erupted.

"Do you like fucking my ass?" the woman asked.

"Yeah," he groaned.

Madison stumbled back to her door, crying. She slammed the door shut and threw on the light. "What an asshole," she muttered.

"I completely agree. Now if you don't mind, some of us are trying to sleep." Ephraim flopped over onto his stomach.

Madison's head whipped back in the direction of his room and back at him. "If you're here then who's-"

"In there fucking the transvestite prostitute?" he finished for her.

"Yes…wait, did you say transvestite?"

"Yes, I did."

"Ephraim, who's in there?"

"Just the guy who's been blackmailing you for the last four months. After tonight you'll never have to worry about him again and you'll have all your money back. Now, could you shut that light off? That prick's kept me up the last two nights."

She looked stunned. "You have Joshua's father in there? Wait, he's not gay."

Ephraim buried his face in the pillow and laughed. "No, he's not. He also doesn't know that she's a *he*. He also doesn't know that I have a camera in there right now with night vision that's capturing this momentous occasion. He will know very soon what's going on. Before he leaves here he will sign custody of Joshua over to you and your grandmother."

"Why..how....I don't understand."

He flipped over onto his back. "It's simple I had the bank account traced to one Trevor McGuire who resides in New Mexico. I did a little check on him, married, two children at home, but he has custody of three children. I did a little more research and found out that Candy lost custody of Joshua when he was six months old."

"She didn't even show up for the court date," Madison whispered.

"That's what I found out. They kept him for four months until his wife put her foot down. She couldn't handle two little boys of her own plus Joshua. So, Trevor pawned Joshua off onto a few relatives, but none of them were willing to keep him. Finally, he gave Joshua to your mother while retaining full custody."

"I didn't know that part."

"I figured. When Candy was eager to move here for the free ride and welfare she forgot one very important thing."

"She didn't have custody and she never asked permission to take Joshua out of the state. She probably figured Trevor would never notice. He hadn't seen Joshua in five years."

"But he did find out. Your mother, even though your grandmother was under the assumption that she had custody of the kids, attempted to get welfare on the kids' behalf. New Hampshire contacted Trevor and Trevor hunted you down and threatened to take Joshua back and put you both in prison for kidnapping."

"He had no case against me and he knew that. He wanted money though."

"And you were to pay twelve hundred dollars a month until Joshua hit eighteen."

"Yes."

"And you really thought that was going to work?"

"I was trying to buy time until I figured out what to do. I can't lose him. He's more than a brother to me. I've raised him. I couldn't give him up."

"So, that's why you put yourself in such a large hole. You didn't want to lose Joshua?"

"Yes." She wiped a tear off her cheek.

"Baby, why didn't you come to me? I would have helped you."

She shook her head. "I couldn't do that to you."

"Were you afraid that I would rip his throat out or lose my job?"

"Both."

He sighed heavily and held out his hand. "Come here."

She walked over to the bed and took his hand. He pulled her onto his lap, making her straddle him. She released his hand and pulled her heels off, letting them drop to the ground.

Ephraim cupped his hands on her hips and pulled her forward. "Can I have a kiss? I've missed you."

Her hands dropped to the bed on either side of his face as she leaned over him. "I don't know. I thought you said you were done with me."

His hands gently caressed her hips. "I'll never be done with you. I'm sorry for being such an asshole, but you hit a bit of a nerve for me."

"About babies?"

"Yes."

"So, you can't have babies? You know that for sure, don't you? You tried with that woman?"

He raised his head to brush his lips against hers. "I don't know anything for certain, baby. I have no clue. As far as that woman is concerned the answer is no. I never slept with her. She wanted to years and years ago. Her Master, who at this very moment is not too happy with me, tried to make a deal with me and offered up twenty females to me to see if I could impregnate any of them. I could keep the babies and in return the master wanted to be like me."

"Did you?"

His fingers threaded through her black hair. "No, I didn't do that. I didn't want a child with a vampire."

"So, how do you know you haven't fathered a child before?"

"That's easy. I never finished inside of a woman before."

She searched his face to see if he was joking. "Never?"

"No, never. It was one of the best ways to prevent by-blows."

"By-blows?"

"Bastards."

"That's not very nice."

"Sorry, that's what they were called back then. My father told us what to do."

"Your father encouraged you?" A thought occurred to her. "I've heard stories that men back then brought their son's to whorehouses, did yours?"

He used her hips to push her up so that her neck was right above his mouth. He began pressing kisses to her neck. "No, he didn't bring me. The last time I saw my father was just before I was taken away. Before that I looked like a little boy. No self-respecting whore would have touched me. He brought my brothers when they were fourteen though so he probably would have."

"Oh."

"So, what did your father tell you to do?"

"Pull out. Never come inside a woman unless she's meant to carry the heir. That's what we were taught."

"So, you never once...." her voice trailed off suggestively.

"Not once." His hands slid down her back until they cupped her bottom. He gently squeezed and caressed her while his mouth licked and kissed her neck.

Madison used her feet to push the covers off Ephraim. She was not losing this opportunity. She'd waited too long for this, for him. Using one hand, she undid the knot on her skirt and pulled it off, throwing it to the ground. She sat back on his lap. She could feel his erection through the material of his boxers.

Ephraim watched hungrily as she slowly unbuttoned her blouse. She threw the blouse to the side, revealing a black bra and matching panties.

"A goddess. You look like a goddess." He was mesmerized by her beautiful black hair and golden skin. He ran his hands down her neck, breasts, stomach and back.

"Do you want to see more?" she asked in a sultry voice.

He swallowed loudly and nodded firmly. "Please."

She reached back with one hand and unsnapped her bra, letting it slide down her arms. Ephraim gently pulled it from her arms and threw it on the floor.

Without waiting, he ran his fingers down to her hips and slid a finger on either side of her panties and snapped the string of the waistband apart. Madison sat up so that he could pull the ripped panties away, leaving her naked.

His eyes drank in the sight of her body. She was so beautiful from her golden brown eyes to her butterscotch nipples. She was everything in the world that was perfect and she was *his*. He growled possessively as his fangs descended. "Come here."

A shot of lust tore through her as his eyes began to glow and his teeth dropped. Madison found herself going to him more that willingly. She leaned down and kissed his lips gently. The kiss was slow and sweet. They took their time enjoying the sensation the teasing sent down their bodies.

Ephraim licked her lips in request. She obliged by opening her mouth. He deepened the kiss. Their tongues moved together, sending agony to their loins. Soon they were both panting and moaning. Madison wasn't aware that she was grinding herself against him. She only knew that she loved the feeling and it wasn't enough.

His arms wrapped around her waist, hugging her close to him. He rolled her over onto her back, never breaking the kiss. Madison grabbed his underwear and pushed it down. When her hands couldn't push any farther she used her feet, frantically kicking them down. She felt his hard shaft against the inside of her thigh and moaned.

He lowered himself and slid his cock against her slit. She was so wet. So fucking wet and he was going to lose it. She was drenching the underside of his cock. The sounds of their panting was loud enough to block out the sounds coming from his room. They didn't care. They were the only things existing in their world at the moment.

"Baby, I have to tell you two things before we do this," his said in a hoarse voice.

"What?" she whimpered. She was squirming wildly beneath him, trying to get him to come inside.

"The first thing you should know, once I put my cock in you I'm not going to stop fucking you until my dick explodes inside of you." His words were like pouring gasoline on the fire that was already out of control in her body. She moaned loudly with anticipation.

"And the second?" She was surprised that she managed a coherent thought never mind a sentence at this point.

He pulled back and positioned himself. "The second is the most important." He kissed her deeply before pulling back to look down at her. He needed to watch her as he told her while entering her. He slowly pushed forward.

Madison gasped loudly. "The second thing, Madison, is that I am head over heels in love with you." With one thrust he was buried inside of her.

Her body tightened around him and began convulsing. "Oh shit!" He touched his forehead to hers while he watched her come apart. She moaned his name while licking her lips. Her body convulsed violently around him. It took everything he had not to explode with her. He'd never been with a woman who came like this, never mind when he entered her.

He waited until her body relaxed before he started moving. His thrusts were slow and shallow, giving her a chance to recover. The entire time his eyes never left her face. "Are you okay, baby?" he asked with a soft kiss.

She bit her lip and nodded. "That's my girl."

"I'm not a girl, Ephraim. That night what you said....," she shook her head. "I'm not."

"Shh, I know, baby. Trust me, I know. You're not some little girl. You're not." He kissed her long and hard before pulling away abruptly. "You've probably never had the chance to be a girl, darling." He kissed her chin, moving down to her neck. "I'm so sorry."

She whimpered as he pulled out. "Ephraim?"

"Shh, it's okay, baby." He moved his mouth down to her breast. His tongue traced a wet circle around her nipple before pulling it into his mouth. It slid in between his fangs. He took two long pulls on her nipple before abandoning it to continue down her stomach.

"So sweet….so beautiful…" He pressed kisses on each thigh.

"Ephraim, please! I need you!" Madison was panting with need. She wanted him back inside.

He chuckled against her skin. His tongue darted out, running over her skin as he made his way to the center of her. "Mmmm." She tasted better than he remembered. He sucked on her swollen little nub, teasing it with the tip of his tongue.

Madison looked down her body. His eyes were focused on her face. He liked to watch. That made her brave. She wanted to please him so badly the same way that he was pleasing her.

His mouth lowered to her entrance where he licked her, greedily. She moaned loudly. Her eyes never left his. He watched her, feeling each moan down to the tip of his erection. He shoved his tongue inside of her.

"Oh, baby, yes!" she cooed. Her hips rose in the air. His hands clamped tightly on her hips and brought her down so he could feast on her.

She ran her hands through his hair, over her stomach and her breasts. When she pinched her own nipples his hips thrust into the bed. He growled low and deep, sending the most erotic sensations through her and setting off another powerful orgasm. Her body arched off the bed.

Before her body fell back on the bed he was back inside of her in one hard thrust. He felt harder than before. She wrapped her legs around his hips, afraid he was going to pull out again. His thrusts were no longer shallow or slow. He moved like a man possessed.

He kissed her greedily as he thrust inside of her. Madison cupped his face as she kissed him. Her fingers gently caressed his skin. It made him feel like a king the way that she was touching him.

She liked to see him out of control and right now he was dangerous. He moved on her like a madman. She whimpered as another climax came and went, leaving her boneless and panting, but still he didn't stop.

His jaw was clenched and the muscles in his neck were taut. He looked like he was in a great deal of pain. That's when she noticed the tears in his eyes. He looked frustrated.

She cupped his cheek. "Baby, what's wrong?"

He shook his head. "I can't....I can't.....fuck I'm so close!"

"You can't come?"

"No. I don't know what's wrong. It's been so long." He moved harder inside of her, bringing her closer to another orgasm. She needed to help him or she was going to die of pleasure.

She pulled him down, tilting his head to the side. "Let's see if this helps." She pressed wet kisses to his neck. Her tongue traced his Adam's apple and up to his chin. His thrusts slowed down into a uniformed cadence. He moaned deeply as her teeth scraped his skin.

"That feels so good," he groaned.

Her hand slid between them. The next time he pulled out she snaked her hand between them and gripped him tightly while her arm circled around his neck and held him down.

She was gripping him so hard. The sensation of sliding through her hand into her wet, tight pussy was too much. The triple combination was too much, too soon. He wanted to pull away from her and take control again, but she held him tightly against her. The sensation was pushing him past the edge. The build up to the climax he knew was coming was too strong.

His body began thrusting wildly into her. She never wavered in her grip. She licked his neck and moaned along with him. "Stop! Madison, stop it's too much!" She only tightened her grip and swirled her hips beneath him.

He broke.

He threw his head back and roared. His hips slammed into her, making her remove her hand or have it broken. She held onto him as he carried her into another climax.

She gasped as he bared his fangs and struck.

Chapter 17

Ephraim was gasping in the crook of her neck. "I'm so sorry."

"Shhh, it's okay." She gently rubbed his damp back. "It's okay."

"I'll replace it. I promise."

She watched as a feather slowly drifted down towards her face. She blew out a stream of air, sending it back up. "It's just a pillow."

"Thank god." He kissed her neck.

"Is it always like that?"

He shook his head. "Never like that."

"Do you always bite in the end?"

He shrugged. "I've never had to bite before. I've never come inside a woman before you. It's never been that powerful before either. You, oh, baby, you don't know what you do to me."

"So, do you always have a problem coming?" she asked shyly.

"No, I didn't, but then again I think the last time I had an orgasm was back in the nineties."

"Oh, so like ten to twenties years ago? That's not bad I guess."

"Wrong century. Try more like a hundred or so years."

"That's a long time." She couldn't hide her smirk.

"Yeah, I guess I had a clog." He laughed and pulled out of her. He looked down at her body as he climbed out of bed. She was covered in feathers. "Let me just go end the charade next door and then I'll help you wash those feathers off."

Ephraim pulled on a pair of dark khaki pants that looked recently pressed and a white tee shirt. "I'll just be a few minutes, baby." He pressed a gentle kiss to her forehead. "I love you, baby."

He felt the change in her. She stiffened beneath his touch. Her breathing ceased. He swore inwardly. She wasn't in love with him. "Madison,-"

She climbed off the bed. "Let me get dressed," she said nervously. Her hands shook as she searched through her drawers and pulled on a tank top and flannel pajama pants.

Warm firm hands gently cupped her shoulders. She began rambling nervously. "You know I really should go in there with you. It's my fault this whole thing happened in the first place, well not really. Candy did all of this, but I don't think she would come in here and help. I mean, we could ask, but she'll most likely throw something at our heads. She hates to be woken up. Do you think we should wake her? Because I can go get her if you think we should. I think she'll just get in the way and-"

His hand covered her mouth, gently. "Shh, baby, I didn't tell you to send you into hysterics. I'm going to take my hand away now so just let me speak, please."

She nodded against his hand. "Okay." He lowered his hand and wrapped his arms around her waist. His lips pressed softly against her neck.

"Now, I'm going to tell you that I love you." She stiffened. "Shh, Madison, let me continue. I didn't say it because I expected you to say it. I knew you wouldn't. You can't, sweetheart. I'm not going to assume you love me and I didn't say it because I wanted to hear you say it. That would make me a bit of a cad."

"I know how freely your mother said that to men. Hell, I've heard her say it about a hundred times to seven different guys since you moved here. I know she thinks she loves them and throws the word around too easily. I also know she never once said those words to you or your siblings. So, I know how foreign those words are to you. I know you don't want to do anything like your mother would, you're afraid of turning into her."

She nodded slowly. "But, Madison, you are not your mother. You're a strong, independent woman. You're headstrong, stubborn, smart, kind, and yes, loving. I know how hard it was for you to allow yourself to give yourself to a man. I'm honored beyond words that I was your first." And last, but she didn't know that yet. "I won't push you or get upset if you don't love me. All I want is to be allowed to show you how I feel about you and to tell you."

"Ephraim, I don't think I'm capable of loving anyone other than my brother and sister."

He pressed another kiss to her neck. "Well, then let me deal with it. I'm not asking you to love me. I'm asking you to let me love you. I'm fine if you never say it. I just want you, Madison."

She gulped. "For how long?"

"However long you'll let me." Forever, but really she didn't need to know that either.

"No pressure?"

"No pressure."

He turned her in his arms. His eyes bore into hers. "Let's just get one thing clear, Madison. I have never told another person that I love them. Not one. I'm not one of those men that come sniffing around your mother. I don't say things lightly and I'm not using you. I won't run for the hills either or become bored. I'm here for you as long as you'll let me and I won't pressure you." He tucked a strand of hair behind her ear. "For as long as you want me, Madison, I am your man."

"But, what if you-"

"I won't."

"You didn't let me finish."

"It doesn't matter. I won't do it if it hurts you." He brushed his lips against hers. She wasn't giving up. He could practically feel her fear.

"What if you get bored with me? I'm not very beautiful and-"

He pulled back to search her eyes. She was serious. She really had no idea. "Madison, let me clear that up for you. You are the most beautiful woman I have ever seen."

She scoffed.

"Madison, I would never tell you otherwise. What makes you even more beautiful and special is your big heart. You're too kind and sweet for your own good sometimes."

"No I'm not. Ephraim, see this is just infatuation for you. You think I'm perfect. I'm not. I'm a woman with many faults, but you don't seem to see them."

"Really? You think so?" he asked, sounding thoughtful.

"Yes! That's how my mother acts with every guy. You don't see the real me."

"Hmmm."

Tall, Dark & Lonely

"I'm not perfect, Ephraim, and sooner or later you'll see that and move on." The words hurt, but they needed to be said. He didn't understand. He couldn't. There was no such thing as love. Affection? Yes, she cared about him deeply. More than anyone, but love? No. There was no such thing as romantic love. It was just infatuation mixed with hormones.

"You're probably right." He pulled away and sat on the edge of the bed to pull on his socks and shoes. "Baby, can you hand me my shirt?" He pointed to a dark grey shirt hanging on the back of the bathroom door. A tie hung around the shirt's collar.

A little confused over how easily he dropped the subject, she handed him the shirt. "That's it?"

"What?" He stood up, buttoning the shirt and unzipped his pants to tuck it in.

She raised her hands slightly and let them drop. "Nothing." She chickened out.

His hands made fast work of tying the tie. "Oh, you mean that nonsense about this being a simple infatuation for me and I don't see your faults? Sorry, didn't know you wanted me to respond to that. Okay, let's see." He wasn't giving her a chance to speak. "You can be bossy at times. You shut down at anything emotional beyond love with Joshua and Jill. When Jill is flipping out and crying, you get annoyed. You hate huge displays of emotion. You're very laid back and relaxed. Well, it appears that way, but you're really protecting yourself and I don't blame you one bit for that."

Her hands shot up. "See that's exactly what I'm saying. You're seeing what you want, and the imperfections that you see, you explain away and excuse things like you're fixing me. I'm not perfect, Ephraim, and I really wish that you would see that."

"You drool."

"What?" That caught her off guard.

"When you're asleep you drool. I've woken up more than a few times with a little puddle forming on my chest." After a thought he added. "And you snore. Not a delicate snore either mind you."

"I do not!" Her face colored with indignation.

He sighed heavily as if the knowledge pained him. "Oh, but you do. I've even heard Jill talk about it. Did you know that's the main reason she was happy about her room. Actually, she and Joshua thanked your Grandmother for putting you at the other end of the house, something about finally getting a decent night's sleep. They compared your snore to a chainsaw. I can see why they'd say that."

"You're lying!"

He chuckled as he attached his holster and badge to his belt. "No, 'fraid not, sweetheart. Also, you pout when you're hungry. Your cute little bottom lip sticks up and you get a frown between your brows right there." He touched the spot with his finger.

She swatted his hand away. "I do not!"

"When you think no one's around and you're drinking soda." She didn't think it was possible, but she felt the blush on her face deepen. "You hold little burping contests."

"How-"

He tapped his ear. "I can hear everything and I can tune things out if I choose."

She dropped her gaze. "One of my mother's old boyfriends taught me how when I was little as a way to relax. It helps with my stress just to focus on doing something silly and stupid."

"You're quite good at it," he commented.

Tall, Dark & Lonely

"Ephraim!"

"I'm serious. I used to know some sailors that you could easily put to shame."

"Stop it!" She suppressed a giggle. She should be mad, she really should.

"Also, you cheat when you play Horse with Joshua. It's sad really." He winked at her.

"How did you know?"

"I've seen you. You distract him and then take a step or two forward, closer to the basket."

She sighed, "I can't stand his victory dance when he wins. It's rather annoying."

He allowed that. "It doesn't hurt that you're also a sore loser."

"I am not!"

"Yes, you are. Everyone says so. I think everyone suspects you cheat at other games as well, but they don't say anything. Mostly because you're such a horrible cheat and you lose anyway."

She placed her hands on her hips. "Should we go over your shortcomings then?"

"Sure, I have a minute before I have to handle your blackmailer. Let's see." He looked at her small make-up mirror and ran his hands through his hair. "I'm arrogant. I'm annoying. I have a hell of a temper that would make the devil quiver. I get extremely cranky when I'm hungry. I hog the covers to keep you in my arms at night. I take too many showers and for far too long. I hog the hot water. I get jealous easily when it comes to other men and you."

"Really?" Her smile was small, unsure and cute as hell.

All humor left his face. He looked at her through intensely possessive eyes. "Oh yes, Madison, you have no idea. I want to tear apart every man that looks at you. I hate it when some other man earns one of your adorable smiles that reaches your eyes, or gets to be there to make you feel better. I hate it, but I accept it. If I didn't, it would drive me to distraction."

"You're also a bit possessive," she added with a wry grin.

"That I am. I'm sorry if it bothers you, but I do love you, Madison. I'm not some controlling asshole that expects to keep you to myself and I would never hurt you or try to control you. I just want to keep you safe. I know I step on your toes sometimes. I'll try to work on that, but not with assholes like Trevor. That I will not tolerate."

She took in a deep breath. "It's okay. I know you only did this to help me. I'm not a complete idiot. I realized that I was in over my head. It's just that I'm so used to taking care of my own problems. I don't like having to depend on anyone."

He pulled her into his arms. "That's because no one's ever been dependable in your life. In time, I hope you'll realize that I am that person, Madison. I'm the man who will always be there for you and I will never consciously hurt you. I do love you, Madison, more than you'll ever know."

She wrapped her arms around his neck and hugged him tightly. "I know. I'm just stubborn."

His chuckle rumbled through his chest. "I know, baby. Now, I have to go take care of a little matter."

Madison pulled back from his arms and looked him over. She didn't realize until that moment that he was wearing his shirt and tie along with his badge and gun. "Are you going to work?"

"No, sweetheart, I have the weekend off. I'm doing this for him." He gestured to his clothes.

Tall, Dark & Lonely

She looked in the direction of his room. "Speaking of which, can I ask what the hell happened? Where have you been? How did you pull this off and most importantly, why is he in there having sex in your room, in this house?"

He looked at his watch. "I suppose I can answer your questions. Quickly though and no interruptions. I really need to get in there. Paula is charging me by the hour you know."

"How much?" She was curious about how much a transvestite prostitute charged. Who wouldn't be?

He winced. "Two hundred an hour. Actually, he is charging me an extra five hundred dollars, because Trevor's an asshole."

"He always was," she agreed on a sigh.

"To answer your questions, and quickly mind you. I went home first. I haven't taken a vacation in three years and I wanted to see my home."

"You went to England? "

He pressed a finger to her lips. "No, interruptions, remember? Yes, I haven't been since the war. I had some thinking to do and I always did my best thinking at two in the morning walking along Hyde Park."

"We have parks here too you know."

He shot her a wry look. "I know, Madison. I needed to go."

"You were thinking of leaving for good, weren't you?"

He nodded, reluctantly.

"Why?"

"The way I feel about you scares me." He held up his hand. "I love you, Madison. I know you don't understand. That's fine, but please let's not argue about it."

"Okay."

"I couldn't stay away, Madison. It took only a minute to know that. The rest of the time I used for negotiations."

"Neg-"

He held up a hand to stop her. "I negotiated with a very powerful group that's been after me for the last hundred and twenty years. A group called Sentinels. Before you ask, they are God's natural defense against vampires."

"Ten Sentinels are born every ten years. They are marked at birth for their position in life. They're not exactly human. They're stronger, more difficult to kill and can heal quicker. They live longer as well and they will look young until they stop fighting and retire."

"Like Buffy the Vampire Slayer?"

He laughed and shook his head ruefully. "I guess you could call them slayers. They also have another very unique quality."

"What?"

"Well, they have to be born as a twin. A human soul has to bring them to earth as a guardian. Most of the human twins die. It's very difficult to share a womb with a Sentinel. The special thing is that they are born with their soul mates already in line. Five males and five females are born. It's a gift. True love from God to keep them dedicated."

"How do they-"

"They know when they find their mates because their marks will change to red, once they're a mated pair it turns black. It's along the same lines as a marriage. Before you ask, the mark is a crescent moon with a tiny cross just below the navel and it's originally a light brown color. Most won't know what they are until another Sentinel finds them and takes them in to train or..." his voice drifted off.

"A vampire finds them. They give off a scent like humans do, right?"

"Right."

"Why did you contact them?" She kept her voice casual, but inside she was trembling. Was he leaving?

He took her hands into his and led her to the bed. He sat down and pulled her onto his lap. "Madison, surely you realize that I don't age. In a few years, I won't be able to explain why I haven't aged. As it is, I look like I'm in my mid twenties. I can only keep it up for a few more years."

"What are you saying?"

"I'm done. I'm done pretending. I'm done starting a life only to end it in five years. I want my own life now. I need it, Madison. I don't want to hide what I am anymore. I don't want to keep running for the rest of my life. With the Sentinels I can have the life I want. I will be given the status of a Sentinel in terms of pay, privileges and resources. I can't change who I am. I'm a Pyte. They need me almost as much as I need them."

"So, you're leaving the country then?" She choked back a sob.

"No, I'm allowed to choose which area I want to protect. That's what they do. That's what I should have been doing all these years. I've just been so damn stubborn."

"But you do protect people! You're a good detective!"

"Shh, no, baby. I've been playing. I do what any human with training and instinct can do. I've been neglecting my calling. I need to help. I need to stop what I can. It's an ongoing war and people are being massacred. I need to do this, Madison."

"So, what now?"

He kissed her chin. "This isn't the end for us, Madison. I'll just be doing something different soon. Something I'm meant to do."

"How soon?"

"Soon, it won't affect us. I promise, baby. There will be a few changes. I've decided that along with doing this I should take more responsibility in my life."

"Meaning what?"

"For starters, I negotiated with Chris's mother over the phone." Her breathing stopped. "I've adopted him, baby. He needs a man to take care of him. He needs a real home and support."

"We're giving him that," she said through clenched teeth. "I'm taking care of him, Ephraim. You didn't have to do this!"

His grip tightened around her, stopping her from jumping off his lap. "Yes, I did. I think it would be a good idea if you and your family continue to treat him like one of your own."

She wiped away a tear. "Why did you do this, Ephraim?"

"Shh, baby, I had to. Don't you see that? I have to protect him now. He knows about me and what's out there. It will be okay I promise you."

"There's something you're not telling me."

He didn't deny it. He pressed a simple kiss to her cheek. "Everything will be fine. Now, would you like to know about our little friend in there?"

He was changing the subject and she knew it. She would allow it, for now. Mostly because she could hear Trevor moaning again and she wanted him out of the house.

Tall, Dark & Lonely

"I decided that the best way to deal with him would be blackmail and a few threats in case that didn't work. I went to New Mexico and told him that I was your boyfriend and that you were struggling. I told him that I was willing to pay him a large lump sum if he came here and signed over Joshua. He's in a bit of a rush to buy a yacht. That's why he's been blackmailing you and that was why he accepted the monthly payments. Seems his wife won't let him buy one. So, he's been doing a crime here and there to save up."

"That asshole."

"It took two days of putting up with his bullshit to get him to come out here. I hired a transvestite to flirt with him and promise him a night of fun. He thinks she just wanted a free trip to New Hampshire. He's been teasing Trevor and offering him nothing but kisses for the last two days. Trevor came willingly."

"The reason we're doing it here is because I was able to set up the equipment here without worry. There's privacy. He didn't want his wife to find out that he was with a woman at a hotel. Apparently she calls the front desk of whatever hotel he's at whenever he's out of town. She hunts him down. He's also a bit whipped and tells her exactly where he stays out of fear of her wrath."

She nodded. "So, that's why they're in my room soiling my sheets, which by the way I am burning and buying new ones tomorrow."

Madison bit her lip nervously. "What is it, Madison?" He kissed her lower lip.

"Since you're in the mood to shop and you've taken it upon yourself to adopt Chris, you should know that he desperately needs new clothes. They're too small as well as ripped and stained."

His lips tugged up into a lopsided grin. "That's all? That's fine. I could use some clothes as well. We'll hit the mall tomorrow under your direction of course."

"What do you mean?"

"I mean, he still needs a mother or a big sister or whatever you've been to him. I don't want that to stop, because you bring out the best in troublesome men." He brushed his lips against hers. "I only took over the legal and financial responsibilities."

"And do you consider yourself one of those troublesome men, sir?" she asked in a teasing tone.

He kissed her more deeply. "God, yes."

She felt him stirring to life beneath her. She wiggled on top of him, testing it out.

He groaned. "Baby, no. I need to end this."

She wiggled again.

He sucked in a deep breath. "You don't play fair."

"Never said I did. If I recall correctly you said that I cheat."

"You do." He chuckled.

He picked her up in his arms and stood up. She smiled, thinking that she won. "I'll be right back." He gave her a loud kiss on the forehead and dropped her on the bed. She bounced a few times before she jumped to her feet to follow him.

Chapter 18

"Come in!" a woman's voice said the same time a man said, "Go fuck off."

Ephraim opened the door to his dark bedroom. He could see everything clearly of course.

Trevor lay on his bed with his hands cuffed above his head. Paula, as he liked to call himself, was between the man's legs, licking his balls while gently pulling on his flaccid cock. It seems Trevor couldn't get it up again.

"Oh, that feels good." Trevor dropped his head back.

"Ephraim, if that's you, man, we'll handle our business later. I'm busy," Trevor said.

"Oh no, we'll handle it now," Ephraim said firmly.

Paula sat up, wiping his lips on the back of one well manicured hand. "About time. You better add a good bonus for this."

"I will."

"What are you talking about?" Trevor sounded confused.

"She's a hooker, Trevor," Ephraim said calmly.

"A hooker? Fuck." He shook his head in disbelief then chuckled. "Thank god I wore a condom then, huh."

Ephraim reached out to flick the light on, but waited. "Just curious, Trevor, did I get my money's worth?" He could feel Madison standing behind him. She was straining to get a look, but it was too dark for her human eyes to see anything.

Trevor laughed. "If you did this to blackmail me out of the money then you're shit out of luck. My wife knows I fuck around. She'll be mad for a while. Make me get tested and then she'll let me between her legs again and all will be forgiven."

"What if I said I had a camera in here? That I caught everything you've been doing on video?"

"It's dark."

"It's a very good camera, Trevor."

He chuckled. "Who cares? Show it to her or put it on the internet. I guarantee that in a month I'll be sliding into my wife's pussy while we watch it together. She gets off on that shit."

"You think so?"

"Hell, yes."

"How was I, sugar? Did you enjoy it? You've said you've had anal before. How did I rate?"

Trevor smiled. "I can easily say that you gave the best head I've ever had and without a doubt the best anal. When we get back to New Mexico I'd love to keep seeing you every week on a purely fuck basis"

"We'll see," Paula said coyly.

"Are you ready, Paula?" Ephraim asked.

"Ready for what?" Trevor demanded.

"Hold on, I just want to do one last thing." He leaned over and took Trevor in his mouth again.

"Oh fuck yeah, suck that cock, bitch!"

Madison fidgeted uncomfortably behind him.

Tall, Dark & Lonely

"You don't have to see this," he whispered.

"I'm fine," she said in a weak voice. She couldn't believe this was happening.

Wet sucking sounds broke the silence followed by Trevor's moans. Ephraim watched as Paula brought Trevor's flaccid cock back to life. At the same time she was palming herself, getting a nice erection for Trevor's eyes.

Madison was mesmerized by the sounds. Trevor seemed to really be enjoying the attention. She pulled on Ephraim's arm until she felt him lean down. "What is it?" he whispered.

"Is that something you would enjoy if I did it?" she asked in a rushed, nervous whisper.

Two red eyes appeared in the dark. "You're killing me, you know that, don't you?"

"Sorry. Just curious."

"Well, stop. I'm trying to focus." He took a deep steadying breath. She watched as his red eyes slowly faded away until she couldn't see anything again.

"I'm ready," Paula said.

"So am I, suck it harder," Trevor moaned.

The lights flicked on.

* * * *

"Stop screaming!" Ephraim snapped.

The high pitched screams slowly died. Trevor's eyes flew from Paula's erection, which incidentally was bigger than his own to Ephraim and Madison.

"Who's that?" his voice cracked as he nodded towards Madison.

Ephraim reached up and shut off the camera before he stepped into the room. "That's the woman you've been blackmailing."

"Madison?" he asked in disbelief.

"Yes," she said and then quickly averted her eyes. The years had not been good to him. He'd gained at least fifty pounds since she last saw him and his hair was thinning and graying. His erection was slowly deflating. "Can someone throw something over him?"

"Sorry." Ephraim uncuffed Trevor and threw his clothes at him.

"I'm leaving!" He pulled on his clothes so fast that he fell over.

"No, you're not."

"The hell I'm not!"

Ephraim stepped in his path. "No, you're not. If you take one more step towards that door I will arrest you."

"Y-you're a cop?"

"Police detective. You've been blackmailing a resident of New Hampshire and I have proof. You're not very good at covering your trail I have to let you know."

"But-"

"But nothing, the arrest will stick. You will not leave the state. You will be convicted and sentenced here and then you'll be extradited to New Mexico where they'll get to convict you as well."

"But-"

"I've taken the liberty of hiring Paul, I mean Paula, to ensure that this goes smoothly. After I'm done with you, this little tape you made will be my insurance that you will never bother Madison or Joshua again."

"But-"

"You don't love him. You've never given the kid a second thought. He's had a good upbringing with Madison doing what you should have done in the first place. You're not going to interfere again. If you ever grow some balls and want to be a real father to the kid, you can contact Mrs. Buckman or Madison otherwise you will stay away."

"But-"

"Just stop talking. If I hear 'but' again I'm going to break your jaw. Now sit down."

Trevor sat down. Ephraim walked over to his computer and turned the monitor on. A bank website appeared on the screen. "What's the password?"

"What?" Trevor looked past him. "Hey, that's my bank!"

"Yes, and that's your account number typed in there. Your password?"

"You can't do this! That's my money!"

Ephraim turned around. "Really? Would you like to argue that?"

"Yes goddammit, that's mine! I don't care what your bitch says!"

That was the wrong thing to say. Ephraim had to force himself not to turn, but he wasn't above kicking this bastard's ass.

"Get up!" Ephraim snapped. He yanked on his tie and pulled it off along with his shirt, revealing the very tight, white tank top that showed off every single muscle to perfection.

"Oh my my," Paula said. His eyes were soaking up Ephraim's body.

Madison had to stop herself from licking her lips. He really was addictive. "Come on, we'll settle this now." Ephraim waited, his hands clenching and unclenching into fists.

Trevor noticeably coward. "I-I-I...That's my money!"

"That's what I thought. You don't know how badly I want you to take a swing at me right now," Ephraim said. "You've made her life a living hell for five months and before that you sat back and did nothing while she struggled to put food in your son's stomach and clothes on his back. You're a piece of shit and you don't deserve him and you should thank her, not steal from her."

He had the good sense to look guilty. "My password is studmuffin69."

Ephraim could only shake his head in bewilderment.

"But she's only given me ten thousand! The rest is mine!"

"I said I didn't want to hear the word 'but' again." Ephraim pulled out a piece of paper with two account numbers on it.

He typed the first one in and entered twelve thousand. "You're paying her twelve grand. She's incurred late charges and fees because you were taking all of her money."

"That's fair I suppose," he agreed in a harsh tone.

Ephraim hit "Send." He typed in the second account number. "This second transaction is to pay back all of those years that you left Madison to support your son."

"What?!"

"I think ten thousand is more than fair to cover clothes, medical bills, food, shelter and other things that little boys need."

"Fine." He bit out.

"This second account is in Joshua's name with Madison as the backup. This will be his college account." He hit send and looked back at Madison and Trevor. "Does that sound fair to everyone?"

Madison wiped her eyes and smiled. She mouthed "thank you." He winked at her.

"Fine. But that's it," Trevor said. He knew he was trapped. "You don't show that video to anyone and I won't bother them again."

"Not quite. Sign this." Ephraim pulled out a clipboard from his desk drawer. "I had my lawyer draft up some papers."

"What are these?"

"You are officially severing ties to Joshua and handing over custody to Mrs. Buckman, his grandmother and she in turn will make sure the boy goes to Madison if something should happen to her. I'll be providing for the boy so you won't need to be bothered again."

Trevor took the pen and signed. "Fine, he was just a tax credit anyway."

Ephraim hit him upside his head, sending him stumbling. "Watch it."

Tears welled up in Trevor's eyes as he nodded. "Paula, if you could?" He held out the paper.

"Don't worry, handsome, no charge for witnessing this. This guy's too big an asshole. Keep him far away from that little boy."

"Thank you, Paula." Madison's voice broke.

"Can I go now?" Trevor bit out.

"Yes, of course. Just remember that if you try to fight the transactions or get more money from her, I'll come back for you with this video."

"Whatever." He paused before Madison.

"Figures you'd turn out to be just like your mother. Spreading to get a man to do whatever you want," he said acidly. Madison flinched back from the insult. "Fucking slut."

Ephraim stormed forward. He pulled out his wallet and tossed it to Madison who barely managed to catch it. "Pay Paula, tip well."

He grabbed Trevor by the throat and lifted him in the air, shoving him violently against the wall. "You don't ever talk to her like that again!"

Trevor could only sputter and choke. "I will fucking kill you! Do you understand?"

Madison's hands shook as she opened Ephraim's wallet. It was filled with crisp one hundred dollar bills. "How much does he owe you?"

"Two thousand," Paula said in a trance.

Trevor's face was turning red. Ephraim wasn't easing up. Madison quickly counted out the money and added five hundred. "Do you have a way to leave?"

"We took two rental cars. I drove one and Trevor the other."

Madison thanked god that Paula was already dressed. She shoved the money in his hand. "Thank you so much for your help. But, I need you to go so that I can handle this."

"You don't have to ask me twice." With money in his hand, Paula yanked open the bedroom door and fled from the house.

All hope that Ephraim wouldn't lose control flew out the window when Trevor's eyes widened in terror and he began kicking and clawing at Ephraim. This had to end.

"Trevor, I'm going to get him to let you go. If you tell anyone about him, I will show the video and he'll probably come after you. Do you understand?"

Trevor continued to thrash, but blinked his understanding. "Ephraim, baby, let go. You're going to kill him if you don't. Look, he's starting to turn purple."

Ephraim didn't look at her, but she could see his red eyes and fangs clearly enough. He wasn't thinking clearly anymore. "He disrespected you," he growled.

"That doesn't mean he has to die. Baby, let go."

"No," the word came out in a loud growl.

She needed to get between them, but Trevor wouldn't stop kicking. If he kicked her, Madison knew without a doubt that Ephraim would rip his throat out. "Trevor, stop kicking so I can get you down."

He didn't hesitate. He froze on the spot. Madison managed to slide between them, but it was a tight fit. Ephraim didn't seem to realize or care that she was there. His eyes were fixed on Trevor's face.

"Ephraim, put him down." He didn't respond. If this didn't work she would have to shoot him. She couldn't stand by and let him kill someone even an asshole like Trevor.

She stood on her toes and pressed her mouth against Ephraim's neck. She licked and nipped at his neck, sucking greedily. She felt his arms lower a fraction. Trevor slid slightly down the wall. He took in a gasping breath. Good, he was able to breathe.

Her tongue traced his Adam's apple while her fingers yanked down his fly. She reached in and pulled him out. He was long and thick, but soft. She ran her hand over him. She'd never done this before, but knew the idea of the matter was to move her hand up and down him.

He growled low and deep as he hardened in her hand. She hoped he wasn't too far gone that he would bite her. That would be the start of a whole other problem. She knew from his description that he was already in bloodlust brought on by anger so she had to tread carefully.

Trevor was slowly lowered to the ground, but Ephraim's grip remained firm as ever. Madison kept gently tugging him forward and his hips moved in response as if they had a mind of their own, but he did not ease his hold or his anger. She could feel it in his neck. His muscles were fixed for battle.

Her mouth found his, effectively blocking his view of Trevor's face. She ran her tongue over his fangs, carefully. All she needed at this point was a drop of her blood hitting the air. Then they'd all be in deep shit. She covered his mouth, running her tongue over his, teasing it to come out and play.

Slowly he melted under her coaxing. He returned her kiss slowly at first until she was gasping for air. He began thrusting in her hand at an even pace. Her intentions may have back fired just a little when his grip tightened on Trevor's neck.

She pulled his free hand up to cover her breast. His body was on automatic. He started kneading and cupping her. She felt Trevor's breath hit the back of her neck. Keeping him breathing was becoming a full time job.

Ephraim watched Trevor's face. He wanted to tear him apart and rip his throat out. He couldn't focus on anything else. His hand squeezed Trevor's throat. He liked the feeling. Liked the way Trevor looked. He was scared. Ephraim could smell it.

He was barely aware of what Madison was doing or how he was responding. His eyes remained open while he kissed her. Trevor's fear was sending endorphins throughout his body. Bloodlust surged through him and he welcomed it.

Trevor's eyes were squeezed tightly shut. Tears ran down his face. His lower lip and chin quivered. Ephraim squeezed a little harder. Trevor made a sobbing pained sound. Trevor's body began releasing adrenaline at an unprecedented rate.

Tall, Dark & Lonely

The smell was overpowering. He was going to tear Trevor's throat out. He wanted that blood, now. He tried stepping forward only to have something stop him. He tried again. His brain didn't comprehend the soft barrier standing between him and his prey.

He tried a different approach. His hand tightened around Trevor's neck and he tried to drag him to his waiting fangs. The soft barrier stopped him, again. He dropped Trevor back against the wall in frustration. A loud menacing growl escaped his lips. Trevor whimpered loudly.

He was about to throw Trevor to the ground and pounce on him to escape the soft barrier when the smell of female arousal teased his nostrils. The growl halted in his throat. It was close, so very close. It was strong and familiar. Something was registering in his brain. It was the smell of a woman, *his* woman.

Possessiveness soared through him. His woman was close by and she was aroused. He was also aware of the scent of another male. He knew that scent to be of his prey, but the scent of sex lingered in the air, confusing him.

Ephraim's mouth stopped moving against hers. He bared his fangs, growling loudly. It was the single most terrifying sound she ever heard. That and the combination of him sliding between her fist turned her on more than she'd ever been in her life.

She needed him, now.

With her free hand, she shoved at the hand that was holding onto Trevor. His grip faltered enough for Trevor to shoot out to his left and towards the door. He stumbled, but didn't stop.

Another menacing growl escaped Ephraim's throat and his hand dropped from Madison's clothed breast and shot out towards Trevor. He missed.

"Run!" Madison yelled.

Trevor scrambled out of the room, leaving behind his shoes. She heard the hallway door slam shut and the sound of an engine turning over. Ephraim tried to pull away to go after him, but he was too confused by bloodlust and competing scents to move.

The soft barrier was stopping him, again. He could still get his prey, could still catch him. A car wouldn't stop him, he knew that. The barrier grabbed him and held on. His hands pushed at the barrier, but it wouldn't move. He was starting to become annoyed with the barrier. He shoved forward, hoping to push the barrier out of his way. Something stopped him. Something was behind the soft barrier cushioning it between it and him.

Shit! He was going to kill her! Maybe she should have grabbed his gun. It was still on his belt. But she couldn't stop. She wanted him. He had her pressed tightly between the wall and him.

She shoved her pants down by wiggling her hips until they were around her ankles and she could step out of them. She released his member and wrapped her arms around his neck as she looked into his eyes.

They were hard and vacant yet determined. Did he even know that she was there? His eyes were focused on her, but unseeing. This had to work. She didn't have any other ideas at the moment and she wasn't really trying to think of any. She wanted him so badly that she ached from it.

She used the wall at her back and his height and strength to pick her legs up while holding onto him tightly. He didn't seem concerned, but his growl was lower. She quickly wrapped her legs around his waist. There was no way she would be able to perform that acrobatic move again anytime soon.

Her arms tightened around his neck as she raised herself up. His very erect member brushed against her slit. She sucked in a deep breath. His growl changed, deepened. Slowly, ever so slowly, she lowered herself onto him.

Tall, Dark & Lonely

She was tight, she knew that. She could feel her body struggling to take him in. Her head dropped back as she licked her lips. He felt so incredible. Using her legs, she pulled him in all the way at last. There was only one problem with her plan.

There was no possible way to move. She was literally impaled on him and stuck between him and the wall. There was only enough room now to breathe. Somehow he managed to move closer when she wasn't paying attention. She tried to wiggle, but her hips were stuck.

She kissed his chin and mouth, but he was still distant. "Ephraim baby, you have to move now."

He didn't move.

"Shit." She grabbed his hands and moved them to her bottom, but it was like dragging a fireman's hose, large, too damn heavy and uncooperative. His hands latched onto her when they made contact, but other than that he didn't move.

Madison kissed him frantically, running her tongue wildly over his lips and tongue, trying to get him to respond. She yanked his hair, he growled viciously, but finally responded. Interesting, he responded to pain. She reached back with great effort and pinched his backside through his pants. He growled again and thrust forward, making her moan. She hoped she didn't have to pinch him for each thrust.

Pain, something was hurting him. He tried to focus, but all he could focus on was the odor of fear left over from his prey and his woman's arousal. He knew the woman was his. He could smell his own scent on her. He tried to focus on the woman. He knew she was in front of him, but he couldn't focus. She was the soft barrier and she was saying something to him and hurting him, but for some strange reason he didn't want to hurt her back or stop her. Something was telling him not to hurt her.

Why was she hurting him? He couldn't focus because with each little shot of pain was a reward of pleasure. Her scent was pushing away everything else now. It was becoming stronger. His own scent was mixing with it. He became aware that he was painfully aroused and enveloped in a tight, wet sheath.

"Fuck me, Ephraim," he heard her whisper against his ear. Her breath was hot, sending shivers down his spine. He thrust his hips forward and he groaned long and loud.

He felt her wet tongue gliding down his neck. His hands gripped her bottom, holding her tightly so that she couldn't move while he took her. He felt her teeth scrape against his skin. He was becoming aware of so many things, but still he was trapped behind a hazy curtain. Dull teeth sank into his neck.

"Shit!" he yelped.

Madison kissed the inured skin. "Good, now that I have your attention, do you mind joining me?"

He blinked several times and stepped back just enough to look down at their joined bodies. He licked his lips hungrily as he watched himself disappear inside her body.

"I'll gladly join you, Madison."

"Good," she sounded relieved. "What are you waiting for, baby? Fuck me," her voice was husky with need.

His hands gripped her bottom tighter, holding her as he pulled back and thrust in. She was talking dirty to him. Many women had talked dirty to him in the past, but he found it annoying and distracting. It wasn't like that with his Madison.

Every nerve in his body was alive. He was inside of her, but felt like he was miles away. He released his hold on her bottom and yanked his tee shirt off. Balancing her weight on his hips, he moved his hands beneath her shirt.

Tall, Dark & Lonely

As his hands slid up so did her shirt until there was nowhere for it to go but off and onto the floor. She looked glorious naked against the wall. He moved closer, one hand going to her bottom and the other to her breast. He squeezed and caressed each area until his mouth decided to join his hand on her left breast.

He pushed her breast up so he could take it into his mouth. She moaned loudly as he took not just the tip into his mouth, but as much as his mouth could pull in. He licked and sucked greedily as he slid in and out of her.

Her hands ran over his back, gently scrapping her nails against his skin. He thrust harder, loving the sensation. Her hands snaked up into his hair and he gently pulled his head back, releasing her breast with a loud sucking sound.

She cupped his face in her hands and caressed his cheeks with her thumbs while he made love to her. Her thumbs gently traced beneath his eyes and then moved down until both thumbs were running over his top lip. They dropped and traced his fangs, carefully. "You're so handsome, Ephraim," her voice felt like a caress.

He turned his face into her palm and pressed a kiss. "Love you, Madison."

Madison pulled him closer for a long, deep kiss. She winced against his mouth. The butt of his gun and the leather holster were digging into her leg and scraping her-*oh shit.*

"Ephraim, stop!"

"What?"

"Stop!"

Ephraim pulled out and lowered her to the ground. "Baby, what's wrong?"

She half bent over and cupped the inner thigh. "Nothing, nothing at all!" She made a mad dash into the bathroom, shutting the door swiftly behind her. She ran over to the sink and raised her foot to the counter to get a better view.

"Thank god." She closed her eyes, relieved. It was rubbed raw, but no broken skin.

"Just like that," Ephraim's deep voice said next to her ear. He was already entering her by the time one hand held onto her hip and the other supported her raised leg.

Her mood had dampened when she thought she was about to send him back into bloodlust. His it seemed hadn't. "I'm sorry about the holster. I'll make it up to you." His hand on her leg gently rubbed the raw area while his other hand moved between her legs.

She sucked in a deep breath and dropped her head back against his bare shoulder. Her arm came up and snaked behind his head, holding on as he gently rocked into her body. "I like watching you." He kissed her earlobe, pulling it between his lips and sucking it gently.

His talented fingers found her swollen nub. They moved in a circular motion, barely touching it and absolutely driving her crazy. She turned her head so she could kiss him. He kissed her deeply as he deepened his thrusts. His fingers continued to rub her at the same slow steady rate.

When he felt her tighten around him, he forced himself to hold out for another minute and make this good for her. The look of fear on her face when he pulled out hadn't escaped him. He was going to make love to her until she forgot that moment, the moment when she realized just how dangerous it was to be with him.

"Do you like that?" he asked in a deep sensual voice.

Her free arm moved back and over his now bare hip. She held on as he moved against her. "Yes," she moaned. She turned the tables on him. "Do you like fucking me, Ephraim?" Her tongue licked his neck, slowly.

Tall, Dark & Lonely

He growled and thrust harder into her. His fingers pressed firmly against her nub. "Yes, I like fucking you, baby. Is that what you wanted to hear? That I love licking and fucking your pussy until you're wet and screaming for me?"

"Oh god!" She started sucking on his neck harder, moaning deeply. Her body was pushed closer to climax. She tried to move against him, but he held her tightly as he quickened his pace. He loved her mouth on him. He wanted it everywhere.

He forced his eyes open so that he could watch her come. She sucked harder and held onto him tightly. "Fuck me, Ephraim….oh, please, Ephraim, fuck me!"

That did it. He couldn't hold back. He slammed into her, lifting her off the floor with each hard thrust. He growled and moaned as she moaned and screamed his name. This time he didn't need to bite to find his moment.

Slowly, he stopped. Her body was still squeezing his in the aftermath of a powerful orgasm. It was too much for his sensitive flesh. He moved to pull back when her body tightened around his still hard member. Her nails pierced his thigh and the back of his neck as another orgasm took over. She screamed and gasped.

He watched her in the mirror, entranced. He pushed forward again and again. He gritted his jaw and continued while she screamed his name. Finally, her hold on him slipped away. She fell forward, slapping her hands against the sink as her leg dropped to the ground.

"That was so good, Ephraim," she said, panting.

"What do you mean was?" He chuckled. His hands gripped her hips as he continued to thrust inside of her.

She whimpered. Her body started to react again. It was too much too soon. "Baby," she said half pleading, half whimpering.

"Yes?"

He was going to kill her with orgasms. There was only one thing to do. She pulled herself off him and turned around. She pressed a kiss to his mouth. His hands moved greedily over her. She caught his hand as it tried to move between her legs.

"Just stand right there," she said with a coy smile.

His brows rose up in confusion as she slowly dropped to her knees, kissing his stomach as she went. "What…" His head dropped back and his mouth formed an "O" in surprise as she took him into her mouth. It wasn't an expert blowjob by any means, but it was the best one he ever received. He lost himself in her beautiful mouth within minutes.

Chapter 19

His arms tightened around her as she shook against him. For the last half hour they sat on her bed, joined. He held her in his arms as she sat in his lap facing him. They kissed slowly and moved even slower. He let her set the pace. It was the most powerful experience he'd ever had with a woman.

He ran his hands down her back as she sleepily laid her head against his shoulder. "Are you tired?" he whispered.

She giggled weakly against his neck. "We've been making love for the last...well, I don't know how many hours and now the sun is up. To say that I'm tired would be an understatement. *I'm exhausted.*"

Ephraim chuckled. "Me too." He pressed a kiss against her forehead.

Madison pulled away from him. Her limbs were so sore and weak from their night of love making.

"Where are you going?"

She looked over her shoulder. "Shower, a nice long hot shower....alone."

He watched as her hips swayed back and forth gently as she walked away from him. Nine times he made love to her last night, a new record for him. After a century of celibacy he had some catching up to do and right now his body was coming back to life, ready to do a little more catching up.

"Hold up. I need a shower, too."

She sighed, "Baby, please I'm so tired. I just want a shower and then go to bed," she said, lightly sobbing. Her body ached all over and she was exhausted. Now that she was away from his body her eyes were fighting to stay open.

He held up his hands. "Just a shower. I swear." She threw him a disbelieving look. "I promise." If he hadn't said it with a grin she probably would have believed him and she wouldn't have looked down.

Her eyes widened in surprise. "Ephraim, please no, sleep! I need sleep!"

"And that's exactly what you'll get after our shower. I promise I'll be good. I just want a shower." He took her hand and led her into the bathroom.

"Fibber," she muttered as her head hit the pillow.

Ephraim laughed weakly as he kissed her wet shoulder. She curled up as soon as he laid her on the bed after taking advantage of her in the shower. That's how she thought of it, especially since he knew that she wouldn't be able to resist him when he put his mouth down there. It was only natural at that point that she allowed him to lean her against the wall and finish the job. She was a helpless victim here of the passion that he invoked in her. She really was. Granted, he had her begging for it, but that wasn't the point.

She looked over at him and sighed. He was out. It gave her some comfort to know that he was as weak as she was on some things, their passion being one of them. He looked so cute and innocent. She rolled over and pressed a light kiss to his lips.

"Give me five minutes and I'll be good to go again," he mumbled, "I swear."

"You're not getting between my legs again until I've had at least eight hours of sleep and some food in my stomach."

"Not fair," this came out as a muffled mutter as he buried his face in the pillow. He was down for the count and not getting back up for a while. Thank god.

* * * *

"Madison, wake up please!" Joshua's banging on the door and sobbing pleas had her sitting up so fast that it made her head spin.

Tall, Dark & Lonely

"Ephraim!" she hissed. She reached over to wake him and practically fell over. His side of the bed was empty. It was twelve in the afternoon. "Damn it," she mumbled. They'd only been asleep for an hour. Well, she had, she had no idea what he'd been doing.

He walked back into the room, yanking up his pants. He wore nothing else. "Baby, get dressed."

"Madison?" Joshua cried louder.

Ephraim yanked her drawers open and tossed clothes to her. "Hurry up, he's upset."

"Just a minute!"

Ephraim walked over to the door, his hand on the doorknob and his eyes on her as he waited for her to cover up. When she had a shirt and pants on, he opened the door. Joshua came running into the room, rubbing his eyes. He didn't see Ephraim as he ran into Madison's waiting arms.

"What's wrong, buddy?" Madison struggled to keep her balance. He wasn't a baby anymore and she wasn't strong enough to hold a ten year old boy for more than a moment or two. She stumbled beneath his weight.

Joshua gasped as strong hands pulled him away from Madison. He opened his eyes in surprise. Then his face crumbled again. He threw his arms around Ephraim's neck and buried his face against Ephraim's bare shoulder.

"Tell us what's wrong, little man," he said in a soothing voice.

Madison rubbed Joshua's back. "What happened?" She tried to ignore the holes in his shirt.

"Gran.......Grand.......Grandma's crying!"

"What?" That's the last thing either one of them expected to hear.

"She's crying. He yelled at her...and then.....she talked to them.......then...then....they left for a little while....then....they came back....and they....she...." He was sobbing so hard that he could hardly get a coherent word out.

Ephraim kissed the top of Joshua's head. "Where's Grandma now?"

He took in a deep breath. "She's downstairs crying, people are yelling, others are crying. It's horrible! I'm so glad you're back, Ephraim!"

Ephraim looked at Madison. "Me, too. Do me a favor and go to your room and relax for a while."

"No! I need to make Grandma feel better and Jill's crying, too!"

"Let's go." Ephraim held Joshua against his body with one arm and held Madison's hand with the other as they made their way downstairs. Halfway down, they heard loud arguing coming from the living room.

He quickened his pace and stepped into the room as Chris threw his hands in the air. "All right, everyone shut up and stop yelling at her!"

Mrs. Buckman, the one woman he thought was tough as nails, was practically backed up against the wall with several of the renters screaming at her, sobbing.

"Rent more rooms because I'm not paying another dime!" one of the men said.

"Stop yelling at her!" Brad snapped. "There are no more rooms available."

"Of course not, there are five rooms being taken and no one is paying."

"I said shut the hell up!" Chris yelled. No one paid attention to him and no one noticed Ephraim in the doorway with Madison and Joshua.

Tall, Dark & Lonely

"Mama, you said I could come here rent free and now you're demanding I pay? That's not fair and you know what? I'm moving out tomorrow. My friend is going to let me crash at his place for a while," Candy sobbed theatrically. "I can't believe my own mother would do this to me!" Most of the people stopped yelling long enough to roll their eyes.

"Look, I said I would try! I can't afford this anymore. I'm sorry," Mrs. Buckman cried into her hands.

"I don't know why everyone is yelling at her. I told you all to come in here and nicely tell that her that we're moving to the boarding house on Smithson, not scream at her!" Brad said.

"You're all moving out?" Candy asked.

Brad nodded. "We can't afford to pay more and the Boarding House on Smithson charges less to start with and has more amenities. We had to make a choice."

"She's going to lose the house," Mrs. Adle said to no one in particular. Mrs. Buckman cried harder and tried to turn away, but the people around her made it impossible.

"If she hadn't taken in that deadbeat and her kids, she'd be fine!" one of them said, looking at Candy who pretended not to hear.

"No, if that dead beat would help out, she would have been fine."

"She was fine before they came. No mortgage on the place. Did I tell you that she tried to get a loan and they denied her?" Mrs. Adle informed everyone as if Mrs. Buckman wasn't there crying.

"This is bullshit. I'm not leaving." Ephraim recognized the newest renter.

Brad scoffed. "That's because they won't take you. You haven't even paid her since you moved in. You're part of the problem."

Jill sat in the corner, crying. Everyone was ignoring her. Chris was trying to push his way to Mrs. Buckman. In a few seconds, he was pulling her into his arms. After a moment of hesitation she wrapped her arms around him and cried against his chest. "Stop it all of you," he said. That sent them off again.

"Do something!" Joshua begged.

That was fine with him. He'd seen and heard enough. He put Joshua down. "Cover your ears," he said softly. Joshua nodded and did as he was asked. Madison didn't wait to be asked before she covered her ears.

"I want my last week's rent back!" some of them started to scream. Then it became a tangle of screams.

"*Quiet!*" Ephraim roared.

Everyone in the room covered their ears and cowered back from the deafening noise. It was probably the loudest and most frightening shout they'd ever heard.

They were still cringing when he walked into the room. Under normal circumstances he was intimidating. Right now he was frightening as hell. He was half naked with every muscle in his body flexing, readying for a fight. His arms were folded over his chest as he stood in an authoritative stance. His eyes had an icy glimmer to them as they scanned the room, challenging anyone to speak.

"That's better. Now, everyone move back so that Chris and Mrs. Buckman can sit down on the couch." The small gathering stepped back in one uniformed move. Chris threw Ephraim a relieved look as he brought Mrs. Buckman to the couch.

Ephraim's eyes moved onto the newest member, a man in his mid thirties. Ephraim didn't have a chance to run a background check on the man as he normally would have done before he left, but he had a feeling that he knew what he was going to find.

"How many weeks do you owe?"

The man's jaw clenched. "That's none of your fucking business, pig." The man had a problem with cops. Interesting.

"Five," Brad said. "He never paid a cent. He gave her a sob story and you know that's her weakness."

Ephraim nodded. "Consider the free ride over. You're to be packed and out within an hour or I will run you and we both know my search will come back with a warrant or two."

The man's mouth dropped open. "Fine, but I'm not paying a cent."

"I never thought you would. Just get out. You only have fifty-nine minutes left."

Jenny, one of the female boarders he couldn't stand, spoke up. "That's not fair! We have to pay so should he!"

He ignored her. "Now, raise your hand if you've made arrangements to move out." Every paying hand went into the air, even Candy's.

He nodded. "When are you moving out?"

Brad cleared his throat. "Tomorrow. They're able to take us then. If we don't go tomorrow we lose our spots."

Ephraim nodded.

"I want my last week's rent back!" Jenny said.

He pinched the bridge of his nose, trying to keep himself under control. "You are leaving with less than twenty-four hours notice. You are not getting your rent back. You signed an agreement for one week's notice. So let it go because she is not giving it back."

"That's not fair!" Jenny yelled.

Ephraim's hand dropped away and he took a step forward. His eyes pierced Jenny's and she stumbled back. "Take it to court then. You signed a binding contract."

Mrs. Buckman sat on the couch, sobbing. He couldn't stand to see a strong woman broken like that. "Has anyone paid for this upcoming week?"

"No," they said collectively. That meant she was completely out of money and no way to pay the bills. It was probably for the best otherwise she would owe them.

"Okay, then you are all free to leave. I suggest you go pack and prepare your rooms for inspection if you want your deposits back," he said dismissively.

They nodded sheepishly and walked out of the room. Candy straightened her clothing and stood up. "I guess I should go pack, too."

"What?" Madison asked in disbelief.

Candy scoffed. "Madison, your grandmother is going to lose the house. I have to find a place to stay. You don't want me to be homeless, do you?"

"What about your mother and your kids? Where do you think they'll end up?" She stepped towards Candy. She was trembling with rage.

Candy backed up and headed for the door. "I don't know what you expect from me, Madison. Really, you're being ridiculous. The kids will be fine. I'm sure the foster homes around here are very nice."

Ephraim reached out and restrained Madison as she swung to hit Candy. She missed, but barely. "Get out of here then! We don't need you!"

"Shh, it's okay, baby. Just let her go." He half dragged her to an overstuffed chair and sat her down. He sat on the arm of the chair and held her hand.

Tall, Dark & Lonely

Mrs. Buckman sat up, looking more composed. "I'm sorry about everything." She swallowed. "Thank you for your help. Ephraim, I think you should go see if you can snag one of those rooms up before it's too late."

Ephraim ran a hand over his hair. "Chris, run up to my room. On the desk you'll find two folders, grab them along with my checkbook and my wallet's up there somewhere I think in my pants. Go grab them."

"Okay." He looked weary as he ran out of the room.

He sat back. "Eleanor, how bad is it?"

She tried to smile, but couldn't quite manage it. "I'm late on the utilities, taxes and insurance, but I'll catch up."

Ephraim looked between Eleanor and Madison. "Would it really kill you women to let me know when you need help? It would make my life a great deal easier."

"This is my problem, Ephraim. I'll handle it. I might have to sell the house. I'll find an apartment big enough for me and my four grandbabies. We'll be fine."

"And what will you do if you can't sell quickly?" His eyes ran over the kids. He noticed for the first time how raggedly they looked. Even Eleanor and Madison looked like they needed new clothes. She told him Chris needed new clothes, but she failed to mention the rest of them.

"We'll manage." Eleanor lied.

"Jesus Christ, Eleanor, I bet you don't have enough money to put food on the table and you think you'll manage? Look at these kids. They need haircuts and clothes, badly. Living in a house without electricity, water or heat is not going to be good for them either."

Eleanor sobbed quietly. "I'll manage. My babies are not going into foster care," she said firmly.

"Foster care? I'm not going. No fucking way," Chris said, walking back into the room.

"Watch your mouth in front of the kids," Ephraim said quietly as he took the items from Chris. "Have a seat, this affects you, too."

He sat down on the arm of the couch with his arms folded over his chest. He looked scared and was trying not to show it. "I'm not going."

Ephraim eyed the four of them before looking down at Madison. "Go sit over there with your family so I can talk to all of you without straining my neck, please."

Madison moved to sit down between her grandmother and Jill. Ephraim sat down in the chair. "Where to begin?" he pondered. His eyes fell on Eleanor.

"How much do you owe against the house?"

"Nothing. I own it outright."

That confused him. "Then why did you get denied a loan?"

Her hands fidgeted in her lap. "My age and I wasn't bringing in enough to cover the bills as it was. The roof cost more than I expected."

"Did they deny you because of us?" Jill asked.

Eleanor reluctantly nodded. "They said they didn't feel right loaning money to me with so many dependants. If I didn't pay on time they didn't want to have to throw kids out of a house."

"Damn it," Chris muttered. "I knew this was my fault."

"No, it's not and don't you dare say that!" Eleanor said fiercely.

"Grandma, I have twelve thousand dollars. You can have that," Madison said, glad Ephraim took it upon himself to get it back.

Ephraim held up his hand the same time Grandma said, "No."

"That's your money, Madison. Keep it in the bank," Ephraim said. He turned his attention once again to Eleanor. "How much debt do you have?"

Her fingers stilled. "Over fifty thousand dollars."

"Grandma." Madison could not believe her ears.

"With the lawyers, then the roof and the foundation the debt added up pretty quickly. Then I couldn't rent out the extra rooms to cover the costs. It just got out of hand."

"And because I was no longer paying for the second room you actually ended up losing money," Ephraim added.

She nodded.

"How much are you going to ask for the house?"

"I'm afraid I won't get much more than two hundred thousand if that. The house is older than most around here. Last year the Thompsons sold their house which was about the same size, but brand new and they only got two-sixty. I don't have high hopes."

"Are we gonna have to go into a foster home?" Jill quietly asked.

"I'm not going and neither are they. I'll get a job," Chris said firmly.

Ephraim sighed as he tossed one folder to Chris and the other one to Eleanor. "What's this?" they asked in unison.

"Open them."

"What does this mean?" Chris asked, frowning as he looked over the legal documents.

"It means you are not going to foster care. It means you are now Christopher Williams."

"What?" his voice rose. "You adopted me? How? Doesn't that take months to do?"

"Yes, I adopted you. I asked your mom and she decided that securing your future was better than abandoning you to the streets so she signed the papers. As for the expediency of the adoption, I pulled a few favors."

"No shit?" Chris asked cautiously, obviously thinking that it might be a joke. He didn't trust easily and for good reason.

"No shit. You are now officially my brat," Ephraim said with a wink.

Chris smiled. "Nice," he said appreciatively.

"I don't understand this. I already had custody. Emma signed it over. I paid a lawyer quite handsomely too I might add."

"I'm afraid Candy lied. She didn't have custody of Joshua. Ephraim was kind enough to secure it before anything happened," Madison explained.

"So, Joshua is mine now?" Eleanor asked with a watery smile.

"Yes, Candy lost her rights years ago. I got the boy's father to do the right thing."

"What about me?" Jill asked.

"Candy signed you over to your Grandmother when you moved here. You're all set as well."

"That's great and all that we all have a family. I'm psyched don't get me wrong, but what good does it do when we're all about to be homeless?" Chris asked as Joshua climbed up onto his lap. Chris hung his arm over the little boy's shoulder.

"You're not losing your home. Things are just going to change." Ephraim opened his checkbook and quickly filled out a check. He handed the check over to Eleanor. "Have the title signed over to me on Monday."

Eleanor took the check with shaky fingers. Her eyes widened at the figure. "Ephraim, what's going on here? You can't afford this."

Ephraim shrugged. "I live here because I don't like living alone, not because I can't afford it. I'm a very wealthy man," he said with an uncaring shrug.

"I'll say." Jill's eyes were the size of saucers.

"Seems I have a rich daddy," Chris teased.

"Are you sure?" Eleanor asked.

"Yes, I love this house."

She smiled and nodded. "Thank you, Ephraim. I'm sure I can find an apartment soon enough."

"We have to move?" Joshua asked. His eyes shot to Madison. "I don't want to move, again."

"Shh, sweetie it's Ephraim's house now," Eleanor said.

Ephraim groaned. "Eleanor, I am not kicking the kids out of their home and I am most certainly not kicking you out."

"You're confusing me," Eleanor admitted.

"I may own it now, but this is your home. You and the children will remain here. The house is no longer a boarding house, although we may have guests from time to time. I'd like the kids to have a home of their own where they don't have to put up with strangers all the time and they're free to be themselves." He stood up and stretched.

"Other than that you run it however you please." He opened his wallet and pulled out several hundred dollar bills and held them out to her. "Take this and the children and go buy some groceries. Tell everyone else that since they didn't pay you for the week they'll have to go elsewhere to eat today. You guys can sit down and have a nice family dinner for once. I'm going to bed now, but when you get back wake me up and we'll hit the mall, okay?"

Eleanor's pride stopped her from taking the money even though the fridge and cupboards were completely bare. Ephraim thrust the money into her hand. "Eleanor, I'm very tired. I've been awake for over three days so let's cut to the chase. You live in my house now. I adore you and your grandchildren, my new bratty son eats like a pig and I'm crazy about your granddaughter. Please take pity on me and just take the money and buy some food so I can go back to bed."

"Ephraim, we can't accept your charity," Madison said.

"Madison, it's not charity. My son needs to eat." He was surprised how easily that rolled off his tongue. Chris turned to hide a smile. "My favorite ten year old and fifteen year old drama queen needs to eat."

"Hey!" Jill gasped.

"Also, Eleanor needs to eat so that she can keep up with the kids and manage this household. It's not charity."

"Yes, it is!"

His hands thrust through his hair. "Have pity, woman. I'm exhausted!"

"Don't do this because of me," she said stubbornly.

"Baby, even if you didn't live here I would still be doing this. Eleanor has taken care of me for the last three years. She's been good to me and I enjoy her company. I would be buying this house just to keep her here. I would also do it for the kids. I don't care who lives here. I am the man of this house. I will pay the bills and put food on the table. I don't expect anything from anyone."

"Thank you, Ephraim," Eleanor said. Her eyes glowed with warmth.

"You're welcome. So, I assume you're going to stay," he said, hoping to end this and crawl back into bed.

She nodded, smiling. "If you'll have us, I would very much like to stay here so the children can have a good home."

"It's your home, Eleanor. Don't ever think it's not."

"But-" Madison began.

He threw his hands up in frustration. "I really wish people would stop starting every sentence with 'but'." He walked over to the couch and took her hands into his as he dropped to his knees.

"Baby, please, you're killing me here. I'm not expecting anything from you. I just want to make sure that we have a roof over our heads. I don't want to come home to an empty house and I want Chris, Joshua and Jill to remain together with their Grandmother. Can you please see that doing this makes me happy? Do you have any idea how lonely I've been and for how long?"

She nodded slowly. She did. He'd been alone for too long. One look in his eyes and she knew that he was doing this for himself as well. He desperately needed them to stay. She sighed, "Okay, but I want to pay for the food then. That's only fair."

"But you'll stay?" He waited nervously for her answer.

"Yes."

"Good, then do whatever you want. But today I pay for the food." He pressed a kiss to her forehead, remembering that they had an audience and stood up.

"I'm going to bed, wake me up later and we'll go to the mall."

"For what?" Chris asked.

"Clothes shopping."

"Oh that sucks. Let's pick up some chicks instead."

Jill reached behind Chris and hit him soundly upside his head.

"What is with you women and hitting me?"

Ephraim shook his head. "I can't imagine."

Chapter 20

"Chris, get back in there! You're not supposed to come out here in your underwear!" Madison hissed. She turned to Ephraim. "Stop laughing! You're only encouraging him!"

"What? Is something wrong?" Chris feigned innocence.

A little girl walking by the dressing room pointed and giggled. Several high school girls went by blowing kisses at him.

Chris winked and flexed his muscles. He was built for a sixteen year old, Madison noticed. That was weird because she knew he didn't work out unless video games were categorized as exercise now.

"Chris," she warned.

"You told me to try on my new clothes and come out here and show you. So here I am." He turned around to show off his underwear.

"You're not supposed to try on underwear and you know you're not supposed to step out here like that!"

Ephraim doubled over with laughter. "Those are his underwear."

"Oh, look at that so they are," Chris said with amused interest. "Hmm, imagine that."

"Stop wiggling your ass!" Madison fought back the laughter, but it was a losing battle.

"Wait, gotta make sure these look good gangsta style." He lowered his boxers to his hips and made mocking gang signs.

The breath caught in Madison's throat. There below his navel was a light brown crescent moon and cross birthmark. Her eyes shot to Ephraim's. He suddenly looked deadly sober.

"Don't," he warned.

"Young man, go back into the changing room, please. This is a family store," a security guard said.

"Oh sorry, my sister told me to do it." Chris gestured to Madison.

"Ma'am, please save the fashion shows for home. I have a lady hyperventilating in my office right now from his little show." Madison's eyes shot daggers at Chris.

"She liked what she saw, huh?" Chris joked.

"Just go," the man said, trying to hide a grin as he walked away.

Madison turned to look at Ephraim. "You knew!" she whispered excitedly.

"That he's a Sentinel? I knew the first time I arrested him. I've been watching over him. Now I had to step up before he gets hurt. He's part of the reason I finally accepted their offer. You're the other. That's also the reason I bought the house. It's going to be turned into a Sentinel home."

"What does that mean?"

"An alarm system, the place will be upgraded. A training facility will be built in the basement and it will be home to a few select clergy to help in the area. This will be our area to protect."

"Are you going to tell him?"

"No, not yet. He has a lot on his plate at the moment." She gave him a disapproving look. "Madison, let him be a boy for a little while longer. He's never had a childhood the same as you. Let him have another year of a carefree life. That was the deal I made with the council. I will protect him and train him myself. He's going to have vampires and minions after him in good time. For now, let him be a boy. Can't you see how badly he needs that? Needs a family? He's already been rushed into adulthood. Let him hang onto the last thread of his childhood before he has to be a man for everyone else. Please?"

She nodded. "You're right. He's been so happy the last two weeks. He only comes to detention now to keep me company and his grades have gone up."

"Exactly, we tell him now and he's either going to rebel hard or get into it too fast and get himself killed. Please don't tell him."

"Tell me what?"

They looked up in time to see Chris coming out of the changing room in his old clothes. Madison had a sneaking suspicion that improved hearing was part of the Sentinel package.

"Are you all set for clothes?" she asked.

"Yes, these all fit." He dropped them back into the carriage. "Tell me what?"

Ephraim stood up. "Well, I guess the surprise is ruined."

"What surprise?"

"You're going with me."

"Where?"

"I'm going to get a tattoo." He reached back to make sure that the two pieces of paper he carefully folded and placed in his back pocket earlier were still there, Sentinel symbols identifying him as a Pyte and a Sentinel by election. The symbols were known to Sentinels and would save him time and energy later on if he had to identify himself or ask for help.

"Really?"

"Yes, I have two symbols that I really like. You can come with me." He raised an eyebrow. "That is unless you're chicken."

"Don't start that shit, man. Let's go!" He practically skipped over to Ephraim.

Ephraim pulled out his wallet and handed over the last of his cash to Madison. "Ephraim, there's like two grand here."

"I know. That should cover everyone."

"That is more than enough to cover you and the kids and Grandma."

"And you. Go buy some clothes." She opened her mouth to argue. "Please just go buy whatever you want. I still owe you a birthday gift. So go buy some clothes."

"You didn't give her a gift? What happened to the ri-"

Ephraim's hand clamped tightly across Chris' mouth. "Let's go before I decide to take Joshua instead of you."

"Thank you." She pulled him down for a kiss. "But you need to stop or you're going to make me spoiled."

"I like spoiling you." He kissed the tip of her nose. "I'll see you later, baby."

She nibbled on her lip. "Are you really getting tattoos?"

"Yes."

"Where?"

"Oh, I think we'll leave that as a surprise."

* * * *

"You said you were only getting two tattoos," Chris said from his stool.

"I lied."

"Apparently."

"I decided on the third one when we stepped in here if you must know."

"I must."

Tall, Dark & Lonely

"You know I've been doing this for ten years" Ed, the man who was filling in the tattoo on his chest, said. "And I can honestly tell you that I've never had a client that stood for his tattoo, never mind two at the same time."

Jeff, the man who was filling in the one on his right shoulder, said, "I would have to agree with that. I like these designs, man. Celtic?"

"Yes, and I'll pay you an extra hundred dollars each never to replicate them for anyone."

"Wanna keep the designs original? I gotcha man. Don't worry about it. We don't use anything here that we don't have permission for. Plus, these damn tats of yours are so fucking intricate I would never be able replicate them anyway."

"I appreciate it, gentlemen," Ephraim said.

"I thought for sure you'd flinch or cry or something. You're really disappointing me, *Dad*." Chris was half teasing, but it was obvious that he really liked calling Ephraim that.

Ed looked up at Ephraim with a curious look. "I would have guessed he was your brother."

"Nope, he's my son."

"I'm adopted," Chris said proudly.

"Well, your Dad's a bad ass. I've had bikers who cry and squirm under my needle. Not your old man. Not one move."

"It hurts like hell, but I don't want to mess it up." He lied. He barely felt the burn of the needle. He'd learned long ago how to block out pain.

"Smart man. One fuck up and this would be totally messed up."

He frowned. "That's what I thought."

"So, Dad, where are you going to put the third one?" Chris asked.

"On my bicep."

"Really? If you think you can handle it, John should be back from his break in a few minutes. He can do that. Jeff, what do you think?"

"Hey, as long as everyone stays in their own space and he doesn't move, we should be good."

"Sounds good," Ephraim said. It really didn't hurt that much. The skin healed as they worked. Plus, he'd had worse from Nichols.

"You know I think you should skip the tribal tattoo on your arm and instead put fangs, bloody fangs, big ones." Chris grinned hugely.

Ephraim narrowed his eyes on Chris. Chris' hands shot up in a gesture of surrender. "Just kidding."

"You want an 'M' in the middle of the tribal band on your arm, right?"

"Yes."

"She might not like that," Chris commented.

"It's not for her. It's for me."

"Okay, whatever you say." He chugged his soda down. "Hey, can I get a tattoo."

"Not without your father's permission and even with that I won't do it until you're at least seventeen," Ed said.

"I can wait. Dad, can I?"

"We'll see how the grades and behavior are. If they're good then I'll take you."

"Sweet."

* * * *

Tall, Dark & Lonely

He groaned. What the hell was he thinking getting a tattoo with her initial in it? The woman hyperventilated just hearing the word "love" and here he was sporting a tattoo with an 'M.' She was going to flip out. He'd be lucky if she didn't kick him out of her bed for good.

A light snore caught his attention as he closed the hallway door. She was asleep thank god. At least he had a short stay of execution. The good news was he could catch up on his sleep and be well rested for the day of yelling that he was going to have to endure tomorrow. That was something at least.

After making sure that she was really asleep and not waiting to ambush him, he stripped out of his clothes and climbed into the bed. He curled up against her and pressed a kiss to her bare shoulder before drifting off.

With his teeth clenched and eyes still shut from sleep, he threw his head back and moaned. This was either the best wet dream of his life or Madison was riding him, hard.

Her hands roamed over his stomach and chest as she moved on him. She was moaning and panting loudly. "Oh, Ephraim! Mmm, baby, you feel so good!" Her body clenched and spasmed around his. She moved harder and faster on him until she was screaming.

Ephraim grabbed her, pulling her down on him and in one move had her on her back. He started thrusting into her. hard, setting off another orgasm and then another until he finally joined her. When his body relaxed he lowered himself on her.

"Good morning, Madison," he murmured, pressing a soft kiss against her lips.

"Mmmm, good morning, I was wondering how long it would take you to wake up and realize that I was taking advantage of you."

He chuckled softly. "I thought I was having the best dream ever," another kiss, "turns out I was having the best morning."

Her hand gently caressed the left side of his chest. "Did I mention that I like your tattoo?"

"Yeah?"

"Mmmhmm, it's very sexy."

He pushed himself up so he could hover over her. "Sexy, huh?"

"Mmm, very." She traced the black circular tattoo with her finger. "It's like a maze, is this Celtic?"

"No, but I guess I can tell you. It's an ancient Hebrew symbol with a slight variation." Holding himself up, he pointed to the symbol in the middle of the maze.

"Hey, I didn't even notice that until you pointed it out. That's really cool....wow...it's the same symbol Chris has."

"Yes, it's the Sentinel symbol. The design prevents anyone from seeing it unless it's pointed out to them or they know to look for it."

"So it will identify you? Can't someone else get the same tattoo and trick them?"

He shook his head. "No, take a better look at the maze on each side what do you see?"

"Words, but I can't read them."

"They're from an ancient language that was forgotten a long time ago. The Sentinel's don't even know what they mean anymore, but it's their motto and would identify me. No one other than a Sentinel knows these words."

"What if they told someone?"

"They wouldn't."

Tall, Dark & Lonely

"But you told me and I wouldn't have noticed them unless you told me. Aren't you breaking a rule?"

His eyes shifted and then took on a guarded look. "No, I told them that I would show you. You haven't told anyone my secret. They appreciate that."

"And if I told anyone those words?" She looked at his chest.

"They would take you."

"Take me?"

"Yes, but I wouldn't let them. Besides, there's nothing to worry about. You won't tell."

"No, I won't, but it's still unnerving."

"I know. I'm sorry. I won't tell you anything else then. I don't want to stress you out. You don't know the words anyway so you're fine."

"Okay."

"Just forget these are symbols and don't point anything out to anyone and you'll be okay."

"So, just let them think my man has really sexy tattoos?"

He groaned, "I like it when you call me your man."

She giggled and wiggled beneath him. "I can tell."

"Good then I won't have to stop and explain how much I like it." He began moving inside her again.

"Oh no you don't! I want to see the other tattoo." Her eyes went to his left bicep. "I didn't get a very good look at that one. Is it a tribal band?"

He pulled out of her slowly and sat on the bed next to her. "Yes, that one is a tribal one. No Sentinel symbols, but the one on my back is the one that identifies me as a Pyte." He turned, trying to distract her from his arm. It worked.

Her fingers ran over the tattoo on his back. "I don't understand why you need this tattoo. Won't they figure it out?"

"I'm wearing this one as a symbol of pride. I didn't have to get this one. The council was showing me some of the books to show me that four other Pytes had joined their ranks years ago and wanted me to see the good they were able to do. I saw that symbol in the book and they told me what it meant. I asked for a copy so I could have that put on my back. It has no hidden symbols and it isn't a secret."

She pressed a kiss against it. "Oh, sorry. Did that hurt? I forgot these things are supposed to hurt for a while."

"No, they don't hurt. I was healed before I left the tattoo parlor. The ink will never fade, thankfully. The damage done to my skin is already repaired."

"This one's sexy, too," she said in a low voice.

"Yeah?" He turned his head back for a kiss. She took his lips in a long sensual kiss before abruptly breaking it off.

"Wait, I want to see the third one and see if it's just as sexy as the first two," she teased.

"No, Madison, wait. Let me-"

Too late, she already moved around him. Her fingers traced over the tattoo and he knew from the way that her fingers shook and her breath caught that she was touching the 'M'.

"Madison, listen before you get mad I was just-"

"Is this an 'M'?"

"Yes," he said carefully.

"Is it..," she swallowed. "Is it for my name?"

"Yes." He prepared himself for screaming.

Her fingers continued to trace his skin until her hand was gliding over his arm, squeezing and caressing his muscles. "You know I'm really surprised."

"I know and I-"

"I really like it. I like seeing it banded around your arm." She pressed a kiss to his arm.

"You like it?" He couldn't disguise the surprise in his voice.

She took his other hand and brought it between her legs. "What do you think?" she moaned as she gently rocked her hips against his fingertips.

He sucked in a breath. She was wet, very wet and very swollen. "I think you better be prepared to spend a day in bed with your legs in the air," he growled as he pounced on her, pinning her to the bed in one swift move and entering her in another.

She was giggling hard until he started moving. Then those sounds of delight turned into sounds of pleasure.

Chapter 21

Don't puke, don't puke, don't puke, she chanted in her head. She took a slow breath and leaned her head against the cool surface of her desk. She sighed as the small comfort calmed her distress, slightly.

"Are you okay, Miss Soloman?" someone asked.

She looked up to see her class staring at her. "I'm fine. Are you done with your exams?"

Most of the class shook their heads. "Okay, you guys have fifteen more minutes. I suggest you use the time wisely. Remember, the highest grade doesn't have to take the final exam next week." That got their attention. They dropped their eyes back to their exams.

She turned her attention to her computer screen, trying to look busy. Her stomach rolled uncomfortably. Four days, four longs days of this. She was vomiting morning, noon and night. This all started when Ephraim left to go to Concord for a conference and training with the State Police.

Madison couldn't believe she could miss one person, a man for that matter, so much. Her appetite was gone and she couldn't sleep. She was love sick. There was no getting around it. She loved Ephraim.

Love.

For the first time in her life she was in love with a man. Ephraim was everything she never thought a man could be, thoughtful, kind, generous, funny and sweet. He was also calm and patient. For the past three months, he'd told her that he loved her without any resistance or expectations and he never once became upset or distant when she didn't say it back. Ephraim never even brought up how she felt. He seemed content with just telling and showing her how he felt.

Tall, Dark & Lonely

He was so unselfish that he made her feel like the biggest bitch. God, she didn't deserve him. She rubbed her hands over her face. Tonight, when he got home she would tell him and show him just how much she loved him. Perhaps dancing and a drive somewhere romantic followed by five or six hours between the sheets. Maybe she should make a romantic meal.

Maybe not.

Her stomach flipped over at the idea. She clutched her stomach and sighed with relief when the bell dismissed her class. Exams were dropped off on her desk as they made their way noisily out of the room.

"Free period, thank god," she murmured, pushing back her chair. She was going to hunt down a can of ginger ale and crash on the couch in the teacher's lounge for the next forty-five minutes.

"Madison!" Chris hissed from the doorway.

She could cry. She really could. "What?"

He ignored the irritation in her voice and took it as invitation to come in, shutting the door behind him. "Has Dad called you?"

"No, I told you last night that he called in the morning."

Chris looked upset. Actually, now that she took the time to really look at him, he didn't look good at all. His hair, which was short and usually swept forward was mussed. He had dark bags under his eyes. He forgot to shave and he was wearing the same clothes he wore yesterday for his date with Amber.

"Fuck!" He shoved his hand through his hair. "Is he still coming home tonight?"

"Yeah. Chris, what's going on? You've been acting funny since you came home last night. Did you and Amber have a fight?" She was a sweet girl even though she had a bit of a reputation.

His eyes widened. "What do you mean?"

"I mean, you don't have to wait for Ephraim to get home. You can talk to me you know."

He crossed his arms over his chest and looked around. "With you?" He looked surprised.

"Yes, me. You used to confide in me you know. I may not be a guy, but I can answer questions about girls, probably better than Ephraim."

His face paled. "I can't talk to you about this."

She didn't have the patience for this today. "Don't you have a class to go to?" she snapped a little harsher than she planned. Her head was spinning almost as fast as her stomach was.

Chris put his hands up in surrender. "Holy shit, I didn't know it was that time of the month, Madison."

Her temper erupted. "Chris, we are in school right now. You know that you are supposed to call me Miss Soloman, not Madison. And for your knowledge I'm sick. It's not my time of the month!" Something clicked, something not good. She sat back down and tore her desk apart, looking for her date book.

"Whoa, calm down, Madison! What's wrong?" Chris moved around the desk, ready to help.

"Aha!" She found it in her bottom drawer and practically ripped it apart opening it.

Chris's finger blocked her view. "What's that sad face mean?"

Madison pushed his finger away and looked. She swallowed as dread sank in the pit of her stomach. "That means I'm…" She counted from that date to today's. "Shit."

"What?" He looked worried.

Tall, Dark & Lonely

"I gotta go."

"Where?" He watched as she grabbed her purse, nearly knocking her computer off the desk with an elbow.

"I have something I really have to do," the words rushed out of her mouth as she stumbled out into the hall.

"Madison, are you okay?" Chris asked, catching up to her.

"Yes, no, yes, I don't know. I have to go."

"You're leaving school?"

"Yes, sick. Going home, good idea," she rambled.

She wasn't aware that he was still with her until she was in the front office. Mrs. Adams, the secretary, waddled over to them. "Good heavens, Miss Soloman, you're pale as a ghost. Is everything okay?"

"Going home sick," she managed to get out.

"Oh, I guess so. I hope you feel better, sweetie."

"That's not very likely anytime soon," she mumbled.

"What's that?" Mrs. Adams asked. "I didn't quite catch that."

Chris did. His brows pulled together as he looked her over.

"Nothing. I'll be back tomorrow." She gave the secretary a weak smile.

"And you, Chris, what can I do for you?" Mrs. Adams asked, looking him over and not happy with what she saw.

"I'm sick, too. I'm going home," he said.

"Not without permission from a parent or guardian."

He gestured to Madison. "You have it from her. She's my dad's girlfriend."

"But-"

"I'll see you tomorrow, Mrs. Adams," Chris said cheerfully. He had to run to catch up with Madison who was talking to herself.

"Just sick. Just sick. Just sick. Nothing to worry about. Just sick." She pulled her keys out of her purse with shaky hands.

"Oh no you don't. You're not driving." Chris took the keys from her hands.

"What?" She looked lost.

"Get in. Tell me where you need to go and I'll take you." He unlocked her door and helped her in. When he climbed behind the wheel her brain started functioning again.

"Wait, you don't have a license. You can't drive."

He turned the car on and threw it into drive. "Hmm, look at that. It seems that I can." She was shocked to see that he could and well.

"It's probably for the best if I don't know the hows or the whys behind your driving abilities." She held a hand over her eyes and tried to relax.

"Yeah, that's probably for the best. Now, where to?"

She bit her lip, thinking. That was a good question. She needed to know badly, but didn't want anyone to know. It was a small town after all. She didn't need this particular bit of news spreading.

"I need to go to a pharmacy," she said slowly. Yes, a pharmacy would do. She looked over at Chris. He seemed at ease behind the wheel. Hmmm, perhaps having him along would work out. "Chris, I need you to run into the store and grab something for me."

"Sure thing, what do you need? Cold medicine? Aspirin?"

"Pregnancy test."

Tall, Dark & Lonely

* * * *

"Are you crazy? I'm not going inside and buying that."

"Chris, we've been arguing about this for a half hour." She looked around the parking lot. "No one's around so just go inside and grab a test, a one minute test preferably."

"Hell no!"

"Chris!"

"No! If I go inside they'll think I've knocked someone up when I can't even....," his voice trailed off, shaking his head he finally mumbled, "I'm not doing it."

"Please!" She pouted.

"No, you go do it. You're the one who needs it."

"No! That's worse!"

He rolled his eyes. "How is that worse?"

She scoffed, "I'm a twenty-four year old single female teacher. How is that not worse?"

He raised a brow, still waiting for a reasonable answer. "If I get it, I'm a slut. If you get it, you're a stud."

His face colored as he looked away. She couldn't be sure, but he looked like he was going to cry. "Chris, are you okay?"

Chris cleared his throat. "I'm fine. Look, this is more important than my problems. You might be carrying the love child of a 206 year old bloodsucker who refuses to raise my allowance," he tried to joke. "I think this takes precedence."

They stared at each other for several long minutes, hoping the other would give in. Finally she broke. "Fine, will you go in with me then?"

"Will it make you feel better?"

"Yes."

"Sure thing. The worse thing that could happen is that people will think that you are carrying my baby. I'm sure it's perfectly normal for a female teacher to be with her male student at a pharmacy in the middle of the day, buying a pregnancy test. What could go wrong?" he asked wryly.

She opened her door. "Fine," she ground out. Damn it, he was too perceptive sometimes. This time it was probably a good thing. "Stay here. You know, you really are a brat and I'm telling your father to cut your allowance, you little traitor," she said out of aggravation. His hand shot out and gripped her arm, stopping her from walking away.

"Chris, I was just kidding." He ignored her and pulled her back into the Jeep.

"What?"

He nodded towards the front of the pharmacy. "Oh....no....is that Mrs.-"

"Stevens? Yes, we need to go somewhere else or she'll spread the news of your purchase everywhere by dinner time. She'll definitely call Grandma as soon as she leaves the store."

"Oh no," she groaned and looked over at him. "Do you feel like a drive out of town?"

He started the car. "I rather like long drives. We'll make a day of it. Shopping, peeing on a stick, and probably a little hyperventilating," he said brightly.

"Brat," she muttered.

Tall, Dark & Lonely

* * * *

"Well?" Chris yelled from the side of the road, startling her.

Madison jumped. "I haven't done it yet. Give me a minute. It's not easy to pee on a stick in the woods you know."

"Oh sure it is. You just unzip, pull it out and-"

"I meant for me, you jackass!"

"Ouch, I hope you don't use that language in front of the baby."

"Little brat," she muttered. After one last look back to make sure that Chris still had his back turned, she emptied her bladder on the stick.

"Please be positive," she whispered, surprising herself.

A baby with Ephraim?

She thought about it, not seriously. He wasn't even sure that they could have a baby together. It was possible, she guessed, but she never took it seriously. She never even considered birth control in the last few months they'd been sleeping together.

She replaced the cap and fixed her clothing before walking back towards the Jeep. Chris was walking around, anxiously and when he saw her, he came right to her.

"Well?"

"It will take another minute." She held up the stick. They both watched, waiting for the digital test to indicate her condition.

"Are you okay?" he asked.

"Yes, I think so. I just want to know."

He put his arm around her shoulders. "It will be okay. Ephraim is a good Dad and you're a really good big sister and you're all motherly so you'll both be fine."

"Thank you." Damn it, he was going to make her cry.

A small beep had them both sucking in air. "I guess we know our answer," Chris said.

"Excuse me?" a man said behind them.

They both jumped and turned around to see a large man with menacing dark eyes standing in front of a black van. Chris automatically pushed Madison back.

"Can we help you?"

He smiled. "Are you Madison Soloman?"

"How did you know that?" She took a step back, dragging Chris with her.

"Oh, no need to run, sweetheart. We're here to give you a ride," the man said.

"Chris, run!" she yelled.

Instead of running, Chris crumbled to the ground next to her. "Chris!" She dropped to her knees next to him. Blood trickled from behind his ear. She looked back to see what caused the injury when a sharp pain shot through the back of her head turning everything black.

* * * *

Madison was pregnant. It took every last ounce of his willpower not to tell her the morning he left. She looked so beautiful sleeping that he hadn't wanted to disturb her.

Tall, Dark & Lonely

He woke up with the alarm at three in the morning and to the change in her scent. It took him a good ten minutes to be sure. He ran his nose over her stomach several times, afraid he'd made a mistake. It took her swatting him away in her sleep to get him to move. He hated leaving her like that.

Now he was rushing back to her. He left the conference early this morning so he could surprise her. He needed to do this right. This was their first baby together and he had to make this right for her. She was marrying him that was all there was to it. He'd been waiting for months to ask her.

He'd been patiently waiting for her to be comfortable with him. Madison was comfortable with him where her body was concerned, god was she ever, but it was her heart that he wanted. Not once had he rushed her, never even asked her to say the words or how she felt. He didn't need to hear it, he knew she loved him. He hoped at least. Now he couldn't wait any longer.

As soon as he saw her, he was going to drop to one knee and propose before she found out about the baby. He didn't want her to think that was why he wanted to marry her. It wasn't. He loved her, worshiped her. She was everything to him. Now if he could only get her to see that.

Speak of the devil. His cell phone rang and he couldn't help but grin when he saw her name on his caller ID. "Hey, baby, you miss me?"

"My, my, my, Ephraim. I don't remember that being your pet name for me," a teasing, sultry voice practically purred.

Cold fear ran through him. "What are you doing with this phone?" he made his voice sound normal.

"What, no 'I miss you Caroline', 'I've been nothing without you', not even 'I miss fucking you'?" she said in a pouty voice followed by a shrill laugh. "Uh oh, seems Madison didn't like hearing the last part. Seems you forgot to tell her about us."

"You know me, I lose interest quickly."

"*Tsk, tsk*, such a shame."

"I don't think you have her."

"Don't you trust me?" She giggled.

"Hell no, you could have any number of minions snatch her phone. Put her on if you want me to even consider your plans."

"Very well, just for a minute mind you, we're not exactly done having our fun with them."

"Them?"

"Two for one roadside snatch job. I'm really rather proud of my boys."

"Prove it."

"Very well, just don't hang up afterwards. I wouldn't want you to miss out on the fun."

He waited for what seemed like an eternity to hear Madison's voice. "Ephraim?"

"Madison?"

"Ephraim, they have Chris, too!"

"Shh, it's okay, baby. I'm coming to get you."

"No! Ephraim, that's what they want. It's a trap! Don't do it!"

"Madison, I'm not leaving either one of you with those sick bastards. I love you and I'm coming for you. Put that bitch back on now."

"Please, Ephraim, don't-"

"Time's up," Caroline said. "If you want them, then come to the old mansion on Drewberry Street. Do you know the one?"

"Yes."

"Good, now remember the faster you come, the faster our fun can begin."
The phone went silent.

"Goddamn it!" He threw the emergency lights and sirens on and floored it.

Chapter 22

Madison and Chris huddled together on the floor as they watched the blonde hair, blue eyed bitch, as Madison liked to think of her, pace the cavernous stone basement. The bitch kept glancing their way, looking thoughtful.

"I'm going to get you out of here, Chris. I promise," Madison whispered.

Chris took her hand in his and raised it, shaking it gently until their chains made a soft clinking noise. "How exactly are you planning on saving me when you can't even save yourself?"

She glowered at him.

"Someone shut them up. I'm trying to think," blonde bitch said.

"If we're making too much noise, we'd be happy to wait outside while you think. Hey, I don't mind chilling in a car if it will help you," Chris said with his most charming smile.

Blonde bitch growled her frustration. "Shut up! Just shut up! The two of you have wrecked my plans!"

"At the risk of pissing you off and you tearing my throat out, I have to ask how exactly did we wreck your plans? You kidnapped us," Chris pointed out.

"I've been planning this for over a hundred and forty years."

"Bullshit, we haven't been alive for a hundred and forty years."

"Ah, Chris, she was talking about Ephraim."

"Oh." He gestured with his hand for her to continue.

Her cold eyes focused on Chris. "The only reason that I'm not ripping your throat out right now is because you're a Sentinel and you will definitely come in handy."

Madison froze.

Chris laughed. "Lady, you're confused. I don't know what you're talking about, but I'm not a Sentinel, whatever the hell that is."

Blonde bitch stopped abruptly to study him. "Don't play coy with me, little boy. I've been alive for over five hundred years and I can sniff out a Sentinel from a hundred yards away and you, boy, are a Sentinel. The only question at the moment is whether or not I have to worry about your mate coming to get you. That would wreck my plans."

"Huh?"

She rolled her eyes and walked over to them. "Let's see where we stand on the mate issue, shall we?" She grabbed Chris by the ear and yanked him up. "Ouch!" Releasing his ear, she yanked his shirt up and his pants and boxers down until they were barely covering his groin.

"Hey, stop that!"

Bitch laughed. "Oh, do calm down. It's not as if you can get it up so I wouldn't worry if I were you."

Chris went utterly still. Madison watched all the blood in his face disappear. "What are you talking about?" he spoke calmly with only a hint of a crack in his voice.

"That you can't get it up? Because I'm not your mate." She ran her finger over his mark. White smoke rose from his mark. She hissed and pulled her hand away, putting her finger into her mouth and sucking it gently before she said,. "The real deal. You are a Sentinel, let me assure you."

"What did you mean by the mate part?" Chris was focused like she'd never seen him before. His eyes never left the bitch.

She laughed. "Were you afraid that your manhood was faulty? Or was your fear that you didn't really like girls?"

Chris' hands clenched into fists.

"I am so happy to be the one to tell you this then, at least some good will come of my night since the two of you wrecked it. You, my boy, are a Sentinel and because of that your packaging only wants one woman." She held up her hand when he opened his mouth to speak. "Your mate was made for you and you for her. I promise you that if I ever let you out of here and you meet her that you'll be able to perform without any problems whatsoever and more importantly, you'll want her."

He nodded slowly as he sat down. "That's good to know at least." He avoided Madison's gaze. "Incidentally, I don't need to have that talk with Dad anymore." He looked thoughtful for a moment. "I believe I will need to have an entirely different talk with him though."

"Imagine my relief," the bitch said, acidly.

"How did Madison wreck your plans?" Chris asked as Madison took his hand into hers.

Bitch gestured towards Madison. "She's carrying his child. The child I want. Granted, it cuts some time off my plans, but now he won't come. He knows I won't hurt her until the baby comes and you are too valuable to me to hurt."

"So, you don't think he'll come?" Chris asked, relief colored his tone.

Bitch kicked a solid oak end table clear across the room, smashing it into the stone wall. "Of course he won't come. Not until the baby comes. That was the only thing I could use to get him to even consider my plan before. Now he has one on the way. He doesn't love women, he uses them. The bastard's cold. Nothing and no one mean anything to him."

"Then why did you think kidnapping us would bring him here?" Chris asked.

Tall, Dark & Lonely

"I didn't want you. My slaves fucked up if you must know, but I am rather happy now. It's not every day that I get an untrained Sentinel as a gift." She didn't know Ephraim had been training him and by Chris' amused expression he was slowly realizing what Ephraim had done. His lips tugged up into a smile, but quickly disappeared, hiding his reaction.

"Fuck!" She kicked the matching table and sent it flying across the room, crashing against the wall with a loud bang. "There's no way that bastard doesn't know she's pregnant. He has the strongest senses of anyone I've ever met. He probably knew the second it happened."

"So, he was using me?" Madison didn't believe it, but the bitch might.

The bitch laughed a cold superior laugh and leaned down, resting her hands on her knees. "Oh, did you think you were special? That he was ever going to love you? Oh, that is rich."

She straightened up and paced again, shaking her head in disbelief. "I'll admit that I wasn't sure what his plan was with you. He usually uses a woman and tosses her aside. Then it dawned on me that he was finally going to try and sire a child."

Her hands came together with a loud clap. "And now that baby will be mine."
She looked lost in thought. A feeling of dread came over Madison.

"And you think he'll want you? That he'll stay with you?" Madison asked slowly.

"Of course he will," she spat out. "Did you think he'd stay with you? You're aging even as we speak. Did you really think he was going to climb between your legs in fifty years and suck on your flattened tits?" She laughed. "No, he won't. Trust me. Ephraim is a cold bastard. He'll stop fucking you the second he loses interest."

"Is that what he did to you?" Madison snapped. Her anger overrode her fears for the baby, Chris and Ephraim. For the last few months, she forced herself to just enjoy the moment and forget about the future. She knew she would age and that he wouldn't. Knowing this woman could offer him something that she couldn't was the final straw.

"You bitch!" She stalked forward with her hand raised, ready to slap Madison. Chris moved in front of Madison, blocking her. Caroline growled and backed off. "Fuck this, cover them just in case."

Two of the men who kidnapped them stepped away from the bottom basement door. Each man positioned himself on either side of Chris and Madison, pulling out a gun and aiming it at their heads.

"Hey! I thought you said you needed us!"

"Oh, I do. There is something you should know. Ephraim is the coldest bastard I've ever met, but I'm the coldest bitch you'll ever meet. If I don't get what I want from him, I'll shoot you first, boy, then the bitch."

"What about the baby? If you kill her you'll kill the baby!" Chris pulled Madison closer, trying to get her away from the gun.

She shrugged. "He'll never die and he likes to fuck. I'm sure he'll knock someone else up soon enough. It won't matter if he finally gives me what I want."

"What's that?" Madison asked.

"Why, what every vampire wants of course, to walk in the sun and live forever." She giggled.

"If I had to deal with a bitch like you day and night I'd turn gay," Ephraim drawled.

Everyone turned to see him casually stroll into the room and plop down in an oversized chair facing them. He leaned back, his eyes never leaving Caroline.

Tall, Dark & Lonely

"How are you, Caroline? It's been ages," Ephraim said casually as if he was running into an old friend at the market.

"How did you get past my security?" Caroline demanded.

"Oh." He looked over his shoulder and waved his hand lazily in the air. "Killed them, you know how it goes," he said with a shrug.

"You killed my vampires and minions?"

"Yes, well the ones who didn't run off anyway. I have to tell you, Caroline, I am a bit disappointed in your selection. They hardly fought back."

"Holy shit!" Chris gasped.

Ephraim shrugged unconcerned. "They were standing between me and my property."

"Property?" Madison's voice sounded hollow even to her.

He ignored her. "So, what is it going to be, Caroline? Are you still hell bent on your petty revenge, is that it?"

"It's not petty."

Ephraim laughed. "You really need to get over it, sweetheart. I'm sure you've fucked plenty of guys and walked off when you became bored."

"Jealous?" She gave him a sensual smile.

"Not in the least. Fuck whoever you want, just don't touch my property anymore. You know the rules."

Caroline walked around his chair, running her hands over his shoulders. "So, which of your property do you want back?"

Ephraim's cold eyes ran over Chris and Madison. If he cared it didn't show. "Tell those assholes to lower their guns or I'll rip their hearts out."

She waved a hand and both guns were lowered. "That's fine, Ephraim, but realize that not even you will be able to get to them before they shoot and you most certainly won't be able to save them both. Now tell me, is it the woman or the baby that you want?"

"Does it matter?"

"No, not really. All that matters is that I get what I want and I don't care how it happens."

"Cut the shit and tell me exactly what you want. I know your little brain has been scheming for the last century."

"Hmmm." She walked away from him and stopped directly in front of Chris and Madison. "Lower them," she said firmly and stepped away. They watched as a set of thick chains lowered two feet from the ceiling in the spot she just abandoned. At the end of each chain was a thick cuff.

"What is that?" Chris asked.

Caroline smiled triumphantly. "I'm guessing from the look of fear on Ephraim's face that it's déjà vu."

Madison looked at Ephraim. His face was pale and his hands were gripping the arms of the chairs. He looked utterly terrified.

Caroline reached up and ran her fingers lovingly over one of the cuffs. "To answer your question, Ephraim, yes these are your old chains. I believe these were the very ones you woke up wearing on that faithful day. Of course, I had them reinforced and cleaned up. They're stronger, much stronger. Granted, it would have been cheaper to buy new ones, but where's the fun in that? I would have missed the look on your face and that is utterly priceless." She winked at him.

Tall, Dark & Lonely

She snapped her fingers and the man that hid in the corner stepped forward, pushing a cloth covered table. "It costs a little bit extra, but I do believe that I was able to recover all of Nichol's favorite tools." She pulled back the cover, revealing at least a dozen sharp barbaric looking instruments. "What I couldn't have repaired I had replaced and of course I've added a few of my own tools over the years in anticipation of this moment."

Ephraim remained quiet. His eyes moved over each tool, slowly. "You don't have to do this. You can get up and leave at any moment we both know that. I'll see you in nine months and we can further negotiate. Until then, I'm sure the boy and your whore will be very happy. I'll take very good care of them."

"Let me do this and I'll let them leave. A fighting chance you might say. She'll have nine months to run and hide and have the little bastard then a lifetime to hide the child from me. It will be her only chance and his as well. Or leave and you can come back for the baby and the bitch will be dead and the boy will be my new bitch."

"Ephraim, just go!" Madison pleaded. She didn't know exactly what Caroline had in mind, but she knew it wasn't good. He had to go. He had to. She wanted him safe and away from here and she never wanted to see that look of raw panic on his face again.

"Don't you dare leave Madison here, you son of a bitch! I don't care if you were using her. Don't leave her here!" Chris yelled.

Ephraim stared a moment longer before standing up. His face was white as a sheet. "I'm sorry," he whispered.

"You son of a bitch!" Chris screamed.

"I knew you wouldn't do it," Caroline said smugly. She didn't seem upset at all. In fact, she seemed relieved. Her eyes darted to Madison for a quick second and it became obvious. She was jealous and worried that Ephraim cared about Madison. Well, she just got her answer. Madison wanted to cry for herself, but she loved him too much even if he didn't love her.

Chris' grip tightened around her. "It's okay, Madison. I'll take care of you."

Ephraim turned around and stepped closer to Caroline. He gripped the bottom of his shirt and tugged it over his head, dropping it on the floor. Then he pulled off the cross necklace before she asked him to do it. "If I were you, I would make it last, because the very second that I escape you're dust." He reached up and clasped a cuff around his wrist. It closed with a sickening "*clink.*" He held up his other wrist and looked at Caroline. "You may do the honors."

With a smile, Caroline did just that.

Chapter 23

"Please stop!" Madison cried. She tried to pull free from her chains and go to him, but they wouldn't give. Chris grabbed her and pulled her back.

"Oh, don't worry, dear, he can't die." With a tilt of her head she considered Ephraim. "I believe I could do this forever."

Ephraim stood erect, looking ahead and seeing nothing. He didn't react. That was one thing he stopped giving to Nichols years ago, a reaction. The bastard might have had his fun torturing him, but he never gave him the satisfaction of a response after the first five years. He would do the same with this bitch no matter how much it hurt.

Holy fuck did it hurt. She was enjoying this too much. The wounds she inflicted on his face, neck and stomach hadn't healed yet and weren't going to for a long time. He was losing too much blood and couldn't heal fast enough. The sound of his blood dripping to the ground let him know that he was standing in a rather large puddle of his own blood.

He heard the whip crack through the air and the snap as it struck his skin. He ground his jaw. "No, please stop!" Madison screamed. When she wasn't screaming she was crying. It was killing him to have her see this.

She dropped the whip to the ground. "Well, that's not working. Let's see what else we have in our toy box, shall we?" Caroline said cheerfully.

She looked over the table and then back at him. A wicked smile tugged at her lips as she walked over to him and unbuckled his belt, slowly.

"What are you doing?" Chris demanded.

Caroline ignored him as she undid Ephraim's pants. He kept his eyes glued to a spot on the wall. "Oh, let's empty the pockets before we continue. Wouldn't want anything to get in our way, now would we?"

She reached into his pockets, making sure to give Madison a good view. Her hands reached in and pulled out his keys, cell phone and Madison noted, his sleek black Sentinel cell phone had a green light blinking. That was odd. It usually blinked red when he had a missed call or a voice mail. Green meant something else he told her. It took a moment before it came to her. He set off an emergency signal. She had to hide her smile as Caroline threw it on the floor with the rest of his things.

"Did you tell her about all the fun things we used to do together, Ephraim?" Caroline asked, taunting Madison who was sobbing softly as Chris held her.

Ephraim ignored her. "It's too bad all those times didn't make the baby we wanted, isn't it?" She smiled. "We must have fucked day and night. I have to tell you it came as a surprise to me that all that sex didn't make a child. I was told a male Pyte could reproduce with a vampire. I guess they were wrong."

For the first time in three hours Ephraim spoke. "Yes, from what I've been told they can," he chuckled weakly. "I have a secret to tell you, Caroline. Do you want to hear it?"

"Yes," she said cautiously.

He leaned forward until his chains tightened. "First off, I only fucked you twice so don't try to cause any bullshit and we both know the only reason I did that was because you lied and said that you could bring me to others like myself. Second, I never came inside you. In fact, I had a hard time keeping my cock stiff in that cold, dry pussy of yours. My palm felt better than what you call a slit. My seed never entered your body."

"Liar!"

"Am I?" He laughed. "Think back, how long did I last?"

Caroline looked like she wasn't going to answer, but then did. She was just as curious as Madison and apparently Chris.

"A minute. You said you were too excited."

Ephraim shook his head. "Chris, block your ears for a minute." Chris covered his ears, too afraid for Ephraim not to do as he asked. "Baby, on a bad day how long does it take me?"

Madison was torn between embarrassment and putting Caroline in her place.

"You're full of shit. You couldn't get it up more than once and you only kept it up for a few minutes at the most," Caroline declared. She ran her eyes slowly over Madison and then scoffed. "Besides, she's not one tenth as beautiful as I am. I doubt you could get it up without the help of a pump."

That did it. "Well," Madison tried to sound and look thoughtful, "you only last a minute, maybe a minute and a half-"

"I knew you were full of shit."

"-when I use my mouth, but I believe the shortest time was ten minutes when you had me bent over the front of your squad car in the parking lot behind the movie theatre." She shrugged and smiled. "The theatre was closing soon. We had to rush."

"You bitch!" She went to slap Madison.

"I thought you were going to torture me some more. I knew *you* were full of shit." Ephraim's weak voice stopped her.

Caroline turned around with a forced smile pasted to her lips. "Oh, I believe I have a wonderful idea. Let's see how long you last after all. Madison can time us."

He laughed weakly. "I would agree that being between your legs again would be torture."

She reached out and ran her nails down his already bleeding stomach and scratched her way down his body, leaving behind five fresh lines of blood behind. His stomach muscles clenched tightly.

"Why don't you tell me how I can be changed into what you are, Ephraim? I know your little secret. Your blood will kill me, but I know there's a way. Tell me." Her hand pushed its way inside his boxers.

Madison felt her heart breaking. She didn't want to see this. She didn't want to see him with another woman no matter what the reason. It damn near killed her when he finally reacted. He dropped his head back and gritted his teeth the way he'd done with her so many times.

Caroline began screaming.

"What the fuck?" Chris crawled on his knees to get a better look. "His pants are smoking!"

"Holy water, bitch," Ephraim ground out. "I knew you wouldn't be able to resist."

She yanked her hand out of his pants and began stumbling around the room while she stared at her hand. "Holy shit! Would you look at that?" Chris muttered.

Madison was looking. Caroline's hand erupted in flames. Seconds later, the flame was gone and her hand was a gray ash color. She stumbled into the wall. The bump was enough to disturb the ash that was once her hand. It crumbled to the ground. New screams left her mouth. "My hand, you son of a bitch! You took my hand away!" All that was left of her hand was a bump at the end of her wrist. Tears streamed down her face.

"That...will...teach   you....to   touch....what   belongs to...another...woman," he said, gasping. The pain in his groin was unbearable. He was burned pretty badly from the feel of it.

"Ephraim, are you okay?" Chris and Madison asked in unison.

He tried to nod. The motion triggered pain in his groin. The sensation shot to his stomach. His legs gave out, leaving his body hanging by the chains. He gasped before he began vomiting blood.

"Oh god, Ephraim!" Madison screamed.

"My hand!" Caroline screamed as she ran out the back door of the basement.

The two men holding guns looked nervous. The third man ran after his mistress.

"What do we do?" one of the men asked.

"We stay here! She'll be back!" The other man fidgeted nervously.

"Holy shit, I'm an idiot." Ephraim chuckled weakly.

"What are you talking about?" Chris asked. His eyes were darting between the two very nervous men. The guns in their hands were shaking. "Hey! Point that damn thing elsewhere before you accidentally shoot her!"

Ephraim sucked in a deep breath as he pushed up with his feet. Once he was standing erect he turned as far as the chains would allow. He studied the two men for several minutes before he realized what didn't feel right about this situation.

He cursed under his breath as he reached up and wrapped a hand around each chain until they were tight. The men watched with wide eyes as every muscle in Ephraim's body tightened and twitched.

"Stop or we'll shoot them!" the man standing over Madison ordered.

Ephraim exhaled before pulling again. This time a loud creaking sound accompanied the action. "No, you won't."

The sounds of guns cocking had Chris and Madison grabbing each other, trying to protect the other. "Ephraim, stop! He'll shoot her!" Chris yelled.

"Not with blanks he won't." A loud painful grunt erupted from Ephraim as he arched himself backwards and broke the chains from the ceiling.

The men turned in unison and began firing at Ephraim. He stumbled towards them, but didn't drop. Madison forced herself to watch. She scanned his body for bullet holes, but couldn't tell if there were any fresh injuries since his body was already covered with large wounds.

Another gunshot and then another. The sound was deafening. With each shot she looked for some kind of sign that he was hit, a jolt, a stumble, a sound, but there was nothing, no reaction.

"They're blanks," Chris whispered.

The two men seemed to agree. They threw the guns to the side and backed off towards the door their master had escaped through. "Go, I'm sure she'll be hungry." Ephraim dropped to his hands and knees, but didn't stop moving. "That's what you were, a meal. She wouldn't hire two idiots who'd never handled a gun before to keep them hostage. You were my meal. I'm an idiot."

"No, she loves us. She would never do that."

"Yeah, keep telling yourself that," Chris said dryly. "She just left you unarmed with a seriously pissed off Pyte. That's real love."

"Oh fuck!" one of the men whimpered.

"Go, just go," Ephraim said weakly. He didn't look at the men as he continued his slow crawl forward. He didn't stop until he dropped his head in Madison's lap. His arms wrapped around her waist. He pressed a tender kiss against her leg.

"Ephraim, oh god, Ephraim," Madison sobbed as she hugged his head to her body.

"We need to get out of here before psycho bitch comes back," Chris said. He jumped to his feet and looked up at the ceiling where their chains hung from. He used his chains to pull himself up to the ceiling. "They're on hooks!" he said excitedly.

"Can you get them off?" Madison asked, her eyes never left the back of Ephraim's head.

"I think so…hold….on….just a little-"

The front door to the basement exploded into the room, startling everyone.

"Shit!" Chris lost his hold and fell the short distance to the floor with an, *"Oomph!"*

Madison sobbed softly as she watched two men and two women in black fatigues enter the room with their weapons drawn.

One of the women spotted the second door and with a signal to the other woman, she moved towards it.

"A vampire with one hand and three of her followers went through that door over five minutes ago," Chris informed them.

The women nodded. "Eric, we're going to see if we can't catch up to them."

"Go," a man with short, spiky, black hair said. "We'll see what we have here." The two men walked over to them and began looking them over.

"This one is a Sentinel, unmated," the other man said after he quickly looked over Chris. He ran a hand through his messy blonde hair, sighing.

"Release him. What about the woman and this man?" Eric ran his eyes over Ephraim's torn and bloodied back. The other man grabbed Madison by the arm, yanking her to her feet. Ephraim rolled off her and onto the ground without a sound.

"Hey, be careful with her! She's pregnant," Chris snapped.

"Sorry," the man mumbled. He looked Madison over for bite marks. "One last thing," he said when he didn't find any. He pulled out a cross and pressed it to her forehead.

Nothing.

"She's human."

"Good, get those chains off her then," Eric said.

"What do we do with this one?" The blond man pushed Ephraim over. He pressed the cross to his head. "I think he's human."

Eric sighed as he bent over and pushed Ephraim's lips apart. "Pretty big fangs for a human, wouldn't you say?"

"Holy shit!"

"What is he?"

"He's some kind of bloodsucker." Eric looked Ephraim over.

"What should we do?"

"What you're supposed to do. Stake him."

"No, stop!" Madison pushed away from the man and dropped in front of Ephraim.

"Stop!"

"Oh great, a fang banger," the blond man said with obvious disgust. "Move. We have a job to do. I don't know what this creature has told you, but you are in very real danger."

"Ma'am, I really need you to move," Eric said as he tried to grab her.

"No! He's one of you! He's a Sentinel!"

"No, ma'am, he's not. He's a vamp or a demon," Eric said softly, probably trying not to frighten her.

Madison wiped her face frantically with the back of her hands. "No look." She pushed Ephraim over onto his back with great difficulty. Chris grabbed a shoulder and helped. "See?" She pointed to his tattoo.

"Ma'am, all I'm seeing is a bloody tattoo," Eric said calmly.

"What?" She looked closely only to realize that it was completely covered in blood. She used her hand to try and wipe it away only to smear it worse. She saw a large bottle attached to the man's belt and grabbed it.

"Ma'am, wait!" She didn't listen to him. She flipped open the cap and poured the liquid over his tattoo. The blood washed away, revealing his tattoo. Then she poured the liquid over his face, washing the blood away from his face and body until his wounds were visible against tanned skin.

"Wasn't that holy water, Eric?"

"Yeah," Eric's voice was shallow.

"Then why isn't he screaming and bursting into flames?"

"Because he's a Sentinel! I keep trying to tell you. Look at the tattoo! He's marked. He's a Pyte!"

"A Pyte? No fucking way." Eric stepped closer and looked over the tattoo. He ran a finger over the intricate design. "I'll be damned. He's one of ours. I haven't seen this mark in fifty years." Madison's brows shot up. The man didn't look older than twenty-five at the most. "I can't believe we have a Pyte. I thought that was make-believe shit. John, look at that." He pointed to the symbol in the middle of the tattoo.

"Please, help him." Madison took Ephraim's hand and hugged it. She was so tired, so utterly tired. "Please." She leaned over Ephraim's unconscious body and began sobbing. "Please, just help him."

Chapter 24

He woke up gasping for air. Someone was going to shoot her. Someone was going to take away his Madison. He'd waited too long. All those months of waiting until she was ready was for nothing. She was going to die.

"Madison?"

His eyes quickly adjusted to his surroundings. He was in her room and in her bed. His hand shot out to her side of the bed only to find it empty. He scrambled out of bed and rushed into the bathroom. Before he even opened the door he knew that she wasn't there. Ephraim ran through the bathroom and into his room, damn near sighing with relief when he spotted her.

Madison was curled up on the overstuffed couch that took the place of his bed, sleeping. The coffee table in front of her was pulled forward and covered with stacks of papers she'd been grading. He moved into the room and noticed her desk was completely covered as well. That was no surprise. She was notoriously untidy when it came to her desk, which was the reason why he insisted on separate desks when they decided to turn his room into an office.

Ephraim walked quietly over to his desk and turned the large chair around so that he could look at her. Right now she looked so defenseless and weak. His heart broke just to look at her and think about how close she'd come to death.

It had been a mistake to keep her in his life before he had Caroline handled. Europe had been a mistake as well. The Sentinels could have waited. There hadn't been any rush. Chris was safe and sound and he would have stayed that way if Ephraim's presence hadn't attracted a fucking Master and her slaves. He dropped his head into his hands. Why didn't he just go kill the bitch when she made her move back in January?

Tall, Dark & Lonely

He'd been an idiot. He let his heart and cock lead him around and now he had a sixteen year old boy on a Master's wish list. It was going to be a race against time now. He had to get Chris completely trained before it was too late. For the last few months he'd taken it slow, trying not to tip Chris off to his plans, but now he had to fucking scramble to get his kid in full fighting mode before they tried to snatch him again and they most certainly would try.

Caroline was a collector. She liked to have unique vampires and people under her control. He should know, he filled a very sought after slot in her collection for a few months over a hundred years ago. An untrained, unmated male Sentinel would be the key to her collection. Once she broke his spirit and his mind that is. Then he would be molded into one of her personal guards or an assassin. He would be perfect for either. Chris' protection would be training. That was the only thing he could do for him. Madison was a different story all together.

He looked up at her. She mumbled something in her sleep and turned over onto her back. Her hand came to rest over her womb where their baby grew. Her life was over as she knew it. That is if she survived the birth, which wasn't possible.

All his research years ago turned up frightening accounts. Impregnating a human woman was a very rare feat for a vampire. It happened maybe two or three times every century. Out of those few times it was very rare for a Pyte to be born, a child born of both worlds with unlimited potential. Most of the babies were either stillborn, killing the mother along with it or a natural vampire was born.

A natural vampire was no different from a regular vampire except that it was born, not made. The mother would also die from the birth. Only the reason of her death was different. She would die from blood loss when her unborn child would rip through the undisturbed womb and attack her heart, the source of the blood.

He already knew what Madison carried, a Pyte, their son. He made damn sure of that the morning he realized that she was pregnant. If he had sensed a natural vampire he would have dragged her to an emergency room and held a gun to the head of any doctor who refused to take it out of her before it was too late.

It was too late to do anything now even if Madison decided to terminate the pregnancy. He could smell the change from here. The womb in a matter of speaking had shut down. The baby's DNA triggered something in her body and there wasn't a weapon on earth that would be able to penetrate that womb. Their child was protected from *outside* interference. Its mother was a different story.

This should have been done months ago. Then he wouldn't have to worry about her day and night. It was frightening to think of all the little ways a human could come to harm. He'd never given it much thought before, because frankly he couldn't have given a damn.

Humans were disposable and easily replaceable in his eyes. They all died at some point or another. It was inevitable. He'd sat back and watched countless generations be wiped out only to be replaced by new ones. There was nothing he could do so he never bothered on an individual level. The only time he stepped in to help was for a monumental injustice.

The American Civil War had him traveling as a ship's cook to Boston back in 63'. After the war he stayed in Boston and took his first policing job. When he couldn't stay any longer he returned home to take up a position with Scotland Yard where he stayed until that one little mishap in November of '88.

He fucked up big time. He was supposed to make the arrest, not drain him, but what else was he supposed to do to the bastard when he was covered in blood? A mistake, it had been a huge mistake to go on duty without eating first.

Tall, Dark & Lonely

They stationed him in Whitechapel to keep an eye on the girls. He meant to get a bite to eat before his shift, but thanks to that notorious little shit all the working women were hesitant to go off into the dark with a man. So, when the little shit he was looking for literally stumbled into him what was he supposed to do? He drained him and tossed his body into a pauper's grave. After that he was too disgusted with his lack of restraint and gave up his human façade.

From there he hid out in vampire covenants, trying to figure out the meaning of his life. He was searching for something or someone. If he had only known the person he was looking for wouldn't be born for another century he would have done a lot of things differently.

He went from war to war, touring the world, looking for the one thing missing in his life. After the second war he found himself traveling back to the states where he'd been ever since, taking up rooms in boardinghouses all over the country. It wasn't much of a life, he was now realizing. Things could be so different for him now and he knew the reason.

Madison.

She could be with him from now on along with the children. They could enjoy life and travel the world. They could make a real difference in this world. He could be happy. They could be happy. He'd been so stupid to wait this long.

Now it wasn't just his happiness at stake, but Madison's life was very much on the line. She was in so much danger and not just from the birth. Caroline was a vindictive bitch as well as a collector. She hadn't taken rejection well all those years ago and his obvious affection for Madison just threw more gas onto the fire. She would not stop now until she had Madison and his son under her thumb.

He couldn't allow that. Madison was everything good in this world. She deserved a long, happy life. She wasn't going to pay for his mistakes or suffer alone for their love. He had to fix this.

She might hate him after this and he couldn't blame her. There was a very good possibility that she would never talk to him again. It would hurt like hell, but at least she would be safe. She would be alive and well. That's all that mattered. She could go on with her life and find another man, live her life and do whatever she wanted. It would hurt every second of every day, but he would find peace in her happiness.

He loved her too much not do this. One day she would understand. She would understand that he did this not only for her, but for their child as well. Their son would need her and he couldn't think of a better mother than Madison. There was no choice, he decided as he brought his wrist to his mouth and sunk his fangs in.

* * * *

Soft lips moved against Madison's. She opened her eyes and smiled. Ephraim was kneeling in front of her, half naked and healed. Not a bad way to wake up, she thought. He pulled his head back and looked into her eyes. He looked so serious, too serious.

"Baby, what's wrong?" she asked, moving into a sitting position.

"Do you know how much I love you?" he asked softly.

"Yes." She ran her fingers along his jaw. "I love you, too," she finally said the words. Instead of the reaction she expected, him taking her into his arms and making love to her until morning, he nodded stiffly.

"You do know that I would never do anything to willingly hurt you or put you in danger, don't you?"

He felt guilty over her abduction. She should have known that he would. "Ephraim, it's okay. We're fine." She took his hand and pressed it to her abdomen. "We're all fine."

His hand gently caressed her still flat stomach while he spoke. "Madison, I have to do something for you. I need you to understand that I've been planning on doing this for a long time now. I should have done it long before this happened. If I had, you would have been fine. Do you understand what I'm telling you?"

She didn't. "No, what's this all about, Ephraim?"

"You may hate me after this and I want you to know that's okay. I just need you and our son to be okay. Just understand that please," he choked on the words.

"Son?" Her eyes watered as she gave him the sweetest smile. She leaned in to kiss him, but he turned his face away.

"Please, Madison, don't make this harder for me than it has to be. I'll already be in hell after I do it."

Things he was saying started to click. "You're leaving me, aren't you? You think if you stay that she'll be after me so you're going to leave?"

"No, baby, I would never leave you. Besides, leaving you would only clear the way for her. Caroline is coming back for you. There's no doubt in my mind. She's more determined than ever now."

She laid her hand over his. "So, we'll sit down and figure something out. We'll figure it out together."

His eyes met hers. His brilliant baby blue eyes darkened into the fiery red she'd come accustomed to during their love making. "I've already figured it out. I should have done it months ago." He kissed her nose. "Remember I love you, Madison. I love you enough to risk losing you."

"Ephraim,-"

"Shhh, all that matters is that you and the baby will be safe." She didn't notice when his left hand gripped her left arm or even when his forearm pressed tightly across her chest. She did notice when he pushed her against the back of the couch and she couldn't move her arms or upper body. He had her pinned.

"Ephraim, what are you doing?" she demanded.

His expression was pained. "I'm so sorry, baby. I never planned on doing it this way, but now there's no choice. I am so sorry."

Something very wrong was happening. She tried to move, but he gave her no quarter. It wasn't until he raised his right hand that had been hanging by his side up to this point that she realized that something very bad was about to happen. Blood was streaming down his arm from a bite.

"I'm sorry," he said again as he brought his arm towards her mouth.

"No! Ephraim, please no!" she screamed. The arm kept coming. "Baby, please, your blood kills people! Please stop! Ephraim, no!"

"You'll be fine. I swear," he murmured. She started kicking him and pushing at him with her feet, but he was like a boulder, he didn't give under her assault.

She opened her mouth to scream one last time when he took advantage and placed his wrist against her mouth. She fought to close her mouth, but his wrist was firmly in place.

Sweet, salty liquid poured into her mouth. She closed her eyes and forced herself not to swallow. Her nose wasn't covered so she could breathe easily. The blood would collect in her mouth and when he pulled away she would spit the blood out and deck him. All she had to do was allow the blood to pool in her mouth and she would be fine, she told herself.

Tall, Dark & Lonely

She tried to scream when she felt his fangs slice through her neck. The move caused the blood pooling in her mouth to pour down her throat until she was practically choking. Tears burned in her eyes as his mouth pulled harder on her neck. Still, the blood didn't stop. She was forced to swallow it or choke.

He had to force himself to slow down. Her blood was so delicious. It sent his body into overdrive. He wanted more, demanded more and he had to force himself to relax. If he drank too fast he would drain her and the baby. He needed to do it slowly until he tasted his blood mixed with hers and then she would forever be safe from even him.

Madison felt Ephraim's teeth pull away long before his wrist left her mouth. He licked his lips and looked oddly relieved. "It's okay, baby, just a little more."

She tried to tell him to go fuck himself, but his wrist made that impossible so instead she settled for loud incoherent mumbles.

"Shh, it's okay, baby. You can yell at me later."

More mumbling.

"If it makes you feel better, you'll be able to kick my ass up and down the street after this."

Oddly enough that did make her feel better. He had a good ass kicking coming for his high-handed behavior. He chuckled lightly. "From the look on your face I'm guessing the idea pleases you." He pulled his wrist away and quickly replaced it with his mouth.

She could taste her own blood on his tongue. It made her stomach drop. She pushed him away. "Why?" she demanded hazily. She felt so tired. Didn't she just sleep? She looked past him at the clock. Yes, she had, for a good four hours it seemed. Why was she suddenly tired now?

Strong arms picked her up. She opened her eyes. When did she close them?

"Shh, baby, you're going to sleep for a while now. When you wake up, everything will be different. You'll be safe. That's all that matters." He pressed a kiss to her forehead.

"I'm so going to kick your ass, Ephraim," she mumbled.

He sighed unhappily, "I know."

* * * *

"Ephraim?" Mrs. Buckman called him as he walked towards the stairs.

"Yes, Eleanor?" He paused at the foot of the stairs.

Eleanor wiped her hands on a kitchen towel. "It's been three days, Ephraim. I think we should bring her to the hospital."

"I'll ask her the next time she wakes up," he lied.

"It's funny. I've been up there several times over the past couple of days and I always seem to come in right after she's fallen back to sleep."

"I think this fever is really taking it out of her."

Her brows pulled together. "If she's so sick then perhaps having Chris in there isn't the best idea. He could end up sick, too."

"He's just worried about her. He's hanging out in the office anyway so he'll be fine." There was no need to tell her that Chris was feeding Madison blood every hour on the hour through a tube to help with the transformation or that as a Sentinel he had natural strength to deal with her if she should wake while Ephraim was out trying to hunt Caroline. So far no luck. He only knew that she was still in the area.

Tall, Dark & Lonely

She crossed her arms over her chest and gave him one of her stern looks. It was the only thing that tipped him off to the real matter at hand. "About that, when exactly are you planning on making an honest woman out of my granddaughter? I'm not too happy that the two of you are sharing a bed. At least when you still had a room I could live in denial, but now you've forced my hand."

"Would it make you feel better to know that I decided to ask Madison to marry me four months ago and the only thing that stopped me from asking was her irrational fear that your daughter Emma created?"

Eleanor wiped her brow. "I was afraid it was something like that."

"I love her very much and already have a ring ready. The moment she says yes, I plan on dragging her in front of the JP before she can change her mind," he promised.

"No, that would never do," she said sternly.

He never counted on her disapproving of a quick wedding. "I have a friend who's a JP. You'll drag him here and I'll set up a quick wedding with the help of the kids. She's less likely to make a run for it if I'm guarding the door."

He chuckled. "Probably."

She nodded. "Okay, then you best get upstairs before your friend gets sick."

"Friend?"

"Yes, the young man who helped you into the house earlier this week after your car accident." That was how Madison explained his injuries when Eleanor stumbled upon them at four in the morning.

"Good. I need to talk to him. Thanks, Eleanor."

"Tell Chris he better get his little buns down here in one hour to set the table or there will be no dessert."

"I will." He was already up the stairs and heading towards their room. One thing he didn't need was a Sentinel involved in this. The council knew what he was donig and was turning a blind eye in his case.

They did not approve of changes. He swore up and down months ago that he would not change anyone else. He only had one person to change into a Pyte. After that his blood would not be as potent and anyone he changed would end up being just a slightly stronger vampire. An army of stronger vampires was a real nightmare for the council.

Now that he was expecting a baby they were ecstatic. They wanted to bring the mother-to-be into their ranks so they could get their influence on the baby early on. As it turned out, this would be the fourth infant Pyte they brought into their ranks. There were three boys in Ireland who were already under their protection.

Their parents were Sentinels. Out of a freak accident with a vampire attack, the female Sentinel who was pregnant at the time was turned into a Pyte. It never happened before in the history of vampires. A Sentinel always died from the attempted change, but the fetuses inside her womb somehow filtered her blood and turned her.

That's how he learned how to change Madison. The female years later turned her mate when he was dying. She wasn't sure at the time of how to do it, but she took a chance. It was the same as a normal vampire change with the exception that it lasted longer and they had to feed from each other at the same time. The key was tasting his blood in hers.

"Hold her down!" he heard Eric yell from the hallway.

"Are you crazy? You hold her down!" Chris yelled back.

"Shit," Ephraim muttered as he ran into the room, throwing the door open.

Chapter 25

"I'm going to kill him!" Madison screamed in his direction. She was standing by their bureau, holding a lamp in her hand. Her eyes were glowing red and a set of long white fangs hung in her mouth. She'd never looked more beautiful to him.

"Stop throwing things!" Eric snapped. That got Ephraim's attention. He looked around the room and noticed the broken glass on the floor along with picture frames, books, CD's, movies and his clothes. She was currently tearing his clothes out of the drawers.

Never a good sign.

The vase went flying in his direction. His hand shot out and caught it easily. He placed it on a table and stepped forward. Eric and Chris were each hovering in front of a door. Chris blocked her exit through the bathroom and Eric was behind him in front of the door he just walked through. They were probably hoping that she wouldn't realize that she could just jump from the window and not hurt herself, best not to tell her just yet.

"Look what you did to me!" she yelled.

"What? I think you look good. A mix between a vampire and a really hot model," Chris said.

She growled in his direction. Damn it, she was turning him on and now was not the time. He had to force Ephraim Jr. to stand down.

Her face turned swiftly in his direction with eyes narrowed. "Are you kidding me? This is turning you on?" She gestured with disgust to her face.

Eric chuckled behind him. He forgot that she would be able to smell every hormonal change in his body.

"I did just tell you that you look hot," Chris said offhandedly.

She screamed in frustration.

"So not helping, Chris," Eric said.

"Did he tell you what he did to me? Do you see this? That bastard did this! Look!"

Chris rolled his eyes. "Yes, we've already established that he did this to you. No need to keep pointing out the obvious."

She grabbed a handful of Ephraim's boxers and threw it at Chris who ducked out of the way.

"Damn it, Madison!" Chris said as he tugged a pair of Mickey Mouse boxers off his head.

"Baby, I know you're upset. I don't blame you. Can we just sit down and talk about this?" Ephraim stepped towards her, trying to get her to calm down.

The rest of his boxers flew in his direction.

"Talk? Now you want to talk about this? Why didn't you do that before you forced this on me? I hate you! I hate you!"

"I told you she'd be pissed," Chris pointed out.

"How very perceptive of you," Ephraim said dryly.

"Well, I did."

Madison turned on Chris so suddenly that she had the boy stumbling back against the wall just from her glare. "You knew he was going to do this to me? You did nothing to stop him?"

"No, of course not!" He frowned. "Well, I just assumed he would change you at some point, but I swear he didn't tell me or I would have talked to you. I swear. Madison. You know how much I care about you. He told me afterwards when he asked me to help take care of you and feed you blood while he went after-"

"You fed me blood?" she shrieked.

"Er, yes?" Chris licked his lips nervously.

"Oh my god, this just keeps getting worse and worse!"

"That's what you eat now. I assumed you knew that," Chris said.

She threw socks at the boy.

"Chris, perhaps now isn't the time to help," Ephraim said.

"Well, I don't know why she's mad at me! You're the one who did this to her!" he snapped.

"I hate you, Ephraim!" she screamed.

"Yeah, I got that." He sat on the edge of the bed and dropped his head into his hands.

"You should have asked me!"

"Why didn't you ask her? I mean, I knew you had to change her, but I think it would have gone easier for everyone concerned if you'd asked," Eric pointed out.

"I panicked. I wasn't thinking straight when I did it. I was so scared...I...I...just couldn't think past making sure that she and the baby were okay."

"Whoa, what do you mean you knew he had to change me? Why did you assume that?"

Eric ran a hand over his hair and sat down in the chair by the door. "You're pregnant with his child."

"So?"

"So, if it's a Pyte in your womb, which I am guessing it is because he didn't try dragging you off for an abortion, you no longer have a choice. The baby is set in your womb and protected. You can't have an abortion now."

"I don't want an abortion! This is my baby and I wouldn't hurt it!"

"Ours," Ephraim said evenly. "The baby isn't going to be human. Are you going to reject it?" he asked casually when inside he felt his heart twist with dread.

"Of course I'll love my baby. I don't care what it is."

"You would have if it had turned out to be a natural vampire. Then you wouldn't have a choice. I'd have a hundred Sentinels here to hold you down while we took it out of you," Eric said matter-of-factly.

Madison's hand went to her stomach. "You'd take my baby? Ephraim wouldn't let you."

"Yes, I would. If it had been a monster, I would have done it myself. A natural vampire doesn't have the same protection a Pyte has." He looked up at her. "Don't worry, our son is a Pyte. They'll leave him."

"Okay," she said slowly. "The baby is a Pyte, everyone is happy so why did you do this to me?"

"Besides the fact that Caroline and every vampire she could get her hands on is currently organizing to attack and take you?"

She swallowed hard.

"You will never survive the birth. I had to change you to save you."

"If you knew…" Her eyes darted to Chris and Eric as she blushed. "Why did you, *you know*," she stressed her meaning with those two words, "if there was a chance of getting me pregnant?"

He folded his hands in front of him. "Because I love you and I wanted a reason to keep you forever."

"No, you wanted a child. You used me."

"Baby, if that's what I wanted I wouldn't have to change you. I would just wait for the birth and be done with you."

"Wow, that's putting it coldly," Chris commented.

"But it's the truth," Ephraim said through gritted teeth.

"I want you out of here. I never want to see you again!"

He stood up and walked over to her. "Baby, just listen-"

She punched him, and not one of those girlie, sloppy punches, but one that would make any professional boxer envious. Ephraim shot across the room, slamming into the wall.

"Holy shit!" Chris yelped.

Ephraim struggled to stand up. He dropped back to the floor and spit a mouthful of blood out. "I guess I had that coming."

"That and more I promise you if you don't leave right now." She folded her arms over her chest. She had to stop herself from doing a little victory dance and running over to him to make sure he was okay. She still loved him so much, but what he did hurt so badly. This was a betrayal, plain and simple.

"I'll sleep in the office for now, but I'm not going anywhere." Ephraim pulled himself to his feet with Eric's help.

"Fine, then I'll leave. I have more than enough money to rent an apartment."

He shook his head, trying to stop the ringing in his ears. "No, you're staying here. You're protected here."

"I thought you did this to protect me. I knew you were full of shit!"

"They can't kill you now, Madison, but they can still hurt you. You can defend yourself well now, but once that baby in your womb starts showing you'll have a harder time fighting back," Eric explained. "If you're hurt badly enough, your body will destroy the baby to heal itself."

"Oh, then can't I move to a Sentinel house and be protected there until the baby comes?"

Eric watched as Ephraim's entire body started to tremble from rage. His eyes glowed red as his fangs dropped. There wasn't a Sentinel on earth who would willingly come between a male Pyte and his pregnant mate. "No, no one will protect you better than the father of your baby. You have to trust me on this." Eric took a step towards the door. "If you need me, give me a call," he said to Chris.

"No problem."

"I'm glad to hear that Ephraim is training you. I was worried that you were defenseless. Now I know better." With that, Eric took his leave.

"Dad, she fed an hour ago and there's still blood in the fridge so I'm going to the training room and work with the knives before dinner."

"That's fine just make sure you set the table. Your grandmother's on a war path." Ephraim managed to say through his rage.

"No problem." Chris looked at Madison who looked just as angry and ready for a fight. "I'm really sorry you're upset, Madison, but I'm glad you're going to be okay now. I was really worried about you." She nodded stiffly to him before he left.

Two angry Pytes stared at each other. No one moved. No one spoke. They were both too furious to do anything other than let the other one know they were pissed.

Tall, Dark & Lonely

Finally Ephraim spoke. "You can still eat food you know. The baby will need both human food and blood. It should solve any nausea you've been experiencing as well as help balance your hormones."

Her eyebrows shot up in surprise. "Really? I thought you couldn't break food down."

"I can't. You can while you're pregnant. Then our son will need both until he makes his change, or he'll be trapped in weak body until the transformation."

She nodded, accepting what he told her. "You know I hate you still."

He turned to walk out. "I know. Believe me I know."

* * * *

"Stupid man," Madison mumbled into her pillow.

"I heard that," Ephraim whispered in the other room.

"I know," she said testily. "Jackass."

He groaned. "Are you going to be quiet any time soon so I can get some sleep?"

"Jerk."

"I'll take that as a 'no'."

She tossed and turned, trying to get comfortable. Great, he even ruined sleep for her. He made her dependant on him to fall asleep. She needed his warm body to curl up against. She curled up on her side and hugged his pillow, hoping it would be a good enough replacement to allow her to sleep. It wasn't.

"Can't sleep?" his soft voice asked.

"Shut up. I hate you."

"Yes, so you keep telling me," he said dryly.

"Jerk."

She heard him move on the couch. He was just as uncomfortable as she was. That made her smile. Good. If she wasn't going to get any sleep then neither was he.

"Are you going to work tomorrow?" he asked suddenly.

"Yes, there's only one week of school left. No point in missing it. Not that it's any of your business what I do anymore."

"Just try not to bite anyone," he said mockingly.

She sat up in bed, growling. She grabbed his pillow, wishing it was him, and threw it across the room. "Jerk!"

"You know what I think?" he asked.

"What?" she snapped.

"I think you still love me."

"Ha!"

"You're pissed. I'll give you that, but you still love me and you know what else?"

"I bet you're going to tell me."

"You want me."

"Ha!"

"I bet your body is missing me right now. It needs me. Think about it, Madison. You know it's true. I've got your body trained to expect me four or five times a day. You haven't had me in a week. You're desperate for me."

"Wow, someone sure thinks highly of himself. I can assure you that sex with you is the last thing on my mind." And it wasn't until he mentioned it. Now she was thinking about it. Damn him!

"You want me, Madison. Admit it."

"Ha! I think it's you that wants me!"

"Oh, you have no idea how badly I want you at this moment," he growled. "I want to come in there and yank that sheet away from you and tear your panties off with my fangs. Then I want to ram my tongue into you over and over again the same way I'd fuck you and I wouldn't stop pounding into you until you squeezed me dry."

What was she supposed to say to that? He sounded so intense that it sent shivers through her body. She wanted him so badly now that she had to squeeze her legs together, hoping to stop the ache.

He chuckled deeply. "Now I *know* you want me."

She turned and buried her face in her pillow. "Jerk!"

Chapter 26

Madison stared in the mirror with her handy tweezers ready, but there was nothing to tweeze. Nothing. It had been three weeks since the last time she tweezed her eyebrows and by now she should have caveman brows, but no, they still looked as they did the morning she was abducted.

She tossed the tweezers onto her small, but expensive, pile of useless cosmetics that she no longer seemed to need. Her skin looked healthy and radiant. She couldn't find anything to touch up or that needed toning. Damn him, she thought as she picked up her pink razor and tossed that onto the pile.

After her forced transformation she decided to stop shaving in hopes that he would be repulsed enough to stop leering at her every time they were in the same room. It should have only taken a few days to grow some decent stubble, but her new change took care of her need to ever shave again. She wondered if her body was frozen as in death from the transformation, never changing.

That thought ended a week ago when she realized that her hair was still growing. Her body it seemed was selective on what changed and what didn't. When she decided to ask Ephraim, one of the very few times she'd spoken to him over the past couple of weeks, the jerk had the nerve to run an appreciate eye over her body.

None of this made sense since he still shaved. She knew he did. A few times she'd shaved him herself. According to Mr. Highhanded, the body would keep itself in what it deemed perfection. Hair and facial hair were things of added beauty. A Pyte's greatest weapon was its ability to attract its prey. So, the body kept itself accordingly.

Not that she was complaining about having an hour a day freed up, but she really was. She didn't like this at all. Her life was changed forever because she fell in love with the wrong man. The only thing good that came out of this was the baby.

Tall, Dark & Lonely

She never thought she would want a baby of her own after raising Jill and Joshua. Joshua still had eight more years before he would be out on his own. She always thought when that time came she would be free to live her life and do what she wanted. Now it seemed that another ten years would be added to her timeline. Not that it mattered in the grand scheme of things now. Thanks to that highhanded bastard she had eternity to live her life. She groaned aloud, no doubt after the first century she would get bored and settle into a life of soap operas and bonbons, correction, blood filled bon bon's. The jerk.

At least it was summer time and she had the next two months off. Her days were filled with sunbathing, swimming and walking. Oh, and of course sneaking away so she could drink a few pints of blood. She learned early on that the more she drank, the more self-control she had.

The first day had been hell sitting in a classroom full of hormone driven kids. Every kid gave off a different mouth watering aroma. It had taken everything she had not to jump over her desk and partake of the buffet. Stupid Ephraim. He had the nerve to show up during her free period with five bags of blood for her. Stupid thoughtful jerk.

He was always doing stuff like that. Whenever they were in the pool swimming, which she never invited him to join her, the kids did, the traitors, he always brought two coolers. A large one filled with juices, waters and sodas for her and the kids and the other was small and locked, filled with bagged blood. He always distracted the kids so she could go off and drink. He never fed until she did and never until he made sure she drank as much as she wanted.

At night he hummed a lullaby in the office for as long as it took for her to fall asleep. He was attentive and sweet when it came to her comfort and care. Other than that he seemed to avoid her just as much as she was avoiding him. It was annoying. She was supposed to be mad at him not the other way around. She was the one who was changed against her will, forced to live a life of a bloodsucker, albeit a bloodsucker with really good pores, but a bloodsucker nonetheless.

340

The bathroom door off the office opened and Ephraim, naked as usual, stumbled into the bathroom. She kept her back to him and pretended he wasn't there, which was their normal routine. Her eyes followed his movements of their own accord and dropped down to his hips. Her mouth watered as it did every time she saw him naked and fully erect. She was starting to think that he was doing that on purpose.

Her hands gripped the edge of the counter tightly as she tried to force her mind to think of puppies and kittens playing with a ball of yarn, anything to keep her mind off of sex. She might lust after him, but that didn't mean he needed to know.

Ephraim chuckled as he passed her. Damn it! The man was irritating as hell! In another week that smug grin would be wiped off his face and he would give in. This surely was a battle of wills at this point. Neither was talking to the other more than what was absolutely necessary. They also seemed to be doing their best to aggravate and tease each other. It was really pissing her off. This was a game and she was not going to lose. She hated to lose so she would start doing what any sane woman in this situation would do.

Cheat.

She would have him on his knees in a week begging for her forgiveness. He'd already apologized and in the back of her mind she understood and even appreciated what he'd done for her and their son, but she was still hurt by his methods. He really scared her that night. It could have been done so differently. That was what hurt the most. The fear and the bitter loneliness she felt while he was doing it.

Madison loved him. Hell, she adored him, but he had to learn that he couldn't treat her like that ever again. She wasn't some child to be handled. He hurt her. He was the one man she trusted above everyone else, the only man she ever trusted, and he did this to her without her permission. She would forgive him, but only on her terms.

Tall, Dark & Lonely

Ephraim was busy relieving himself when she put the first part of her plan into motion. He had a routine that he never faltered from. He woke up, drank two pints of blood, relieved himself and took his shower before he did anything else. Nothing came between him and his shower.

Last week when the city had to shut the water off to fix the main he sat on the bathroom counter for four hours, waiting for the water to be turned on. It seemed to be his weakness, well one of his weaknesses. With a coy smile, Madison stripped out of her tee shirt and pajama pants and stepped into the shower. She turned on the water and smiled. He was going to be rip roaring mad. She looked forward to it.

"Pass the soap?" he asked from behind her.

She shrieked and jumped. How did he do that? She had super sensitive hearing thanks to him and he kept sneaking up on her. After she was done being mad at him and he sufficiently groveled, she would have to ask him to show her how he did that.

"Stop doing that!" she snapped. It was hell on her nerves. It really was.

He yawned loudly. "Sorry," he muttered. He reached past her for the soap, brushing his stomach and other *things* against her. Then he stepped back as if it was nothing. Her body on the other hand was on fire now.

"Ephraim, what are you doing in here?" she asked, making sure to sound put out.

"A shower. What does it look like? You know I always take a shower first thing in the morning."

"But *I'm* in here," she pointed out irritated.

"Hmm, so you are. How about that?" he said in an amused tone.

She looked over her shoulder, giving him her best scowl. "Get out."

"Of course, how rude of me."

"I agree. Now get out."

"I'm leaving….right after my shower," he said with a straight face.

She groaned. "You can't be in here. I'm naked!"

His eyebrows pulled together as his eyes ran down her body, slowly. "Look at that you are. Hmm, imagine that."

He lowered his head over her to wet his hair. When he straightened again he wiped the excess water off his face. Since he was no longer looking at her, she decided to give up glaring at him and finish her shower. This match was lost.

Ephraim watched as the water ran down her smooth, darkly tanned skin. Her skin reminded him of mocha, it was only a touch darker than his own, but he liked it nonetheless. Toasty, that's what he thought of when he saw her skin. It looked warm and inviting and in fact it was. He missed holding her at night. He longed to hold her in his arms with her bare back warming his stomach while her very delicious bottom kept his pelvis snuggled in heat.

Every time he thought of sucking up his pride and apologizing and begging for her forgiveness she would say the phrase that broke him, "I hate you." She didn't mean it. He knew that, but those three little words were enough to keep him at bay. They hurt more than anything.

He'd heard those words hundreds of times before, probably thousands of times if he was being completely honest with himself. While his brother was alive, Ephraim had been a cold bastard to the women who shared his bed. Shared was too generous of a word. They only spread for him so he could give them pleasure. Once that was done he left. He'd never slept with any of them. That was too personal. It made him feel weak and scared to give that trust to anyone.

After Marc died, he turned into the cold bastard Caroline came to know. He didn't care about anyone or anything except what he wanted, company from his own kind. He didn't care if it was a human child he created or another Pyte, he just didn't want to be alone anymore.

Tall, Dark & Lonely

The only person who could manage to handle him and put him in his place was Eleanor Buckman. She'd seen through his bullshit the first day and let him know it. She never quivered away from his temper. Her stubborn brown eyes would set and her fists propped on her hips while she would wait for his little tirades to finish then without a word she would reach up and slap him upside the head. Was it any wonder that her granddaughter would be the only other woman able to manage him?

"Madison, you have tree pitch on your back from yesterday," he lied. He wanted to touch her, needed to touch her without giving into her demands. If they were going to settle this it was going to be on equal terms. He wasn't about to spend eternity whipped. Well, anymore whipped than he already was. A man had to draw a line.

Her hands shot back, trying to find the phantom sap. "Where?"

He ran his finger in the middle of her shoulders where he knew she wouldn't be able to reach. She knew it too. "Here let me."

"Fine," she said evenly.

Ephraim had to work on not grinning like an idiot while he soaped up his hands. He was going to touch her again, on his terms. She looked back over her shoulder. "Just the tree sap, nothing else."

"Nothing else," he repeated in a bored tone. She studied his face a moment longer before turning around.

His fingers itched to grab her, caress her, and squeeze her, but he had to behave. He started by gently rubbing a circle over the area. "Is it coming off?" she asked.

"Nope." He was going to drag this out until he got his fill of touching her. Three weeks was too much.

He spread his hands over her back so he could use his thumbs to caress the area. Her breath caught. Damn, it felt good to touch her. After a few minutes he decided this was not enough. "Oh, I missed some."

"Huh?" she said in a daze.

"Hold on, I'll get it." He gently ran his hands over her back, caressing every bit of skin. Madison's breathing sped up as his hand moved down to caress her bottom. Before she could register the touch, his hands moved back up. Then he slowly reached around until he was caressing her stomach in a circular motion.

She could feel his hot breath on her nape. "Better make sure there's no sap over the baby," he whispered near her ear.

She could only nod, it made sense, she thought. Better to be safe than sorry. There was nothing worse than sticky sap on skin. He was just helping her out that was all.

His hands moved up and cupped her breasts. Her nipples were already hard from his attentions. He rubbed her nipples between his fingers pinching and teasing them as his mouth found her neck.

He sucked and licked her skin slowly, sensually. Madison licked her lips and dropped her head back against his shoulder. "What are you doing, Ephraim?" Her voice sounded dreamy.

"There's some sap on your neck. I'm cleaning it." He used his hold on her breasts to pull her firmly against him. "I think there's one other spot that I've neglected."

She gulped nervously. "There is?"

"Mmhmmm."

Tall, Dark & Lonely

He kept one breast firmly in hand as his other hand smoothly made its way between her legs. Ephraim used his foot to push her legs open for his intrusion. A long finger ran across her slit, teasing her until she moved her legs further apart to give him more room. He slid his finger in, teasing her little, swollen nub.

Madison moaned softly as he ran his finger over the nub, teasing it until it was swollen almost painfully. She gasped as his finger slid inside of her. His tongue traced a line to her earlobe and then flicked it, making her groan and move against him.

As he worked a second finger into her, Madison reached up and grabbed his hair, yanking his mouth down to hers. He eagerly took it. While their tongues wrestled for control his fingers thrust inside of her, hard. Ephraim ground his erection against her ass, forcing her to move against his fingers.

The sensation of his hand on her breast, tongue in her mouth, fingers inside of her and his large hard shaft sliding against her bottom was too much. Madison screamed into his mouth as her body gripped his fingers. He moaned along with her.

"That's it, baby, come for me," he whispered against her mouth. She screamed again as another orgasm hit her harder than the last one. "Tell me you miss me…tell me that you love me…."

"No," her voice cracked.

"Tell me!" He began thrusting harder against her, sending her towards another orgasm.

Her pride found its way to the surface. She was not going to give in no matter what he did. He'd been wrong, not her. This was not the way this was going to end. Even as he had her on the verge of another mind blowing orgasm she set her heels into the ground. "No! I hate you!"

She stumbled forward and had to put her hands out to stop from falling. Confusion set in. The absence of his touch from her body was so sudden. She looked back, expecting to see him ready for another argument, but he was gone. The bathroom door slammed shut, making her jump as dread filled her.

* * * *

"Too far," he bit out as he walked down the hall, towards the front stairs. She'd pushed him too far this time. He rounded the corner, never relenting in his fast stride.

Chris was in the hallway, wrestling with Joshua. He stood up with Joshua hanging over his bare shoulder and whirled around. Joshua laughed gleefully. "I'm getting dizzy!"

"Body slam!" Chris roared playfully.

Joshua yelped in alarm. "No!"

Chris pretended to break the giggling child over his leg. When the boys noticed Ephraim's presence they sobered immediately.

"Dad, what's wrong?" Chris placed Joshua gently on his feet. Joshua staggered drunkenly around until Chris placed a hand on his head and held him still. The little boy's thin bare chest was heaving from exertion. The men of the house seemed to go around half naked all the time now. He never could have pulled it off when Eleanor owned the house, but now that his name was on the deed she didn't say a word. Soon Chris and Joshua joined him. The only time Eleanor put her foot down was at the table. The boys were expected to come to meals fully dressed.

"Nothing. Do you feel like a work out?" He was full of rage and needed to work it out.

"Er, normally yes I would love to, but you look like you're ready to tear something apart and no offense, Dad, but I don't want to be the rag doll."

Nothing was going his way today. "I'm not going to hurt you. I just want a workout."

"I'll workout with you, Ephraim!" Joshua said cheerfully. They let him come down to the basement just to appease him now and then so he would feel like one of the guys, but he was not allowed down there during serious workouts.

"I don't know, little man. You're brutal. I'm afraid you'd hurt me." Ephraim cowered back from the boy.

Joshua grinned hugely and charged at him. Ephraim caught him around the waist and hung him upside down. He swung him gently from side to side like a pendulum. "If I take most of it out on the weights and bag first, will you come down for a workout?" he asked Chris.

Chris tapped his chin thoughtfully. "You know what I'm thinking, don't you?"

He was almost afraid to ask. "What?"

"If I had some tattoos I could go down there and not have to worry about any bruises showing from the ass whooping you're bound to give me."

"So, you're willing to go one on one right now if I bring you to get a tattoo?" he asked, chuckling.

"It does seem fair."

"You know what else sounds fair?"

"No, what?" Chris asked warily.

"That we stick to the original deal and I take you next November when you turn seventeen. I'll even pay for the tats."

Chris seemed to think it over. "Can I get two?"

"If you don't cry like a girl after the first one you can have a second one. That will be your birthday gift." Chris was turning seventeen and would need a car, especially for patrol. "Well, one of your gifts anyway."

"Okay." He nodded his agreement.

"Ephraim, can I get a tattoo, too?" Joshua asked between giggles.

"When you're seventeen."

"Oh man! That's like seven years away!"

"If Chris doesn't mind, you can come with us, but you can't tell any of the women, okay?"

"I won't tell, but you just did," Chris said.

Madison's scent drifted towards him. He turned around to see Madison watching them with an amused expression. "Why don't you boys go downstairs and get a snack. I need to talk to Ephraim."

"Come here, squirt." Chris took Joshua by the ankles and carried him down the stairs that way. They could hear Joshua giggling and pleading with Chris to put him down all the way to the kitchen.

"Eph-"

He held up his hand, still listening. "It sounds like the boys have just found your stash of candy bars."

She waved the comment off. "I don't care about th- they're touching my chocolate?" She was momentarily distracted. She'd been looking forward to her collection of Mounds bars and peanut butter cups.

He pointed to his ear, indicating that she should listen. "You hear that?"

"Yes, those little punks. They should know better than to come between a woman and her chocolate."

"I'll buy you more."

She stomped her foot. "I don't care about the chocolate. I want to talk to you!"

He turned his back on her and headed down the stairs. "So you can tell me you hate me again? I can never get enough of that," he said dryly.

"Would you please stop?"

"No, just say what you need to say and get it over with. I'm warning you, I will snap if you tell me you hate me one more time."

Madison slammed into his back when he suddenly stopped at the bottom of the stairs. He turned around to steady her. "Are you okay?"

She didn't hear him as a really annoying sound teased her too sensitive hearing. "What is that sound?"

Chapter 27

"Crying and by the sound of it, somebody's doing a piss poor job of faking it." He knew who it was of course. The scent of cheap perfume that tainted the air told him.

He headed for the closed parlor doors and yanked them open. Eleanor sat on the love seat looking at a loss while she watched Candy sob theatrically into her hands.

"Mama, I need to come back just for a little while. Things just went a little badly."

"Emma, things didn't go badly for you. It's all over town that he found you in bed with another man," Eleanor said in a strained voice.

"But what did he expect?" Candy wailed. "He left me alone every day and I got lonely."

"Work, Emma. It's called work. That's where he went. If you had kept your job then you wouldn't have been so bored."

She sniffed. "They fired me."

"Please tell me you didn't get caught stealing again."

Emma sat up, wiping at her eyes. "Just a misunderstanding. They simply miscounted."

"I really don't know what you expect from me, Emma," Eleanor said, sounding exhausted.

"Well, I was hoping to come back here for a little while. I just need time for myself to refocus and find myself, you know? I just really need to get in touch with who I am so I can get on the right path and do something with my life."

Tall, Dark & Lonely

"You really expect to come here after you left your children high and dry? You didn't even care where their next meal came from. For all you knew these last five months they could have been on the streets, scrounging for food."

"Oh, mama, you're being so ridiculous. I knew you would never let them go hungry."

"I'm sure you did," Eleanor said tightly.

Emma stood up, smiling and probably thinking she'd won. "I'll just go get my stuff. Since those people moved out I'll take a room at the other end of the house, you know so I can have some privacy."

"I wouldn't bother getting your things." Ephraim's deep voice echoed in the small room.

Both women turned to look at him. Eleanor looked embarrassed while Emma's eyes ran over his naked chest, hungrily. Neither woman could see Madison. She was in the foyer, leaning against the wall and trying to reign in her temper. Her eyes were squeezed shut and her tongue ran over her fangs, trying to send them back the way Ephraim showed her. It wasn't working. With each word that left Candy's mouth her temper flared.

"Hey, Ephraim, looking good," Candy purred. The red in Eleanor's face deepened.

"As I'm sure you're well aware, I purchased the house off your mother months ago so you can stop badgering her."

"Oh?" She sat back down and crossed her legs slowly as she leaned back, giving him free reign to look her over.

"Yes."

"Well, maybe you and I can come to some sort of....arrangement?"

She was going to kill her. That was it. Madison was going to bitch slap her mother. After all the years of sacrifice this was how she repaid her eldest daughter by hitting on her man? She opened her eyes and took a deep fortifying breath.

"Madison, what's-*whoa*!" Chris came to an abrupt halt in the foyer.

"Wow! Can I get contacts, too?" Joshua asked excitedly. "That is so cool!"

"Maybe later, little man." Chris tried to play it off.

"Oh, fangs too! Cool!"

"Oh no," she mumbled, wincing at her brother's excited expression.

"Yeah, she looks cool, huh? Why don't we go upstairs and play a video game?"

"In your room? You have the best games. Da- I mean Ephraim won't buy me any of the cool ones."

"Sure, in my room." Chris herded the boy to the stairs and threw Madison a look that inquired if she was all right. She nodded.

She closed her eyes again. That was too close. Thank god it hadn't been Jill. She would have flipped out into hysterics.

Ephraim didn't say anything for a long moment. He was too busy listening to the conversation in the foyer. That had been a close call. Everyone would have to be told sooner or later what they were and what Chris was. It was imperative for their own safety that they had the facts. But they were children and Eleanor knew nothing of the real world that she lived in. She had no idea that she shared this world with the likes of him. She would soon enough.

Emma was on her feet again, walking towards him. "Why don't I go pick out my room and you and I can discuss the terms of my stay?" She licked her lips invitingly.

Tall, Dark & Lonely

"Don't you have any pride, Emma?" Eleanor asked in disgust.

Candy shrugged uncaringly. It seemed she was done playing nice for her mother. She saw a new mark. From the look on her face and her body language she had every intention of getting what she wanted.

Ephraim gently pushed her away when she stepped too close. "Emma," he said it because he knew how much she hated it, "I'm with your daughter so your little offers are wasted."

Candy laughed haughtily. "She's just a girl, Ephraim. You need someone with experience, someone who will please you."

"Emma!"

His jaw clenched tightly. "Come on, Ephraim. Let's go talk about it. Shall we?" She reached for his hand, but he drew away and stepped back.

In a restrained voice, he addressed her. "Emma, let's be perfectly clear, even if I wasn't with your daughter, you would never catch my eye." That didn't seem to disturb Candy. She continued to smile knowingly at Ephraim. She seemed to think her charms would work at attaining what she wanted, free room and board and maybe some cash.

"I am in love with your daughter and when she stops being so damn stubborn I plan on asking her to marry me. I've had the ring ready for months now," he said the last part for Madison. Her gasp was rewarding enough so he continued now that he made his feelings known on the matter.

"As far as you joining this household, there's not a chance in hell that is going to happen. I don't think it would be good for Joshua and Chris to be around a woman like you and I know from what happened with Jill in New Mexico it certainly wouldn't be good for her." Eleanor's brows creased in suspicion. He'd forgotten that she didn't know about her daughter shoving her youngest granddaughter towards a thirty-five year old man.

She scoffed, "They're used to me. When I lived here we barely spoke so that's nonsense. They don't care what I do. There's no reason I can't come back."

Ephraim ran a hand through his hair in aggravation. This woman was really trying his patience. "Fine then! You're not coming back here because I do not want you near my baby. There is no way in hell our baby is going to be subjected to someone as selfish and depraved as you!"

Emma recoiled as if she'd been hit. "You've made me a grandmother?" she shrieked as it was the vilest thing in the world.

He ignored her and the choking sound of outrage coming from the hall and focused on Eleanor. She suddenly looked every day of her fifty-eight years. It looked like she'd finally been beaten. Ephraim didn't have to ask to know why.

She thought she failed. Her granddaughter was unmarried and pregnant. History was repeating itself and she was helpless to stop it. She didn't want to see another child go through life without a real family, without love.

Ephraim took a knee in front of Eleanor. He took her trembling hand into his. "Eleanor, she's not Emma. She's not Emma."

Eleanor looked so lost. "Eleanor, she's not sixteen and she's not alone. You know how much I love her. I'm not one of the men that Emma hangs around with. I wanted to marry her anyway. You need to know that she will be taken care of and want for nothing in this world. Our child will grow up in a loving home with both parents. We will never hurt our child the way Emma hurt Madison. Do you understand?"

"Yes," she whispered.

"You, me, Madison, the baby, Chris, Jill and Joshua are going to stay right here and be a family. The three of us are going to raise them together. I promise you I will be the father to all four children that they deserve."

Eleanor gave him a watery smile. "You have been a good father to them and I thank you for that. It's been good for the kids to have a good man around."

Tall, Dark & Lonely

"Thank you, but you're forgetting the best part."

"Oh?" She looked confused.

"This will be the first grandchild you get to hold as a baby since Madison. The first of many I hope."

He watched as realization shot through her. She sucked in a deep breath. "That's right." She grinned hugely. "Can I help with the nursery?" Her eyes brightened with excitement.

Ephraim pressed a kiss to the back of her hand. "I'm sure you, Madison and Jill will do a splendid job."

"Oh, there's so much to do!" Eleanor jumped to her feet. "I've got to call the girls so we can start on baby blankets and clothes."

"You can't do this! She can't have a baby!" Emma snapped.

Eleanor ignored her as she left the room. He knew the moment she spotted Madison. "A baby! We're having a baby!" the older woman cried happily. He heard all the air rush out of Madison's lungs from the intense hug Eleanor gave her.

"And a wedding! Don't forget the wedding!" Ephraim yelled. He didn't want her to forget that part. He was sure Madison would come around eventually.

"I'm so happy! A baby and a wedding!" Eleanor said as she hurried to the kitchen no doubt where she would be making several dozen calls.

"Ephraim, you don't know what you're doing!" Emma shrieked.

He turned his attention on her. "Oh, what don't I know?" His voice was deceptively calm.

"I'm going to tell you this for your own good." She pushed her thick, dyed blonde hair back over her shoulder. She spoke in a calm confiding manner. "She's done this before."

356

"Excuse me?" That was a little confusing and unexpected.

Candy nodded sympathetically. "It's true. Madison is a pathological liar. It pains me to say this, but it's true."

"Enlighten me." He knew Madison had stopped breathing and wondered how long it would take her to calm down before she stormed into the room.

"Very well, I was hoping I wouldn't have to, but apparently she's got you under her spell." She sauntered over to the couch and sat down. He took the seat Eleanor vacated minutes earlier and waited.

"Since she was very young I've had to deal with her problem with lying. She would steal and I would have to of course cover for her. Things got bad when she hit puberty. She slept around with every boy she encountered. Soon she began drinking and doing drugs."

"I have never seen her take so much as a sip of alcohol since I've known her," he pointed out sharply.

She ignored his tone. "She drinks in secret since the last time she was pregnant."

Holy shit, this woman was the bitch to end all bitches. He shifted on the couch, trying to focus on what she just said. "You're saying she's been pregnant before?"

"Yes, she didn't know who the father was then either. When she couldn't get any money from the men, she had the baby aborted. That was one of the reasons we came out here. I had to get her away from all of that."

"I thought you came out here because you were homeless and penniless."

Tall, Dark & Lonely

"That too," she ground out. "Of course I was penniless. Madison took every penny I brought into the house. It was so hard putting food on the table for my two little ones. Once I got here I needed to get away and clear my head. I know I should have gotten her help." She added a slight sob to the end of her little act.

"So, what are you trying to tell me?"

She moved down the couch until she was sitting close to him. She reached out and took his hand, he let her. "If she is in fact pregnant, the baby may not be yours."

Candy began running her fingers suggestively up and down his arm. "You think she's been cheating on me?" he asked softly.

"I didn't want to be the one to tell you, but she's been with so many men since she's moved here that she's developing quite the reputation. This baby *could* be yours."

He folded his hands together and looked down, ignoring her cold touch. Her hand was now caressing his muscles. "What do you suggest I do then? If she's been unfaithful to me I won't stand by her."

"Oh, and I don't blame you. You're such a strong, good man. You shouldn't have to take that," she crooned.

"What should I do?"

"Well, I think space might be the best option. She's saved plenty of money and has a good job. You should ask her to move out."

"What about the baby?"

Candy shrugged. "She's been cheating on you? Do you really want to see her? If she is pregnant she'll be fine. She'll take care of the baby. She's good at that and you shouldn't have to be hurt by this. It's not like she's your wife or anything, thank god. Can you imagine how humiliated you would be if she was?"

"So, you suggest I throw a woman out who might be pregnant?" he asked without any emotion.

She squeezed his bicep to reassure him. "I think it might be best."

"I can't believe this." He shook his head in disbelief. She took it the wrong way, which was the way he intended for her to take it.

"I know. I never thought she would do this again. I hoped and prayed that you would be enough to turn her around, but I was wrong. It's not your fault. You're such a good man." She placed her other hand on his knee.

"What about the kids?" He knew he was speeding up her little game.

"Well, I wanted to move back here anyway. Granted, I didn't know she was playing this game again, but I would be willing to help out with them and I'd be there for you as well." Her hand moved up his inner thigh where he caught it.

Ephraim chuckled darkly "Oh, Candy, how you amuse me." He pushed her hand away. He looked her in the eye. "Let's start with the basics. Madison doesn't lie. She's a bad cheater when it comes to games, but she doesn't lie and she never stole a penny. I've never seen a woman work harder to make sure her siblings were taken care of before. She even stretched herself to the max when she took Chris in, but she never once complained."

"She's fooled you." She gave him a look of pity.

"Candy, I can tell you right now without a doubt that Madison was a virgin the first time I took her."

"Oh, you poor thing. Woman can fake that," she said confidingly. He had a feeling that she probably knew that from experience.

"Do you remember that doctor's appointment at the OBGYN?"

"Yes," she said hesitantly.

Tall, Dark & Lonely

"Well, the doctor confirmed it to my face that she was a virgin, not that I had any doubts. From the look on your face, you really didn't know she was a virgin, did you?"

"I-"

"So, when you realized your mother was no longer able to give you a free ride you thought I would if you offered yourself. Then you realized your possible meal ticket wasn't interested and you thought to get rid of what you deemed to be your competition, didn't you?"

"Ephraim, don't be like that," she purred.

He abruptly stood up, putting more space between them. "Did you really think I would throw the woman I love and my unborn baby out on the street based on your word?"

She looked nervous for the first time since their conversation started. "She's just using you Ephraim," she argued desperately.

"No, she's royally pissed at me at the moment and I don't blame her. I did something stupid without asking her first. Even if she never wants me again, I would never touch you."

"Ephraim?"

"You never deserved her you know. You used her and discarded her and those two great kids. She gave up everything to put food on the table for those kids and you never once thanked her. Now, you repay her kindness by coming in here and trying to throw her in the street? You disgust me." He turned his back on her to discover that Madison had moved from the foyer into the doorway.

"Oh! Madison, we were just talking about you," Candy said cheerfully, trying to pretend that nothing happened.

"I heard," Madison said dryly.

Candy's face dropped. "It's not what you think. I…I…was just testing him to make sure he was good enough for you."

"How kind." Her eyes were locked with Ephraim's. "Can I talk to you for a moment?"

"Of course."

"Wait, what about me?"

Madison finally looked at her mother and saw nothing. She was nothing. Finally after all these years she didn't feel anything when she looked at her mother, not love, pity, or even guilt. Candy's pull over her was gone.

"What about you?" she asked in a cold voice.

"I have nowhere to go. You're really not going to throw your mother out on the street, would you? What will your baby think when it finds out you threw its grandmother out or Jill and Joshua?" Candy asked, playing the game she knew worked so well with her.

"You've never been a mother to those kids and you certainly aren't this baby's grandmother," Madison said in the same cold voice.

"How could you! I have no money and nowhere to go! Stop being such a selfish little bitch!" Candy snapped with the knowledge that whatever control she had over Madison was gone.

Ephraim put a hand out to stop Madison from doing what he would like to do at that moment. "I'm going to give you five thousand dollars on the agreement that you will leave the state. I am going to go talk to Madison and when I get back, you better have made your selection, because this is a one-time deal. I will purchase a one way ticket to the state of your choice. I will give you some money to cover the first two days at a hotel. Once I hear from you, I will send a check to you. This will be the last time you bother us. I will never give you another cent so you better make it last until you get a job."

Tall, Dark & Lonely

"You're giving me five grand?" Candy's eyes lit up.

He nodded. "It's your choice, five grand and you leave or nothing and can stick around somewhere else so you can be near your kids. What's it to be?"

She didn't even blink. "The five grand!" She clapped her hands together. "This is so exciting!"

Neither one of them was surprised. "Fine. Stay here and I'll be back when Madison is done talking to me."

She waved them off. "I'll be fine, don't worry about me." They weren't.

Ephraim led Madison into the foyer. "Where do you want to talk?"

"The training room."

"Okay." He wasn't looking forward to this, but it was better to get it over with so he could start groveling and begging her to come back to him. He would, too. He couldn't live without her and he didn't give a damn if he made an ass out of himself to prove it.

He punched the code into the alarm pad. At the beep, he opened the door and held it open for her. The door shut with a click and a beep behind them before they reached the bottom step.

"So, what did you need to talk-" She grabbed him by the shirt and slammed him into the wall as her mouth closed over his.

Chapter 28

Madison trailed kisses down his chin and neck. "Not that I'm complaining, but I thought you wanted to talk."

"Mmhmm." She ran her tongue over his flat nipple on her way down his stomach. She nibbled and kissed each rippling muscle.

"I'm really sorry about everything, Madison. I know I should have done it another way and I know you know all the reasons so I'm not going to get into that again. If you could just see it in your heart to forgive me I will spend the rest of eternity making it up to you."

She laughed against his skin. "What do you call this?"

He sucked in a harsh breath as she unzipped his pants. "I-I don't know what it is just p-please don't stop."

His pants dropped around his ankles followed by his boxers. Madison pulled them off and threw them to the side, leaving him naked and fully erect. Several drops of excitement oozed from the tip of his erection. Madison looked up and met his eyes as her tongued darted out to lick it up.

A long, loud, pained moan escaped him. His erection jerked under her touch. She ran her tongue from tip to base and back again, leaving him panting until he couldn't take it anymore.

"Enough!" he growled as he yanked her off her feet and threw her over his shoulder.

She giggled breathlessly as he carried her further into the training room. He stormed past the exercise equipment, knives table, the guns table, and holy weapons table until he came to the matted section of the large room.

"Four weeks is too long, baby." He gently placed her on the mat.

"I agree so don't piss me off again." Her voice was low and urgent as she ran her hands over his chest and arms. He stripped off all her clothes. She was still sitting up when he dropped his head between her legs and ran his tongue between her slit.

She slowly leaned back until she was resting on her elbows. Her legs were bent at the knee and spread wide for him. Ephraim lapped the sweet nectar between her folds like a man dying of thirst.

Madison moaned as she rocked her hips against his mouth. Ephraim slid his tongue inside her core while his thumb took over rubbing her swollen nub. "Ephraim...oh Ephraim!" she screamed as climax took over. Her hips rose off the mat, riding his mouth to the end.

Ephraim removed his tongue as the climax ended and covered her body with his. He hooked her legs over his broad shoulders, opening her wide for him. "Tell me, Madison." he demanded in a strained voice as the tip of his manhood rubbed against her slit.

"I love you, Ephraim. Please!" she begged. He thrust his hips forward, burying himself deep in one motion.

"I love you, Madison. I'm so sorry. So sorry," he said as he pulled out all the way only to enter her slowly, allowing every sensation of sliding into her tight wet heat to register.

Her head dropped back. He watched as she licked her lips. Her fangs descended as another climax hit her. She moaned and arched beneath him. He slowed his thrusts, planning to make her come one more time before he lost it. As it was, he was dangerously close to coming too soon.

"Do you forgive me?" he whispered against her neck.

"Mmmhmmm, I forgave you upstairs when you said I was stubborn."

He laughed weakly against her skin. "That's what it took?"

"That and you've never doubted me and even with a mother like Candy you're willing to take a risk with me."

"There's no risk with you, Madison. I adore you, sweetheart. I'm so sorry, baby, please believe me. I'm such an idiot. I-"

"Shh, shouldn't you be fucking me instead of talking?" she asked with a sultry smile.

He growled against her skin. She knew what dirty talk did to him. She loved his reaction. It threw him off his steady cadence until he was pounding into her without finesse or rhythm.

Ephraim let go. Everything he'd held back the last four months to make sure he didn't overwhelm or hurt her was released. He thrust into her harder than he'd ever thrust into any woman before. She moaned and cried out his name. He knew she liked it when her body gripped him tightly, trying to keep him from pulling out even to thrust back in. She was drenching him and making every slide into her body more intense. She was so damn wet he could cry.

His fangs lowered and he decided to show her exactly what it was like to be fucked by a Pyte. He sank his teeth into the crook of her neck. His eyes squeezed shut with pleasure. It had never been like this. He'd bitten plenty of women while bedding them, but he'd never gained any pleasure from the bite. Now he was ready to explode.

Madison gasped as his teeth sank into her. It intensified what he was doing between her legs. It sent a thousand sensations throughout her body. She desperately wanted to move against him, but he had her pinned to the ground with her legs over his shoulders. She managed to turn her head so she could lick his neck. He moaned and shuddered against her. She licked again and was rewarded with a harder tug on her neck and a more violent thrust between her legs. It was too much, she couldn't hold back.

Tall, Dark & Lonely

Ephraim thrashed wildly on top of her as her fangs pierced his neck. It was the most erotic sensation of his life. They fed off each other while he made love to her.

Their loud moans vibrated pleasantly throughout the room as a powerful climax claimed them both. Madison's nails scraped down his back, driving him on until the last tremor subsided. They released their bites and kissed each other slowly as they tasted the mixture of their blood.

He pulled back to smile down at her. Madison bit her lip and looked embarrassed.

"What is it?" he asked soothingly.

"We were rather loud," she mumbled

He grinned arrogantly. "We definitely were."

"Everyone on the first floor probably heard us." She looked horrified.

He kissed the tip of her nose. "Impossible. I've had the basement soundproofed."

"You have?"

"Mmhmm, otherwise Eleanor would kill us for firing guns inside the house."

Somehow she managed to pull her legs off of his shoulders and gently push him off so that she could sit up. "You said 'us', you mean Chris is firing guns?"

He exhaled loudly. "Madison, he's not a boy. We've talked about this. He's a Sentinel. This is what he's meant to do and he's very good at it. They all are, but he has to practice to improve his skills."

She took his hand into her lap and began playing with his fingers.

"Madison? Do you understand?"

After a moment she spoke. "Yes, I don't like it though. Chris is like a little brother to me and he's my best friend. It scares me when you take him out on patrol."

"I know that, baby. You need to remember that he's my son and I take every precaution to keep him safe. I would never let anything happen to him, okay?" His voice was tender.

She looked up at him, smiling sweetly. "You really love him, don't you?"

His lips pulled into a lopsided grin. "The brat's definitely grown on me." In a more serious tone he continued. "Yes, I love him very much as I love Joshua and Jill as if they were my own."

Madison tugged on his hand until he leaned forward for a kiss. "You're a very good man who does very, very, very, very, very stupid things." She half teased.

"I'm an idiot." His eyes were focused on her lips. "You're really going to have your hands full keeping me in line." He brushed his lips against hers.

"What do you suggest I do to keep you in line?" her voice was low and husky.

"Marry me. Make an honest man out of me," he proposed against her mouth as he laid her back onto the mat.

She pushed him onto his back and quickly straddled his hips. "I tell you what, if you can make me scream your name three times I'll marry you."

His hands cupped her hips. "Is there a time limit on this deal?"

She leaned forward, sliding against his already hardening length. "Oh no, actually taking your time is encouraged on this deal and if you make me scream your name four times I'll marry you tomorrow."

He gripped her hips and brought her forward as he thrust inside of her. "Better get ready to repeat your vows, Madison, because tomorrow you're *mine*."

Tall, Dark & Lonely

"Nice!" Chris said appreciatively as Joshua took out four bad guys.

Joshua was in the zone. Nothing outside of the video game mattered to him. He leaned back against the foot of Chris's bed as he readjusted himself into a new sitting position, his eyes never leaving the screen.

"Hey, loser." Jill knocked on his door and came in without waiting for an invitation. She flopped down on her stomach across his bed.

"He's not a loser," Joshua said automatically.

"Thanks, little man." He looked back at Jill. She was watching them play. "Whatcha need?"

"Grandma's on the phone calling everyone she's ever met. She told me to order pizza for dinner."

"Sweet," Chris said. As much as he loved grandma's home cooking, he missed junk food. She didn't let them order out very often unless something big was going on. "What's up with Grandma? Did the reverend finally make his move?" he teased.

Her eyes shot to Joshua. "I'll tell you later." That piqued his interest.

"Tell me now. Give me hints." He tossed his controller on the floor and turned in his game chair to face her.

"No, order the pizza first."

"You."

"No, you do it," she said dismissively. Every chance she got she talked down to him. It was irritating. He often wondered what he did to get her panties in a bunch.

"Fine, hand me my phone. It's behind you."

She looked over her shoulder at the silver phone on his nightstand. "Just use the one in your pocket."

He pretended not to hear. He wasn't really supposed to talk about *that* phone. It was his Sentinel phone, GPS, and emergency beacon; basically it was his lifeline to the council. "It's my work phone, Jill. I'm not allowed to use it for ordering pizza. Just throw me my phone."

She tossed the phone to him. "I don't understand why Ephraim quit his job with the police department to work with a sixteen year old working security?" Disbelief filled her tone.

"Believe what you want." That was the cover story they gave. Luckily they wouldn't have to use it much longer. The clergy needed to enter the house soon to add protection. The house required prayer guards and extra support. Ephraim said they would need to know the truth soon and he was thankful for that, because even he wasn't buying it.

He placed the order and tossed the silver phone back her way. "So, tell me what I want to know."

Gossip. That was Jill's best friend. As long as you allowed her to report it or gave it to her, she would be your best friend. "Well, it seems that in seven and half months they will be letting out another room."

Chris rolled his eyes. "Oh, that? I already knew about *that*."

"You're such a liar."

"Puhlease, I was the first person after the two of them to know three weeks ago." In fact, Madison had twisted his arm, literally, and made him go into a Wal-Mart an hour away to buy the damn test.

"Liar, why would they tell you and not us?"

He gave her a 'duh' look and spoke slowly to her in much the same manner. "Because he's my father and she's my best friend."

"Hey!" Joshua griped.

"Besides you, little man, of course." Chris reached out and gently punched Joshua on the shoulder.

Joshua nodded firmly, satisfied with the correction. "Of course."

She snickered.

"What?" he asked, mildly annoyed.

"He's not really your father you know."

"Tell that to our legal system," he said dryly.

"Ephraim is too his Dad! You're just jealous! He treats me like his son too and you like a daughter so I don't know why you're complaining, Jill. I think you're just mad because he didn't adopt you, too." Joshua's voice was crisp.

"I am not! I just think it's weird! I mean he's only what twenty-six! He can't have a sixteen year old for a son. It's weird!" Jill might have denied it, but the dark blush on her cheeks gave her away.

Chris didn't correct her and tell her he was really 206 years old that was beside the point. Instead he shrugged a shoulder. "If it doesn't bother me then why does it bother you?"

She looked around his room pointedly. "Of course it doesn't bother you. He spoils you rotten."

Chris followed her gaze around his room. Ephraim bought him a flat screen television, video games, DVD player, posters, clothes, computer and all the other stuff he never had before. When he lived with his mother he slept on old blankets on the floor of the trailer in a corner of the living room. He'd never even slept on a mattress before Madison and Ephraim took him in.

He kept his eyes on her face as he pointed lazily around the room. "If memory serves me correctly your room looks very similar to this one."

She averted his eyes. "That's not the point."

"Oh, then pray tell what is? Are you pissed because I knew about the baby first or because Ephraim is my Dad?"

"Shhh!" Jill hissed, pointing to Joshua.

"It's going to be a boy," Joshua said offhandedly.

"What? How did you know?" Jill demanded.

"When Ephraim and Chris aren't at work or training, he takes me with him to run errands. Chris was with us and he complained that Madison keeps hitting him upside the head for stealing her 'pregnancy food'." He shrugged unconcerned. "It was really me, but I didn't say anything."

"You little punk," Chris said, chuckling. He was impressed. The kid was coming along nicely.

"Hey, junk food is junk food, brother."

"You knew and you didn't tell me?" Disapproval heavily coated her words.

"Why would I? You have a big mouth and you throw tantrums like Candy. I also didn't tell you that Ephraim wants to marry her and *I* don't care what you think about that!"

"So, what is it, Jill? What's your problem?" Chris asked. This spoiled brat act was getting old. Actually, it was old months ago.

"I think she's just jealous. I'm going to ask Ephraim to adopt me, too. Then Chris and I can be brothers and Ephraim will be my Dad for real."

"He can't adopt you!" Jill shrieked.

"Yes, he can! He likes me, too! He introduces me to everyone as his youngest son."

Tall, Dark & Lonely

Jill rolled her eyes. "You're such an idiot. Don't you see what he's doing? Remember when you were little and all of those guys bought us things or took us places?"

"Yes," Joshua answered slowly. Chris didn't like where this was going.

"He's just using us to get to Madison. As soon as he gets bored with her or finds someone else, he'll stop being nice to us."

"Liar!" Joshua yelled, but his lower lip trembled. "He bought this house so we could stay here."

"No, he bought this house so he could stay here. As soon as he's done with her, we're out."

"That's not true! He loves me! He even told me so!" Joshua dropped the game controller and started wiping frantically at his face.

"You can be a real bitch, you know that?" Chris told Jill as he pulled Joshua onto his lap.

"I'm just warning him. It's best he finds out now instead of when we're given the boot."

"Save your warnings. They're not necessary." He put his arm around Joshua. He hated this bullshit that Candy did to them. His mother did her fair share of bullshit throughout the years, but at least he could tell when someone genuinely cared about him.

"H-h-he lied?" Joshua looked up at him through a rim of tears. Chris swore inwardly. Jill was lucky that he didn't hit girls.

"No, he didn't lie to you. If you want to ask Dad to adopt you I'll go with you. If for some reason he can't like maybe Grandma is going to do it or something, you and I are brothers no matter what, okay?"

Joshua smiled weakly and stopped crying. "Really? You'll be my brother?"

"Yes."

"I don't want Grandma to adopt me. I want her to be my Grandma and Ephraim to be my Dad."

"What about Madison? Did you think about that? If he actually marries her, which I doubt he'll go through with it, she'll be your step-mother." Jill really could be a bitch. So much like Candy sometimes it was scary. He hoped she didn't follow other traits.

That didn't seem to disturb Joshua at all. "So what? I already see her as my mom. She's not really my sister so it won't bother me." His eyes shot to Chris. "Can we ask tonight?"

"Sure."

"Kids, I think your food is here. Go answer the door," Grandma said as she walked down the hall. They heard her busily talking on the phone as she headed for her room.

Chris placed Joshua on his feet. "Food, let's go." He grabbed his wallet and knelt down. "Alright, climb up." Joshua didn't need to be told twice. He jumped on Chris's back with a choke hold around the neck.

He threw an annoyed look at Jill. "Let's go, you can carry the pizza." With that he took off running, making Joshua laugh and screech the whole way.

"Alright, team work. I'll bend and you open the door."

Okay!" Joshua said excitedly.

Chris bent over and heard Joshua open the door followed by Jill's scream and felt Joshua tighten his grip around his neck. Chris looked up to see the barrel of a gun aimed at him.

"Stand up and move back, now," the man said in a crisp military tone.

Tall, Dark & Lonely

Chris stood up slowly, keeping his eye on the man in front of him. "Slide down Josh and stay behind me." Josh did as he was asked. His little hands gripped Chris's back pants pocket tightly.

"Move back," the man said, again. Chris slowly backed up, giving Joshua time to move.

"Is anyone else in the house?" the man asked as six armed men flanked him into the house.

Before Chris could lie, Grandma walked down the stairs and Candy walked out of the parlor. He hadn't known she was there.

"You two women, come here and join them" He used his gun to gesture his request.

Candy's eyes took in the men and guns and began to sob. "I'm not with them! I don't live here. Just let me leave and I won't say anything."

"Join the group or I'll shoot you, bitch." He leveled the gun on her. She stumbled into the middle of the foyer and threw her arms around Jill. "Oh my god!" she sobbed against Jill who was reaching out blindly for Joshua to pull him behind her, but the boy wouldn't give up his hold on Chris' pants.

"What's going on here?" Grandma demanded.

"Everyone, take off your crosses now," he demanded as the men broke off to search the house.

Chris pulled his cross off and tossed it forward. Joshua, Jill and Grandma did the same. The man kicked the crosses towards the wall.

"All clear," he called out. Then with an evil grin he said, "I'm inviting you in."

"About time," a familiar voice said.

"Oh shit," Chris groaned.

The blonde bitch stopped in front of them. Chris' eyes dropped to where her stub should be. Damn it, her hand had grown back. "What? You're not happy to see me?"

"To be honest? No, not really," Chris answered.

"Chris, do you know them?" Grandma asked.

"Don't worry, Grandma. I'll take care of it," he said firmly.

Caroline laughed. "Oh Chris, you are so funny. We both know that before the night is over that I'm going to tear your family limb from limb."

"Oh god," Candy said before she passed out. Jill did her best to catch her, but in the end could only guide her to the ground.

"We'll kill her first," Caroline ordered. A man stepped over to Candy. As soon as his hand touched her arm she jumped back. "Ah, a little faker. Good to know."

She looked Chris over. "Where's Ephraim?"

"Fuck you."

Caroline ran her fingers over his jaw and sighed heavily. "Shoot him." She stepped to the side. Chris pushed Joshua back hard and stepped forward. The searing pain in his chest sent him collapsing to the ground before he heard the sound of the gunshot.

Chapter 29

"I love you, Ephraim," Madison said between kisses. Her hand darted down to the fly of his pants. She gripped him, giving him a gentle tug. "One more time?"

"Baby, I have to get Chris and get ready for patrol." He hated leaving her now that they'd made up. "Plus, we should really save some of it for the wedding night." He wiggled his eyebrows.

Madison giggled at his leering gesture. "I guess I have a lot to do anyway."

"Yes." He grinned arrogantly. "You have an entire wedding to plan and pull off in less than twenty-four hours." She bit her bottom lip nervously at his words. "But, if I know Eleanor, and I think I do, she's probably upstairs planning a wedding for tomorrow even as we speak."

"You think so?"

"Yes, she's been itching for this wedding for quite some time. Now that you're pregnant she'll want to rush it to make sure neither of us changes our minds." He kissed her lips gently.

"I won't."

"That's very good to know," his voice was hoarse, more intense.

Madison flattened her palm against the growing hardness when a loud piercing beep made her jump back with a yelp. Without a word, Ephraim reached into his pocket and took out his Sentinel phone. The light flashing was green.

"Shit," he muttered. "Looks like we're heading out sooner than later." He pressed his thumb to the small piece of glass on the back of the phone and waited for it to scan his fingerprint. With another small beep the phone slid open.

"Where are you going?" Madison asked curiously.

"One sec..I just have to...there." A text message with the Sentinel's name that was in trouble, current location and directions from his location to the Sentinel's was given. "Oh fuck."

"*What?*" she asked anxiously.

"It's here. Chris is in trouble." He swore under his breath as he walked to the weapons area.

"Maybe it's an accident. Joshua or maybe Jill were playing with it and set it off."

He shook his head. "That phone never leaves his sight. He's very good about that. Besides, no one can open his phone except for him or another Sentinel. It's also impossible to set off the emergency signal by accident. He has to press his finger on the scanner while pressing eleven twenty-five."

"The day every Sentinel is born," she stated.

"Exactly. They're upstairs right now. Someone let them in the house. I need to get up there before someone gets hurt." He poured a bottle of holy water over his head, allowing it to drip down his back to his jeans.

Madison watched as he attached two ankle holsters with guns already secured to each foot. He placed a large gun in the front of his waistband and a matching one in back.

"I thought bullets didn't kill vampires." Her voice shook.

"They don't. These are for Minions."

"But they're human!"

He nodded. "They're also slaves and probably upstairs. They gave up their rights as far as the Sentinel is concerned when they took their oaths. In my opinion they gave up their lives when they came after my family." He pocketed a cross and several small bottles of holy water.

Tall, Dark & Lonely

Finally, he pulled on a bullet proof vest. She knew it wasn't meant to save his life, but to stop anything from slowing him down. A bullet in the heart could knock him out for several hours as she learned several months ago.

She reached for one. "I'm going, too."

His hand wrapped around her wrist. "No, you're to stay here. I need to know you're safe."

"Ephraim, you said I can't die and nothing can hurt the baby. I'm going."

Hard cold blue eyes met hers. "You can't die, you're right. It's another thing to suffer pain with absolutely no relief. You are not going. I will not have you hurt. You will stay down here and wait. I'm going to try and get the kids down here safely." He pulled out his phone again. She watched as he pressed his thumb to the screen while typing in four numbers.

"What are you doing?"

"Two Sentinels asking for help in the same location will get a bigger response. I'm leaving this phone with you. If something should happen to prevent me from coming back for you they will find you."

She knew what he meant. He meant if they managed to take him away. "You're not going to let yourself get taken, are you?" She eyed him accusingly.

"No, but if they leave the house with anyone I'll have to go." He pressed a swift kiss to her forehead. "Just please stay here." He didn't wait for her answer before he flashed away.

* * * *

A low whistle caught his attention. He turned just as Ephraim slithered behind him. With one swift move Ephraim had the man disarmed and pulled back against him in the dark corner of the dining room. His fangs scratched the man's neck, making him shudder.

"Make a sound and I'll make this a very painful death."

378

The man only nodded.

"Good, how many are in my house including vampires?"

"Five men and the Master."

Ephraim chuckled darkly. "You're not lying to me now, are you?" He allowed his fang to drag across the skin, leaving behind a small paper thin cut that he knew would sting. The man gasped.

"I'm not lying," he hissed.

"Then why are you telling me the truth?"

"She said you would change all of us. That we would all be day walkers like you."

"You're taking a chance telling me her plans."

"Yes, I don't see any reason not to tell you." The man's voice was unsteady.

"Because you want to remain on my good side so that I'll change you?"

The man nodded.

"What's the plan for the women and children?"

He didn't answer. His entire body went rigid. "She told you that you would feed off of them?"

The man nodded stiffly.

"Did she fail to mention that a change takes several days to occur?"

"N-no."

"But you came here with the intentions of killing and feeding from my children?"

Tall, Dark & Lonely

He smelled the first real wave of fear spread through the man's body. "I-I...no...I..."

"Thanks for your help." He covered the man's mouth with his hand and sunk his teeth in his neck. He needed sustenance to endure anything he was about to encounter so he did what he hadn't done in over a century. He drained the body until the man's heart stopped. For his family he would do anything.

With that done, he moved into the kitchen after the next man. Four dead bodies later he moved around the second floor. He quietly crawled up the wall towards the ceiling and glided across the ceiling, making sure to keep away from the chandelier that hung in the middle of the foyer.

Silently, he rolled over onto his back so that he was looking straight down at the scene bellow him. His eyes took everything in. The first man had lied of course. Below him were five heavily armed men with their guns aimed at the small group huddled in the middle of their circle. The scent of blood hit him hard.

Sentinel blood.

His eyes focused on the half naked body lying in Eleanor's lap. In that moment he thanked god that the boys copied his dressing habits. He could see the wound clearly, a shoulder wound. It was a bad wound nonetheless. From the burn marks around the wound he knew it had been a close range shot. It probably cauterized the wound enough to slow the bleeding.

Chris' left arm hung uselessly by his side. His right hand was clenching and unclenching into a fist. He kept his eyes focused on Caroline as she paced the large foyer. Satisfied that Chris was fine for the moment, he looked at the rest of the hostages.

Joshua knelt by his Grandmother in the middle of the circle where he would be more protected if they started to shoot. Jill cried softly as she kept her back pressed against Joshua's side, keeping him covered from yet another side. He was so proud of her at that moment. In spite of all the shit Candy put those kids through and Jill's trust problems and pessimism, she was turning out be a really good kid.

Candy he was going to kill. She was slowly adjusting herself behind Joshua not to protect him, but to push him slowly out of the middle of the circle to take his spot. He watched with fury as she gently, but insistently pushed at Joshua's back. With each movement she moved in to take his spot until Jill and Grandma adjusted to cover him again. They shot Candy a warning look.

"I'm scared!" Candy cried. "Just let me take his spot. Look, he's not even upset! I am! Let me sit there!"

Joshua nodded. "She can have my seat. I'm not afraid. I don't care if she's a vampire or not. I'm not scared." His small eyes were focused on Caroline in an act of defiance.

"There's no such thing as vampires, Joshua. Stop trying to scare me!" Candy screeched.

He went to move out of his spot when Chris reached out and grabbed his arm. "You sit right there and do not move!"

"But,-"

"But nothing. If you really want me to be your big brother then you'll listen to me. You do not move an inch for her or I'm telling Dad and you know he'll be pissed. You keep your little ass in the middle and do not move. She'll be fine!"

"I don't care about her. I just don't want her panicking and getting you guys shot," Joshua muttered.

"We'll be fine. Just stay put so we know you're okay," Chris said, sucking in a deep breath. The movement had cost him.

"So, you want him to be your brother, do you?" Caroline asked. "Does that mean you want Ephraim to be your Daddy?" she asked mockingly.

"Yes," Joshua said firmly.

Ephraim quickly took in the rest of the room. No vampires other than Caroline. He was not surprised. She wouldn't want to share. Her aspiration was to be the most powerful vampire with large armies beneath her. In short, she wanted to be Queen with him as her king.

She wouldn't take the chance of involving another vampire, afraid the chance would be stolen from her. He closed his eyes and listened. He couldn't hear any other heart beats inside the house. He focused more on the outside and found one, probably the driver.

"What if I told you that your *Daddy* was just like me, but worse?" Caroline asked, clearly enjoying tormenting his little boy. He was absolutely going to kill her.

He watched as Joshua folded his arms across his bare chest. "You're a liar."

Caroline giggled. "Oh, I assure you I'm not. Why do you think we're here? We need his blood."

"He's nothing like you!" Joshua yelled.

She threw her head back and laughed harder. "Oh, we'll see, won't we?"

"What's going on here?" a new voice asked.

Ephraim's eyes shot to the hallway beside the stair. He was going to spank her ass until she couldn't walk, then he was going to do it some more.

Madison stepped into the room.

* * * *

Did he really think that she could sit back and wait? She spent the last half hour pacing the room before she had enough. After sticking a small cross in her bra and a stake in the back of her pants she decided enough was enough. She crept up the stairs and then rushed into the foyer, knowing that it wouldn't take Ephraim more than a few seconds to sense her and force her back.

Her only hope was that Caroline wouldn't be able to sense the change in her. Ephraim promised that vampires couldn't smell Pytes only shifters could. Their scents were invisible to vampires. Madison prayed that he was right. He said all vampires suspected they were human until they tasted their blood or if they changed in front of them.

Caroline smiled triumphantly in front of her, showing her fangs off proudly. With a wave of her hand she sent two men to drag Madison into the small group sitting on the floor. The scent of Chris's blood hit her, hard. She didn't have a lot of practice with the scent of blood, but she knew enough to know that his was different. It smelled sweet and inviting, too inviting. It was a natural booby-trap Sentinels had. The blood would kill a vampire on the first bite.

"So very nice of you to join us. You've just made my job of hunting you down a lot easier. Now we just have to wait for Ephraim. I assume he's going around the house, trying to kill my men?"

"I have no idea where he is," she said.

Caroline stepped in front of the guns and bent down. She closed her eyes and inhaled deeply above Madison. She knew. Caroline knew that she'd been changed. Her plan failed. Madison was about to hit the woman, hoping to knock her out so she could save her family when Caroline reacted a bit differently than she'd expected.

"You bitch!" Caroline snapped. She stepped back with her eyes shimmering silver. Damn it, she did know. They were going to shoot the kids now.

Tall, Dark & Lonely

Madison put an arm around Jill and Joshua, hoping it would be enough to protect them. She knew it wouldn't be. She had to figure out a way to use her new abilities to get them out of here.

"You've been with him! I can smell him all over you! You bitch!" she shrieked again.

Madison turned to look at Caroline and did her best to hide her relief. "He's mine," she said firmly, hoping to keep the woman distracted long enough to figure out how to get everyone to safety.

Caroline's face contorted in anger. "Not for long, I guarantee that." She walked away until she stood directly in front of their little group. She snapped her fingers and one of the men lowered his gun and brought her a chair. She sat down, crossing her legs at the ankles and leaned in with her chin resting on her fists.

"I want to see the looks on their faces when you tell them what Ephraim really is." When Madison made no move to speak, Caroline added. "If you don't tell them I'll shoot them one by one starting with the old woman."

Chris tried to sit up. "You lay still," Eleanor hissed.

"I'll tell them," Chris said, sounding a little stronger.

"Even better." Caroline grinned. "I would love to hear this explained by a Sentinel."

"Sentinel?" Jill and Grandma asked at the same time.

"Er…" Chris was at a loss where to begin.

Caroline jumped in. "I'll explain him and then he'll explain Ephraim."

Ephraim watched carefully. His mind calculated every single possibility while he kept track of the conversation. He knew Madison was going to throw her body over her brother, sister, Chris and Eleanor too if she got the chance. He also knew that if she was severely injured her body would reject the baby.

He should have reminded her that her body would reject the baby to heal itself, but there hadn't been enough time. There were no words to describe the pain from a bullet or a knife wound and he didn't want her to find out first hand either. If she was shot, her body would rush to fix itself and kill their son.

Now he was kicking himself for his stupidity. If she'd known how painful an injury was as a Pyte she never would have come out here. Well, that wasn't true. She probably would have for the kids. He made a rule right then and there to always tell her everything from now on and make damn sure that she listened.

"I'll give you the quick version so we can get to the real juicy stuff." Caroline said in a tone that was friendly and excited as she let them in on what she probably thought was a juicy secret. "Chris here has a big secret."

Out of the corner of her eye she saw Candy inch further away from Chris. She probably thought he was a monster in disguise ready to pounce on her.

"Chris is what we call a Sentinel. I'll explain Chris, but no interruptions. I want him to explain Ephraim as soon as possible." She cleared her throat. "Thousands of years ago, Lucifer found a way to place a demon in disguise among humans." She raised her hand when Jill's mouth opened. "I said no questions." Jill shut her mouth and reluctantly nodded.

Caroline's minions looked very interested in this tale. Something told Ephraim that she didn't like sharing information. The men took small steps closer to their Master in hopes of not missing a single word.

"Now this is just the story. I obviously wasn't there when all of this went down. I'm just a result. God found out and was pissed. He decided to send, I guess you would call them half angels, warriors in his place to earth. He couldn't on his own interfere. It's a long ago agreement that earth was a chess board. They could add, but not subtract. They also couldn't interfere once the game was in play."

Tall, Dark & Lonely

"Once Lucifer released his demons he knew that he would never be allowed to release anymore. Rules as I said." She waved a dismissive hand. "As I said it's all very complicated. So he made sure his demon could multiply on his own through a blood exchange."

"Now, God had to play by these rules as well. I know, doesn't seem fair does it?" she asked with a wicked smile that showed her fangs. "Instead of depositing all of his half-angels at once he set it up so that ten of these half-angels would come to earth every ten years."

"Five pairs of mates made up ten warriors. They're born as a twin to a human mother. They require a human soul to bring them to earth. I believe Chris's twin died in the womb." She looked at Chris for confirmation. He nodded. "Our Chris here is an unmated Sentinel. You see, he has never met his mate and probably never will." She threw Chris a taunting smile. "Mostly because I plan on hunting her down and tearing her throat out for fun."

Chris' scream was feral as he tried to get to his feet and attack her. Grandma, Madison and even Jill held him down. It took Joshua's little hand in his to finally calm him down. Caroline continued as if nothing happened.

"Now, normally a Sentinel will live to be around two hundred and look about twenty-five for the rest of their lives. They'll begin to age quickly when their job is over. Then they are sent back. Rumor has it that they are born again. Their mates are also born again as their mates. They're what you would call soul mates. Now unfortunately for Chris, he is not going to live to see his mate never mind tomorrow morning."

She clapped her hands together. "Now, I believe Chris has a tale to tell us."

From above them, Ephraim's voice echoed throughout the room. "Oh, I believe I'm more qualified to tell that story, wouldn't you agree?"

Everyone looked up and gasped.

Chapter 30

Madison was surprised to see Ephraim lying across the ceiling with his hands folded behind his head and his ankles crossed. The perfect picture of leisure, if one did that sort of thing on the ceiling that is. She had to remember to ask him to show her how to do it.

She dropped her gaze to take in everyone else's response. Caroline looked torn between anger at not knowing he was there and excitement that he was. Her men looked nervous and awed. She knew what they were all thinking. Caroline no doubt promised to have them changed and they all thought they were looking at their future.

Candy cowered back even more. Madison saw Candy's eyes take in everyone's position. She inched away quickly while she could. Madison didn't say anything. If Candy managed it, good for her, otherwise drawing attention to her right now would set off guns in their direction. If Candy was going to get herself shot, Madison would rather she did it away from the kids.

No one else seemed to notice that Candy was no longer part of their group. Caroline kept her eyes on Ephraim, probably expecting her men to watch the small group. Of course they weren't.

Ephraim watched Candy sneak away out of the corner of his eye. She didn't even look over her shoulder again to give her kids one last look never mind taking them out of there to safety. If Chris hadn't been injured, he could count on the boy to take the younger children to the training room where they would remain safe until help arrived.

Chris looked relieved to see him. Eleanor looked relieved as well as she tightened her grip around Chris and reached out to take Joshua's hand in hers. Joshua beamed up at him. He winked at the little boy. Jill just looked astonished. She didn't look frightened just surprised.

Candy was just making it past the stairs when Caroline's gaze dropped to her.

Tall, Dark & Lonely

"Kill her."

Everyone in the group except for Madison and Chris whimpered and ducked down, trying to cover each other. Madison threw a pleading look at Candy. "Get back here before they kill you!"

Candy hesitated at the stairs and looked back. She was deathly pale. "No, I'm not dying for anyone." She turned to run. "I'm not going to die!"

One of the men chased after her. Madison was frozen on the spot. She couldn't risk running after Candy to help her and give herself away. She had to stay and protect the children. She knew that instinctively just like she knew that if she ran, Ephraim would stop her.

Ephraim watched Candy run. One look at Caroline let him know that if he went after Candy that Caroline would kill everyone. If it had been anyone else he may have risked it, but Candy wasn't worth it. She just abandoned her own children to certain death.

A few moments later they heard several gunshots. The kids and Eleanor jumped. Chris swore. Madison wiped away a tear. He knew it was the hardest thing she'd ever done, sacrificing her birth mother to save her family, but he was glad. He couldn't lose any of his children or Eleanor.

The guard walked back into the foyer and nodded. Caroline looked pleased. "Next time any of you fail to do your job I will personally rip your throats out." The guards backed up a bit and refocused their attention on the group.

"Why don't you come down here, Ephraim, and tell your story? Or we could just shoot the little boy. Both would be entertaining."

Joshua swallowed loudly as he cowered back. With grace a dancer would be jealous of, Ephraim fell to the ground, landing on his feet without a noise. Caroline smiled wolfishly. "Oh, how I look forward to being able to do that."

"I bet," Ephraim said smoothly as he stepped in front of the group. He stood no more than an inch away from them, blocking Caroline and the front two men's view of the group. His legs were less than an inch apart, further blocking their view.

"You three cover their backs. I don't trust him," she said to the other three guards.

"I want you to take off your vest and remove your weapons, slowly. Then turn around or I tell those three to start shooting," Caroline ordered, her eyes followed Ephraim's every move.

Ephraim slowly removed the vest, knowing how much Caroline appreciated a man's chest. While he had her distracted, he pressed his left leg against Chris's side, knowing the back of his lower legs and Chris's hands would be blocked. A few seconds later he felt his pant leg pushed up from the back and his gun removed. He'd left both guns unstrapped for this reason. A few seconds later the second gun was gone. He heard Joshua and Jill's small gasp of surprise and so did Caroline.

"What is it? Turn around now!"

He turned around, giving Caroline a view of his back. He saw Chris tuck the guns in the waist of his pants. He nodded, one. Ephraim winked at the kids as he tossed his bullet proof vest, carelessly, but purposely, on Joshua. Eleanor released the boy's hand and with Jill's help, they quickly had the boy inside the vest as fast as they could.

"Master, they're putting the vest on the boy," one of the men pointed out. Ephraim's fangs lowered as he eyed the man. He growled viciously in warning. The man took an unsteady step back.

Caroline laughed it off. "If he wants to give the boy false hopes let him."

Tall, Dark & Lonely

Ephraim heard Caroline approach. She removed the gun from the back of his pants and threw it back. It hit the wall before it fell to the floor. Her fingernail traced lines on his back. No doubt she was cautious about touching his skin after the last time. He also knew what she was looking at.

"Hmm, I see you've turned into quite the passionate lover, Ephraim, if these scratches are any indication. That's good to know."

"You'll never know," he said in a bored tone.

"His eyes," Eleanor whispered.

He looked back down at her. "It's okay. I promise." She nodded slowly. Jill did as well. Joshua just grinned hugely.

"Cool!" the little boy said. Hope filled his eyes. Ephraim only hoped he didn't let him down.

Caroline's hand snaked around him, still careful not to touch him, and removed the second gun. She threw it across the room. "We're all waiting for an explanation, Ephraim." She backed away, giving him room. Apparently she wasn't completely stupid. That was a bit of a surprise.

Ephraim walked around the room, careful not to go near the armed men. He didn't want to make them anymore nervous than they already were. He decided to buy some time by doing what she wanted, for now.

"What you need to know is that I would never hurt any of you. I was born this way. I was born in London, England during the winter of 1803." He paused to give them time to adjust to this knowledge. "My father was a vampire and my mother was human. I don't know the details of their relationship. She was married to a Duke whom she already bore two sons for. I was very different, small."

"When I was sixteen I went into a coma and a month later I awoke like this. I will never die, but I can be hurt. I walk in the daylight and I drink blood. I have killed, but only when needed and for good reason."

"I was planning on telling you shortly. As you know, Chris is a Sentinel. We both work for a special council. Our job is to kill violent vampires, demons and shifters. This house you are in is an incomplete Sentinel home. I say incomplete because the Pope and the council have been working hard to set up a proper household for us. It's taken a lot longer to do than it normally should have because of the baby."

"Is the baby.." Eleanor's voice trailed off.

He nodded. "The baby is like me. The Pope and Council want the baby safe and under the protection of Sentinels with the hope that one day he will join their ranks as I have done." He gestured to Caroline. "Masters like Caroline want the baby for themselves to make as many powerful vampires as possible. She hopes to get her hands on the baby and turn him into her servant."

"You're forgetting something, Ephraim. You will turn me or I will kill your family."

"Ephraim, why can't you kill her and them before they hurt us?" Jill asked, trying to sound brave.

"Because if he makes a move against me, they'll shoot you. He can't save all of you and he knows it," Caroline said smugly.

Jill bit her lip and nodded. Chris held his gaze for a moment and nodded. He slowly turned until he was propped up in Eleanor's lap while his legs spread out in front of Joshua and Madison.

If they were going to do something, it had to be now. Chris was losing too much blood and was at risk of passing out. Ephraim watched as Chris laid both of his hands in his lap. Moving the left one caused him pain, but he pushed through it.

Ephraim turned and punched a hole in the wall. Everyone jumped at the unexpected move. Chris took advantage of the distraction and finished positioning himself.

Tall, Dark & Lonely

"Fucking hell!" He pulled his hand out and stalked towards Caroline. "I'm sick of these fucking games, Caroline. This is bullshit. If I had known you were going to stalk me for eternity I would have just given you my blood a century ago."

"You'll do it now?" she asked cautiously.

He looked like he was thinking it over as he looked back at the small group. With a tired sigh, he nodded. "Let's just get this the fuck over with. Are you going to want me to turn them into vamps?"

"Wait what does he mean by vamps? You promised we would be like him!" one of the men said.

"You will of course," she purred. She threw Ephraim a warning glare. If he told them her plans she would kill them now.

Ephraim nodded.

"Let's get this over with."

"Fine, now I know your blood will kill me if I drink it straight, so what do I have to do differently?"

"I have to feed from you first. It will mix with my blood. Then you can feed." He lied. They had to feed at the same time and it wouldn't work even if they did. He'd already turned Madison. His body would safely take her blood as a meal. He could easily feed off vampires, but preferred human. Caroline didn't realize that his stomach would digest her blood, slowly. If they were doing a dual exchange her blood would shoot through his system fast enough so that it would mix with his and make her stronger.

"If this doesn't work kill them all," she told her men. They all nodded as their eyes shot from the two of them back to the group.

"Turn around," Ephraim said.

"No, I want you to feed from me while I'm in your arms," she argued.

"No, it will be easier for me this way." Before she could argue, his hand shot out and yanked her to him. His fangs sank into her neck. His eyes darted from Madison to Chris. Chris nodded. He prayed that Chris wouldn't hesitate when it came time to act.

He pulled quickly on her neck, draining her. The more blood she lost the quicker her death would be when she took his. She winced and groaned in his arms. "Enough!"

He ignored her and continued to feed. After a few more minutes when he knew her body was all but drained and his stomach was uncomfortably full he pulled back and offered his wrist. "Take your fill." He had to make this convincing. "After this is done stay the hell away from me. I don't want to see you for the rest of eternity."

She nodded her agreement as she pulled his wrist to her mouth. Caroline was too excited to make the moment last. She'd waited so long for this. She sank her teeth in and swallowed as fast as she could. Some of his blood leaked from her mouth, but she was unconcerned as she drank greedily.

After a minute he pulled his arm away. "That's enough, if you take any more I'll end up having to drain those men before you get your fill. You don't want to go away hungry."

She laughed triumphantly. "There's more than enough here to meet my needs."

"If you don't mind…" He let his voice trail off while he cocked his head towards the men.

"Certainly." She smiled, not knowing her blood had settled in his stomach and not his veins, leaving him too full to take even one more drop of blood.

Ephraim walked over to the men. "Let's get this over with. I want you all out of my house."

Tall, Dark & Lonely

The men looked at him nervously, but no one moved. Ephraim started with the one at the far left, the one covering Eleanor and Chris. He needed to be taken out first. Ephraim had to move quickly if they were going to manage to pull this off without his family getting hurt.

"Put down your weapon. I'm not having you accidentally shoot my children while we do this."

The man nodded and put the gun in his holster. The other men watched anxiously. Ephraim stepped up to the man and took the man's head firmly in his hands. "Are you ready?" he asked.

The man nodded, but it wasn't him that Ephraim was asking. Madison watched as Chris reached down and pulled out two guns. With his left elbow, he shoved Eleanor down, causing her to fall backwards. With his left leg he knocked Joshua and Jill out of the way. It was easy with the way they were sitting. They all fell at once. Chris took aim while Madison covered the kids with her body.

"Now!" Ephraim yelled when Caroline screamed in pain. Madison looked over at the woman as Caroline dropped to the ground. Her body convulsed as smoke rose from her skin. The men shouted orders as Chris began shooting.

Ephraim snapped the man's neck. He lunged at the next man before the first man's body hit the floor. A bullet hit him in the side of his leg, but he barely noticed it. "Don't stop no matter what!" he yelled at Chris. Another bullet tore through his right bicep, but he didn't let the pain slow him down.

Madison looked over at Chris as he fired his guns. His left hand wasn't as fast as the right one, but he seemed in control. She heard more shots fired behind her. They had to take the men out before one of them managed to shoot her family.

Ephraim moved towards the last man standing. The man was already hit several times, but wouldn't stop firing. Chris cried out in pain the same time as the man fired another round as Ephraim reached for him. He took out the man with a quick snap of his neck.

"Chris!" Madison screamed.

"Oh fuck," Chris muttered. He was hit in the same shoulder as well as the stomach. The gun in his left hand dropped to the ground. He kept the right one pointed at the slumped bodies on the floor even as his hand shook. He was going to pass out soon and he was fighting it. She could see from his expression that he wasn't quite there anymore.

"Chris!" Joshua screamed.

Madison turned to find Caroline sitting on the ground. Heavy, white smoke rose from her body. Some of the smoke cleared from her hands as she raised one of her arms. Madison saw the gun too late.

Chris slowly swung his hand around. He muttered a curse and flung himself in front of the kids, taking her down to the floor in the process and out of the line of fire. Several things seemed to happen at once. Ephraim roared in anger, continuous gunshot echoed throughout the room, Chris's body went limp and then jumped several times as if it had been struck violently. The last thing to occur was the front door crashing open.

Ephraim jumped over the small group, taking a bullet from Caroline's gun in his leg before it could hit its intended mark. Caroline screamed in pain as she turned to face the intruders.

Eric stormed in, aiming a crossbow at Caroline. He pulled the trigger, sending the arrow flying through the air. It hit her in the heart, slamming her backwards, but not before she managed to pull the trigger one last time. Ephraim dove over her falling body, taking the bullet in the chest that was meant for Eric.

He saw Eric flinch as he expected the shot to complete its aim to his head.

"Fuck," Eric muttered unsteadily, taking in the scene. Men and women stormed the house as Eric helped Ephraim to his feet.

Tall, Dark & Lonely

"It's Chris." Ephraim ran, half stumbled back to the group. Eleanor was fussing over Chris's body. He could already see that Chris was unconscious and loosing far too much blood.

Eric dropped by Chris' side. "I need a medic!" he yelled.

Another man dropped next to Chris. He opened a backpack and began securing the wounds. "Two in the shoulder, one in the back, one in the stomach, one in the leg and the last one on the side of his neck.

Madison reached up and took Ephraim's hand. He gave it a reassuring squeeze and sighed with relief when he didn't smell her blood. Chris had saved their baby.

Ephraim watched helplessly as the boy who'd become his son lay dying on the ground. There was nothing he could do to save him. "Joshua's been shot!" Jill's voice broke through his anguish.

He reached out and yanked a very pale Joshua from the middle of the chaos. He was covered in blood, but from the smell of it, it was Chris' blood. His eyes ran over the frightened little boy. "Where?"

"My tummy hurts," he cried. "Is Chris going to be okay?" His chin wobbled.

"I hope so." Ephraim yanked the vest off the little boy and sighed with relief. Joshua had a hell of a purple bruise on his stomach, but no penetration.

"Looks like the vest saved him," Eric mumbled as he poked his finger in the vest where the bullet entered. "He needs to go to the hospital as well."

"Chopper's here."

"That was quick," Madison said as she struggled not to cry.

"When two Sentinels are in danger we don't play around. I'm just sorry it took so long to get here. We had a false alarm in Boston. We were halfway there when your calls for help came through. We double checked the situation in Boston by phone and found out that it was bogus."

"A trick to divert you," Eleanor guessed.

"Yes, ma'am. I do apologize," Eric said.

She waved him off. "Just get my grandsons to the hospital and you're forgiven."

"He's packed up. Let's move him out," the medic said.

Several men moved in, but Ephraim blocked them. "I've got him." He scooped Chris up, ignoring the pain that shot through his body. It wasn't as bad as it could have been since he'd overfed. His wounds were already healing.

He looked at the men evenly who were still reaching to take Chris. "He's my son."

After a moment's hesitation, they nodded and moved back as he ran with Chris in his arms to the waiting chopper. Eric ran behind him, carrying a crying Joshua.

Ephraim held Joshua in his arms while they strapped Chris to a board and started an IV. "He needs blood!" the medic yelled.

Eric held out his arm. "Take it! It's our blood he needs anyway! If they give him human blood it will kill him." The medic nodded his agreement as he set to work. Ephraim and Joshua watched as the medic attached an IV from Eric to Chris.

"Ephraim!" Madison yelled over the sounds of the chopper. He turned to see her healthy and well. "We'll meet you there!"

He nodded.

"I love you!" she yelled.

"I love you, too. Be careful."

"I will." She turned to leave.

"Oh, Madison?"

"Yes?" She turned back around.

"When this is all over and Chris is better, be prepared to have the spanking of a lifetime for not listening to me *and scaring the hell out of me!*"

Her mouth dropped open to argue, but she only nodded. It was the smartest thing she'd done all day, except for agreeing to marry him of course. He watched her as the helicopter rose.

She went back towards the house. There were dozens of Sentinels running around now, trying to clean up the mess. He knew his family would be safe. His eyes moved back to Chris. His color was coming back.

"It's the blood. It will help heal him quickly. My blood is stopping the bleeding, see?" Eric pointed to a still white bandage on Chris' neck. The bleeding was slowing down. He just prayed that it was enough. He couldn't lose Chris.

A loud, steady beep went off from one of the machines they had Chris hooked up to.

"Shit, he's coding!"

Ephraim heard Chris's heartbeat sputter. "No! Chris, no!"

"Clear!" the medic ordered before he shocked Chris.

His heart flat lined.

Epilogue

"Dad?" Ephraim looked up from his infant son. Joshua strolled into the nursery and sat down in the other rocking chair.

"What's up, little man?" he asked, gently rocking the baby in his arms.

"Nothing, I just miss Chris." He looked around the baby's room and frowned. "Whose idea was it again to go with a teddy bear theme?"

Ephraim chuckled. "Your mother's."

"Figures. Mom's always been partial to teddy bears. She used to buy me clothes with teddy bears all over them."

"I'm sure you looked cute."

"I did," he agreed, giving Ephraim a grin that would one day make the girls melt at his feet. Ephraim knew that day was coming soon. At eleven, the kid was already too damn good looking and charming for his own good.

Jill walked into the room. "Madison is asking for you, Dad."

He nodded.

It was funny how quickly and eagerly Jill and Joshua came to regard him as their father. Joshua easily made the adjustment to place Madison from sister to mother. Jill hadn't. She was too old for that change and saw Madison as a sister and friend, but still allowed Madison to adopt her. She said it just felt right.

"Do you mind taking little Marc Christopher for me?" He stood up and carefully handed his son over to Jill.

"Of course." She smiled at the baby. "Hey, baby brother, you are so cute."

"Of course he is. After all he's named after me," Chris said as he walked into the room. He messed up Joshua's hair on his way to his youngest brother.

"Hey, little man. Did you miss me while I was out on patrol?" Marc gurgled and grinned hugely. "That's what I thought." He kissed the baby's head.

"Well?" Ephraim asked.

"Nothing to report. Quiet as a church on Sunday. How did your patrol go?" Chris asked as he rubbed the ugly pale scar on his neck.

"Fine. Nothing. Are you still sore?"

"Yeah. The muscles are tight." Chris winced.

"You know I've been waiting for you all night," Joshua complained.

Chris's lips tugged up into a smile. "I can see that."

"Let's go, I only have a half hour before I have to go to bed."

Ephraim cleared his throat. "More like you were supposed to be in bed an hour ago. It's ten."

"Aw, Dad!"

"Go."

"Damn it," Joshua muttered. Chris hit him upside the head, gently. "Watch it, punk."

"You're the punk," Joshua said with a fond smile.

Chris walked with Ephraim across the hall to their new room. Madison insisted before Marc was born that they move their room closer to the rest of the family. He agreed, but only after she twisted his arm, literally.

"So, Dad, I was thinking."

"Yes?" he asked cautiously. It was always a good idea to be cautious when it came to his seventeen year old son's "thinking". He swore if Chris asked for a third tattoo again he was going hang him by his ankles in the foyer and leave him there.

"I was thinking instead of taking my own Sentinel home next year that I might hang around here for a while and make sure everything's okay."

Ephraim hadn't expected that.

"Chris, I would love for you to stay, but I don't want to hold you back."

"You're not holding me back, Dad. You know as soon as I leave they'll set up another Sentinel home close by to protect Marc."

Ephraim sighed. "I know. We thought of moving to start over somewhere else, but this is our home. Madison and your Grandmother want the kids to finish growing up in one home. No more moving around for a while."

Chris smiled easily. "I'm not complaining, Dad. I don't want to move out just yet. I would like a few more years with my family before I have to go out on my own."

Ephraim cupped the back of Chris' neck. "Are you sure? You know I will never stand in your way."

"I'm sure, Dad."

"Okay." He pulled Chris into a bear hug. "I'll see you tomorrow. Get some sleep, we have a vamp nest in Concord to help clean out tomorrow."

"Night, Dad." Chris headed back to the nursery where he would most likely stay for the rest of the night. The kid was a natural when it came to kids. Ephraim hoped he wouldn't have too long of a wait to find his mate.

He turned to head into his room only to pause as he spotted the pictures that covered the hallway walls. A sad smile tugged at his lips as he looked at the enlarged photo of him with his two brothers when they were children. His eyes shifted to the next blown up photo of him standing with Marc and his family. Marc looked so happy with one arm hung around his shoulders and his other arm cradling his youngest child.

Tall, Dark & Lonely

Ephraim chuckled, wondering what Marc would have thought about the hectic day Madison gave birth. Marc would probably be jealous as hell that Ephraim was the one that delivered his son into the world. Not that he had much of a choice since Madison went into labor downstairs while she was watching Chris struggle to re-learn how to walk.

It was the best day of his life, seeing his son take his first steps again after seven months of surgeries and grueling physical therapy. The doctors hadn't held out much hope that Chris would ever walk again. Hell, more than half of them didn't think he'd make it through that first night, but in the end Chris proved them all wrong. He'd never been prouder of Chris as the boy dragged himself across the floor and then forced himself through the pain to walk up the stairs in order to get help for Madison.

He reached up and traced a finger over Madison's smiling lips in their wedding photo. She looked so happy in his arms. He just hoped he could keep her that way forever.

With a smile, he walked into their room and closed the door. He wasn't too surprised to find Madison on the large bed, waiting for him.

Ephraim pulled his shirt off and crawled across the bed, predatorily towards the beautiful woman in his bed. "Is this what you called me for, my beautiful wife?" He gently pulled the sheet covering her body away, exposing bare skin. He licked his lips as two gorgeous breasts were revealed.

"Perhaps." She laid back as he crawled over her.

"Perhaps?"

She laughed. "Well no, I wanted to tell you that Father James told me that another Priest will be joining the household tomorrow. He'll be taking over my old room."

"Ah I see. Then you don't want any of my wares tonight?" he asked, wagging his eyebrows.

"I didn't say that." Her fingers found the zipper of his fly and gently pulled it down. Her hand brushed his already hard shaft before she reached in and pulled it out.

Ephraim's hips pushed forward, knocking her hands out of the way as he entered her in one smooth thrust. Madison's fangs dropped. "You are far too good at that, Ephraim."

"And you feel too damn good, darling," he growled.

"Yeah?" her voice was thick and husky.

His head dropped back in pleasure as he moved inside of her. "Oh yeah, you feel wonderful."

"You're sure you're not going to get bored of me in say, a hundred years?"

The muscles in his neck strained as he growled long and loud, "Hell no."

She moved beneath him, meeting his every thrust. "How about a thousand years?"

"No."

"How about a million years?"

Ephraim lowered his weight on top of her. He gently brushed her lips with his as he moved with lazy thrusts in the way that he knew she liked. She licked her lips, moaning continuously beneath him.

"I will never grow tired of you. Not in a million, zillion, quadrillion years."

"Why?" She looked serious for a moment.

His expression softened. "Because I absolutely love and adore you, Madison."

"I love you too, Ephraim. So much." He took her mouth in a searing kiss.

She pulled back after a few minutes. Giggling uncontrollably as she asked, "What about a zillion, billion, million, quadrillion-"

He sighed in exasperation. "I see I'm not doing this right if you're still able to talk." His arms wrapped around her.

"What-ah!" she gasped as they were suddenly floating in the air towards the ceiling. He effortlessly turned them over so that she was lying on top of him. Her back touched the ceiling as he took her hands into his and pinned them against the ceiling above their heads.

"Now let's see if we can't find something more interesting to do than talk, shall we?"

A sneak peek at the first Sentinel Novel:

Without Regret

Chapter 1

Present Day

Seattle, Washington

"Okay, this probably wasn't such a good idea," Isabella murmured softly to herself as she gripped the worn shoulder straps of her favorite backpack, tightly.

She stumbled and quickly righted herself. She straightened her baseball cap as she quickened her pace. Okay, so she admitted she probably had no business being in this area at three in the morning by herself. She was too short, had two large melons that somehow passed for breasts that constantly threw her off balance, and had the fighting skills of a day old baby. Why she ever thought agreeing to this meeting was a good idea she really didn't know.

Well, maybe the prospective buyer of her program had something to do with it. Normally her potential buyers met her at restaurants, downtown offices and a few times she was flown to Europe. What she wouldn't give to meet a client in a stuffy office during the day for this sale. Of course that couldn't happen with this particular program, it being extremely illegal and all.

Not that she was in the business of creating illegal programs or anything. This one time had been a complete mistake. Okay, illegal might be a poor choice of words, but she was pretty sure that was the point the FBI Agent was getting to the other night. She hadn't been happy finding her small apartment ransacked. It was more insulting that anything. Did they really think she kept her work in her apartment?

That would be pretty stupid considering how many Fortune 500 companies were after her work. A few of them didn't take being outbid well. Just over this past year her apartment had been broken into thirty-seven times. The only thing they found was a small collection of CD's she may have set up to look like her programs. What they got if they stole them, and they did each and every time, was a dummy program full of virussy goodness. They could scan those discs until the cows came home and they'd never detect their true nature until after the damage was done.

It took her program twenty-two point six seconds to infect a large network. The sweet part of her viruses was that she was the only one in the world that could put a stop to them and recover all the work. Well, recover might be an overstatement since what her program really did was create the illusion of destruction. All she required was an apology and a check to cover the damage to her apartment and time before she fixed it.

A large figure suddenly stepped in front of her, scaring the living hell out of her. Isabella screeched and stumbled backwards, falling flat on her ass. She pushed her tan baseball cap up carefully so she could see the imposing figure. The heavy B.O. followed shortly after, making her gag.

"Have you seen my kitty?" the gruff voice demanded.

Isabella shook her head.

"He's around here somewhere. He ran out of the house when I was going out to milk the cows. Now I've got to look for him and the cows are gonna have to wait to be milked. They're gonna be mighty angry with their tits sore from the milk."

"Oh, ah....I hate when that happens," Isabella said, not really knowing how she should respond. She didn't speak crazy, but if he let her live she'd be willing to learn.

He nodded firmly as he sighed heavily. "I guess I should go check the barn," he said, heading back into the alley between two brick buildings.

Isabella jumped to her feet, fixed her hat, and moved her ass. The last thing she needed was for him to come back and mistake her for a cow that needed milking. She made her way to the small park and found the bench for the meeting place five minutes later. She sat down and hugged her backpack to her chest, trying to catch her breath.

In no way was being in a rundown park at three in the morning a smart idea just because she was desperate to get rid of her program. It wasn't over money, she was far from poor, but she couldn't stomach destroying one of her babies or allowing the government to take it from her. It was pride. Stupid pride that was going to get her a slot on the ten o'clock news tomorrow night when they found her nude body in some embarrassing position tomorrow, well, really today.

"This is stupid," she decided to say out loud just to add emphasis to something she already knew. She couldn't let her program go to someone who needed to meet in places like this. What in the hell was she thinking? In the wrong hands her program could do so much damage.

This really was not one of her finer moments, she decided.

Groaning, she got to her feet. Well, she'd have to chop this up to a life lesson and figure something else out. She started towards the street, hoping she'd spot a taxi that could take her safely back home. She was not looking forward to the return walk. She idly wondered if her farmer buddy had any luck with his kitty when several figures stepped out of the darkness in front of her.

"Miss. Smith, you weren't leaving, were you?" a tall thin man with a slight accent she couldn't quite place asked in an amused tone.

"Ah, no?" She forced her eyes to focus on anything other than the scar running down his face and the one across his throat. Something told her the man wouldn't appreciate staring.

"That's very good," the man said, gesturing to one of the other men to take her bag from her. She resisted the urge to fight him, reminding herself that she really sucked at fighting. Seriously, it was sad. Her only move was a cross between a windmill motion and bitch slapping, which usually missed its mark and sent her stumbling.

The man took the bag and opened it. He tossed her candy bars to the ground and she almost bitch slapped him then and there. What kind of sick bastard came between a woman and her chocolate? Her copy of *Lord of the Rings* soon followed along with her iPod, bottle of water, and cell phone. When he pulled out her Netbook she nearly winced at the thought of that getting tossed into the pile. It wasn't her main computer. It was just a cheap little computer that she used when she was out and wanted to play around with some code. Still, she loved it. It was small, cute, and had a picture of a baby groundhog standing on its hind legs eating a carrot set as her wallpaper. It was really cute.

He handed the computer off to one of his men. A moment later he pulled out three CD cases. "I presume this is what I'm after?"

Nope, but Isabella nodded slowly. She forced herself to remain cool. If they were going to kill her than at least she could die knowing they just screwed themselves over with no way to repair it. Ever.

"That's it. Where's my money?" she asked, trying to sound sufficiently afraid, no problem there.

The man smiled a truly ugly smile. Were those canines long and pointy? She gave herself a mental shake. Her mind was obviously messing with her in its panicked stricken state.

"Oh, I have something much better for you. You see your skills....well, they're very useful to my employer. He'd like to offer you a permanent place in our *company*," he said the last word as if it amused him.

The other two men snickered.

Oh, that couldn't be good......

"Um, thanks, but no thanks," she said, backing up.

One of the men grabbed her and hauled her back against his chest. One arm went across her chest, keeping her arms pinned to her sides while his other hand gripped her chin and tilted her head back and to the side.

"Seriously, I don't make a good employee....I'm always late, I take long breaks, I suck at office politics, my desk is always messy, I get cranky if I don't have a constant flow of caffeine, I've even been fired from volunteering, twice. I mean seriously that should tell you something. Who gets fired from volunteering? If you just let me go I'm sure we can work something out on a contractual basis," she rambled on nervously.

"Shhh, you're annoying me. Now shut up and let me do this. When you wake up everything will be fine," he said as he leaned in.

Isabella's eyes widened to the point that she was actually afraid her eyes might pop out of her head. Either she was in a fear induced hallucination or those two teeth were fangs. She didn't have much time to contemplate her situation before those very long and very sharp teeth were in her neck.

She screamed as sharp pain tore through her. Isabella tried to breakaway only to find herself in a death grip. She immediately stopped fighting when the grip became more painful than the bite and stood there whimpering as the man drank her blood. There was no doubt in her mind that's what he was doing.

He was making slurping sounds!

The man suddenly stumbled back from her. She felt two small drops of hot liquid run down her skin beneath her shirt. *Ew!* The man clutched his stomach, gasping.

"What's wrong?" the man holding her asked.

He sucked in a hard breath and managed to say, "Sentinel."

"Oh shit!" The man holding her shoved her away into the other man who shoved her right back. Great, they were playing keep away. Nice. Between that and blood loss she was seriously ready to puke.

"Kill her!" the man on the ground roared.

The two men stopped shoving her and pulled out guns. Isabella squeaked as she covered her head and dropped onto the ground in the fetal position. From her position she watched in horror as the man who'd been drinking from her started to smoke. Seconds later he was on fire.

"Sentinels!" one of the men yelled.

"You bitch! You tricked us!" the other man yelled.

Isabella squeezed her eyes tightly shut as the sounds of flesh hitting flesh, gunshots, and blood curdling screams tore through the night. Something heavy landed on her legs, earning another frightened scream from her. A few seconds later it rolled off.

"Grab her!" a new voice said.

She gasped as she was hauled to her feet. A man with spiky blonde hair pressed a cross to her forehead. A freakin' cross! He pulled her collar down and ran a finger over her bite marks.

"Hmmm," the man said. Intense blue eyes met hers. She squirmed under the rather unnerving observation. He was looking at her like he could see her, really see her. Without a word, and much to her embarrassment, he yanked up her tee shirt and pointed a flashlight at her navel.

"Hey!" she said as she tried to shove her shirt back down.

He ignored her as he ran a finger over the birthmark below her belly button. "You're unmated," he said.

Okay.......This night was just getting weirder and weirder. What next? Would he check the bottom of her foot to see if she was a chocoholic?

She finally managed to shove her shirt down and took several steps back and nearly tripped over her bag. Keeping her eyes on the four new people, two men and two women dressed in black fatigues, she bent down and quickly reloaded her bag with shaky hands. They made no move to stop her, but just watched her as if they were waiting patiently for her to finish.

When she was done she stepped back, too afraid to take her eyes off them. She didn't feel like being anyone else's late night snack again and she had no idea if these people were like whatever the hell those three guys were.

"Well, um, thanks. I'll just be going now," she said, taking several more steps back.

The man who helped himself to her navel took a careful step forward. "We need to talk to you," he said slowly as if he was afraid of frightening her off.

She cleared her throat nervously, taking another step back. "Sure. Yeah, that sounds like great fun, but right now I have somewhere to be."

"I'm afraid that I must insist that you stay," he said more firmly the same moment his three friends broke off and started moving towards her.

"Okay, I guess I could-," she suddenly pointed behind them, "Look! Behind you!"

The four of them shared a bored look before looking back at her. She smiled sheepishly.

The leader of the group folded his arms over his chest and tilted his head to the side to study her. "You really didn't think that would work, did you?"

She made a pinching motion with her thumb and index finger. "Maybe just a little?" It had worked on Angela Briggs in the fourth grade when the much larger girl cornered her against the building and demanded her lunch money and her shoes.

He sighed wearily as he pinched the bridge of his nose. "Grab her."

54005422R00233

Made in the USA
Columbia, SC
24 March 2019